Mage Academy 5

A LitRPG Magic Academy Light Novel

Kal Griffith

Copyright © [2024] by [Kal Griffith]

All rights reserved.

No portion of this book may be reproduced in any form without written permission from the publisher or author, except as permitted by U.S. copyright law.

Contents

The LitRPG Group	V
Important Links	VI
1. Not Yet Used To It	1
2. The Battle Ahead	11
3. Homecoming	19
4. Hero's Duty	28
5. Nothing To Chance	37
6. Towards Achievement	46
7. Unexpected Dungeon	55
8. Tor-sava	64
9. Dead Mountains	73
10. City Under Siege	82
11. Relucent Professor	91
12. Turning Over	99
13. Lessons In Survival	109
14. Unraveling Secrets	118
15. Crumbling Defenses	126
16. Horde	135
17. Rally	144

18.	Touch of Healing	152
19.	Finest Hour	161
20.	Price Divided	170
21.	Unknown Device	179
22.	Lessons With Daggers	188
23.	Estate Survivors	196
24.	Temple Price	206
25.	Discovery	214
26.	Reckoning Loss	223
27.	Hunger	232
28.	Dragonrider	240
29.	Orders	249
30.	Things Known	258
31.	New Plan	267
32.	A Reach	276
33.	Stone Lesson	285
34.	Walls Rise	294
35.	Redirection	303
36.	Calm	312
37.	Storm	321
38.	Nations	330
39.	Red Dragon	337
40.	An End of Things	348

THE LITRPG GROUP

"To learn more about LitRPG, talk to authors including myself, and just have an awesome time, please join the LitRPG Group ."

Important Links

If you want to keep up with my work, associated work, or in general want to get better in touch, join me or my peers in basically any of the following places online.

1. GosuVerse (Discord) – https://discord.gg/w5uG2hRrtr

2. LitRPG Books on Facebook: https://www.facebook.com/groups/LitRPG.books

3. LitRPG Society on Facebook: https://www.facebook.com/groups/LitRPGsociety

4. LitRPG Releases on Facebook: https://www.facebook.com/groups/LitRPGReleases

5. LitRPG subreddit: https://www.reddit.com/r/litrpg/

6. Amazon Book Club: https://www.amazon.com/abc/detail/amzn1.club.bookclub.7aba3a46-af44-70be-7bf8-5f91cf522ead?ref_=abc_aa_bdp_r_ds_imw_ibc

7. Webpage – https://fantasyunlimited.org/

ONE

NOT YET USED TO IT

"Master Youngblood, prepare yourself."

As the words echoed in the heavy air, Danny let out a long breath. He still wasn't used to being called Master, though he took the title in stride.

At that moment, he, Ascended Mage Obadiah Flamekeeper, Margot, Radiance, and Master Barrydew knelt on the top of a small rise overlooking the entrance to a dungeon. Standing in front of the doorway covered in dark runes and carvings of skulls, Danny steadied himself.

The area around them was covered in a light smattering of trees, with the grove giving way to grassland as the landscape ran down and away from the dungeon. The sun was just cresting the horizon and hadn't yet burned away the layer of dew that covered everything.

Sounds were muffled, and Danny's armor felt heavy. "I'm ready," Danny said firmly. "Everyone else?"

Master Barrydew only shrugged. Margot let out a long breath while next to her, Radiance drew out her sword and prepared several ice spells in her hands.

It was a major attack to be taking so many students on, but... desperate times called for desperate measures.

"Just so we're clear," Obadiah said, his voice hanging in the air. "When the dungeon breaks, we're to clean up everything we can, then retreat to Flathammer."

"There are three other dungeons due to break today, so once we get back to the city, we'll engage in the defense there. Tess is already there with my soldiers."

"We've got it, dad," Margot whispered. "You've drilled it into our heads for the last three hours."

"I don't want to leave anything to chance." Obadiah set his jaw.

Danny nodded resolutely, though the gravity of the situation weighed on him. The circumstances were dire any way you looked at it, that was for sure.

All across the Empire, dungeons were beginning to break open. He knew his duty was to be here, on the front lines, fighting alongside his fellow mages to protect the innocent.

[Notice: The Warped Flesh Dungeon will now begin to overflow!]

Danny slowly rose to his feet, along with the other mages. The ground trembled, and with that... A great horde burst forth from the ground.

It was an Undead Dungeon, with a Crypt layout. The monsters that roared along the ground, clambering and snarling and waving their arms wildly, were all zombies, skeletons, wraiths, revenants and other such creatures.

As the ground continued to shake, Obadiah nodded. "Let's do this!"

He raised his hand and magic flared across his palm. At that moment, a great many traps that he had previously laid across the bottom of the path that led to the dungeon went off.

Brief flashes of light dazzled Danny's eyes before a great blast echoed through the air.

KA-BOOM!

Fire rolled across the ground, turning the first several dozen creatures into nothing more than ash. As the creatures screamed and looked around, Obadiah advanced.

While flames rolled down from his hands, he threw several great fireballs into their midst, the subsequent explosions taking out a dozen monsters at a time. Margot formed a flaming bow in her hands and launched arrow after arrow into the horde, doing plenty of damage on her own.

Radiance joined the fray by creating a layer of ice across the ground, making countless undead slip and fall across one another, piling them up for the two fire mages. Master Barrydew, meanwhile, raised his hands and kept his eyes focused on the trees.

Here and there, when the monsters made a break for the safety of the ridge line, he threw bolts of lightning that cut them down.

"Alright." Danny rubbed his hands together. "Let's do this."

"Patience." Master Barrydew held up a hand then flung another bolt of lightning. "Your time will come."

Danny let out a long breath and balled his hands into fists. The horde was still coming hard and fast from the dungeon, but the others had it contained.

And then, with a roar, something huge came stomping out.

[Monster Identified: Rotting Troll. Level 52. Hp: 5,400]

"And there you go, Danny!" Master Barrydew called out. "Knock yourself out!"

Danny snapped his fingers, and with a flash, a stone golem formed behind him. He poured an extra hundred mana into the thing, making it grow to a height of twenty feet and adding the **Boss Attribute**, **Storm Attribute**, and **Magma Attribute**.

Fire glowed from between the cracks in the stone, lightning flickered from its hands, and it thumped its chest. Down below, the Rotting Troll (which stood around the same height) turned and looked up at it as the stone golem leapt into motion.

It tore down through the battlefield, smashing the smaller undead into bits without even noticing that they were there. Several of them were incinerated by simply getting hit by the flares of lightning trailing off the thing.

Danny grinned as the stone golem punched the Rotting Troll as hard as it could. The massive troll came crashing to the ground, flattening dozens of the other undead underfoot.

It then raised a foot and smashed the head of the rotting troll flat, killing it in the blink of an eye.

[Creature Absorbed: Rotting Troll]

[Traits: Troll Torso (Lv. 52) (Already Owned), Troll Legs (Already Owned), Troll Head (Already Owned), Troll Arms (Already Owned), Undead Attribute (Already Owned)]

[Mana to Quicksummon: 1,400]

Danny nodded with a smile until the ground shuddered again. With an even louder roar, a troll half again as large as the first one came running out and threw a punch straight into the chest of Danny's golem.

The golem was lifted off its feet and came down smack in the middle of it all. Once more, it did quite a good bit of damage, but it wasn't quite the same.

As the golem struggled to stand back up, the troll grabbed it and threw it into the tree line, not all that far from the mages. Lightning exploded across the area as the golem roared.

The light inside its body began to glow brighter, and the hands of the golem turned bright orange. As the troll thundered forward, it leapt back upon the thing, grabbing its head.

Smoke poured upward as the **Magma Attribute** did its job, burning deeply the flesh of the mighty beast. The troll (which Danny realized was a Stone-Fleshed Troll) snarled and punched the stone golem several times.

Finally, it broke the hold of the golem and shoved it backward, near the trees once more. With that, the troll snarled and rushed at it.

The golem glanced around then grabbed hold of a large sapling. With a single twist, it ripped the tree out of the ground and used it as a spear, plunging the weapon into the heart of the troll.

NOT YET USED TO IT

The great, flabby creature groaned and flopped to the side. Danny beamed at his handiwork.

"Leave it for later!" Master Barrydew cut loose with another blast of lightning, taking down several zombies that were attempting to flee around the back of the dungeon. "We've got work to do!"

Danny couldn't disagree, and he spawned in a second stone golem, sending it charging into battle. Obadiah pressed his relentless attack, unleashing enormous gouts of flame, while Margot and Radiance ran cover from above.

Slowly, the horde began to dwindle, until, finally, the tide was stemmed. The last, lonely zombie staggered out of the dungeon and looked up at the mages and golems facing it, and let out a single squeak before being curb-stomped into oblivion.

Danny smiled and turned to his companions, all of whom looked rather exhausted. "And that wraps up this one."

Obadiah turned and started walking back toward their horses which were stabled nearby. "We need to get back to Flathammer before-"

Flap.Flap.Flap.

The noise was low and steady, and the company froze. Master Barrydew turned and looked toward the south, in the direction of the dungeon, but Danny didn't hesitate.

He ran forward and leapt into the air. As one of his stone golems caught him and lifted him above the level of the trees, his blood turned to ice.

"Dragon!" he bellowed. "Dragon incoming!"

"Where in the Empire did that come from?" Obadiah snapped.

"Does it have anything with it?" Master Barrydew demanded.

Danny squinted. It was still a couple miles off, but was coming low and fast, and heading straight for them.

"Nothing else with it. Looks to me to be Level 80, if I had to guess. Green scales, only two wings, maybe sixty feet in length. The system can't tag it yet, so that's just a guess."

With a mighty roar, the beast let out a gout of flame that stabbed down at the ground, burning through the trees. It then swept straight toward them, continuing its assault.

Danny leapt down. "Brace yourselves!"

He raised a hand and re-absorbed the stone golems (which allowed him to regain the mana he had used to summon them). As they vanished, he hit the ground while Obadiah and Master Barrydew formed a shield over the group.

And then, there was flame. Fire raged against the small shield, blasting trees apart and scorching the earth.

As it faded away, the beast landed only a few hundred feet away. It bent down and snapped something up, and a moment later, about half a horse landed on the ground next to them.

"Well, there goes our ride," Danny muttered.

"We can live with that." Master Barrydew charged at the beast. "Come on!"

[Monster Identified: Green Dragon Scorcher. Level 100. Hp: 100,000]

"Any idea how we're going to kill this thing?" Obadiah called out. "Fire dragons are immune to flame!"

"I can immobilize it," Master Barrydew called out. "Danny? Any chance you can do something?"

"I'll give it my all," Danny said resolutely. "Let's take this beast down."

"You'd better!" Obadiah called out as he and Margot drew to a halt. "We can shield you, if nothing else!"

"Much appreciated!" Danny and Master Barrydew charged forward.

Radiance came along as well, though further back. She let out a blast of ice crystals, which stung at the dragon's face but didn't seem to do much damage.

Master Barrydew raised his hands, and threw a mighty blast of lightning that wrapped around the dragon. In an instant, it tightened around the beast, pinning its wings to its side and knocking it to the ground more fully.

Danny let out a breath, then raced forward as fast as he could. "What's my mana level?"

[Current Mana Reserves: 1410/1412]

A determined smile came across Danny's face. He could remember when he had started out, a mere ten mana or so to his name.

He drew in a deep breath then let it out. "I need a stone golem summoned with 1400 mana."

He had never gone so large before but figured that it would be worth it. He added all the attributes as before but with a few others this time.

With a mighty roar, the creature formed around him, and he felt himself carried up into the air. One of the perks of being able to summon monsters was the ability to be absorbed into the summons, when he desired to do so.

At that moment, he suddenly felt his senses expand, and he came into control of a forty-foot-tall stone golem that practically crackled and blazed with energy.

The dragon looked up and snarled at him, and Danny balled his huge hands into fists. Time to get to work.

He smashed his foot down onto the dragon's head, then punched it as hard as he could. The lightning net broke, and the dragon was sent rolling along the ground.

It flipped around and righted itself, spreading its wings. A great tongue of flame stabbed outward, washing over Danny's body with a heat of unfathomable intensity.

Danny charged straight into it, grabbed the dragon around the neck, and lifted it up into the air. Almost instantly, it roared and lashed out, beating at the stone golem with its wings and tail.

It clawed at him with its massive claws of steel, scraping along his armored body.

"Danny!" The voice echoed in his ears. "There's a pond right over here!"

Danny turned to see a small body of water. It was tiny, but... Maybe it would be enough.

The dragon flapped about, and Danny charged forward, barely maintaining his control of the beast. As he reached the water, he dove in, plunging down to the bottom of the small lake.

The dragon snarled and thrashed about, and Danny felt the water grow cold around him. Likely, Radiance was freezing the lake over top of him.

Not ideal, but it would work if it meant killing the beast. The dragon suddenly twisted around, and through the murky water, Danny saw its eyes settle upon him.

FOOOM!

A blast of flame, more powerful than before, lit up the lake, and almost all the water was burned away within seconds. Danny found himself lying on a dry lakebed, half-sunk into what had once been mud, with the dragon on top of him.

It snarled and lashed around, then wrapped its tail tightly around his arm. It gave a single, sharp twist, ripping the left arm of the golem clean off.

Danny felt no pain, but the beast was able to launch itself up into the air, shooting high into the sky. Danny bit his lip, then allowed himself to be extruded from the summoned creature.

He raced across the dry lakebed as the dragon peaked high in the air and dove straight back down, aiming straight for the golem to deliver a death blow.

"What are you doing?" Master Barrydew asked as Danny reached the edge of the lake and dove behind some cover.

"Something clever, I hope." Danny said through gritted teeth. "Plug your ears."

Master Barrydew nodded and covered his ears, motioning for the others to do the same. After they did so, Danny let out a long breath.

With that, using five of his remaining ten mana, he summoned a Nightingale of the Snow.

It was a tiny creature, with very little health and no combat abilities... Except for the fact that it could put creatures to sleep. Granted, the effect could vary depending on a great many factors, but... Still.

He summoned it onto the side of the dragon's head, and it began to sing its sweet song. Meanwhile, the stone golem tore itself up from the bottom of the lake, stepped forward, and threw a massive punch up to meet the falling dragon.

The dragon likely hadn't been put entirely to sleep, but it did seem to stumble slightly, and didn't react quickly enough to loose any further flame.

The stone golem's fist hit the dragon at a combined speed of what must have been a thousand miles per hour. A shockwave exploded outward, flattening Danny, Master Barrydew, and the forest for half a mile around.

Needless to say, the golem was entirely destroyed. As Danny picked himself up, a flickering shield around him being projected by Master Barrydew, he found that the lake's crater was now almost twice as large as before.

The dragon lay at the bottom, stunned and nearly dead, and a smile came across Danny's face. Master Barrydew drew himself up, and slowly raised his hand.

A single bolt of lightning to the back of the skull killed the beast, and it collapsed. Danny let out a long breath of relief as a handful of notifications appeared.

[Notification: Monster Summoning has increased to Lv. 40!]

[Reward: Mana Increase: 1412 -> 1486]

"Yes!" Danny beamed. His mana automatically refilled with the level up, which was a nice bonus even of itself.

As Obadiah and the girls joined them, Master Barrydew frowned. "I repeat Obadiah's earlier question. Where did that thing come from?"

"I don't know." Danny turned to nod toward the distant town that they were supposed to be guarding. "But I do know that we need to be getting back to work."

Auto save - [Savefile: Information]

- **Health: 74%**
- **Mana: 100%**
- **Quest: Protect the city of Flathammer!**
- **Location: Flathammer Plains, Western District of the Empire**
- **Inventory: Essential Supplies, Basic Armor, Iron Sword, Sword of the Wasp, Aquamarine Sword, Frostbite Sword**
- **Skills: Monster Summoner (Lv. 40), Flame Combat (Lv. 2), Wind Combat (Lv. 5)**
- **Relationships: Friendly with Margot, Friendly with Radiance, Friendly with Master Barrydew, Speaking Terms with Obadiah Flamekeeper, Ascended Fire Mage**
- **Time of Day: 8:27 a.m.**

Two

The Battle Ahead

Danny summoned in several skeletal horses, and the group flew back toward town just as fast as they could go. The beasts were far from comfortable to ride on, but they didn't exactly have a lot of options.

The forest fell behind them as they flew across the prairie, and Obadiah stood up slightly. "I'm getting a message from Commander Johnson. There are already monsters attacking the city."

"He's handling defense on the northern side, Tess is engaging the beasts on the eastern side."

"Then you two head around to the north," Master Barrydew said. "Danny, Radiance, and I will take the east."

"Right you are!"

With that, they split off, flashing across the plains. Danny lowered his head as they flew along.

Ahead, as the town of Flathammer rose, Danny bit his lip. It was a small town with only a small wooden wall protecting the area.

It hadn't needed greater protection for the last... Well, however long it had been in existence. The people who lived there were mostly shepherds and farmers, along with a few traders that went to the larger cities to pick up supplies to bring back to the other residents of the city.

They weren't warriors, and they weren't mages or soldiers or anything other than just people. Ordinary people, who were about to be eaten by a horde of monsters summoned by the people who ran the Empire.

Danny's heart hammered as they raced around the side of the city and found the defense. Monsters, mostly large beasts like scorpions, spiders, and rhinos, threw themselves against the city walls in a desperate bid to break through.

On top of the wall, archers fired arrows desperately into their midst, while a handful of soldiers stood their ground in front of the gates itself. Tess was among them, her blade a beacon of light amidst the chaos.

"We're coming in hot!" Master Barrydew raised his hands, and lightning flickered through the sky. "Better let Tess know we're coming."

He snapped his fingers, and lightning came crashing down, killing several of the beasts right around Tess and her warriors. They glanced over and waved, and Tess threw herself further into the battle.

As mighty beasts turned to regard the newcomers, Danny grinned. He was ready for the challenge.

"Alright." Danny spread his arms and called up his interface. "What should it be?"

"Whatever you do, make sure it's epic." Radiance raised her hands and launched a crystal of ice into the side of a rhino, freezing the creature at least halfway.

She smiled and nodded as it stumbled and fell to the side, its other legs flailing frantically as it fought to regain its balance. "Wouldn't want me showing you up, now would you?"

Danny chuckled and nodded. "Alright, then. I want an army of Rockworms. Two hundred Mana apiece. Make them fast."

With a rumble, the ground underneath of him heaved. He could, of course, only summon seven of the creatures, but that would have to be enough. There was a long pause as he came to a halt...

THE BATTLE AHEAD 13

And then, with a great blast of earth, the creatures exploded from the ground. Each was about a foot across and armed with a tooth that could eat straight through solid granite.

Now, of course, it plunged into the flesh of the mighty creatures, eating through their bodies as if they were paper bags. The monsters let out roars of pain, and flailed around as they tried to fight back, but the worms were too quick, and dove back underground in the blink of an eye before the monsters could kill them.

All across the battlefield, the seven worms burst here and there, struck, and dove back down once again. It was a slaughterhouse, and great beasts died left and right.

Tess and her soldiers advanced, killing anything that Danny wasn't able to take out, and within a few minutes, the last creature, a Wooly Mammoth, fell headlong across the field.

Tess sheathed her sword, and Danny re-absorbed his worms and approached. "Thanks for the help." She muttered, glancing around the battlefield. "Wish you could have gotten here earlier, but I suppose you did what you could."

"Sorry. We got tied up by a dragon." Master Barrydew raised an eyebrow in frustration.

"Dragon?" Tess's head whipped around. "Where did that come from? The closest dungeon that could spawn a dragon is over a hundred miles away, and I didn't think it was set to overrun for another month."

Master Barrydew could only shrug. "In times like these, I'm afraid we can't take much for granted. It showed up, and now it's dead, and I presume that Danny has a new dragon summon as a result."

Danny frowned and checked his interface. He hadn't seen the notification, but there it was; **Green Dragon Scorcher, Level 100**, capable of being summoned with fifty thousand mana.

"Yeah, but I'm not going to be able to summon it for a while." He shook his head. "Even with mana crystals, I'm pretty limited in what I can do. I'm running pretty low."

"I wish I could get you more." Master Barrydew grimaced. "Unfortunately, with the war, mana crystals have suddenly become far more valuable. Do you have any left?"

"I have three Purple crystals, each worth around 10,000 mana," Danny said. "Enough to cast my dragon hatchling in a pinch."

"Good." Master Barrydew sighed and sent up a pulse of magic. He paused for a few moments while he waited for it to come back down.

When it did land in his palm, he nodded and continued. "Alright. Obadiah's soldiers more or less have the northern border secure. There are two more groups coming up from the south, though."

"Two?" Tess snorted. "Alright, I'll get my soldiers. You three head out and do what damage you can on the way in, and I'll stop them at the city."

"You got it." Master Barrydew wheeled his horse around, and he, Danny, and Radiance shot off once more.

As they flashed along, Danny remained focused and determined. So much death already, but things were really just getting started. He had to stay strong to protect the innocent people counting on them.

As they flew across the landscape, they saw the next wave of creatures approaching. These creatures were mostly insects, each the size of a horse. Across the prairie, a band of goblin-like figures prowled in the distance.

"I've got the bugs!" Master Barrydew called out. "You take the gold-lovers."

"Got it!" Danny turned slightly and raced in that direction, running through his lists of summons.

He needed something that could do large, area of effect attacks. The dragon hatchling was an obvious one, except that...

Well... It did take an extraordinary amount of mana, and he wanted to save it for a truly dire time. Did this count? It was hard to say, but Danny suspected that there were better ways.

"Let's just dial this in," Danny said. "Cave crows, loads of them, all equipped with Fire."

A flash of light burst across the sky, and hundreds of creatures descended from the heavens. Flames trailed from their wings as they slashed through the prairie.

In an instant, the tall grasses ignited, roaring with fire that crackled toward the goblins. The cave crows swooped through their ranks, setting many ablaze.

In mere seconds, the goblins fell in droves, reduced to charred corpses upon the ground. Danny watched intently as the swarm of fiery cave crows circled back, ready to strike again, scorching the prairie as they relentlessly pursued their prey.

Suddenly, a great roar echoed across the landscape, and Danny turned to see several trolls lumbering forward, trailing the goblins. They snorted and hefted their clubs, prompting Danny to sigh.

With a quick gesture, he unsummoned the cave crows and rode toward the trolls. If it was a fight they wanted, it was a fight they would get.

Tess was guarding the town walls, and although he hadn't wiped out all the goblins, he had thinned their ranks significantly. She would have to handle the rest.

Fortunately, the trolls didn't pose much of a challenge. They were only Level 30, and he dispatched them with ease.

The last one, with its stony flesh, resisted most of his stone golem's attacks, but eventually, it fell, and life moved on. Danny turned his attention back to the city, where Tess and her soldiers were locked in battle with the goblins at the southern walls.

No gate blocked the southern wall. Goblins hurled grappling hooks, scrambling to scale the barrier, while Tess's soldiers frantically hacked at the ropes and fired arrows into the throng below.

Outside the city walls, soldiers battled fiercely, but the goblins cared little for direct combat, swarming around them and clambering up the walls, making it difficult for the soldiers to land effective blows.

As Danny approached, he quickly summoned a fresh swarm of cave crows. The crows dove with ferocity, tearing into the beasts, and Tess's soldiers cheered at the much-needed support.

An archer on the wall finally felled the last goblin, and Danny exhaled in relief. "Where were you?" Tess demanded as she strode across the battlefield, strewn with bodies and blood. "We could have died!"

Danny blinked, taken aback. "I was off fighting them in the prairie, like I was supposed to be doing."

"Well, it wasn't enough!" Tess snapped.

"What are you talking about?" Danny asked. "We saved the city, didn't we?"

"Some of my men are dead," Tess retorted as she turned and stomped away. "That's entirely unacceptable, no matter how many or few it is."

Danny frowned, puzzled by her harsh reaction. "I'm sorry you lost men, but I killed several hundred of the things out on the prairie! I'm not really sure what more you wanted me to do."

"I don't know, Master Youngblood!" she snarled, coming back after him. "That's your title now, isn't it? Master? I don't know that you've earned it, but-"

THE BATTLE AHEAD

"Incoming, ma'am!" a soldier up on the wall called out. "Barrydew and Silver did a good number on the insects, but they're coming now!"

"Good!" Danny turned and held out his hand, unsummoning his cave crows and preparing to summon another stone golem.

"Don't bother," Tess snorted. "You'd only get in the way."

Danny raised an eyebrow then snapped his fingers and spawned in a stone golem anyway. As it thundered off across the prairie, straight toward the attacking insects, Tess spun toward him.

"You just have to come in here, upending everything, don't you?" Her hand went to her sword, and she tightened her fingers on the hilt. "You're nothing more than a showoff, using a crisis for personal gain!"

"I don't know what you're talking about!" Danny cried out. "I-"

Suddenly, his eyes narrowed. He could feel Tess's presence... along with something else. Something dark.

"Get away from her," he snarled softly. "Your fight is with me, not with her, and not with the Empire. Get away from her!"

As Tess took a step back and drew her sword, Danny pulled out a purple mana crystal. "I'll use it!" Danny barked. "You know I will."

A brief second passed, and something like black smoke drained out of Tess's eyes. She blinked a few times then looked down at her sword.

"Monsters incoming." Danny put away the crystal and gestured across the grasses. "Fight now, talk later."

"Works for me," Tess muttered.

With that, she formed up her soldiers while Danny's stone golem engaged the monsters. The shouts and screams of monsters and men pierced the sky as Danny gritted his teeth.

This was a battle for survival, a desperate struggle to hold their ground against the abyssal beasts. Humanity's place in the world hung by a thread as monsters, both human and beast, fought to push them into oblivion.

Danny could only hope that, in the end, they would prove strong enough to endure.

Auto save - [Savefile: Information]

Health: 71%

Mana: 2%

Quest: Protect the city of Flathammer!

Location: Flathammer Plains, Western District of the Empire

Inventory: Essential Supplies, Basic Armor, Iron Sword, Sword of the Wasp, Aquamarine Sword, Frostbite Sword

Skills: Monster Summoner (Lv. 40), Flame Combat (Lv. 2), Wind Combat (Lv. 5)

Relationships: Friendly with Radiance, Friendly (probably?) with Tess.

Time of Day: 9:37 a.m.

Three

Homecoming

They spent the rest of that day cleaning up monsters around Hardhome. When they finished, they remained on patrol for several more hours, trying to make sure that nothing would be forgotten in the end.

Danny stayed vigilant, determined to protect every soul in the city. By the end of the day, all seemed normal, and Obadiah called them to the gates of the city.

"On behalf of all my people, I thank you." The city's governor bowed deeply to the warriors. "We're deeply indebted to you."

"Just doing our jobs." Obadiah flashed a smile at him. "Just let us know if you see anything out of the ordinary, alright?"

With that, they set out across the plains of the Empire toward the Imperial City. The ride would take nearly a week, with several dungeons to clear along the way.

The next morning, they reached the city of Donahue, where they spent the entire day battling a swarm of kobolds that surged from a dungeon beneath the city. Exhausted and weary, they rode out again that night, arriving at another nearby dungeon by midnight, where they narrowly averted a breach into the wilderness.

Only then could they rest, camping until dawn before setting off once more. By the time they cleared the final dungeon, the convoy was drained.

As the day waned, they rode into the rolling hills surrounding the Imperial City. Approaching from the west, where dense forests interspersed with sparse farms dotted the landscape, they now saw large encampments—refugees fleeing the monsters' advance.

"This is incredible," Tess murmured as they rode through the thick trees, smoke intertwining with the leaves overhead. It was late summer, and the smells of roasting animals filled the air.

Danny worried about how the camps would sustain themselves once the air turned cold and food became less abundant.

"I've never seen anything like this," she continued. "I've never even heard of something like this happening in the entire history of the Empire."

Radiance rode up next to them, her horse limping slightly. In better circumstances, they would have given the beast a rest.

Now, they could do little but to push it on.

"I've often wondered what it would be like to have been around when the Empire was formed," Radiance said. "Now, I suppose we'll get to tell our children stories of how it ended."

Tess snorted. "Let's not get hasty."

"I'm not being hasty! Just realistic." Radiance sighed. "I dunno. Just frustrated, I guess."

"Danny! Tess." Obadiah came riding up, a serious look on his face. "I'm afraid I have to ask for some privacy."

"But of course." Radiance nodded and allowed her horse to fall back, and Obadiah took her place.

Danny glanced over and saw a grave look on Obadiah's face.

"What's the matter?" Tess asked. "Something about the dragon, I assume?"

"Yes. I just received a communication as we entered the encampment area." Obadiah sighed.

"I think we found where the dragon came from. There was a dungeon break in the eastern province, the Cherry Mountain Dungeon."

"It was known to have contained a dragon, and forces were brought appropriately. In the chaos of the battle, though, the dragon managed to escape, and made a direct line west."

"It was unknown until now exactly where the dragon had gone."

"Hmm." Danny frowned. "But then... Why would it come straight to us? Why not attack the Imperial City on the way?"

"Or any number of other large, unguarded settlements?" Obadiah added. "I wish I knew. I can only assume that dark forces are at work."

"There's still one Deepcorp Lord on the loose. Perhaps he had something to do with it."

Danny glanced at Tess, who looked down at the ground. Obadiah sighed, then shrugged.

"Anyway, I thought you two ought to know. If that is the case, keep your eyes open. No telling what will happen next."

He started to ride away, then paused and fell back. "Also, I have your orders for the next few days in the Imperial City. Look them over, make sure you follow them precisely. That's all."

He passed small pieces of paper to the two warriors, then rode off sharply. Danny glanced down at his own orders, and frowned.

"It looks like I have three days in the Imperial City. Tomorrow I have a meeting in the Imperial Palace, and then I'm riding out with the Twelfth Legion."

Tess frowned and looked at her own orders. "I'm riding out in four days, it looks like I'll be with the Fifth Legion."

"Ahh!" Danny shook his head in frustration. "In that case, this may be the last time I see you for a while. I doubt we'll see each other much in the city."

"If I don't see you for a time, know that you're the best mage I've ever fought with." Tess held out her hand, which Danny grasped. "Master Youngblood."

Danny snorted and looked down, then frowned and looked back up. "I've been hesitant to ask, but since we won't be seeing each other much after this, I-"

"You have every right to ask." Tess shook her head. "You want to know what was happening with me?"

Danny nodded. "Pretty much. It was... It was weird. I thought you'd been possessed, but-"

"I thought the same thing at first, when you ordered him away." Tess paused. "I could feel him leave my mind. I'm sure it was a he, but I can't tell you how I know that."

"I think..." She bit her lip. "I think he entered my mind three days earlier. I can't prove it, I just have that feeling."

"I don't think he did much, he just watched, and... I had this sense during that time that something was off, but you know how things are in a war like this. Everything seems off, no matter how hard you're desperately trying to make sure it's not."

"Anyway, there are a few decisions I made in that time, mostly in where I sent my soldiers, that I look back on now and wonder why I did things that way. All I can figure is that whoever it was planted suggestions, here and there, to direct things as he wanted."

"And then he revealed himself when it looked like the city wouldn't fall." Danny frowned.

"That's my guess," Tess said. "Look, if you're really up against this dark lord, you're going to need everyone behind your back."

"I know," Danny replied resolutely.

Tess shook her head. "I think you miss my point. You're going to need to suspect everyone."

"Maybe not Ascended Mages, they'd probably be strong enough, but... If they're not that powerful, assume that he could at least be watching you through someone else's eyes."

"Wonderful," Danny said dryly. "Part of what's made our fight against them, this time, is the fact that I can trust people."

"And I'm not saying to stop. Just only trust them, not the thing that could potentially be mucking around in their brain," Tess said then shrugged. "Simple."

"Yeah. So easy a child could understand it," Danny said, forcing a wry smile. "Thanks for telling me, anyway. I appreciate it."

Tess nodded. "Well, we're almost home. Let's just enjoy the rest of this ride."

Danny could only nod wearily. He was exhausted from the tour, and as they rode through increasingly hilly land, he felt himself nodding in the saddle.

Tess slapped him across the cheek to wake him up, and Radiance, upon rejoining them, hit him with a blast of ice that did a good bit of work, too. In any event, he was soon able to make it up and into the city, where things were generally in a state of utter chaos.

People were packing into the city just as tightly as they could make it. Tents filled the alleys while small shacks were being built out of crates and blankets.

It was dire, no two ways of looking at it. People were even building homes on rooftops and out in the streets, anything to get inside the city and away from the growing chaos outside.

Danny dropped off his horse at the local stable where the stableboys started doing their best to get the great beasts rested enough that they could ride out on another tour of duty. After that, he headed across the city, making his way to his old family home.

He bade farewell to Tess and to Radiance, both of whom had their own places to be, then soon staggered up the stairs to his boyhood home. As a light flickered within, he pushed open the door and stepped inside.

"Danny!" Zechariah, his father, looked up from the kitchen table covered in scrolls, maps, and other such documents. "I wasn't expecting you until tonight!"

"It is tonight." Danny nodded out the window where the setting sun cast long shadows across the city.

Zechariah blinked a few times then glanced back down at his maps. "Well, now. It is. Wow. Time flies when you're having fun, I suppose."

"And you're having fun?" Danny dropped onto a couch which felt good after being in the saddle for so long.

"No, but someone must be if time is moving so fast." Zechariah sighed. "Grab down some spices from the cabinet. I'll go out and buy something for us to eat. Maybe a rabbit or quail or something. Get some water boiling in the hearth."

Danny did as he was instructed, and around an hour later, they had a stew that was passably edible. Both were fairly good cooks, they had learned out of necessity after Danny's mother had passed, but in desperate times, food was the last thing to take priority.

Zechariah kept working on the documents even as they ate, and Danny leaned forward, curious.

"So what are those?"

"The short answer is that I'm crunching some numbers and planning out the next several tours of duty," Zechariah murmured. "There were a few dungeons that broke early, delaying the return of the Eighth Legion, so I have to adjust some schedules."

"The Emperor wants someone familiar with the battlefield to make those plans, which, consequently, falls onto the shoulders of whoever happens to be in the city at any time. Barrydew will get the pleasure of doing this for the next few days, but for now, I'm stuck with it."

"When do you ride out again?" Danny asked.

"Tomorrow morning. I'm heading for the northern plains, two weeks," Zechariah answered with a sigh. "Your tour is going to be three weeks, I'm afraid. It'll be difficult, but I have little doubt that you can do it."

"Are you supposed to be telling me things like that?" Danny asked.

"No. You'll find it out officially tomorrow morning in your audience with the Emperor, but you can't blame a father for giving his son a heads-up." He sighed and crossed his arms, momentarily putting down the documents.

"Forgive me for intruding, but... Obadiah sent me a fairly cryptic message, it sounds like you had some trouble out in Flathammer? I thought that would be one of the easier parts of your tour."

"Something like that." Danny explained quickly about the dragon and Tess's odd behavior.

When he finished, Zechariah crossed his arms. "And that was a week ago?"

Danny nodded in confirmation. "Yeah, why?"

"Because from what I saw when I got into town three days ago, you were originally assigned to go along the shoreline. It was a fairly simple tour, but with several S-ranked overflows that you would have been dealing with."

Zechariah shrugged. "About a week ago, your tour was changed to do a southern tour. Three weeks, through the jungle and parts of the wasteland. Only one S-ranked overflows to deal with."

"Longer, and probably more grueling, but less strategic. I wondered about it, but was told that it had been analyzed intensely and it was decided that you'd be heading that way."

"Interesting." Danny crossed his arms. "You think that someone is intentionally sending me down on a different tour?"

"I think that with what you told me about Tess, it's not out of the question to think that the dark lord may have had a hand in changing your orders," Zechariah answered. "All I'm thinking is that if that happened, and at this point I would probably classify it as an if instead of an absolute, you should be careful."

"Three weeks is a long time, and there are a lot of places out there that would be perfect for an ambush."

"I'll keep my eyes peeled," Danny said.

"Good." Zechariah sighed and blinked sleep out of his eyes. "Well, I've only got a couple more things to figure out, and then I'll be free for the evening. Feel like a board game?"

Danny glanced longingly at his cot. He rather wanted to collapse on a real bed and fall deeply into the bliss of sleep, but at that point, meetings with his father were rare, and he never knew if it would be the last time he'd see him or not.

"That sounds like a good plan to me," Danny said with a smile as he slowly rose. "I'll go get checkers."

A few minutes later, they'd cleared all the documents away and settled in for a quick game. Both were exhausted, and so neither of them played particularly well (resulting, eventually, in a draw), but it was fun, nevertheless.

Finally, worn away by the stress of their current lives, they staggered to their cots and fell fast asleep. The next morning would bring his official orders, along with a great many other things.

Where would those paths lead? There was no way of knowing... except to stick to the path and simply follow it as closely as possible.

Auto save - [Savefile: Information]
Health: 100%
Mana: 100%
Quest: Go to the Imperial Palace to receive orders
Location: Youngblood Residence
Inventory: Essential Supplies, Basic Armor, Iron Sword, Sword of the Wasp, Aquamarine Sword, Frostbite Sword

Skills: Monster Summoner (Lv. 40), Flame Combat (Lv. 2), Wind Combat (Lv. 5)

Relationships: Friendly with Radiance, Friendly with Tess. Family Bond with Zechariah, Ascended Fire Mage

Time of Day: 10:49 p.m.

Four

Hero's Duty

The next morning, Danny rose early. Zechariah was already gone, though there was a note on the table promising to catch him at the Imperial Palace.

Danny smiled, ate a bit of bread and fruit for breakfast, and slipped out into the city. All around him, the city bustled as people continued to flood into the safety of the walls.

Do-gooders walked around handing out baskets of food to anyone who needed it, while vendors called out their wares and did their best to sell to the masses that, increasingly, had no money whatsoever. There were a few construction projects underway, which Danny suspected were being funded by the city in order to push money into the floundering economy, but that was just speculation.

His business was killing monsters, not managing economics. As he strode through the city, pushing his way toward the Imperial Palace, the streets became more and more packed.

By the time he reached the palace itself, there were so many tents, vendors, and people that he imagined it would have been impossible to ride a horse through the tight area. The palace itself was surrounded by a great wall, forming a citadel that would provide the final standing point if the city was breached.

The gates into said citadel were guarded by a handful of the Emperor's Guard, who were... Well... In a word, very impressive. Their armor was sleeker than that of the average soldier, and it was patched with colored plates that clearly signified they were different.

Their helmets were a bit taller, and were topped with feathered crests. At that moment, half a dozen of them stood at attention, keeping back the crowd that was more than ready to demand their safety from the Emperor.

When Danny approached the gate, one of the guards turned to him and placed his hand on a sword. "No admittance without proper credentials," he barked in a gravelly voice.

Danny reached into his inventory, pulled out a small badge, and showed it to the guard who gave a small nod.

"Master Youngblood, I see," he said, straightening his posture. "Please, proceed."

Danny tucked the badge away and slipped through the gate which another guard opened just enough for him to enter. Once inside, he did his best not to simply look around to stare in awe.

The Imperial Palace stood as a marvel, unmatched in its grandeur. A stone bridge spanned a moat twenty feet wide and fifty feet deep, an imposing barrier against any potential breach of the city.

Beyond lay what had once been a broad courtyard, now transformed into a maze of barricades and defensive fortifications. Behind it, the palace towered, a mountain of golden spires and silver domes, with the banners of the Imperial Family and the Empire fluttering in the wind.

The sight was breathtaking, and as Danny reached the stairs and ascended into the entry hall, he had to remind himself to breathe. The palace's interior matched its exterior in splendor.

The entry hall, slightly smaller than the Grand Hall at the Academy, dazzled with tapestries, paintings, statues, and more. Ahead, diamond-encrusted doors led to the Throne Room, guarded by half a dozen of the Emperor's elite soldiers.

They inspected his badge, cross-referencing it with a list of those permitted to see the Emperor that day. Satisfied, they swung the doors open, and Danny stepped into a meeting already in progress.

The throne remained vacant, yet the gilded hall shimmered in its presence. A table had been set up at the base of the small stairs leading to the throne, where the Emperor stood surrounded by mages and soldiers.

Tess, along with Zechariah and Obadiah, also stood nearby. Emperor Ezra turned slightly as Danny approached and greeted him with a smile.

"Master Youngblood! So good you were able to make it! I trust you slept well last night?"

"As well as can be expected," Danny said as he approached the table. "And... you know, I'm not really a master."

"I am the Emperor of this land." Emperor Ezra smiled softly, his boyish eyes taking a moment of levity before returning to their hardened state. "If I say you're a master, then you're a master, and that's the end of it."

"He's got you there," Obadiah commented. "Hate to tell you, Youngblood, but if the Emperor says jump, you ask how high. If he says-"

"Yeah, I got it." Danny sighed and crossed his arms behind his back. "I apologize, your majesty."

"Please, feel no guilt. We're all under a great deal of stress." Emperor Ezra sighed and turned back to the table with a great many documents, all of which were more or less identical to the ones that Zechariah had been messing with, albeit containing slightly different information.

"Now, Danny, I assume you know that you'll be traveling with the Twelfth Legion, leaving in three days?"

"Yes," Danny said. "Why am I being given so long in the city? Most other people get two days' rest."

"And while I'm sure you can handle it, the simple fact of the matter is that the Twelfth isn't due to arrive until today at some point, and they need the rest," Emperor Ezra answered gravely. "You'll be proceeding on a march far to the south."

"There will be multiple loose hordes that you'll need to mop up, a handful of dungeons I'd like you to contain as they break, and one in particular that I'd like you to clear out before it breaks."

"Before it breaks?" Danny bit his lip. "Forgive me for speaking out of turn, but I thought we weren't going to do that. Too risky, and it takes too long."

"And while that's true in most cases, I believe that you were attacked by a dragon and narrowly escaped," Emperor Ezra said. "There's another dungeon along your route that will spawn a dragon, and I believe you'll arrive three days before it erupts."

"I'd like you to clear out the dungeon, just enough that it doesn't break. Don't engage the dragon unless you have to for some reason, but... I can't let another of the beasts escape, not if possible."

"I understand." Danny nodded resolutely. "I'll see what I can do. Will I have any other mages with me?"

"Mages? No, but you'll be traveling with Isa Fireworth. I believe that the two of you are acquainted," Emperor Ezra said.

"While she can no longer create more of the crossbows, which we believe to be somewhat of a travesty, she's expressed interest in rumors of an old artifact located down in this portion of the country. It was for this reason that you were diverted to this location."

"You'll escort her down there and assist in her research, in the hopes that it can help turn the tide of the war."

"I'll do what I can," Danny confirmed.

"And..." Emperor Ezra added. "If I can provide a word of warning, Master Youngblood? I personally fear that traps are being laid for you."

"I can provide no justification for this line of thought, but I strongly suspect that there are forces within the army that seek to lay you low. For the sake of our world, do not allow that to happen."

Danny frowned. He wanted to ask more questions about why the Emperor himself thought such a thing, but it wasn't the time.

Emperor Ezra moved on, and Danny folded his hands behind his back once again.

"Next, we move to the matter of Tess Stoneflower." Emperor Ezra turned. "As you know, you're being reassigned to the Fifth Legion, which gets into town tonight as well."

"This isn't just a random move from one to the other. I'd like you to take personal command of the unit."

Tess's jaw dropped. "But that's-"

"A promotion to Commander for starters, as well as a pay increase..." He chuckled. "From absolutely nothing to a handshake with the Emperor. Sorry, but we really will get you all compensated when this is all over. In any case, do you think you can handle it?"

Tess blinked a few times in shock. "I... I'm honored, and I'll do my best, but why-"

"The very simple answer is that the Fifth Legion lost their commander when they were ambush by trolls," Emperor Ezra answered. "He was a good man, but he's gone now, and from what I can tell, you're as good a replacement as any."

"As soon as they get into town, you'll meet with the men and make yourself acquainted with them, then move out as assigned. You'll be taking the seaboard route that Danny was originally assigned, along with both Masters Barrydew and Flamekeeper."

Danny frowned and took a step back as orders continued to be handed out. Soon, everyone had received their instructions, and he turned to leave as everyone departed.

In the doorway, he could see more people waiting to enter, likely civilian leaders wanting help managing everyone coming into the city, but Emperor Ezra held up a hand. "Please, Danny. Wait for a moment."

Danny paused and held himself back, and everyone else filed out of the room. When they were gone, Emperor Ezra motioned for the doors to be closed, then turned fully to Danny.

"Thank you, first of all, for all that you've done. You know that I hold your personally responsible for freeing me from the influence of the Deepcorp."

Danny nodded. "I know that's what you think."

"Everyone else whom you would credit with assisting you has been amply rewarded, and will continue to be." Emperor Ezra folded his hands behind his back. "Now, I know you're wondering what I know that you don't know."

"I'll admit, it crossed my mind," Danny said.

"And I wish I could give you more answers, but..." The emperor shrugged and shook his head. "What I know is that someone has been appearing around the palace, usually at night in my quarters, to give me messages."

"Most of them pertain to you, a few of them pertain to the broader war or to the missing Deepcorp Lord. Whoever it is smells of dragon ash, which I believe to me more of an identifying marker that they keep about themselves as opposed to actually being covered in dragon ash."

Danny felt his heart leap. "Nicodemus. Well, or Barbara. Or both, I suppose." He sighed. "I'd be lying if I said I knew which one."

Emperor Ezra frowned and nodded. "Anyway, whoever it is wants you to know that the Lord is watching, and preparing to move. He said that the missing lord isn't a patient man, and that you should watch your back at all times."

Danny snorted and shook his head. "More warnings. Got it! I'll watch my back."

Emperor Ezra raised an eyebrow and Danny sighed. "Sorry. First Tess was warning me, then my father, and now you…"

"I see. Well, you can never be too careful, I say." Emperor Ezra clapped Danny on the shoulder.

He started to turn away, then paused. "Oh. He also said that the artifact that Isa is heading to recover could be the tipping point in the war. I don't know more than that."

"Then it's important that Isa bring it back," Danny surmised.

"At any and all cost," Emperor Ezra confirmed. "I'm doing the best I can, but the city is filling with people, and reports of death and destruction are rising every day."

"Your patrols are the only ones I can count on to come back more or less successful, I'm afraid."

"I'll do everything in my power to ensure we succeed," Danny said firmly.

"If it's up to me, and pretty much everything in this Empire is, I'll put a lot more weight than just that upon your shoulders before it's all said and done." Emperor Ezra patted Danny's shoulder.

Then, as Danny turned to leave, the emperor spoke up. "One last thing."

"Yes?" Danny turned slightly.

"While I don't want this to be public knowledge, I want you to know that if you determine that a course of action is better than your orders, you're to feel free to take it." Emperor Ezra's voice was grave.

"If you think that the Dark Lord is hiding in a cave, and tarry for a few hours to check it out, feel free. If you believe that you're coming upon a trap, and divert the entire unit, you're more than free."

"Your new commander knows this as well, though she'll be maintaining control unless you very specifically countermand her orders. She would appreciate it, though, if you talk to her before simply marching off into the wilderness."

Emperor Ezra paused. "Understand that this isn't being given to you lightly, and is authority that I expect you to use only in times of uttermost danger."

He sighed. "Basically, if you feel you need to do something, do it, and if anyone tells you that it's a problem, just bring it back to me and I'll make sure that you're exonerated."

"Fair enough," Danny said.

Emperor Ezra waved a hand to dismiss him, and with that, Danny broke and walked away. Soon, he was out of the grand Throne Room and in the entry hall once more as a whole new group of people filed in to take up the ear of the Emperor.

"Times of war, mmm?"

Zechariah's voice sounded behind him, and Danny turned to find his father striding toward him. He was in fresh combat robes, and his eyes looked far brighter than they had done the previous day.

Danny gave him a nod, and they embraced in a quick hug.

"And how was your meeting with the Emperor?" Zechariah asked as they started walking back through the entry hall.

"Well enough," Danny said with a grin. "I never thought that a sentence like that would be used in casual conversation."

"Oh, I know," Zechariah said. "We live in odd times, but it's times like this that make the greatest heroes."

Danny shook his head. "I'm no hero."

"What's to say that I was talking about you? Don't let that ego go to your head." Zechariah answered.

After a moment, he laughed, and Danny shook his head in exasperation. "Look, get along, and I'll see you soon, I hope. I don't think we'll overlap the next time I'm in town, but perhaps the time after that."

"I'll see you then!"

Zechariah walked along a bit faster and soon vanished out through several side doors. Danny watched him go then folded his hands behind his back and walked out into the city.

He had a few days to rest and relax before he would hit the trail once more. While he had many things that he could have filled his time with, soldiers and mages alike were largely encouraged to actually use the time to rest, ensuring that they would be as good as possible on the grueling trail.

Danny would use the rest of the day to rest, then meet with his new commander bright and early then next morning. And then... Then, it would be back to battle in the war for civilization itself.

He could only hope, with unwavering determination, that it was a battle they could actually win.

Auto save - [Savefile: Information]
Health: 100%
Mana: 100%
Quest: Meet your new captain
Location: Imperial Palace, Entry Hall
Inventory: Essential Supplies, Basic Armor, Iron Sword, Sword of the Wasp, Aquamarine Sword, Frostbite Sword
Skills: Monster Summoner (Lv. 40), Flame Combat (Lv. 2), Wind Combat (Lv. 5)
Relationships: Speaking Terms with Emperor Ezra the Fifth, Family Bond with Zechariah, Ascended Fire Mage
Time of Day: 7:29 a.m.

Five

Nothing To Chance

The next morning, as Danny rose, he found the house quiet and forlorn. He ate breakfast in silence and sighed deeply as he realized that it would likely be months before he saw his father again.

After eating, he wearily changed into his combat robes and belted his sword to his side, then staggered out into the street. There, he made extra certain to lock the door behind him.

While the vast majority of the people flooding into the city were simply trying to stay safe, there were always a few bad actors amidst a crowd that large. Plus, people were getting desperate, and an empty house was an immense temptation for someone with children to shelter.

Frankly, Danny and Zechariah had talked about just selling their house to give to the refugees, but they had decided against it on account of the training center in the basement, as well as the assorted secrets that Zechariah had accumulated over the years. Plus, they did need a safe place to withdraw during their times in the city.

In any case, Danny headed up toward the Academy, which was now serving as a command center of sorts for the efforts. It was still being used for an actual academy, mostly for first and second year students who were still too weak to send into battle, but those classes were largely confined to the First-Year Wing.

Everything else was being turned out for the war effort. As Danny strode up the stairs to the academy, he sighed deeply.

Banners fluttered from the parapets; banners of the Empire, banners of the mages, and banners of the Imperial Corp. Never before had Danny seen so much cooperation between the different branches of imperial forces, which he had to admit he rather liked.

As he walked up and into the Grand Hall, he found soldiers bustling this way and that, and he turned and walked over to the receptionist.

"Can I help you?" she asked, looking up from a pile of paperwork deeper than some oceans. "Please do be quick about it."

"I'm just looking for the commander of the Twelfth Legion," Danny answered.

"Ahh... Let me see. They just got in last night, as I recall." The woman flipped through a few pages then nodded.

"Yes. The soldiers are camping out in the barracks in the History Wing. The commander, one Captain Anne, was assigned to the Research Wing for something. Couldn't tell you what."

"I think I've got an idea." Danny felt a smile break across his face from ear to ear. "Thanks!"

He felt a distinct spring in his step as he swept through the lobby and made his way up the stairs. It didn't take him long to reach the Research Wing.

When he had first arrived at the Academy, the reclusive and strange wing of the building, the only wing to allow non-mages to work and teach, he had been inherently distrustful of it. Now, he found that it was among his favorite wings in the building.

Once he arrived, he spent a few moments checking around, eventually making his way to a large laboratory near the rear. With a flourish, he threw open the doors and strode inside where Isa and Captain Anne looked up from a map that was tacked to a table near the rear of the room.

"Danny!" Isa beamed from ear to ear.

"Master Youngblood," Anne corrected her, and stood at attention, though she, too, had a smile upon her face. "It's good to see you."

"You, too." Danny embraced Isa as she ran over to him then shook Captain Anne's hand. "I've been wondering how you two were doing."

"Just us?" Captain Anne raised an eyebrow.

"Okay, you and just about everyone else I've had any contact with." Danny sighed and walked over to look down at the map that depicted the entire Empire as well as the handful of lands that were known beyond the Empire's borders.

"Strange times we live in."

"You can say that again." Isa grimaced. "When I first arrived here and you drove an evil spirit out of me, I thought that was crazy."

"Now... I don't know. Makes me terrified if I think about it for more than three seconds at a time."

"Courage." Captain Anne crossed her arms. "We'll make it through. The Empire has gone through hard times before."

Isa raised an eyebrow. "Tell me one other time, in the history of the Empire, where the dungeons began overflowing at an uncontrollable rate, threatening the entire human population."

"Ahh..." Captain Anne shrugged. "Maybe there was another Empire before this one?"

"And it was completely and utterly overthrown, resulting in the need to completely rebuild a new one?" Isa laughed. "You're not exactly making me confident here."

Captain Anne turned to Danny and nodded. "I was glad to find out you've been placed under my command. Pretty much everyone's been campaigning to get you in their unit."

"We took quite a beating last time."

Danny grimaced and sat down in a nearby chair as Isa turned back to the map. "What tour did you take?"

"We were on a long one, and on our own, without a mage. That's what our legion has been pegged to do, mostly."

Anne sighed and sat down as well. "We went down to the wasteland, down near Castle Rock, actually. We could see it in the distance, though I suppose that doesn't really narrow it down all that much, since you can see the thing from so far away."

"Anyway, we were doing well at first, mostly containing C and D-ranked Dungeons, but then we had an A-ranker that we had to stem."

"An A-rank dungeon, without a mage?" Danny's jaw dropped.

"It wasn't supposed to overflow until next week," Anne said. "There was another group coming through that was going to take it, I think the Tenth Legion, but then it burst, and we had a town to save."

"I lost almost a quarter of my men in that battle. We were able to limp back and mostly did the rest of our duty, but it wasn't easy, and we lost a whole lot more people on the way back."

"I'm sorry to hear that," Danny murmured.

"It's alright." Anne sighed and turned away from the table. "Anyway, today I've got replacement troops heading in. A few of them are coming from the Twenty-First, but most of them are new recruits from the Imperial City and the surrounding area."

"I've got to go get them integrated. Make sure you ride out with us when the time comes."

"I'll be there." Danny waved.

Anne strode from the room, waving once more at Isa.

As the door fell shut, Isa flashed him a smile and turned back to the map. "I suppose you're wondering what this mysterious artifact that I'm chasing happens to be."

"I'll admit, I've been rather curious about it." Danny chuckled and climbed to his feet, stepping up to her. "Where's it located?"

"Somewhere right... Here." Isa pointed at the map, down to the south. "There's a small mountain range right here, the Dead Mountains."

"Ominous, I know, but it's named for a mountain that looks sorta like a skull if the light is right."

"And you think there's something there?" Danny asked.

"Well, you remember my research that I've been working on for the last few years? The impact of dungeon artifacts on the progress of society, and vice versa?" Isa asked.

"Well, I was digging around, and I found something that was buried pretty good in some of the files. You remember Marshal, of course?"

"The mage who created the Desert Sapiens and tried to overthrow the Empire?" Danny raised an eyebrow. "Sorta hard to forget him."

"Well, he was hard to forget in his own time as well," Isa answered. "About twenty years after he vanished, another student rose up who tried to press onward with his research."

"That student became an Ascended Mage by the name of Thurston, specializing in the study of dungeon artifacts. He was formally a wind mage, but he had a fascination with all things that came from the dungeons, and actually made a lot of headway in the science of what we now know as Dungeon Analysis, Dungeon Tactics, and that sort of thing."

"Hmm." Danny frowned and crossed his arms. "So, when did he go crazy?"

"That's the thing. He never did," Isa said. "He spent a distinguished career in the field, did a ten-year research stint where he mostly just traveled from dungeon to dungeon to dungeon collecting information, and then became Headmaster and spent the rest of his career putting the information together."

"The only reason I found him was because he referenced Marshal extensively, as being a pioneer in the field while Thurston himself was a mere follower. I digress, though. The point is that, beyond what I've just told you, the file was empty."

"Empty?" Danny frowned. "Someone did so much, and contributed so much, and the file was empty?"

Isa nodded. "Exactly. It made me wonder what he might have dug up, so I started going through the library."

"It wasn't easy with Master Barrydew gone, and the new librarian under strict orders not to allow anyone into the Forbidden Archives, but I did manage to pull a few strings. Eventually, I found that he had formed a group of students known as the explorers."

"A terribly generic name, but they apparently roamed far and wide for him once he became tethered to his desk in the spire, and often reported back to him on their findings even after they became full mages. They were loyal to him, and apparently received prominent placings in the army as a result."

"Anyway, toward the end of their career, it seems that they discovered something in the Dead Mountains. They brought it back to the Academy, where the report goes dead."

"I haven't a clue what they found, or what they did with it once they got here, but several generations later, another Headmaster made the note that he discovered a secret room in the Spire that contained something. He then reported that he had it transferred back to the Dead Mountains where it belonged."

"I can only assume that they're the same things."

Danny crossed his arms. "Did you bring this to Headmaster Bluestream?"

"I did. He looked like he wanted to throw me out of his office for merely suggesting it, but he went ahead and looked through his files for me."

Isa shrugged. "For what it's worth, he was able to find a few documents that mentioned the secret room, and actually opened it up for me. It's pretty cool. Totally empty now."

"He's clueless about what it could be, but desperately wants to find it."

"I see." Danny frowned. "What do you know about where to find it?"

"I have those clues in a sealed envelope I keep in my inventory," Isa answered. "No one else except myself knows what's inside it, and I don't plan on telling anyone. I'll reveal the information, a bit at a time, where we get there."

"Sounds harsh." Danny climbed to his feet.

"We're being watched, you know," Isa commented.

As Danny started to walk toward the door, he paused, then turned back. "Watched?"

"I know you've felt him. He's watching us, through the eyes of others." Isa shrugged.

"I was able to resist him, since I knew the moment he tried to enter my mind, but others aren't so cautious. I don't know that you're so cautious, since you've never had an entity mucking about inside your head."

Danny bit his lip then nodded. "Fair enough."

Isa gave him a small nod then turned back. "Now, if you'll excuse me, I have some work I need to get squared away before we depart."

"As it turns out, a lot of people at this academy have been looking forward to my reports on a wide variety of subjects, and if I don't get them turned in before I go, half a dozen people are going to want my head on a silver platter when I get back."

"Fair enough!" Danny laughed, quickly turning and stepping into the hall. He immediately noticed Captain Anne leaning against the wall, waiting.

Danny frowned as she glanced his way.

"Walk with me?"

"Ah... sure." Danny started down the hall, and she joined him. Her slightly tense posture made him wonder.

"What's going on?"

"What's going on is Isa," Captain Anne murmured. "I don't know if you've noticed, but she seems... Strange. Extra secretive."

"She wouldn't tell me where the artifact is located, even though I know she knows. I was wondering if she happened to tell you."

"No." Danny decided to play along. "She didn't."

"I just..." Anne sighed and shook her head. "I'm worried about her. I know she's struggled with evil spirits in the past, and now with this dark lord popping around in people's heads..."

"Make sure you keep a close eye on her, alright? If she blinks wrong, or if I give the order, I need to know that you'll be with me."

"I'll be with you." Danny turned and gazed into her eyes. "Anne."

Anne blinked a few times, and Danny shrugged and turned back straight. Her steps seemed to pick up again, and her posture resumed a more normal stance.

As they swept out through the halls and toward the front of the Academy, Danny struggled to keep his mind focused. It was enough to make him want to scream with rage, but... what could he do?

The Dark Lord was doing everything possible to bring ruin upon them, even when things were falling apart around them. It wasn't enough for the Deepcorp, who wouldn't dare stop until the last remnants of the Empire were completely and utterly crushed.

Thankfully, he wasn't perfect. Anne couldn't have known about the whole dark lord possessing people, since she hadn't been in on those conversations.

The only reason Isa knew was because she had recognized him when the lord popped into her head. Anne had no way of knowing.

It was a tip of the lord's hand, but it was still far from comforting to Danny. In fact, it only made him more nervous.

Whoever it was, he was leaving nothing to chance. Danny could only hope that as events continued to play out the man would eventually make some small slip, just enough that they could catch him.

If he didn't... Well... Danny was afraid that they were looking at the later days of the Empire.

Auto save - [Savefile: Information]
Health: 100%
Mana: 100%
Quest: Prepare for Departure
Location: Research Wing
Inventory: Essential Supplies, Basic Armor, Iron Sword, Sword of the Wasp, Aquamarine Sword, Frostbite Sword
Skills: Monster Summoner (Lv. 40), Flame Combat (Lv. 2), Wind Combat (Lv. 5)
Relationships: Friendly with Isa, Friendly with Captain Anne
Time of Day: 6:58 a.m.

Six

Towards Achievement

When the morning of their departure came, Danny made his way to the Town Square, where soldiers were being assembled. The Twelfth Legion, along with the First Legion, were both making themselves ready.

Danny caught sight of Captain Anne mingling with some of her lower officers, and he waved and made his way over toward her. She waved back, then motioned for him to come and meet with some of her soldiers.

"This is Sergeant Haley, and this is Lieutenant George," She said nodding her head at the men. "This is Master Youngblood."

"The strongest mage in the whole Empire, from what I hear," Sergeant Haley joked, tucking his helmet under his arm. "You think you'll be able to take care of us, kid?"

Danny laughed and shook his head. "I'm just here to do my job, alright?"

"Hey! So are we." Lieutenant George waved and started back into the crowd. "You watch our backs, and we'll watch yours. Got it?"

Danny nodded and waved after them, then turned to Anne. "How are things looking?"

"As good as they can be." She sighed. "We've got a long march ahead of us, and we're going to have to do it mostly on foot. We have horses to pull the baggage wagons, but that's it."

TOWARDS ACHIEVEMENT   47

Danny's jaw dropped. "We're walking the whole way? What happened? The last three tours I've done have all been mounted, at least mostly."

Anne could only shrug. "Horses are dying faster than soldiers, I'm afraid. We still have to maintain the same schedule, so..."

She turned and gestured south. "We're to contain a B-rank dungeon tonight, twenty miles south. We'd better get moving."

Danny nodded wearily. Marching the distance in a single day wasn't the problem.

No, it was marching that far and then having the strength to still fight.

"Let's get moving," Danny said resolutely.

The caravan set out promptly at 8:00 that morning, sweeping out of the city gates and heading toward the hills at a brisk pace. Danny marched near the front, alongside Captain Anne, while Isa rode on the baggage train, perched next to the coach driver amid the numerous tents, food supplies, and extra weapons.

Danny had traveled south from the city many times during his academy years, and the path felt mostly familiar as they crossed the barren hills and descended toward the south. Limestone boulders dotted the rolling slopes, now accompanied by tents—some forming small, bustling encampments, others pitched in isolation.

The tents stretched up to the edge of the scorched landscape where the dragon had attacked, a place still too inhospitable for even the hardiest travelers. As they moved further south, the landscape grew wilder, and Danny shuddered at the sight.

They didn't halt until they reached a small settlement with an inn where Danny had stayed during his first academy trip. Weary and broken soldiers were just returning from battle as the caravan arrived.

After some brief exchanges between the groups, Danny frowned when Captain Anne pulled him aside with one of the commanders.

"What's going on?" Danny asked as the other soldier, Captain Jacobs, crossed his weary and battered arms. "Did you guys fall behind your main unit?"

"I wish." Captain Jacobs sighed. "This is all that's left of the Sixth Legion."

"All that's left?" Danny's eyes widened, his mouth opening slightly as he tried to find the right words. His breath caught, and for a moment, he could only stare, completely taken aback.

"There are only like... Fifteen people here!"

"Seventeen, including myself," Captain Jacobs confirmed. "We ran into an ambush on the mountain slopes, about a day's march south of here."

Danny frowned. "A dungeon broke that wasn't expected?"

Captain Jacobs shook his head. "No. Once more, I could only wish. It was a band of thugs. Must have been a hundred of them."

"They started an avalanche that buried half my men. We fought them off as best we could, but had to retreat when it drew a handful of werewolves from the hills."

"Last I saw them, they were carrying off our armor, weapons, anything they could grab."

"People are getting desperate," Danny muttered through gritted teeth.

"That's one way of putting it." Captain Jacobs shook his head in frustration. "Look, I'm... I'm angry, but there's nothing I can do."

"Tomorrow morning, I'll march the last of my soldiers back to the Imperial City so we can get outfitted with another group. At least, that's the plan."

He kicked at the ground. "Almost makes me want to give up, but then I'd still just wind up fighting for my life somewhere else. I'd rather pick my battlefield than have it chosen for me, you know?"

"Good man," Captain Anne said. "Keep up the good work."

Captain Jacobs sighed then turned to Danny. "I don't think I need to tell you, Danny, that you're our last hope."

With that, Captain Jacobs took his men and made his way into the inn while Anne started issuing orders. The dungeon they were supposed to take on was located just half a mile away, and they quickly made themselves ready and started marching in that direction.

"It's a magic dungeon!" Anne called out above the crowd as they came into view of the dungeon. "Probably a higher concentration of wraiths and that sort of thing than normal. Prepare accordingly!"

The soldiers nodded and began to make themselves ready, applying silver power to the weapons and such things while Danny set his jaw.

"You know, it's strange," he murmured to Captain Anne. "When I first got to the academy, everyone looked at me like I was going to end the world. Now that the world is ending, I'm seen as the only hope."

"Strange, isn't it?"

"You could say that." Captain Anne flashed a small smile. "I'm just glad you didn't get discouraged and turn against us."

Danny had more to say, but at that moment, the dungeon broke open. As monsters came screaming out, Danny charged into motion.

The number of magical monsters was unusually high. Griffins streaked across the sky, their feathers raining fire on the soldiers below.

Wraiths surged forward, unleashing bolts of lightning, frost, and flame, while darker creatures slithered out, hurling themselves against the lines of soldiers, clawing at their shields and tearing at their armor. Danny's stone golems smashed through the enemy ranks, crushing them with relentless force.

He held his breath, tension gripping him.

The dungeon didn't take long to clear, and not a single soldier was lost. As they returned to the inn that evening, Danny felt a measure of relief about their chances, and the soldiers seemed reinvigorated.

As the sun set, they gathered for a brief meal, preparing to rest for the night ahead.

"I heard you were really something today," Captain Jacobs said as he stopped by Danny's cot underneath the stars. "I just want you to know that it's an honor to have met you. Really makes me think we can do this."

Danny nodded and shook his hand. "Can you tell me how much longer people are going to be willing to fight? How much longer before people do start giving up?"

Captain Jacobs puffed out his cheeks. "Honestly, I don't know. Pretty much everyone is concerned that this fight isn't sustainable."

"We can war against the dungeons all we want, but if they're popping at this rate... I don't know. Doesn't seem to me like we can win in the long term, but if we give up, we're just going to allow them to kill us all, so..."

"Beats me. Quite a predicament, and most of us are just so tired all we can do is keep fighting."

As Captain Jacobs walked off, Danny bit his lip.

"At least for now," he mumbled to himself.

The next morning, they marched south as quickly as they could. There was only one dungeon on their schedule for that day, a C-ranker that was about a mile off their path.

As they approached it, Danny glanced at Anne and leaned over.

"You know, I can take this one by myself if you want to keep the rank and file moving onward. Might give them a bit of rest."

"Not to mention the fact that it'll only increase your legend among them." Anne smirked at him.

Danny felt heat rise to his cheeks. "I didn't mean-"

"I know, I know." She laughed. "Go. We could use the break."

Danny nodded and split off from the main group, making his way toward the location, which was a Labyrinth-style dungeon nestled next to a rather picturesque lake. There was a local fisherman sitting in a small boat, happily reeling in catfish as the dungeon broke open and minotaurs came pouring out.

When Danny's army of stone golems had done their work, he thanked Danny profusely, and promised to get to proper civilization... Right after he'd brought in the year's harvest, and made sure that he'd stored up enough for winter. Danny had to laugh at the man, who apparently had no concept of the fact that the world was ending.

When Danny got to camp late that evening, he opened his inventory and tossed several minotaur heads onto the ground, eliciting quite a few cheers from the army. He then took out several catfish that had been given to him in thanks, and passed them to the cook before going to join Captain Anne, who was looking at the mountains to the south.

They were huge and foreboding, and Danny could hear the distant roars of creatures that were taking up refuge within their protective borders.

"Sounds like you had quite a time," Captain Anne murmured as they looked up at the immense mountains.

"First time I've ever gotten freshly-caught fish as a reward for clearing a dungeon." Danny laughed softly. "Oh, and I leveled up again."

"I'm glad. Happy for you." Captain Anne frowned, not looking away from the mountains.

"Sorry to be a downer, I just... Tomorrow, we'll go through the pass where the Seventh Legion was ambushed."

Danny winced. "That's not going to be good."

"I've half a mind to take an alternate route, and half a mind to stick to the course," Anne said. "Alternate routes are more dangerous, but also... We're not going to have time to stop to mourn them, or to bury them."

"We've got to stick to the course," Danny said firmly. "At least, that's my opinion, for what it's worth. We'll find some way to make a memorial for them, as we pass."

The next morning, despite Anne's misgivings, they set off as planned and soon entered the narrow pass. Barely half a mile in, they reached the site of the ambush.

Thankfully, they were spared the sight of their companions' decaying bodies; it seemed the remains had been devoured. Out of respect, they gathered the scattered armor pieces into a large heap as they passed, and that was that.

Danny could only imagine how many similar monuments would be erected across the Empire before the war's end.

As they descended from the mountains, they turned east, setting a direct course for the Dead Mountains. The march took a week, leading them through several small towns and one larger metropolis, almost half the size of the Imperial City.

Known as the Lesser City, it had once served as a secondary throne for the Emperor, governing his more distant lands. Now, like the Imperial City, it was overflowing with people, and they passed through it as quickly as possible.

The other towns they encountered were as varied as could be imagined. Some villages remained picturesque, their residents knowing of the war only through the passing soldiers.

Others lay in smoking ruins, devoid of life. Most, however, were somewhere in between, with frantic inhabitants either erecting barricades and practicing with swords or loading up wagons, seeking safer lands.

Finally, after a week and a half, a mountain loomed on the horizon. As they marched toward it in the morning light, the sun's rays from the east revealed two deep hollows in its slopes that resembled eyes.

From such a distance, the mountain truly looked like a skull, and Danny shuddered at the sight.

"And there you have it," Isa commented as she walked up next to him, leaving the baggage train. "The Dead Mountains.

They formally separate the central plains from the jungles of the south, at least in this part of the Empire."

Danny tried to see behind the stony edifice. He could just make out another mountain behind it, and perhaps one more beyond that.

All looked as if they harbored a deep evil, though that might have simply been his mind impressing that fact upon the mountains.

"Now do we get to know where this thing is located?" Danny asked, half-joking.

Isa shook her head. "Not yet. Just stick to the scheduled path, and I'll tell you when it's time to do something."

Anne turned and glared slightly at Isa, but Isa didn't seem to notice. Danny thought he saw a few faint wisps of smoke dancing around Anne's head, but he couldn't tell for sure.

Either way, they were almost there, almost to whatever was hidden within the rocky slopes. Maybe it would be nothing and they would have to keep fighting the war in their desperate bid for survival.

On the other hand, maybe it would indeed turn the tide of war against the great beasts. He had no way of knowing... and they wouldn't know until they had managed to find what centuries had covered over.

Time to get to work.
Auto save - [Savefile: Information]
Health: 100%
Mana: 100%
Quest: Located Isa's artifact
Location: Southern Plains, Steppes of the Dead Mountains
Inventory: Essential Supplies, Basic Armor, Iron Sword, Sword of the Wasp, Aquamarine Sword, Frostbite Sword
Skills: Monster Summoner (Lv. 41), Flame Combat (Lv. 2), Wind Combat (Lv. 5)

Relationships: Friendly with Isa, Friendly with Captain Anne
Time of Day: 5:47 P.M.

Seven

Unexpected Dungeon

The next morning, they rose to face the dawn with a sense of unease. Armor clattered as the soldiers gathered their gear, and the baggage crew quickly packed up the tents.

The army began to move out, drawing closer to the looming mountain, its skull-like shape glaring down at them in the morning light. Danny joined Anne at the front, nodding toward their destination.

"What's our target?"

"Our first stop is a dungeon in the foothills," Anne replied. "It's about an hour's march from here. A-ranked."

"Piece of cake." Danny rubbed his hands together.

"Just be careful," Anne cautioned. "I have a feeling things won't go as planned today."

Danny frowned. "Premonition? I don't really believe in such things, but-"

"I don't know." Anne shook her head. "Sometimes, at nights, you can tell that something's about to happen because the insects stop chirping."

"Sometimes, when you walk into a city, you can tell that things are about to go sideways because you see more people clustered around the taverns than ought to be right. I can't put my finger on it, but I have a feeling that this day will end with blood."

"Well, I hope you're wrong," Danny said.

Anne nodded. "As do I, as do I..."

They moved swiftly, covering ground with purpose, and soon reached the foothills. The army kept pace, energized and seemingly ready for the battle ahead.

Danny's breath caught as they crested a large rise, revealing the dungeon entrance below. The entrance was imposing—a massive, dark arch framed by two heavy wooden doors etched with ominous runes.

The doors loomed before them, radiating an unsettling energy. Danny knelt in the grass, eyes narrowing as he studied the ancient symbols.

Anne stopped beside him, raising a hand to halt the advancing army. "How tall would you measure those doors to be?" Anne asked.

Danny squinted his eyes then shrugged. "I wouldn't know. Fifty feet or more?"

"That's what I thought, too." She balled her hands into fists. "That looks to me like an S-ranked dungeon."

Danny nodded slowly. "I was thinking the same thing. We can take it, though."

"Can we?" Anne spun back around. "We left all our gear for S-ranked raids back in the baggage train."

"S-ranked dungeons are a whole new level of chaos. We can't just go at it. We can't just brace for impact."

"True enough." Danny paused then slowly climbed back to his feet. "Have everyone fall back. Line the ridge, be ready with bows to get anything that slips past me."

"You're seriously going to try to stem the tide of an S-ranked dungeon all by yourself?" Anne blinked a few times like he wasn't serious.

"I always keep a few items on me in case of an emergency." Danny opened his inventory and pulled out a purple mana crystal as he started down the slope.

"If we're wrong, and it is just an A-ranked dungeon, I'll just spawn my normal monsters, and you all can engage as you see fit."

"Alright." Anne bit her lip. "Be careful, Danny."

Danny waved over his shoulder and soon reached the bottom of the slope. Once he was a good fifty feet below his friends, he paused on the low, rocky trail.

The doors of the dungeon began to tremble, and he held out his mana crystal.

[Notice: The Oak Door Dungeon will now begin to overflow!][Warning: This is an S-Ranked Dungeon]

Danny tried to think through all the S-ranked dungeons he had learned. The previous two years, he had been required to memorize a list of every single one in the land.

The Oak Door Dungeon didn't sound to him like it fit on that list, though he certainly hadn't been the best student in the class. In any case, there he was, and there it was, which didn't leave him with a lot of options.

"Then let's get this show on the road." He activated his purple mana crystal and let the energy flow down into his arm. "Dragon Hatchling."

With a flash, the creature appeared in front of him. Smaller than most dragons, it was a good twenty or thirty feet long as it spread its wings wide.

It had blue scales and snarled at the open door. It was quite handy in a fight, by far the most powerful thing that Danny had ever absorbed.

Well, until he had acquired the attributes for the green dragon, which would have been nice, except for the fact that it was just so hard to create. In any case, the blue dragon spread its wings and drew in a deep breath, and the dungeon doors burst open.

Rrrrrrrrrrrrrrrrrraaaaaaaaaaaaaaaarrrrrrrrrrrrrrrrrgh!

A gout of dragon fire rolled across the ground, burning away the grass and melting rocks into nothing but slag. The first line of monsters out the door, trolls that looked to be Level 80 or higher, hit the wall of fire and collapsed into ash, white bones clattering to the ground before they'd made it a full ten feet out the door.

The dragon kept up the burst of fire for almost thirty seconds, as monsters continued to pour out through the doors and the dragon continued to incinerate them.

[Notification: Monster Summoning has increased to Lv. 42!][Reward: Mana Increase: 1562 -> 1640]

Danny smiled and punched the air in delight. At the end of the blast, the dragon hatchling allowed the fire to die away and shook a bit of smoke out of its nostrils.

With that, it charged forward, throwing itself into the fray. The dungeon continued to produce mostly trolls, golems, and giants.

They were all humanoid, in any case, sprinkled with a good number of Goblin Lords and Massive undead and things of that nature. The dragon tore straight through them, clawing them to bits with iron claws.

It was really quite impressive, on a great many levels. Gore filled the small ravine, massive heads thunked against the ground and rolled across the stone.

Danny smiled at the incredible sight. Wham!

A huge troll, larger than any Danny had ever seen before, came charging out of the dungeon. It stood almost as tall as the doors themselves and had black scales across his skin.

The club it carried whacked the dragon hard, sending it flying back across the ground to land more or less where Danny was standing.

[Monster Identified: Dragonskin Troll. Level: 100. HP: 200,000]

The dragon took another breath and launched another blast of flame which roiled and churned around the monster with unfathomable fury. Monsters on either side of the troll fell, but it began to press forward.

Slowly, against the rage of the beast, it fought toward the dragon and raised its club once again. "No!" Danny ran to the side, and the dragon darted to the other side.

The club came crashing down between them, sending out a shockwave that flattened Danny and knocked the dragon asunder. The troll glanced back and forth between the two, then snorted and turned toward the dragon.

By that time, the army up top was starting to pass out their S-ranked gear, having apparently had just enough time to catch up with the wagon. Magical arrows flew down, exploding against stony skin, while staves allowed the non-magical soldiers to launch high-level spells.

Danny watched it for a second, then frowned as several large spider-trolls clambered up the other side of the ravine and escaped. "Go after them, Danny!" Anne called out to him. "We've got this!"

Danny flashed her a thumbs-up, then spawned in a stone golem. He leapt up into the creature, and went charging off up the slope.

The dragon was still engaged with the dragonscale troll, neither of which paid him any attention. Soon, he was racing across the rolling hills, chasing after the trolls as quickly as he could.

That was when he caught sight of something. Ahead, a small caravan was winding through the hills; five wagons and a handful of people.

The trolls were bearing down upon them, while he saw several of the people turning and running for the hills. Danny gritted his teeth, then put on a burst of speed.

He caught up with the trolls right as they reached the caravan. The lead troll bent down to snatch at a wagon, but Danny leapt past the rear trolls and punched it as hard as he could.

The troll was sent tumbling, and he spun around and smashed a fist into the face of the next troll. As Spider-trolls, each had four arms (which were a good bit more spindly than normal).

They snarled and leapt upon him as he threw himself into the fight. For the next several minutes, Danny and the trolls crashed around the neighboring hills.

He was knocked down time and time again, only to get up to slam the trolls to the ground. The civilians stood there, just watching, unable to turn away from the horrific battle around them.

Finally, Danny grabbed a large boulder, hefted it over his head, and smashed the head of the last troll flat. As it collapsed, breathing heavily, he turned toward the caravan.

Everyone there flinched in fear, and he allowed himself to step down from the golem. What they would have seen was the golem, which was a good forty feet tall, bending down and holding out its palm.

With a flash of light, he appeared in the palm then hopped down. The bystanders stared at him in awe, and one of them, an older man, slowly stepped forward.

"You're Youngblood, the summoner."

Danny sighed. He hadn't realized that his fame had spread so far. "That's me."

"Well! What do you know about that?" The man laughed and took off his hat. "I've been hearing rumors about you ever since you entered the Academy! Lotta folks thought you were going to go nuts and burn the nation down! Guess you decided it was more fun to save it instead, that right?"

"Something like that." Danny shook his head then sighed. "Well, we'd better get you on the road again."

"Much obliged to you!" The man waved and started making his way back to his wagon. All around him, the other members of the caravan started gathering up items that had fallen on the ground.

"I'd have hated to be so close to safety just to get squashed!" Something about the way the man said it made Danny pause.

He looked out across the rolling hills where the dragon and the troll were still duking it out, then turned back. "What exactly do you mean by that?" Danny asked.

"Well, just that we're almost to safety, and then those things appeared, and I thought we'd been fools to wait until morning to leave." He sighed as he climbed up onto the wagon box and took up the reins of the head wagon.

"What do you mean by safety?" Danny demanded. "You know of a safe place?"

"I reckon we do." The man nodded. "Tor-sava! I don't blame you for not hearing about it, we only just learned about it a little bit ago."

"Tor-sava?" Danny shook his head. "I'm confused. What... Where..."

"Please." A woman walked up, sighing. "You have to forgive my father, he doesn't always explain things the best."

"About two weeks ago, someone came to our village, telling of us a safe place where we wouldn't have to worry about the monsters. A mountain city called Tor-sava."

"Right down this road, it's nestled in the heart of the mountains. We're told that we won't have to worry about... Anything, really."

Danny bit his lip. "And what do you know of it?"

"Nothing more than what I've told you." The woman answered. "Thing is, I don't care. Maybe it isn't safe, but from what I've heard, the Imperial City isn't exactly a beacon in these trying times, either."

"We've had a dozen attacks against our village, lost half our population. Any chance that we can find is worth it."

"Fair enough," Danny murmured.

A few moments later, the caravan resumed its march, and Danny turned back toward the battle. His stone golem thundered along beside him as he sprinted over the ground.

Minutes later, they reached the fight, where the army struggled to hold back an ever-growing wave of trolls, while the dragon clashed furiously with the dragonscale troll. Gritting his teeth, Danny watched as his stone golem charged into the fray, smashing through the ranks of trolls and easing the pressure on the beleaguered soldiers.

'Come on,' he murmured. 'Don't let me down.' The dragon snarled, then lunged upward, scaling the troll with terrifying speed.

In an instant, it coiled around the troll's neck, tightening its tail in a crushing grip. The troll staggered, teetering on its feet, before the dragon unleashed a blast of fire directly into its face.

The troll crumpled to the ground in a lifeless heap, and the dragon leapt back, ready to take on the remaining beasts.

[Notice: You have defeated an S-Ranked Boss solo! Please name your reward]

Danny's jaw dropped. "Name my reward?"

[Yes. Defeating an S-ranked boss solo entitles you to a reward of your choosing. If you do not select, a random S-ranked item will be given to you.]

"Right." Danny frowned. Should he ask for a sword? A better summons? Or...

"I want a purple mana crystal strong enough to spawn my green dragon," he finally said. With a flash, a huge crystal appeared on the ground in front of him.

It was almost two feet in any given dimension, and as he picked it up, he found it so heavy that he could hardly lift it. When he stuck it into his inventory, he found that it took up every last bit of his free space, but he didn't care.

Quickly, he crossed his arms and started down the hill as the battle played itself out. The dungeon had been defeated, and he was walking away with quite a prize.

Now it was time to figure out what exactly was going on.

Auto save - [Savefile: Information]
Health: 92%
Mana: 51%

Quest: Figure out what happened to the dungeon

Location: Southern Plains, Steppes of the Dead Mountains

Inventory: Essential Supplies, Basic Armor, Iron Sword, Sword of the Wasp, Aquamarine Sword, Frostbite Sword

Skills: Monster Summoner (Lv. 42), Flame Combat (Lv. 2), Wind Combat (Lv. 5)

Relationships: Friendly with Isa, Friendly with Captain Anne

Time of Day: 11:37 a.m.

Eight

Tor-sava

"Well. That's done." Danny grimaced, standing on the charred ground in front of the now-closed doors.

"All thanks to you," Anne murmured.

"Guys!" Isa flew down the slope, a book tucked under her arm. She flipped it open as she arrived and passed it across to them.

"I just wanted you to know that I just checked on it, and I can confirm that this thing was listed as an A-rank dungeon in the last three surveys of the land performed over the previous hundred years. The fact that it's S-ranked is new."

"Can dungeons spontaneously change from one rank to another?" Danny asked, concerned.

"It's not unheard-of," Anne said, crossing her arms. "That said, it's not common in the slightest. The fact that it happened here and now makes me suspicious."

"I agree," Isa confirmed.

"And here's something even stranger..." Danny quickly told them about the caravan.

When he finished, Anne stroked her chin in thought. "The combination of all of this has me extremely worried. I fear a trap."

"I think this was the trap." Isa pointed at the doors and laughed. "You don't get much more of a trap than this!"

"Whatever it is, it smells of the Deepcorp to me." Danny crossed his arms and slowly turned to look across the mountains. "What's your route now?"

"We're passing between the mountain of the skull and the second mountain, then we'll come around the southern slope and continue on eastward," Isa answered. "Three days, and then we'll be moving on. Why?"

"Because I'd like to go check out this location." Danny answered. "This... Tor-sava. I don't know what it is, but I almost think that it might have something to do with the Deepcorp."

"That city could be as much a trap as anything else," Anne said. "If it really is some sort of safe haven being run by the Deepcorp... I don't know. Or it's just a trap, or it could just be bandits luring desperate pilgrims."

"I think I need to go find out," Danny said resolutely. "Please."

Isa sighed then nodded. "We don't have anything major that we'll be doing for the next three days. Make sure you're back with us by the fourth morning. We'll be heading for the Snakeskull Dungeon, which is listed as an S-ranker."

Danny nodded. "I'll do it."

"Any chance I could come with you?" Isa asked. "Just... Because?"

Anne frowned, but Danny nodded quickly. "Of course you can," he said with a smile.

When Anne snarled softly, Danny briefly considered calling the dragon over to him. It was still sniffing around the base of the doors, making sure it was, indeed, over.

After a moment, though, she relaxed and nodded. "I'll see you both on the other side," she said. "Don't leave me hanging."

Danny nodded, and they took a few moments to gather up their belongings. After unsummoning the monsters, he and Isa struck off across the hills.

A few of the soldiers glanced off after him, but they were too well-trained to question it. Soon, they were out of sight, heading for the same road where he had found the pilgrims.

"What do you think we'll find?" Isa asked as they moved along, wandering down through the hills until they reached the path.

They turned toward the mountains, and Danny thought he could see the wagons just off in the distance, slowly mounting the slopes as they climbed upward.

"I don't know," Danny murmured, as if afraid that the Deepcorp Lord would be able to hear him. "Do you think it's something to do with the Deepcorp?"

Isa shrugged. "I don't know. What I do know is that dungeons aren't likely to just change shape and size. The only way to do that would be to affect the Dungeon Core itself."

"And... The only way to do that, at least as far as I know, is to be a very powerful mage."

"Right." Isa frowned. "And what would the purpose of it be?"

"Well, I suppose that's what we'll find out," Danny said. "Come on."

They moved along the road quickly and lost sight of the wagons as they entered the steep mountain passes. As they reached the mountains themselves, they moved along a bit slower, not wanting to be seen by the civilians.

Danny had no particular worries about the intentions of the civilians themselves, but he had a great many worries about the people that the refugees might speak to. In any case, as the pass wound through the mountains, sometimes crossing the edges of immense cliffs and other times wandering across small meadows, they sometimes caught sight of the wagon train.

Finally, Danny held up a hand, and they paused in a small, rocky meadow dotted with yellow flowers. "Here." He pointed at the ground where the grass was slightly bent-over.

He scanned the meadow carefully, spotting the faintest trail winding through the grass. Across the way, a narrow crevice branched off from the main path.

Isa frowned, then nodded, and they quickly moved toward it. As they entered the crevice, the first signs of danger appeared—large, sharpened poles wedged into the stone walls, acting as deadly spears meant to impale any large monsters that dared to pass.

Many of these makeshift weapons were already stained with blood. They soon passed barricades and archer nooks carved into the rock.

Finally, they rounded a bend and found an iron gate blocking their path. Danny couldn't see anything beyond it, so he approached cautiously.

No one appeared as he neared the gate. Danny reached out and knocked, the sound of his fist creating a hollow boom that echoed ominously through the pass.

A small panel on the door slid open almost instantly, and two eyes peered out. "How many?" a voice asked.

"Two." Danny answered smartly.

"You seek sanctuary in Tor-sava?"

"Why else would we be here?"

After a pause, the panel slid back shut. With a louder boom, the door slowly swung open, and Danny and Isa stepped inside.

Danny whistled sharply as the door swung shut behind them. They found themselves in a stunning little valley.

A waterfall trickled down the far end, splashing from tier to tier until landing in a pool. From there, the water ran through a groove cut through the town before splashing down and out through a grate off to one side.

Meanwhile, the town itself was... Well... A town. The buildings were small, with tiered roofs covered in red tiles.

Cherry trees were planted here and there in large garden boxes, while a handful of guards wearing black armor marched around the perimeter. Danny felt his blood turn to ice as his eyes settled upon the armor.

Deepcorp Knight armor.

"Welcome." A guard stepped up to him, the same guard who had spoken to him through the door. The man wore the same black armor, but had the visor raised, and his voice was cheerful.

"I'm glad you could come here. Here, you will find a place of safety, a place where you can ride out the coming storm brought upon us by the corrupt and complicit Empire."

Danny bit his lip. So this was the Deepcorp's gambit, now. Provide places of refuge, wait until the Empire was gone, and then settle the land once again with loyalists.

Brainwashed loyalists, perhaps, but he imagined that beggars couldn't be choosers. "Thank you for having us!" Isa beamed.

She turned her head back and forth, then sighed. "It's even more amazing than the way it was described to us. Who's in charge?"

The knight frowned, and Isa shrugged. "I just mean... Who put this together? They must be very powerful, and very generous."

"Ahh! But of course." The guard gestured at the waterfall. "Behind there are where his chambers lie, though he isn't here often. He has many such refuges throughout the nation, and is actively running around from place to place trying to ensure that everything is in place to survive the wave of monsters."

"Now, since you're here, just head over to the central building, where you can register and get a home. After that, you're free to do as you please, as long as you get along with everyone here."

"You can also, if you wish, take up some training. When the Empire has fallen, every sword will be needed to reclaim our place. It will be years before we depart this home, but in that time, we'll need to be as strong as possible."

Danny nodded. "Thank you."

The guard bowed then snapped down his visor and returned to his post. Danny struck out through the city, with Isa following along closely.

"What are you thinking?" Danny asked, glancing over at her.

"I'm thinking we need to get a look at those private chambers," Isa murmured.

"Yeah, me too," Danny confirmed. "Alright. I'll go first, maybe I can use a goblin to-"

"No." Isa shook her head. "There's a much easier way."

Danny turned to her. "There is?"

After a quick survey of the city, they located the building where the sets of armor were stored. Slipping inside unnoticed was easy, and soon they were dressed in the Deepcorp armor.

With their new disguises, they set out for the waterfall. "Bleh. This smells like someone died in here." Isa coughed as they kept to the edges of the wall.

A few people saw them and waved, obviously happy to see the symbols of protection clomping around. Danny didn't wave back, but only because he hadn't seen any of the other knights waving at people, either.

"Maybe they did," Danny said. "Being a knight for the Deepcorp probably isn't a way to ensure you're long-lived."

"Don't say that. I'm going to be sick."

When they reached the pool, they found a small path that wound around the backside of it. There, they ducked behind the waterfall, where a narrow tunnel led down to a set of double doors.

Two more guards stood there, hands on their swords. Danny raised a hand, and a Nightingale of the Snows flashed from his palm.

The soldiers, both quite confused, glanced at each other... And then fell upon one another, asleep before they hit the ground.

"Nicely done," Isa said. "Anyone tell you that you're sorta overpowered?"

"All the time." Danny grinned. "Thing is, I like it that way."

It took them only seconds to find the keys and unlock the door. Stepping inside, they entered a bunker-like complex.

The Nightingale flitted ahead, darting through shadowed doorways. The clatter of armor echoed through the corridors as soldier after soldier collapsed where they stood.

Danny glanced into the rooms as they passed, finding only storage and nothing of interest. Finally, they reached the last room, which held a few basic amenities and a large table with a map spread across it.

Danny paused, his gaze fixed on the map as he frowned. The map depicted the Dead Mountains, with a mark showing their current location.

Other marks dotted the mountains, a few circled and several crossed off. Isa leaned over the sketch, her brow furrowing in thought.

"He's going after the artifact, too."

"How close is he to finding it?" Danny asked.

"Close. Looks like he had three places left to search." Isa looked over the three remaining circles that hadn't been crossed out. "The middle one there is where we're heading."

"We can swing by that location on the way to meet with Anne," Danny said. "You're sure that's it?"

"Quite so," Isa confirmed. "Since there's no one else here, and I assume we'll be going straight there, no reason to keep it hidden any longer."

"Mm." Danny frowned as he looked over the map, then turned and looked at their surroundings. It was simple, but it was a base.

"What do you make of all this?"

"Other than the fact that he's making sure that he'll have people ready to supplant the Empire, loyalists who will back him, along with the fact that he's building a standing army for that occasion as well, I'm not sure I really get much of anything from this." Isa answered. "You?"

Danny snorted. "That about sums it up. He's crafty, that's for sure. Crafty, and powerful if he can just jump around the Empire like that."

Suddenly, something caught his eye, and he frowned. Off to one side, there was a pedestal covered by a cloth.

Glancing around, he walked over and slowly pulled the cloth off, revealing a black mana crystal. It wasn't terribly large, but he could feel the air trembling with power.

"Wow," Isa breathed as she stepped up next to him. "I never thought I'd see one of those in person."

"Mind telling me what it is?" Danny asked.

"In layman's terms, it contains an infinite amount of mana." Isa paused. "Technically, it taps into the latent mana of the universe, so you really only have enough as is in existence, which by definition can't be infinite, but you get what I mean."

Danny frowned, confused. "Why wouldn't he take it with him?"

"Because if you're close enough to one for too long, the mana radiating off the thing will burn through your body," Isa answered. "No, I'm serious. Put that thing in your inventory, and you'll be dead in a week. Maybe less."

"You think he has more of these?" Danny pressed.

"It would make sense," Isa answered. "If he's teleporting all over the land checking up on these hidden refuges, while poking around in the minds of people, he'd have to have a near-infinite source of energy."

"Which, all things considered, gives me hope. He's powerful, but he's obviously not all powerful." She paused. "Why?"

"Same reason. Just trying to get a gauge for how powerful this guy really is." Danny paused. "I'm going to leave him a little message, I think."

"Why?" Isa scowled. "We could get out of here without him ever knowing we were here."

"Yeah, or we could mess with him for a change." Danny raised his hand and quickly tied a summon spell to the crystal. "The next time he uses it, it'll activate a little present for him."

"Something that will kill him?" Isa asked hopefully.

"I can hope," Danny said. "Probably not, but it'll mess with his head. Come on." He turned away, and sighed deeply as he strode back out.

"Let's get out of here before anyone wakes up and realizes what happened. You know how to get to your artifact?"

"I think so." Isa smiled. "I definitely could if we could fly."

"No can do. My cave crows aren't strong enough." Danny paused, then continued. "That said, I bet riding a stone golem would be fun."

Auto save - [Savefile: Information]
Health: 100%
Mana: 99%
Quest: Get the artifact and get out of there.
Location: Tor-sava, Private Chambers of Evil Lord
Inventory: Essential Supplies, Basic Armor, Iron Sword, Sword of the Wasp, Aquamarine Sword, Frostbite Sword
Skills: Monster Summoner (Lv. 42), Flame Combat (Lv. 2), Wind Combat (Lv. 5)
Relationships: Friendly with Isa, Friendly with Captain Anne
Time of Day: 1:28 p.m.

Nine

Dead Mountains

If anyone had been watching the desolate slopes of the Dead Mountains that evening, they would have witnessed a most unusual sight: two stone golems racing across the rugged terrain, as if in a competition to reach some distant goal. Atop the golems rode two students, laughing and smiling, treating the wild ride as if it were a carefree adventure.

"And... Brace yourself!" Danny called out as they approached the edge of a narrow ravine. It was perhaps fifty feet across, and lay at the bottom of an already-steep slope of the mountain.

The two golems were sliding down the side, and as they reached the edge, they both sprang out into space. "Hang on!" Danny shouted.

The two monsters sailed through the open sky then slammed into the far walls. Their massive hands grabbed hold of the thin cracks, the narrow holds that they could manage, and they both slid slightly down the wall.

Stone cracked and exploded underneath their grasp, but they held firm, and a moment later, had pulled themselves up. With that, they raced along the top of the ravine on the far side, then turned and raced across the rough and jagged terrain leading onward.

They flew across the top of immense cliffs that fell to sparkling waters below, they passed above small and hidden meadows that had likely never seen another human before. More than once, they passed large monsters roaming about free, likely escapees from the many dungeon breaks that were taking place across the landscape.

"We should be getting there soon!" Isa called above the wind. "Turn right!"

Danny nodded, and the two golems responded accordingly. Soon, they reached the top of a cliff more massive than they had yet seen, one that ran down the full southern slope of the mountain.

Far below, Danny could see a thin path that wound along the edge of the immense jungle, which stretched out like a carpet of green to the very horizon. He thought he could see flickers of light from the army's armor, but it was hard to tell for sure.

"Wow," Danny murmured. "This is... This is incredible."

"It's amazing what you can see when you do simple things," Isa commented. "Like taking a golem ride through forlorn and dead mountains."

Danny chuckled and shook his head then sighed and glanced down the cliff. "Now, where are we headed?"

"See that cave, about halfway up the cliff? Below us and off to the left?"

Danny frowned as she pointed across the stone. Sure enough, there was a small hollow in the rock, maybe a hundred feet below them.

"We have to get to that?" he scowled.

"Yup," Isa confirmed. "Now do you want to fly us there?"

"I'd happily fly us there if I could, but like I said, I don't really have any way of doing that. Guess you'll just have to hold on."

With that, the stone golems leapt into motion. They jumped down the side of the cliff, digging in their hands and feet to slow their descent.

It actually worked surprisingly well, and within a few seconds, both of them caught hold of the small cave. As they swung inside, Danny and Isa dropped to the ground.

Danny squinted his eyes as he looked around the little area, and he re-absorbed the golems with a wave of his hand. "What is this place?"

The front of the cave looked to be set up like a sitting room with a handful of chairs carved into the very stone of the mountain. There was a table, barren and windswept, and at the back there was a door that led deeper into the mountain's face.

"This was a base for that group that I told you about," Isa murmured, walking up to the door. She placed her hands upon it, where Danny noticed that there were no doorknobs.

"Give me just a second."

Danny frowned and nodded as Isa tapped her fist against it several times. There was a long pause while she pounded out a specific rhythm, and then...

And then, with a rumble, it slowly swung inward. Danny's jaw dropped as he found himself looking at a stairwell that led down into the stone.

Isa motioned for him to go first. "As they say, ladies first. I'd hate to take the honor from you."

"And I'd hate to get eaten when there's something waiting down below," Isa responded. "You're a whole lot better at fighting things than I am."

"Fair enough." Danny chuckled. He stepped into the stairwell and started down, one foot in front of the other.

It was dark, and he pulled out a torch, using it to light more torches that were still hung in their fittings on the wall. At the bottom, there was another door, this one with an actual doorknob, and through that Danny found himself in what could only be described as a laboratory.

It wasn't large but wasn't all that small either. Maybe thirty feet on a side, there were a handful of tables covered in old, dusty pieces of equipment, along with a great many maps tacked up to the walls.

The maps depicted the jungle, showing all the different dungeons and rivers and other such formations within the location. Several were crumbled and faded to the point Danny could no longer read them, but others were legible.

"This is amazing," he mumbled.

Isa walked over and turned a crank on the wall, opening up several slits in the ceiling. Sunlight flickered inside, and Danny's jaw dropped.

How far beneath the surface were they? He didn't have a clue how the group had managed such a thing, but he was looking at it, which made it possible.

Somehow.

"Alright." Isa murmured as she started walking around the area. "Look for anything that seems out of the ordinary. We know that this artifact, whatever it was, was put here once again after the headmaster discovered it at the Academy."

"How big is it?" Danny asked, looking over the equipment on the tables. There were quite a few spyglass-looking things, all of them connected to assorted measurement rods and compasses and other such items.

"Do we have any idea?"

"The floor of the hidden room had marks on it that showed a table about... Oh, I'd say five feet across." Isa answered. "Circular. I don't know whether the table was just used to hold the artifact, or it was the artifact."

"And what exactly do we know about this mystery artifact?" Danny asked, glancing at all the tables. None of them really fit the bill, but there was a section of wall that was empty, looking to him to be rather like a hidden doorway.

He walked over and ran his fingers across it, possibly finding a hidden seam.

"Is there something you're not telling me?" Danny asked. "All this seems like a lot of trouble for something whose main feature just seems to be being mysterious."

"A fair question," Isa said then sighed. "The simple answer is that, based on a few offhanded references that are made, I'm fairly certain it's a weapon of some sort, but beyond that, I'm in the dark."

"The Headmaster and the Emperor are both convinced that any old weapon is needed at this point, and thus, here we are."

Danny nodded, then tapped out the rhythm Isa had used earlier on the front door. She noticed, frowned, and walked over.

Placing her hand on the stone, she tapped out a slightly different, yet familiar pattern. With a low rumble, a hidden door slowly swung inward.

Isa shrugged, a hint of a smile on her lips. "Guess it's all about the right touch."

"Someday, I'll ask you how you knew that." Danny shook his head and stepped inside.

The room was dark, even with his torch. He frowned and held it around, noticing a small trough filled with something oily around the outside of the room.

Carefully, he touched his torch to it, and with a flicker, flames roared around the edge of the room, illuminating... Something.

"What in the Empire?" Danny murmured as he stepped forward. It was, indeed, a circular table about five feet across, but it was much more than that.

Instead of being a flat plane, like most tables, instead there was only a circular ring of wood around the outside, while the middle was an enormous sphere about four feet across. The sphere had a rod that ran through the middle of it, which in turn was connected by brass fittings to several concentric circles made from iron.

It allowed the sphere to be spun on multiple axises, more or less allowing a person to spin it any which way they chose. That, though, wasn't the interesting part.

The interesting part was the fact that it displayed a map of the Empire. Well, the Empire and a whole lot more.

"It's a globe." Danny murmured as he stepped up to the thing. He carefully laid his hand upon the upper portion, which depicted a huge body of land that he recognized well from the many maps throughout the Academy.

Below it, though, stretched out another body of land almost twice as big, with an assortment of notations carefully carved into the surface of the wood. There were deserts, forests, mountains, and a great many more things that were listed.

Even cities, here and there! He spun the globe slowly, moving past the great western ocean, and came there to a long string of islands, then even more continents, swirling together into an immense body of lands that he couldn't imagine had ever been seen by someone from the Empire.

"It's amazing." Isa frowned, touching the item as well. "I've heard it theorized that the world was round, and even seen calculations about how far it would be to sail from one side of the Empire around the far side of the world to the other, but... This is beyond any of that."

"Do you think it's just speculation, or do you think it's accurate?" Danny asked. He pressed his palms against the wooden item, almost hoping that it would do something magical, but nothing happened.

"I'm leaning toward believing that it's accurate. The only question is why it would be here." Isa frowned and crossed her arms.

"The headmaster who sent it back here clearly said that it belonged in the Dead Mountains, and the mage who put all of this together very clearly had some sort of fascination with this area."

"I don't know." Danny shook his head. "Maybe the answer lies with the maps out there?"

"I'll go see if I can take any of them." Isa shrugged and turned around. "You see about fitting this thing into your inventory."

"Into my inventory?" Danny blinked a few times. "Even if I dropped everything else out of my inventory, I don't know that this would fit."

"Oh, come on!" Isa called from the other room. "I've seen you fit mammoth tusks in your inventory before! You're not nearly as much of a hoarder as some people."

Danny couldn't disagree with that. He opened his interface and tried to import it, but was told that it took up **10 Units** of space (he had never quite been able to figure out what a Unit of Space was, nor had he cared enough to try), and that he had only half a unit left.

After spending a few long moments scrolling through his inventory, he decided upon dumping out a handful of monster trophies that he had collected, including several minotaur heads and the scales of several basilisks. When he was done, he was just able to slot the thing into his inventory, and with that, he headed back out into the main room.

"Alright, I think I've got it." Isa carefully pulled down one last map and tucked it into her inventory. "The trick is going to be getting it somewhere safe at the Academy, but that'll be a problem for me to deal with at that point. Ready to leave?"

Danny gave a small nod, and together they headed back up and out of the room with Danny making sure to close up the secret room. Not that he really imagined the Deepcorp Lord would miss it, but if there was a chance that he arrived and didn't catch it, he felt it was better to make sure that it was harder to find than easier.

Soon, as they stood on the precipice of the cave entrance, Danny snapped his fingers. The two stone golems appeared once more, and they all quickly started down.

It took them another thirty minutes to reach the camp of the army. They arrived just as night was falling.

Guards looked up in initial fear as the two monsters loomed out of the darkness, but they soon relaxed as they realized it was only Danny and Isa. Danny unsummoned the monsters, and he and Isa quickly reached Anne at the middle of the camp.

"Did you find what you were looking for?" Anne murmured, her voice barely audible over the crackling of her campfire.

"We did," Isa confirmed. Danny bit his lip, hoping that Anne wasn't being actively probed by the Deepcorp Lord.

He doubted it, but it was always possible. "Should be good to go," Isa continued.

"And what did you find out about... What was the name of that city again?"

Danny quickly explained what they had seen in the secluded location. He kept things rather vague, not really wanting to give any free information to the Deepcorp Lord if he did happen to go poking around in Anne's mind.

When he finished, Anne nodded tightly. She seemed aware of the fact that Danny was holding out, but being a soldier, she didn't seem to mind terribly.

"Good work. I'll report this to my superiors." Anne rose and started to walk away, heading back toward her tent.

"For now, get some rest, both of you. We've got an early march in the morning. I want to make sure that all of us make it back to the Academy in one piece."

Auto save - [Savefile: Information]
Health: 100%
Mana: 100%
Quest: Complete the tour of duty
Location: Army Camp, Northern Jungle
Inventory: Essential Supplies, Basic Armor, Iron Sword, Sword of the Wasp, Aquamarine Sword, Frostbite Sword

Skills: Monster Summoner (Lv. 42), Flame Combat (Lv. 2), Wind Combat (Lv. 5)

Relationships: Friendly with Isa, Friendly with Captain Anne

Time of Day: 7:12 p.m.

Ten

City Under Siege

It took them a week and a half to return to the Imperial City. They skirted the Dead Mountains, clearing several more dungeon breaches along the way, and wound their path back across the plains, stopping at small towns to assist with rebuilding and fending off monsters.

With each stop, Danny noticed fewer and fewer people. Some secluded villages seemed untouched by the chaos, but most were rapidly emptying, residents fleeing as fast as they could pack their belongings.

By the time the Imperial City came into view, Danny was exhausted, and the situation appeared even more dire. In the three weeks since he'd left, the refugee camps had swelled, sprawling across the hills for miles around the vast city.

As they marched in, Danny observed the refugees using white limestone to construct a new wall, stretching for miles around the entire area. The work progressed swiftly, driven by desperation and the lack of other tasks.

Although he didn't see anyone actively coordinating the effort, the smooth progress was a welcome sight. Upon reaching the Imperial City and receiving his orders, Danny wasn't surprised to find that his first task was to help Isa set up the artifact.

After that, he had a meeting with the Emperor. Oddly, there were no further orders or scheduled deployments, but he assumed he'd learn more during his audience with Emperor Ezra.

He marched with the army into Town Square, where Captain Anne formally discharged them for their allotted rest. "Get some sleep," she ordered. "You've earned it."

As they all nodded and began to wearily march off toward the barracks, Anne turned to Danny and Isa. They both folded their hands respectfully behind their backs as Anne gave them a nod.

"You both did good work out there over the last few weeks." Her voice was soft but grave. "I assume you've noticed you don't have any exit orders?"

Danny nodded. "Strange tidings. Do you know anything about it?"

Anne shook her head. "I don't. Look, if things go sideways at any point, know that I want in on the fight."

"Officers are boarding at an inn just adjacent to the Academy. Make sure you find me."

"Will do." Danny started to turn away then paused and turned back. "Do you really think it's going to come to something like that?"

"At this point, I don't know what to think," Anne murmured. "All I know is that the world feels like it's ending, and that sort of thing will make a lot of people do things that they'd never consider in a normal situation."

Danny couldn't argue with that, so he gave a small nod. He and Isa then turned and began making their way through the crowded city, heading back toward the academy.

Progress was slow, as the city was more congested than ever. People surged through the streets, pushing and shoving as they scrambled to secure even the most basic necessities.

Soldiers and mages struggled against the tide, trying to maintain order, but the scene was utterly chaotic. More than once, Danny felt overwhelmed by the crush of bodies and the frantic energy all around him.

When they finally pushed through the academy doors, Danny felt a wave of relief, as if he had returned home. They quickly made their way to the Research Wing, where Isa beamed as she opened the door to her laboratory, and they stepped inside.

"Isa!" Marcella's voice rang through the air, and Isa turned to find her friend sitting there, dressed in semi-combat robes.

As the two girls embraced each other, Danny nodded to Marcella. "How goes it? I haven't seen you in ages."

"Ahh, it goes," Marcella said with a shrug. "I just got back into town two days ago. I've been running research on combat missions in the area, mostly just local tours trying to clear out the immediate area."

"I've been studying the monsters, mainly just making sure that they're all doing the things that we would expect them to do."

"Is there concern that they might not?" Danny asked. He glanced around then grabbed hold of a table and started pushing it to the side, making room for the massive globe.

"There were some soldiers reporting that monsters were starting to behave erratically. Goblins acting like undead, or undead acting like beasts," Marcella said.

"I can't say that I've seen every monster in the land, but from what I did see, it's my opinion that it mostly adds up to stress on the soldiers. I didn't see anything out of the ordinary, and I've been taking samples for a month."

She frowned. "What exactly are you two doing?"

"Setting up... This." Danny opened up his inventory and pulled out the globe.

With a flash, it appeared on the ground in the middle of the laboratory, and he turned and bowed. "Ta-da!"

"Wow!" Marcella walked over and looked down at the globe. "This is the world?"

Before Danny could answer, the door to the laboratory opened and Master Barrydew poked his head inside. Danny felt himself light up as the old master smiled and walked inside.

"I heard you two just got back into town. I knew you wouldn't be expecting me, so I figured I'd just pop down." His eyes settled upon the globe, and he froze.

"Is that what I think it is?"

"If you mean... Is that a depiction of what might just be the entire world, beyond the borders of the Empire, then yes!" Danny nodded and patted the thing.

"Now, what does it do beyond that? Not a clue in the slightest. Maybe it's just a fancy map, in which case I don't really understand how it can be a weapon except for maybe dropping it off a roof onto someone, but-"

"I can sense something inside of it." Master Barrydew frowned and placed his hand on the surface. "There are mechanisms. Gears, cogs... A handful of mana crystals."

"So it's some sort of device." Isa frowned and walked over to it. She crouched down and stared at it for a long moment, then looked back up at Master Barrydew.

"Is it active right now? Like a clock or something?"

"I can't tell, but it seems inert to me." Master Barrydew shook his head. "I also can't tell how you'd access anything on the inside. It feels solid to me, but then, I haven't done a detailed scan of it."

"I'll get to work on it right away." Isa promised.

"I wouldn't trust the work to anyone else." Master Barrydew shrugged and started to walk away.

"Please do let me know if you need anything else, at any time. I have a feeling that this project will be more important to the war effort than just about anything else."

Danny frowned, but nodded. Isa nodded back, and he quickly followed Master Barrydew out into the hall.

The door closed behind them, and the two mages slowly started to walk off. As they did so, Danny glanced at his master, but Barrydew beat him to the punch.

"You're wanting to know, first of all why I'm here, and second of all why I'm talking like I'm still going to be here for a while longer."

"That about sums it up." Danny confirmed.

"Unfortunately, there are many things I cannot tell you." Master Barrydew sighed. "Do you have an appointment scheduled with the Emperor?"

"Tomorrow morning." Danny frowned. "What's this all about?"

Master Barrydew bit his lip. "Probably best that you wait until then."

Danny didn't sleep well that night, nor did he really think that he could be expected to. When the morning came, he went to the Imperial Palace just as early as he thought that he would be allowed to do so.

The guards let him in, and soon, he found himself walking into the grand Throne Room. It seemed, somehow, less grand than before.

Perhaps the floor was more sullied from so many feet, or perhaps the windows dustier and dingier, but somehow it felt as though it was losing the shine that had so set it apart once before. A small group of mages and captains, including Captain Anne, stood around the small meeting table.

It still depicted a map of the Empire, though there were now a handful of bright-red markers across the land. As Danny took up his place, a lone trumpet blew, and Emperor Ezra the Fifth came marching in.

He wore tan robes girded about the waist with a leather belt, looking like he was marching to his doom. As he approached the table, he nodded respectfully and folded his hands behind his back.

CITY UNDER SIEGE

"Thank you all for coming," he began quietly. "I know some of you have heard rumors, and some of you have merely noticed a few things that are off about the Imperial City. To answer everything as quickly and as precisely as possible, all of you are formally relieved from your tours of duty, though of course not from your posts."

"The Imperial City has formally been designated as a fallback point, and the last point of hope for the Empire, where we will make our stand."

Danny's jaw dropped. One of the other captains smashed a fist against the table, and Emperor Ezra held up a hand.

"Please. I know it must make many of you angry." His voice was soft, but firm. "That's just how it has to be."

"We're abandoning our people?" Captain Anne snapped. "We're abandoning the Empire?"

"We are not abandoning our people." Emperor Ezra snapped. "We are bringing them all here, to the Imperial City, where the combined might of our forces will face off against the monsters as they come."

"Why the change?" another commander who looked as displeased as Captain Anne asked.

"The change is because of these." Emperor Ezra pointed to the table. "Tell me, all of you. How many red markers do you see on the map?"

Danny leaned forward and counted quickly. "Eighteen," he answered after a moment.

"Correct," Emperor Ezra said. "Eighteen A- or B-ranked dungeons that, upon investigation within the last month, have turned out to be S-ranked instead. If I included the number of C- and D-ranked dungeons that had been upgraded to A and B, this map would be covered so thickly you wouldn't know it was anything more than a modern art project."

"So, the dungeons are becoming more powerful?" Danny surmised.

Emperor Ezra nodded. "Yes. We're losing men faster than we can possibly replace them. The simple fact of the matter is that the situation is rapidly spiraling out of control, and the plans that we initially laid, where rotating bands of soldiers and mages kept the monsters at bay throughout the land, has become entirely unfeasible."

"It was never going to work long-term anyway, it was just too grueling, but now? Now, it's entirely impossible."

"Then we just wasted all that time? All those lives?" another captain snapped.

"No," Emperor Ezra said firmly. "First and foremost, if nothing else, it provided valuable stress training. More importantly, though, it also provided the cover necessary for countless civilians to retreat to this city. Countless people are alive, here, because you were able to escort them, to free their towns."

He leaned over the map. "As near as my tacticians have been able to tell, every single village in the Empire with a population larger than 50 has been visited in the last few months. Everyone knows the situation."

"If they've chosen to remain out in the wilderness, that's been their choice, and their risk. The time has come that we must withdraw. We make our stand, and then, just as was done in the early days of the Empire, we will fight our way out from here."

"We'll claim land one mile at a time, one dungeon at a time, until we've reclaimed our borders. Is that clear?"

Heads nodded around the table, but Emperor Ezra didn't seem satisfied. "I asked if that was clear!"

They all snapped to attention. "Yes, sir!"

"Good." Emperor Ezra nodded. "This is not a retreat. This is not giving in. We will not succumb to the darkness. This is merely a tactical decision to make sure that our forces can fight, and will keep fighting as we press forward into this new land. Dismissed."

CITY UNDER SIEGE   89

As everyone turned to leave, Emperor Ezra held up a hand. "Youngblood, remain."

Danny nodded and folded his hands behind his back, waiting as everyone else filed away. When they were gone, Emperor Ezra approached him and lowered his voice.

"I'm told that you helped uncover a weapon?"

"Maybe," Danny said. "I wish I could tell you what it does, but the simple fact of the matter is that we don't know."

"Well, you have permission to do whatever you need to do," Emperor Ezra murmured. "I will not allow the Empire to perish, not on my watch. My lineage can be traced in an unbroken line back to that very first Emperor of old, and I will not suffer so many long years of work to be undone by the whims of a dark lord."

"I'm here to help, and I'll do everything I can," Danny confirmed then crossed his arms. "Was there something specific you were wanting?"

Emperor Ezra shook his head. "No. Merely to confirm that I plan on holding this city here. In that defense, you will be invaluable. Anything you need, it's yours. Anything you desire, name it only, and you will have it."

"This is the battle for civilization, the battle for the world." Emperor Ezra's hands tightened on the edge of the table, and he snarled softly. "And I want you to be my sword, striking back anything and everything that dares even think about plunging our world into darkness."

Auto save - [Savefile: Information]
Health: 100%
Mana: 100%
Quest: Defend the City.
Location: Imperial Palace, Throne Room
Inventory: Essential Supplies, Basic Armor, Iron Sword, Sword of the Wasp, Aquamarine Sword, Frostbite Sword

Skills: Monster Summoner (Lv. 42), Flame Combat (Lv. 2), Wind Combat (Lv. 5)

Relationships: Friendly with Isa, Friendly with Captain Anne, Friendly with Master Barrydew, Speaking Terms with Emperor Ezra the Fifth

Time of Day: 8:14 a.m.

Eleven

Relucent Professor

The audience with the Emperor had left Danny reeling. As he returned to the Academy, frustration gnawed at him—an uneasy blend of confusion and resignation.

The Emperor's plan was sound, but it stung nonetheless. Danny knew there was no other choice; holding the distant plains, the jungle regions, and the wastelands was a losing battle, especially with the mass exodus of residents fleeing to more fortified lands.

The Empire's borders, once the bastion against the beast hordes, would soon shrink, forcing them to retreat, conceding territory mile by mile. Back at the Academy, Danny wandered the halls, feeling adrift without a class schedule or the familiar discipline of a marching regiment.

He knew he should rest, conserve his strength for when he'd be needed, but the thought of lying down while others toiled to build protective walls with their bare hands gnawed at him. The weight of the world pressed down, and aimless wandering seemed the only escape.

Eventually, Danny found himself in the library, where the stillness of the room offered a rare moment of peace. The chaos outside felt distant here, as if the library stood as a sanctuary amidst the storm.

Master Barrydew, sensing Danny's turmoil, looked up from his work and slowly approached, his presence a quiet anchor amid the uncertainty.

"It's incredible, isn't it?" Master Barrydew sighed and slowly walked over to sit down at a nearby table. "I don't know about you, but sometimes, I feel like I can hear the wisdom of so many years speaking to me."

"In the quiet, when everyone else is gone, I can sit here amidst these volumes and just soak it in, letting the words penned so many years ago just drift around me."

"Poetic, but I'm not reading any of them, so I'm not getting any of their wisdom," Danny said dryly.

Master Barrydew flashed a thin smile. "None of my pupils have yet taken up academic work. I suppose that smashing monsters is more fun, but I'll certainly say that bookwork has a way of calming the mind in times such as these."

Danny frowned. "How can you just sit here when everything's falling apart out there?" He pointed at the window.

"There are people, refugees, who are lifting boulders and cementing them into place with mud! They're building a wall because they have nothing else they can do, nothing else that gives them any hope of survival."

"For what it's worth, I'm not just sitting here." Master Barrydew motioned for Danny to stay put then returned to his office.

A moment later, he came back with several ancient books. One of them was on the Dead Mountains, another was speculation about the lands beyond the Empire's borders.

"I'm doing research to see if I can pin down what that globe happens to be. I know Isa's working on it from her own end, but I wanted to see if theory and old books might be able to give me an edge on her."

Danny chuckled softly. "And what have you found?"

"Precious little," Master Barrydew admitted. "In this book, the one about the land beyond the Empire's borders, it goes through a handful of the theories that have been put forward over the years."

"It was written about a hundred years ago, I believe. Anyway, it goes through things like the circumference of the world and how such things were calculated, but..."

"It also has a handful of maps that are eerily similar to that globe. From what the book mentions, and from what I can tell, it was written by the apprentice of one of the students involved in the Explorer group that Isa discovered."

"That doesn't seem like a coincidence." Danny frowned.

"I thought not, as well." Master Barrydew shrugged. "Now, importantly, it doesn't really explain how he came to the conclusions that he did."

"Moving over to this book on the Dead Mountains, the only thing that I can find is a report of an herb that, when consumed, had the effect of increasing your perception stat temporarily by a factor of almost fifty. At least from this report here, upon eating this herb, you could see a..."

"How did it put it? You could count the hairs on a fly at a distance of four miles."

"That doesn't explain how you could find a map of the rest of the world, though," Danny said.

"No, indeed. Four miles is a far cry from the thousands of miles you'd need to see to make something this detailed." He shrugged.

"Anyway, not important really, I just thought you might want to know what progress I was making. Which is to say, not much, but I really am trying."

"I know." Danny slowly rose from the table. "I know." He turned and looked up at all the old books then waved.

"Bye, ancient wisdom. Hope you can flutter your way into one of our heads, so we can get to the bottom of all this."

Master Barrydew chuckled as he climbed to his own feet. "Master Youngblood?"

"I don't like the sound of that." Danny muttered, pausing on his way to the door.

"You need something to keep yourself occupied, or you're going to go just as crazy as a loon." Master Barrydew crossed his arms. "I hereby appoint you to teach the First-Year class on... Monsters."

"You want me to teach a class?" Danny raised an eyebrow.

"You remember your first-year monster theory class, right?" Master Barrydew shrugged. "Master Black was your professor, I believe. Or was it Longbeard?"

"Neither of them are with the Academy anymore. In any case, with your father still gone on patrol, the class has been somewhat lacking. I'd like you to go and teach it."

"It'll give you something to do, and hopefully keep you out of trouble as we try to plan our next move."

Danny shrugged and nodded. He didn't like the idea, but it did give him something to do. "When's my first class?"

"Two hours." Master Barrydew flashed a crooked grin. "Best go start preparing."

Two hours later, Danny stood at the front of the same, old classroom where he had started his career as a student five long years earlier. Students were still filing in as the class session began, but he could hardly blame them for being late given the circumstances.

As they took their seats, he folded his hands behind his back then slowly looked around at them all. "Welcome to Monster Theory," he began.

"Ahh... Forgive me, I've had a very short length of time to prepare for this class. It looks to me like you've been going through humanoid monsters?"

The class nodded, and a girl at the front of the room stood up. "We've had five different professors this year, and we've only been here for a month."

She flashed a small smile. "At this point, whatever you teach us, I'm sure will be fine. Each professor has just sorta been doing what they see fit."

"Well, no time like a crisis to completely throw lesson plans out of order." Danny shrugged and crossed his arms. "Let's just focus on humanoid monsters, then. Everyone cool with that?"

They all nodded, and Danny turned to the chalkboard. "Now, the important thing to remember is that humanoid and undead are two very different things."

He wrote the distinction as quickly as he could. "A lot of people get the two confused, since undead are usually humans, but the two different types of monsters react differently to things, can be harmed differently, have different attack patterns, and so on."

The girl at the front of the class raised her hand. "So, what's technically classified as humanoid?"

"Excellent question." Danny snapped his fingers, summoning a goblin.

It hissed as it looked out at the class, and most of the students shrieked. At that moment, Danny realized that most of them probably didn't realize who he was.

As they settled down, he decided to just play it as if he had planned to scare them. "Humanoid monsters include anything that has two legs, two arms, walks upright, uses tools, or at least has the capability to do so, and isn't dead."

"On a practical level, that means goblins and trolls primarily, but can also include kobolds, lizardmen, orcs, gargoyles, harpies, and so on."

"And what's the best way to kill a humanoid monster?" the girl asked.

Danny wasn't sure if she was just naturally inquisitive, or was trying to suck up to him. Suddenly, he realized just how challenging being a professor really could be.

"As a very general sort of suggestion, if it would hurt or kill you, it'll probably hurt or kill a humanoid monster," Danny answered with a small chuckle. "Most of them have organs in similar places to us, and wear armor in similar manners."

"With humanoid monsters, really don't give it too much thought, is my best advice. If it's shooting arrows at you, duck. If it has a sword, prepare for a fight. So on and so forth."

With that, he launched into the lecture as best he could, detailing a few minor points about goblins and other such creatures. When he wrapped up with humanoid creatures, the class asked him to touch on undead monsters as well.

They were supposed to have been covered the previous week, but from what Danny could gather, the professor had been running through between tours and hadn't really been able to do much. Danny was happy to oblige, and he quickly ran through some of the more common forms of undead.

By the time he finished, the bell had rang, and the students had scurried out. Danny nodded and watched them go then raised his voice.

"If anyone has any questions, feel free to come and ask me! I'd tell you to prepare for a test, but I don't have the faintest idea when or if there will be one, so... Just do your best, and know that if you don't pay attention, you'll probably die!"

The girl laughed along with a few of the other students, and they soon all filed out and into the hall. With that, Danny crossed his arms and leaned back against the blackboard as Master Barrydew poked his head inside.

"If you don't pay attention, you'll probably die?" Master Barrydew asked.

Danny shrugged. "I'm new at this, alright? Don't judge me too hard."

Master Barrydew laughed. "I wasn't judging! That said..." He walked into the room and slowly shut the door behind him.

"If you liked doing it, from what I could see, you were pretty good."

Danny frowned. "You want me to actually take this up long-term?"

"At least until your father gets back into town." Master Barrydew answered. "You know monsters better than almost anyone. If there's someone who could teach this course and do a good job on the fly, it would be you."

"Oh, I don't know about that." Danny shook his head. "There's a difference between popping in once, and teaching it long-term."

"I couldn't agree more." Master Barrydew placed his hand on Danny's shoulder. "Please, do consider it. I'm in dire need of new professors, given how many are currently either in battle, or have resigned their service because of the war."

"It would give you more of a purpose, at least until we know more on the war's front."

Danny sighed and nodded, then wearily walked over to the desk and sat down. The top of the desk was rather disorganized, likely on account of the revolving door of professors who had come through.

Not knowing what was what or how to even begin to act in the manner of a professor, he started sorting through the files and looking at what exactly each one happened to be. "And what do you think that the course of the war is going to be?" Danny asked as he set aside several lesson plans that detailed what monsters to cover on which days.

It looked quite familiar from his time as a first-year, and a nostalgic smile came over his face. Ahh, those were simpler times.

"I wish I could say." Master Barrydew shrugged. "I could offer you my personal opinions or insights, but that's all that they would be. Speculation, hardly worth your ears."

He nodded down to Danny, then turned away. "Just let me know if you need anything, Master Youngblood. We'll make you worthy of that title yet."

Danny flashed a small smile, but hardly noticed as Master Barrydew left. As the door swung shut behind him, Danny sighed.

So, this was his new life, now. Teaching monster theory while waiting for monsters to attack the city so he would have something to do. Or, at least, while waiting for orders to be given to him informing him of some new course of action.

It was far from a bad life, far from unpleasant. He only hoped that, in the midst of it all, he would be able to keep his head and would be able to respond when the time came.

Auto save - [Savefile: Information]

Health: 100%

Mana: 100%

Quest: Prepare for the next lecture.

Location: Monster Theory Classroom

Inventory: Essential Supplies, Basic Armor, Iron Sword, Sword of the Wasp, Aquamarine Sword, Frostbite Sword

Skills: Monster Summoner (Lv. 42), Flame Combat (Lv. 2), Wind Combat (Lv. 5)

Relationships: Friendly with Master Barrydew, Friendly with [Class]

Time of Day: 10:37 a.m.

Twelve

Turning Over

Several days later, Danny awoke with an odd feeling in the pit of his stomach. He felt as though he had just gone through some sort of nightmare, but when he thought about it, he couldn't quite figure out what had happened.

Carefully, he swung his feet off the side of his bed and climbed to his feet. The house creaked around him as a powerful wind blew against the aging and uncared-for frame, and he frowned.

And then, something clicked in his mind; the smell of dragon ash. He balled his hands into fists and spun, finding a dark figure standing in the corner of the room.

It was tall, far taller than Barbara, and wore a cloak with a deep hood. Danny stared at the form apprehensively, and, slowly, Nicodemus stepped forward, reached up, and drew the hood back.

Danny gasped softly. Nicodemus had been burned, badly. His features were almost unrecognizable, and he gave a small nod.

Danny couldn't tell whether he was smiling or scowling, so bad were the man's burns.

"Sorry." Nicodemus croaked out, his voice parched. "Turns out that dragon fire isn't actually all that good for the complexion. Should have read the fine print."

"Nicodemus!" Danny beamed and took a step forward, but Nicodemus raised a hand.

"I can't come too close to you." He shook his head. "I'm risking a lot by even being here."

"What are you talking about?" Danny asked. "What's going on? Where have you been? I'm so confused. Nicodemus, I miss you."

"I miss you, too." Nicodemus sighed. "There is much I cannot explain, not at this moment. Suffice it to say that I am being watched, very closely, by someone who has a keen interest in you."

"You, and the whole of the Empire."

Danny grimaced. "The Deepcorp Lord."

"Do not say his name, or his title." Nicodemus instructed. "He doesn't have the power to place the same taboo on it that he once did, but that doesn't mean that he's powerless."

"Do not give him anything that he can use."

"I see." Danny paused. "And if you get too close to me..."

"I'd rather not take the chance. As I said, I am risking a great deal by even being here." Nicodemus looked down at the ground, then balled his hands into fists.

"I am here for a reason. Your father, my son, is in trouble."

"Son-in-law," Danny corrected.

"He's become as much a son to me as my own flesh and blood." Nicodemus set his jaw. "His unit is returning. They've met up with Tess's legion, but are being pursued."

"Head due west. You won't miss them."

Danny nodded. "What about you?"

"I am prohibited from helping." Nicodemus looked down at the ground then back up at Danny. "As I said, there are many things that I cannot tell you."

"What you need to know now is that you have to go, and go quickly."

"I will." Danny started to leave but paused and turned back. "What of Barbara?"

"She is alive." Nicodemus answered. "That is all I can tell you at this moment."

With that, he raised a burnt hand and snapped his fingers. A flash of light exploded through the room.

When it faded away, Nicodemus was gone. Danny bit his lip then turned and flew out of the house just as fast as he could.

Danny ran through the city at a breakneck pace, or at least as close to one as he could manage in the cramped quarters. He soon drew near to the academy, where he was able to see the nearby building being used for officer lodging.

The guard merely gave him a nod as he flew past, and he was soon banging on Anne's door as hard as he could. "What's going on?" Captain Anne poked her head wearily out of her room.

"Danny, do you know how early it is? I was up until midnight in the Imperial Palace, attending a meeting to coordinate-"

"My father is heading into the city, but his legion is being chased." Danny spoke quickly. "That's all I know."

"What road?" Anne asked, her eyes opening slightly.

"West."

"Head that way. I'll be there with as many soldiers as I can muster." Anne ducked back into her room.

Danny spun on his heel and bolted down the hall. By the time he reached the stairwell, Anne had already burst out, fully armored and ready.

Danny didn't waste a second. He sprinted into the street, heading straight for the stables.

Bartering for a horse took only a moment, and soon he was galloping through the crowded city streets, charging toward the western gate. Once outside the city, he pushed the horse to its limits, urging it to run faster.

The horse, slightly injured—likely the reason Danny had managed to get it so quickly—still powered forward with determination. They raced down the long road, now lined with countless tents and makeshift shacks.

Two miles out of town, Danny shot past the newly erected wall and plunged into the trees, driving the horse to its maximum speed. The ground fell away behind him as he raced on westward, through the rolling and twisting hills that lay there.

Three miles went by, then four. He was starting to wonder if Nicodemus had been right when he began to hear grunts and snarls and snorts from ahead, and he put on a burst of speed.

He flew up and over one last rise, and there he saw them. The army, or what was left of it, staggered along at top speed, but as they had no horses, it wasn't fast at all.

A row of soldiers in the rear fought off a horde of goblins and undead, all of which were clawing desperately at the retreating men. Near the front of the procession, quite a few stretchers were being carried, while at the rear, the soldiers were rotating to keep fresh men at the line of battle.

Danny quickly drew to a halt and leapt down from his horse, then ran down toward the procession.

"Danny!" Tess called out. "We're making for the Bone Dungeon! Any chance you can cover us?"

"You've got it." Danny raised his hands, and light pulsed across his fingers.

There was a brief pause, and the trees around them began to quake. The goblins actually paused their attack...

And with that, a great pack of wolves burst from the trees and tore straight into their midst. The mighty beasts were a good three feet at the shoulder, and armed with teeth that were practically steel.

They sent the goblins and zombies sprawling, and quickly formed a line across the path. With that, the army began to move on a bit faster, and Danny assessed the situation.

"BLARGH!"

A huge troll came stomping along behind the horde of goblins, swinging its club. Goblins were knocked high into the air under the blow, and the troll chuckled then grinned down at Danny.

"I killed a troll three times your size just a month ago," Danny said.

The troll blinked its beady eyes but apparently decided that the threat wasn't enough to take credibly. It lunged forward, and Danny snapped his fingers.

A huge, stony hand stopped the club halfway to Danny's head, and the troll blinked its stupid little eyes as a stone golem stared it down. A moment later, the troll was flat on its back, dead, and the goblins were sent screaming.

Danny sent his wolves after them then turned and ran after the army. The Bone Dungeon wasn't far away.

It wasn't set to overflow, but it did have a handful of buildings that could be used defensively. By the time Danny got there, Tess had led her soldiers inside where stretchers were laid in the back, secure rooms and barricades were thrown across the doors and windows.

Danny raced inside, and Tess nodded to him. "I can't thank you enough," she murmured. "You just saved our lives, at least for a bit."

"Just for a bit?" Danny asked. "I just killed the horde chasing you."

"Problem is, they're not the only horde that was chasing us." Tess sighed and sat down on a windowsill, looking out at the forest.

"My long-range scanner can still see them. There were like three dungeons that all overflowed right as we were passing through."

"I mean... We're at the end of our tour, we were caught entirely flat-footed. I lost half my men, probably, and so close to home."

She snarled, balling her hands into fists. "This war isn't sustainable."

"Well, you and the Emperor agree on that matter, for sure." Danny patted her on the shoulder, then paused. "Where's my father? I thought he was with you."

Tess turned wordlessly and pointed at one of the stretchers. In that instant, Danny's world seemed to stop.

He flew over and knelt down by the side of the cot, which held a man covered in so much blood that Danny hadn't even remotely recognized the man. Several arrow shafts still stuck out of his body, though the ends had been snapped off to prevent them from catching on things.

"His unit met up with ours when we realized how much trouble we were both in." Tess sighed. "Danny, you should have seen him. His hands were charring, he was using so much fire."

"I've seen some impressive fire mages in my time, but I've never seen someone who could do so much. It was incredible... And then this black skeleton appeared."

"It was immune to flame, at least I assume it must have been. It hit him in the shoulder, surprised him, and then... And then, they all just focused their attacks on him." She sighed.

"He's the only reason any of us are alive."

"We're getting him back to the city." Danny nodded tightly. "All of you. Anne is heading this way with reinforcements."

"Good." Tess murmured, then paused. "How did you know where we were, anyway?"

Danny opened his mouth to reply, but was cut off as something came tearing through the woods. It was humanoid, tall and lithe, and ran headlong at them at a speed that made Danny's head hurt.

He snapped his finger, and it ran straight into the fist of a stone golem. The massive golem smashed it into the ground then slung it into a nearby tree, killing it.

With that, it stomped on it a few times then braced itself and turned away from the buildings.

"What was that?" Tess whispered. "See, that's the thing! New monsters. Deadly monsters. Dungeons that aren't the same level they once were."

"Trust me, I know." Danny gritted his teeth as a familiar style of message appeared.

[Creature Absorbed: Slender Runner]

[...]

Danny frowned. "It's listed as an undead of some sort. Human body, undead attribute, something called a Slender Attribute. Never heard of it before."

"Me, either." Tess gritted her teeth. "Danny, I don't like this at all."

"Neither do I." Danny shook his head. "Let's just make sure that we survive until our escort arrives, or until we kill enough that we can get out of here."

"I couldn't agree more."

Danny spawned in several more stone golems, and called back his wolves. As they all approached, more monsters came racing through the trees, and the battle was on.

The forest itself seemed to quake under the battle, as more of the runners, countless undead, wargs, orcs, spiders, and a great many more things came charging at them. Danny's monsters whirled and struck, fighting desperately to kill everything that came their way.

The stone golems ripped up trees to use as weapons, or even just smashed the trees flat to crush their enemies underfoot. It was truly incredible to behold, and the warriors under Tess stared out through the windows, watching it all in equal parts horror and amazement.

"Why don't all mages have powers like yours?" One of them finally muttered. "Forget all the old tensions between the Corp and the mages. This war would be over by now."

Danny chuckled and shrugged. "For what it's worth, I'd gladly share the power with a few others."

The soldier laughed and patted Danny on the shoulder, though Danny wasn't quite sure what the gesture meant. Outside, suddenly, Danny caught a flash of silver, and he smiled.

"And here we go! Anne! Bring them in!"

Danny's monsters leapt forward, clearing a path. Anne's soldiers rushed through the battlefield, slaying everything that happened to get through Danny's armada.

A few moments later, they were inside, with Anne and Tess shaking each other's hands. Tess nodded gratefully.

"Glad to see you."

"Glad to be here." Anne frowned. "Though it looks to me like Danny more or less has this all taken care of."

"Looks can be deceiving," Danny said.

Outside, a huge lizard (though not a dragon) crashed through the trees and snarled at the building before charging at it headlong. One of the stone golems leapt forward, smashing a boulder over its head before spearing it with an oak sapling.

"In this case, they might not be, but..."

Before Danny could finish, Anne interrupted. "And there we have it." She shook her head then turned to Tess.

"What can we do?"

"You can get the wounded out of here," Tess answered. "I'd love nothing more than for you to escort our entire force back to the city, but at the moment, we're safe enough with Danny here, and the wounded need taken care of."

"My soldiers are too exhausted to keep making the run, so if you can take them and get them to safety, I'd sure appreciate it."

"Be extra careful with him." Danny pointed at Zechariah.

Anne followed his gaze, and her jaw dropped. "Oh, no. I'll make sure he's given the finest care."

Danny shook his head. "He won't want special treatment. He just needs taken care of."

"Any one of these men would cede their place to him," Tess said. "If for no other reason than the fact that he's worth thirty soldiers if not more."

Danny sighed. "That's fair."

A few moments later, Anne and her soldiers had gathered up the injured, fifteen in all. One of the stretchers was left behind as it was discovered that the woman on it had died in the midst of the battle.

Danny watched the group as they ran back out while his monsters gave them cover on either side. Anne knew her work.

Four men carried each cot, while the rest of her forces formed a line on either side to keep them safe. They ran from the battle, charging up onto the road and back toward the city.

Tess sighed as she watched them go, then sat down in a chair. "And now, the rest of us are going to take a much-needed break while you deal with all the chaos out there."

"Me?" Danny put his hand over his heart, pretending to be offended.

"Oh, come on. You're the most powerful mage in the Empire, and you could do your job laying on the couch sipping a goblet of wine," Tess snorted. "Boo-hoo."

Danny couldn't argue with that and flashed a smile as he turned back toward the battle.

[Notification: Monster Summoning has increased to Lv. 43!]
[Reward: Mana Increase: 1640 -> 1720]

His mana refilled, and he blinked a few times. He had previously used up almost all 1600 mana spawning in the current batch of monsters... And now he had another 1700 to work with.

Tess raised an eyebrow, and he shrugged. "Time to finish this battle."

He held out his hands as all around him monsters roared through the trees. He only wanted to defeat them all so he could follow his father to make sure that he would be okay.

Until then... Well... Nothing else mattered all that much.

Auto save - [Savefile: Information]
Health: 98%

Mana: 1%

Quest: Get everyone back home safely.

Location: Bone Dungeon, Imperial City Agricultural Area, West Side

Inventory: Essential Supplies, Basic Armor, Iron Sword, Sword of the Wasp, Aquamarine Sword, Frostbite Sword

Skills: Monster Summoner (Lv. 43), Flame Combat (Lv. 2), Wind Combat (Lv. 5)

Relationships: Friendly with Tess, Friendly with Captain Anne, Family Bond with Zechariah, Ascended Fire Mage

Time of Day: 9:48 a.m.

Thirteen

Lessons In Survival

Danny held his breath as he slowly walked down the hallway of the Research Wing, making his way toward the hospital. A few nurses looked up at him, and a few of them immediately glanced away and got out of his path.

That fact made him nervous, and he let out a long breath as he approached the room number. A messenger had come to him the moment that Zechariah had been deemed stable enough to have visitors.

As Danny reached the door, he knocked softly on the frame then slowly stepped inside. Zechariah lay on the bed, breathing softly, eyes half-open.

The blood had been cleaned off him, and he was bare to the waist. Dozens of bandages patched over his chest and torso, closing the wounds that had been opened by the arrows.

His beard had been shaved off, which Danny knew he wouldn't be terribly fond about. As Danny walked up beside him, Zechariah's eyes flickered open slightly more, and he smiled weakly.

"I'm told that I have you to thank for my survival."

"And I'm told that Tess and a lot of the other soldiers have you to thank for their survival," Danny countered.

"Maybe so." Zechariah groaned and let himself sink slightly back into the pillows. "No good deed goes unpunished, and all that."

"I'm just glad you're alive," Danny said. "When I first saw you..."

"I'm so sorry." Zechariah's voice was weak. "But we're all alive. The doctors say that I should be back on my feet inside of a week."

"They don't want me fighting for a while after that, but I'll be able to get out of this room to at least help... I don't know. Advise on the battle, or something."

"I'll be able to assist in some respect. Just need to get all these arrow wounds sealed over so I don't start bleeding like a stuck pig."

Danny chuckled softly. Zechariah suddenly frowned, and his eyes sharpened.

"I've already heard the story twice, and something had struck me both times. How exactly did you know that I was out there? How could you possibly have known I was in trouble?"

Danny held up his hands and smiled. "Can't a guy just have a lucky guess?"

Zechariah scowled. "Don't hide something from me, Danny. I need to know what-"

Suddenly, he paused, and his eyes opened slightly in understanding. "He's alive."

"And for whatever reason, he feels as though he can't show himself," Danny said.

"Did he say anything?" Zechariah asked. "Anything that might give you a clue about why he's afraid? He just killed multiple Deepcorp Lords, and survived a direct blast of dragon fire."

"That ought to more or less seal his reputation."

"I wish I knew." Danny shook his head. "The only thing he said about the matter was that he was being watched by the surviving Deepcorp Lord."

"Wonderful." Zechariah murmured.

"Mm. You haven't heard everything we've learned." Danny sat down on the edge of the bed, being careful not to bump his father.

"It's actually even worse than we thought, believe it or not."

He quickly explained what they had learned about the hidden refuge and the likelihood that the Deepcorp Lord was building an army to use against the Empire once everything was settled. When he finished, Zechariah frowned then shook his head.

"At this point, I'm just going to be satisfied with the fact that he's saving people. We can worry about the specific details at a later date. If even one extra person manages to survive this chaos, I'll be glad about it."

"True." Danny hadn't thought about it quite like that. "I just hope that we don't have to kill them on the field of battle after this is all over."

"Well, that will be a problem for future Danny and future Zechariah." Zechariah sighed and shook his head weakly. "For right now, you should leave me be. I have a great deal of absolutely nothing to get to doing, and I'm sure you have other duties."

"I do, I just..." Danny shrugged.

"I'm glad you came," Zechariah answered. "I truly am, I simply don't wish to keep you from what you need to be doing. Go get back to work, I'm sure Master Barrydew has you running circles around yourself."

"I'm actually teaching your class," Danny commented as he walked up to the door.

"Pfft. I take a couple arrows, and he already goes and gives away my position," Zechariah snorted, though with a smile on his face. "No wonder Nicodemus chose me for his daughter instead of Barrydew."

They both laughed. Danny was just happy that his father had his sense of humor back.

With that, Danny turned and slipped out into the hall, traveling down the long corridors and making his way back to the classrooms. As it happened, he really did have duties that he needed to be attending to.

He soon reached the Monster Theory classroom, where, as he stepped inside, he found his students looking up at him in expectation.

"My apologies." He flashed a thin smile as he walked over to the desk. "I know I'm a bit late. My father was severely injured as he returned to the city, and I received word that he was awake and accepting visitors right as this class began."

"We'd have all done the same thing!" One of the students called from the back. A smattering of laughter ran through the room, and Danny gave a small nod.

"And, in all seriousness, I'd not have counted it against you. Now that we're all here, though, we need to press forward. Today, I think we're going to start with beast-type monsters."

The girl at the front of his classroom, the same one who had spoken up in his original lecture, raised her hand. "Master Youngblood, we've already covered beast-type monsters."

Danny frowned and nodded then gestured to her. "What's your name? You've been very helpful, but I'm afraid I don't actually know which student you are."

She flashed a smile. "Trish. Trish Greymountain."

"Well, Trish Greymountain, I'm well aware that you've already covered beast-type monsters," Danny said. "That said, from what I can see, you covered it with Master..."

He paused and glanced down at some notes on his desk. "You briefly touched upon it with Master Herring, and from what I can see from his lesson notes, it was far from comprehensive."

"Perhaps you've gone over the material from the perspective of the curriculum, but I'm not here to make sure that your education ticks all the boxes that the paper lists. I'm here to make sure that you learn enough that you survive in the dungeons."

Trish nodded and raised her hand. Danny nodded to her.

"From your experience in the dungeons, what's the most important thing that we need to know?"

Danny thought for a moment. That was an odd question, but an important one.

"I just mean..." she pressed. "Is it better to know the monsters and their attack patterns? Is it better to known your own personal fighting style?"

"Is it better to know the layouts of the dungeons?"

"First off, it's a composite issue," Danny answered. "As I've been entering the field more and more, I find that each and every class that I've taken contributes to my success on the field."

"I know that makes me sound like the Headmaster or something, like an inspirational speech, but I promise, it's true. That said, if I did have to pick one..."

He paused, then nodded. "It would be knowing the monsters. If you know the details on the dungeons, you'll know what sorts of monsters you'll be facing."

"If you know your fighting style, you'll know how to approach different sorts of monsters, but at the end of the day, the monsters are the things that you'll actively be engaging. Being able to size them up as they come at you is essential for making sure you survive and they don't."

Danny paused and waited to see if there were any further questions. When he saw that there weren't, he pressed forward.

"Now, that brings us to beasts. The classic definition of a beast is pretty simple: Anything that looks like it could exist in nature."

"You see a zombie walking around, and it's pretty obvious that the thing isn't natural. You see a giant rat, and like... I don't know. Maybe it's just a species that hasn't yet been discovered or classified."

Danny paused and crossed his arms. "Because of that, generally speaking, beasts are made of flesh and blood, which means that the very general rules apply in the same way as humanoid monsters."

"If it would make sense for it to hurt, it'll probably hurt it. Most of them have one heart, blood that flows through their veins, so on and so forth."

Danny paused, then frowned. "The real trick with beasts is Attributes, which is where they can change themselves dramatically and really mess up a raid. Have you covered attributes yet?"

The class collectively shook its head.

"Great!" Danny clapped his hands. "Then that's what we're going to do here. Ahh... Let's just go with a giant rat. The very first monster I ever killed was an Enraged Rat, actually."

With a flash, five different Enraged Rats appeared on the floor at the front of the classroom. The students at the back craned their necks, and Danny waved them up.

"Here! Come on up, and make a circle. Push some of the desks back if you have to."

The students quickly obeyed. It wasn't every day that they got to see actual monsters in their classes, that was for sure.

The rats snarled and snapped at the students as Danny nodded to them. "Now, we'll have this one serve as the control."

He waved his hand, and one of them reared up, hissing and spitting. "Behold! The Enraged Rat. Very simple. Stab it in the heart or the lungs, and you've got a sure kill. Now, though..."

He turned and motioned at the next rat. It suddenly turned white, and crystals of ice slithered down from its mouth.

It let out a hiss and spun around, and the students drew back slightly. "This is now an Enraged Frost Rat," Danny explained.

"If you were to see this thing coming at you, there are a few options. First thing to know is that, if it bites you, the wound will freeze, and there's a chance that you'll be infected with Frostbite."

"That can slow your attacks, which automatically puts you at greater risk. Also of note is the fact that the skin of the rat will be covered with a layer of ice, making it harder to stab through it."

"The rat will be weaker against Flame and Lightning attacks, but it will be stronger against most other forms of damage."

As the students were pondering that fact, the third rat burst into flame. "This is an Enraged Fire Rat. A bite from this creature will deal more raw damage, but it will actually be a cleaner wound."

"Chances of infection from a fire-type creature is almost nonexistent, and it's pretty much a guarantee that it won't bleed. Getting too close will probably deal you some area of effect fire damage, which makes ranged attacks preferable."

"It will actually be almost entirely immune to frost attacks, mostly immune to lightning attacks, but slightly weaker to physical attacks."

The fourth rat suddenly became slimy and matted, displaying open sores. A dark liquid dripped down from its fangs, and it fought to break free of Danny's control.

The fifth rat grew a layer of armor that sealed it up tightly, and the sixth rat withered to the point that it almost looked like a skeleton. Danny spent the rest of the class period talking through the different methods of attacking and killing the monsters.

He despawned them creatures and spawned in new ones here and there, running the gambit as much as he could. When the bell finally rang to let the students know it was time to leave, the classroom left rather reluctantly indeed.

Danny waved as they all left... And then frowned as he caught sight of Master Barrydew watching him through the door.

"Checking up on me?" Danny raised an eyebrow as the master walked inside.

"No, not at all." Master Barrydew shook his head, then smiled. "Well, perhaps slightly. I asked a visitor to my office how your class was looking, he had just come from this hallway after all, and he told me that it looked like the students were actually having fun."

A small smile came across his face. "Not many professors bring live monsters into the classroom. Don't tell the health inspectors."

Danny laughed and waved his hand, dissolving all the creatures. "Don't worry about a thing. I won't breathe a word of it."

He paused as he walked up to Master Barrydew. "Thanks for giving me this task. I think I probably needed it."

"I would tend to agree." Master Barrydew crossed his arms. "Now, if you'd like, I can take your next class. I know your father just woke up. If I'm being honest, that's the real reason I came."

"I heard that you went to visit him, but were called away by your class."

Danny flashed a smile. "Thanks, I appreciate it, but I can stay."

"You sure?" Master Barrydew asked. "I really can help."

"My father isn't going anywhere, and I think he'd prefer that I was being useful," Danny said. "He wouldn't want to feel like he was hurting the war effort, you know."

"Fair enough. I suppose I'd be the same." Master Barrydew shrugged and turned away. "Well, if there's anything I can do, please let me know."

"Have some sort of food delivered to the hospital room for dinner tonight, so I can eat with him," Danny answered. "That would be great. And maybe send a Daggers board along, too. I'm sure he's bored and wouldn't mind a game."

Master Barrydew bowed his head. "I'll make sure it's done."

With that, Master Barrydew walked away, and Danny felt a ray of warmth wash over him. Maybe things weren't so bad after all.

Outside the city, it felt like things were falling apart, but here there was still life. And he would fight with all his might to make sure that that life was never diminished.

Auto save - [Savefile: Information]
Health: 100%
Mana: 99%
Quest: Teach your next class.
Location: Monster Theory Classroom, Introductory Wing
Inventory: Essential Supplies, Basic Armor, Iron Sword, Sword of the Wasp, Aquamarine Sword, Frostbite Sword
Skills: Monster Summoner (Lv. 43), Flame Combat (Lv. 2), Wind Combat (Lv. 5)
Relationships: Friendly with Master Barrydew, Family Bond with Zechariah, Ascended Fire Mage
Time of Day: 11:53 a.m.

Fourteen

Unraveling Secrets

The next few days slipped by in relative peace, though an uneasy quiet hung in the air. Danny continued his teaching duties and met with Zechariah in the evenings—and sometimes in the early mornings as well.

Outside, rumors of the war swirled like a storm on the horizon. News of small towns falling filled the air, while conflicting reports about the fate of various legions spread like flocks of crows.

From what Danny could gather, the current strategy was to withdraw all remaining legions into the Imperial Capital. However, with several legions either trapped or delayed, the process proved anything but simple.

Danny, eager to help however he could, found himself chafing at the bit. He wanted nothing more than to ride out and rescue the stranded legions, but his orders kept him firmly anchored in the capital.

"Why can't I just go out there to see what I can do?" Danny asked Master Barrydew several days later as word reached the Imperial City that the Third Legion was alive but trapped inside the Falling Rocks Dungeon.

They were not too far from the Imperial City but surrounded by a horde of S-ranked creatures.

"Because the Emperor believes... And I frankly believe as well... That we're being watched." Master Barrydew sighed.

UNRAVELING SECRETS 119

"The moment you leave the city, we have good reason to believe that a massive attack will be levied."

"I agree, I don't like it, but all these reports you're hearing... Most of them are impossible to verify anyway, and even if we could confirm them, they're likely just a plot to get you out of here."

Danny frowned. "I understand, but it's still frustrating to be stuck here."

"So did Nicodemus, and he wasn't around in a time of war," Master Barrydew said. "I can only imagine what he would have done if he had been placed in your shoes. In any case, this is what's being ordered, and I expect you to follow orders."

Danny knew that he was best off to listen. The near-omnipotence of the Dark Lord was worrisome, and it was a sure bet that the moment Danny left the city, it would be known.

That didn't stop him from fantasizing about it or trying to make plans just in case he had to leave, but he did his best to obey and stay put. Through it all, Isa continued to work in her own lab.

Almost three weeks after his return to the Imperial City, Danny found himself wandering over to her room and knocking on the door. She pulled it open a second later and beamed as she motioned him inside.

"Danny! Please, come in, come in." She stepped back, allowing him to slip into the room.

The moment he was inside, she closed it and locked it tight. Danny's jaw dropped.

The huge globe had been taken apart. The lower half of the globe still sat in the fitting while the upper half of the casing had been removed and now sat in a corner off to one side.

Meanwhile, the interior of the globe, a massive network of gears and cogs and mana crystals, was on full display. It looked like Isa had taken apart a good chunk of it, judging by the carefully-arranged gears that were spread across several nearby tables, along with the countless diagrams that she had drawn up showing how this or that thing went back together.

"This is incredible." Danny gaped at the thing. "How'd you get it apart?"

"It wasn't easy." Isa shrugged. "I spent almost three days just looking the thing over, comparing maps, diagrams, and things, and then I happened to see the thinnest little crack that ran around the middle of it."

"I could only see it across one of the oceans, it must have just been damage from sitting there so long. Took me another two days after that, but I managed to pry it apart, and here we are."

"So, what is this?" Danny leaned over the contraption, making sure not to touch anything.

"Believe me, Danny, if I had even the slightest idea, you'd know by now." Isa answered with no little exasperation. "From what I can tell, all these gears were mostly used to spin the globe about."

"When we found it, you could just reach out and manually turn it this way and that, but I think that it could just do it automatically. Like... You'd tell it to show you the Imperial City, and it would spin itself to show you."

"Fascinating!" Danny shook his head, then pointed at the mana crystals. "And it would use these to power itself?"

"That's my best guess, yes." Isa confirmed. "Now, I haven't been able to access the lowest portions yet, but from what I can see, there are twenty-one fittings that can hold mana crystals in this thing."

"This crystal here..." She pointed at one right at the top, which still gleamed in its fitting. "This is a telepathic stone. You can use it to talk to people across long distances, that sort of thing."

"They're super rare, I think only one gets pulled out of the dungeons every year or so, across the whole of the Empire."

She paused. "The problem is that it's just about the only stone that I can identify."

"A lot of the mana crystals seem to have degraded over the years. Like... Look at this fitting. There's a bit of dust left in it, but the crystal itself has just crumbled away."

"Or this one." She pointed at a grey mana crystal off to one side. "This one has lost all its power without crumbling. I can tell it's a mana crystal, but all the mana itself is gone, I don't have a clue what sort of mana might have been contained within."

"So, what are you doing right now?" Danny asked, taking a seat off to one side.

"Right now, I'm tearing this whole thing apart, making a many notes as I can, and then I'm going to try to put it back together." Isa answered.

"My hope is that I'll be able to deduce what sort of crystal to put back into each fitting. Like, I'm pretty sure that this one here is a fire crystal, but..."

"First off, I don't know what a fire crystal would be doing inside a globe, nor am I confident enough to just wing it. Put the wrong type of mana in the wrong place, and you're looking at a bomb instead of... Well, instead of whatever sort of weapon this thing actually is."

"Mm." Danny crossed his arms and frowned. Something inside the machine caught his eye, and he leaned forward. "What's that at the center?"

"I wish I knew, I truly do," Isa answered. "It's a massive fitting for something, but whatever it holds is completely encased, so I can't tell what it holds. If it is a mana crystal, it has to be one that holds at least five thousand mana, but like I said, I just don't know."

She paused, then suddenly brightened. "You want to see something super cool, though?"

"I'd love to." Danny stood up slightly as she walked to the other side of the room.

"Then come over here." As he joined her, she gestured at a collection of odd things she had apparently pulled out of the machine.

Each one was a flat piece of metal, two inches wide by three inches long, and was covered in tiny little grooves that had been meticulously carved into the surface. Danny frowned and carefully picked one up, shaking his head.

"Alright, I'll bite. What's this thing?"

"That, my friend, is something that I'm calling a circuit," Isa answered. "These things are connected to the fittings with the mana crystals, at least most of them."

"Each of them has three inputs, one on a side, and then an output on the fourth." She pointed to small brackets on the sides of the things.

"They all connect to other fittings that are attached to the gears. Basically, if the machine moves in a certain way, the gears move into place and come into contact with these things."

"The mana from the crystals, at least from what I can tell, moves through the gears. If the gears then come into contact with these circuits, it sends the mana up through them and into the other mana crystals, which then (probably) either activates them or turns them off, or whatever."

Danny blinked as he tried to wrap his mind around the concept. "That's amazing, if it's true..."

"Oh, it's true," Isa said. "I don't yet know why it works like that, though I do have some theories. This machine... Whatever it is, it's so far ahead of our time."

"I mean, seriously, it's like it came from the future or something. I mean, just look at clocks. Clocks were only invented about a hundred years ago."

"If someone at the start of the Empire had seen a clock, they would have been amazed, and like... I feel like I'm staring into something that shouldn't yet exist."

"Isn't your whole thesis about how dungeons can affect the progress of civilization?" Danny asked with a small smile.

"Indeed it is." Isa nodded then paused and turned to look at him. "What did you just say?"

"That things you find in dungeons-"

"Can affect the technology of a civilization." Isa snapped her fingers. "Okay, not exactly what you said, but that was the gist. I've been looking at this all wrong!"

Danny frowned and crossed his arms. "Do tell?"

"I've been trying to figure out who built this, and why. I still need those answers, but also..." Isa spun to him.

"Inspiration rarely happens in a vacuum. Whoever built this probably had a reason for doing so, and it probably has something to do with something that he or she found in the Dead Mountains."

"There are a whole lot of unknowns in that sentence," Danny commented.

"Trust me, I know." Isa sat down on a seat and stroked her chin. "I need to know what can come out of those dungeons. I need to know what makes them special."

"What was pulled from them that made someone build this thing?"

Danny shrugged. "Master Barrydew mentioned an herb that improves eyesight."

"Yeah, he told me about it. I'm pretty sure that's not what's going on here." Isa bit her lip, stood, and started pacing.

"Danny, could you do me a huge favor? Like just a colossally large favor?"

"Possibly, provided that it doesn't compromise morals or national security," Danny joked.

"If I get you a list of books, can you go find them from the archives?" Isa asked. "Better yet, if I give you some general topics and places to look, can you just bring me a ton of material?"

"I'm sure that Master Barrydew can help you."

"I'd be happy to." Danny nodded. "What are we looking for?"

Isa walked over to a desk that was still somewhat empty, and she quickly began to write down things on a piece of paper. When she was done, she passed it to Danny, who blinked in surprise as he looked down at the list.

It was really quite long, and he tucked it into his inventory. "I'll see what I can do," Danny confirmed. "Anything else I can do?"

"Find me an extra set of hands." Isa chuckled as she turned back to the globe. "I could sure use an assistant in taking this thing apart, but I need someone who responds to my exact thoughts."

"Marcella tried to help me for a while, but it was more trouble than it was worth. I feel bad, I sorta yelled at her, but…"

"If I don't know exactly where everything is placed, I won't be able to put this all back together."

Danny paused for a moment then slowly held out his hand. With a flash, a goblin appeared next to Isa.

She gave a small jump, but Danny shook his head. He connected to Isa's presence, a technique that he was getting rather comfortable with as he became more and more powerful, and, after a moment, he had bonded the goblin to Isa instead of himself.

She blinked in surprise as it was given to her command. Danny lowered his hand. "There you go. You should be able to order him to do what you want, and he'll respond to your thoughts."

Isa looked down at the goblin then at Danny. "I didn't know you could do that."

"In fairness, neither did I," Danny said. "I guess we can all still give surprises. Maybe that's what'll keep us ahead of the enemy."

Isa shrugged, and with that, Danny turned and walked out of the room. As he did so, he sighed deeply.

Isa was making good progress, but it probably wasn't fast enough. He had to help her if at all he could...

The Empire, and likely the world, depended on it.

Auto save - [Savefile: Information]

Health: 100%

Mana: 99%

Quest: Take Isa's list to Master Barrydew.

Location: Hallways, Research Wing

Inventory: Essential Supplies, Basic Armor, Iron Sword, Sword of the Wasp, Aquamarine Sword, Frostbite Sword

Skills: Monster Summoner (Lv. 43), Flame Combat (Lv. 2), Wind Combat (Lv. 5)

Relationships: Friendly with Isa, Friendly with Master Barrydew

Time of Day: 4:27 p.m.

Fifteen

Crumbling Defenses

Several days later, Danny slowly walked into the library to find Master Barrydew looking with equal parts pride and worry at a large pile of books almost three feet tall. It sat upon one of the many tables in the library.

He turned to Danny with a small nod. "I think this is everything that Isa requested." He sighed and started running his finger along the spines of the books.

"Dungeon Logs for the Dead Mountains and surrounding areas going back almost eight hundred years... Lists of unique artifacts... Lists of Rare and Very Rare treasures... What exactly does she need this for, anyway? I'm a little confused, if I'm being completely honest."

"I think she's mostly grasping at straws, and the only reason I'll say that is because I think she'd agree to it," Danny said. "She's trying to find anything at all that will link a dungeon artifact to that globe."

"So, she really does think it's something more than just a fancy map?" Master Barrydew asked.

Danny nodded. "I believe so, yes. As far as I know, she believes it to likely be an accurate representation of the world, and the land beyond the Empire's borders. She also believes that it could take verbal commands."

"You'd tell it to show you a part of the world, and it would spin in that direction."

CRUMBLING DEFENSES

"The question is what else it could do," Master Barrydew murmured.

"Indeed, that is the question. And that's what she's trying to figure out. If we can find record of a stone that allows you to see around the world, or..."

"Or a stone that allows you to kill things across the world." Master Barrydew looked at the stack of books with some concern. "I'll admit, Danny, this makes me worried. I'm afraid of what will happen if we truly find something to unleash, some sort of weapon that should have just been locked away."

"The only reason I'm allowing this research is because, indeed, if the dungeons continue to grow more and more powerful, I don't know what else we might be able to do to survive."

Danny nodded and started to open his inventory to transfer the large pile of books. Suddenly, footsteps echoed in the hall as Tess came running into the library.

"Danny! Been looking for you."

"What's up?" Danny frowned and turned around. "Trouble?"

"Depends on how you define trouble." Tess looked down at herself and chuckled. "I know it looks like I'm probably running here to give you desperate news, but the reality is that I'm just being impatient and don't have much time."

She sighed. "Several of my guards were injured last night in a small attack against the wall, but my unit still has to go on patrol today. Would you be willing to come out with me? Might be good for the town to see you in action anyway, and I could sure use the help."

Danny nodded. "Sure, I just need to get all of this down to Isa."

"Oh, you go. I'll take this down to her." Master Barrydew waved his hand. "I'd like to talk over the project with her, anyway."

Danny nodded, and he and Tess turned and made their way quickly out of the Academy. Soon, they were out in the city, making their way toward the outer walls.

"Any major attacks expected?" Danny asked as they slipped out through the southern gates of the main body of the city.

Of course, that only put them inside the larger, walled-in area that had now ballooned to a truly extraordinary size. He could see the outer walls rising rapidly, a true testament to the spirit of endurance that could be found in emergencies.

"No, just routine," Tess said. "Things are getting nasty out there, though. You'll see in a minute."

When they reached the outer wall, they quickly slipped through another gate and out into the wilderness beyond. There, several guards stood at the ready while a small group gathered for patrol.

Danny looked up at the new wall, and winced slightly. It had quite obviously been built rapidly, and was far from what could be considered exceptional craftsmanship.

Impressive, yes. Would it survive a major attack? That was another question entirely.

He and Tess, along with several other soldiers, began to march around the outside of the wall. It wrapped through the prairie, rising and falling over the hills.

Danny gazed out across the wilderness as they marched. It truly was a wilderness, now.

Large claw marks marred the ground just about everywhere while rotting corpses of both man and beast could be seen across the hills. Giant bones lay here and there where the monsters had laid for long enough to decompose almost entirely.

A few cottages stood here and there, now little more than ruins, the remnants of the farms that had once provided food for the entire land.

"How long is this wall?" Danny asked as they moved along. "Does anyone even know for sure?"

"The short answer is no," Tess replied. "The longer answer is that we can estimate it at about thirty miles."

"Thirty miles?" Danny's jaw dropped. "How do you come up with that number?"

"The Imperial City itself is about six miles across." Tess answered. "The walls go about two miles beyond the city's walls at any given point, making for a total of ten miles across. Got it?"

"Got it." Danny frowned. "I think."

"Well, if you were paying attention in math class, you can find the circumference of a circle by taking the radius and multiplying by six." She shrugged.

"It's not exact, but it's close enough for most practical purposes. Five miles from the center to the edge, multiplied by six, makes for about thirty miles of wall that we now have to patrol with very few men."

Danny grimaced but nodded. The unit continued to walk along, past the desolation, making their way toward the next gate.

He didn't even know if it would be possible for one person to walk the whole length of the wall in a single day. Well...

It would probably be possible for one person to walk thirty miles in a day, but would they be able to actually defend the wall at the end of it? He didn't know, and hoped that they wouldn't have to find out.

In any event, they wrapped around the southern side of the city toward the west, over the rolling limestone hills. Off in the distance, Danny saw several monsters wandering here and there, wolves and bears and things, but they kept their distance, so the army didn't approach.

"Policy is to only engage if they're heading straight for the city, or within a distance of one hundred yards of the wall." Tess explained. "We just don't have the manpower to do anything more."

Danny nodded, then pointed ahead. "So that would be a problem?"

Tess followed his gaze, and nodded wearily. Ahead, several trolls were stomping through a ravine, making for a low point in the wall.

Several civilian guards began to fire arrows at the things, but they fell short. "Civies." Tess grumbled as the army picked up speed.

There were about ten of them, and they all drew their swords. "Always wasting resources. I know it makes them feel better, but they'd really be better off to just leave the fighting to us."

"Yeah, but you know how stressful things are right now." Danny tried to defend them.

"And that's the only reason I don't yell at them more." Tess started to break into a jog. "Come on."

"Maybe I should go on ahead?" Danny suggested.

"By all means." Tess slowed. "But now showboating. Just do the job and do it quickly."

Danny nodded and ran down the hill. The trolls were large, but far from the largest things he had ever taken down.

Quickly, he snapped his fingers, and a stone golem formed, racing across the landscape with powerful footsteps. The civilians on the wall cheered as it ran down toward the trolls.

The trolls, meanwhile, drew up short. Apparently, they were confused by the thought of someone cheering over the fact that they were about to die.

Their confusion was abated a second later when a limestone boulder smashed into the head of the closest one, leaving nothing but air upon the troll's neck. It collapsed with a loud thud, and the other trolls spun toward their attacker.

Danny felt a pang of sympathy for them, but it quickly passed. The stone golem charged forward and threw a punch into the second troll that killed it in a single instant.

CRUMBLING DEFENSES   131

The third troll roared and swung a huge club at the golem, but the golem simply raised a hand and caught the club in its palm. It twisted sharply, ripping the club out of the hand of the troll then hit the troll over the head with its own weapon.

The club broke, the troll's skull shattered, and with that, it hit the ground as well. "And there we have it." Danny smiled and nodded to Tess. "No showboating."

CRACK!

Danny spun as a huge crack spread up the wall. It ran from the ground all the way to the top, causing the men on top of the wall to scream.

Several of them started to climb down while the others turned and ran along the top of the wall in either direction. A second later, about twenty feet of wall just crumbled, collapsing in an immense pile of dust.

The stone golem lurched forward and caught two of them men before they hit the ground, one or two of the defenders made it safety to part of the wall that stayed put, while the others vanished into the great plume of dust and debris. Screams filled the air as Danny rushed forward.

He suddenly found himself looking through the gap into the vast tent city, into the eyes of mothers, fathers, and children, all of whom were utterly defenseless against the beasts of the wilderness. With the stone golem looming in the gap, people screamed and started to run away, and Danny sighed.

"Please!" A man covered in dust leapt through the rubble and pointed frantically at the stone. "My brother is trapped under there!"

Danny nodded, and the stone golem lumbered forward, effortlessly hefting large pieces of rubble and tossing them aside. After a brief hesitation, Danny summoned several goblins to assist.

They scurried around, quickly clearing the smaller debris and making swift progress. Tess and her soldiers plunged into the work, driven by urgency.

Danny was about to join them when a low rumble caught his attention. He froze, turning slowly to see a bear cresting a nearby ridge, followed by a pack of snarling wolves.

Their eyes gleamed with predatory intent, sensing a vulnerability in the city's defenses.

"Danny!" Tess called out. "I know you've already provided a dozen hands, but I really wouldn't mind it if you came and helped out personally."

"Yeah, I'm a bit preoccupied at the moment," Danny called back.

"With what?" Tess was invisible amidst the dust which was only just now starting to settle.

"You just focus on you, and I'll focus on this," Danny said. "Deal?"

"What? No!" Tess called out. "Youngblood!"

As Danny snapped his fingers, rockworms burst up from the ground, punching holes straight through the bear and two of the wolves. The other wolves snarled and raced forward, leaping across the ground just as fast as they could go.

The stone golem threw a large chunk of the wall, smashing one of them into the ground, and then threw a punch that splattered another one across the ground like paste. A third wolf leapt past it, and the golem spun and snatched at its tail.

The jaws of the wolf snapped shut only inches short of Tess's face as the golem caught hold of the beast, and her startled scream echoed across the landscape as the golem spun and threw the wolf up into the air, flinging it out over the wastes.

"And here I didn't think you even could scream," Danny commented as more creatures came to see what all the fuss was about.

There was a goblin lord, a few wraith-like creatures, a swarm of giant rats, and some other small monsters. They all looked down at the gap hungrily as Danny nodded to the golem.

"Go get them!"

Rockworms burst up from the ground, chewing through whatever they could reach, and the golem charged into battle. Danny watched closely as the fight raged on.

Finally, as his golem stomped the last rat into pulp, Tess gave a cry. "And that's the last of them!"

Danny nodded and turned back where the dust had finally settled down, and he could see a handful of people laid out on their backs, gasping for air as a handful of other people worked to attend to them. "Are they okay?" he asked.

"Most will pull through," Tess replied. "There are a few that could use medical attention, but I'm not sure that they're going to get it."

"Can't we just take them back to the city?" Danny demanded. "There are hospitals there that-"

"The hospitals in the city are full to overflowing." Tess shook her head. "There's the medical ward in the Academy, but that's for soldiers and mages only, and even it is overflowing."

"The other hospitals literally have stretchers lined up on the streets. Moving them would only damage them more."

She sighed. "There are medics here in the camps who will do what they can, but that's all that we can do."

Danny grimaced. He didn't really have any healing spells, nor did Tess.

Radiance knew a few of them, as did Margot, but they weren't around. Danny reluctantly nodded as he watched a few civilians, mostly older women, doing their best to bandage the wounds.

Tess turned and looked up at the crumbled wall and shook her head. "The bigger issue is this wall. We had to build it the way we did, but it's just not built very strongly."

She simply held up her hand. "Not much we can do now. I wish we could help rebuild this section, but I'm not even sure we can do that."

"I just got a message that there's a herd of rhinos angling for the wall about a mile ahead, we need to get there before they do."

Danny nodded and started to follow as Tess walked away... And then paused. He snapped his fingers, and with about half his mana, he spawned in a handful of massive bees.

The crowd screamed as the monsters looked down at them... And then, without another word, the bees flew down and began to pick up the pieces of the wall. Exuding wax, they stuck the pieces of the wall back together.

In front of the army and the crowd, the great barrier was slowly rebuilt. "Now that's what I'm talking about." Tess held out a fist which Danny bumped.

"Come on, let's move on and stomp some rhinos."

With that, they took off. Danny's heart pounded, and he did his best to stay focused.

He was glad that he could help, but he also desperately wished he could do more. If he ever did catch up with that Deepcorp mage, well...

The dark lord was going to have a lot of blood on his hands to answer for.

Auto save - [Savefile: Information]

Health: 100%

Mana: 45%

Quest: Protect the Imperial City

Location: Imperial City Agricultural Area, Southern Side

Inventory: Essential Supplies, Basic Armor, Iron Sword, Sword of the Wasp, Aquamarine Sword, Frostbite Sword

Skills: Monster Summoner (Lv. 43), Flame Combat (Lv. 2), Wind Combat (Lv. 5)

Relationships: Friendly with Tess, Friendly with Master Barrydew

Time of Day: 2:47 p.m.

Sixteen

Horde

And that... That concludes our lesson on undead." Danny nodded, gesturing to the Skulking Zombie that stood at the front of the classroom. It was truly a grotesque thing to look at, as one eye was missing and great flaps of skin hung loose.

Its jaw was wide open, capable of latching down onto a rather enormous portion of a warrior's body. "Are there any questions?"

Trish's hand shot up, and Danny nodded to her. "So, you're saying that the type of undead relates to the level of that undead? I just want to make sure I'm understanding that correctly."

"Exactly," Danny confirmed. "The same is true of goblins. A level 1 Zombie is just a zombie. Level 2 Zombies are called Strong Zombies, and so on."

"Level 90 and above can use magic, that's typically when you start getting liches and things of that nature."

Trish nodded. "Got it. And you said that mummies are just zombies with an attribute?"

"Correct," Danny said. "The Mummified Attribute can be applied to any and all zombies, and basically just makes them immune to piercing damage but weak to slashing and fire damage."

"And one final thing," the eager student continued. "You said that the undead attribute can technically be added to any monster throughout the land? Have you ever seen undead versions of other creatures?"

"Yes-ish." Danny crossed his arms. "Normally, the Undead attribute is applied to a Level 1 Human Body. Important to note is that this human body will never spawn without the Undead Attribute, the dungeons don't just go around kicking out humans."

He chuckled slightly, and the rest of the class tittered lightly. "Now, it's more often applied to monsters of a humanoid form. Goblins, trolls, orcs, that sort of thing."

"Each specific monster type has its own dice roll, but..." He paused for a moment in thought. "I want to say that the average chance of a non-human humanoid to spawn with the Undead Attribute is around 0.001%."

"I.e., out of every one hundred thousand humanoid monsters you encounter, one of them will be undead. Of course, most people will entirely miss the fact that they've encountered one, since they often come in swarms, and because undead are often seen with normal humanoids."

He paused. "As far as non-humanoid undead, I once saw an undead wolf, out on patrol just a few months ago, but that's the only one I've ever encountered."

"I think outside of non-humanoids, the percentage drops down to something like 0.00001, or one out of every ten million monsters you encounter."

"And how many monsters will the average warrior kill in his lifetime?" another student asked.

"On average?" Danny shrugged. "I could run some numbers, but I honestly don't know. I wish I had a better answer."

Trish cupped her hands around her mouth. "Lame!"

The rest of the class laughed, and a few others made mock signs of disrespect. Danny laughed at it then waved them out of the classroom, and it quickly emptied.

After they were gone, he sighed deeply and walked over to his desk where he sat down and started to mull through his assorted reports. He had been working for almost fifteen minutes when he noticed there was another student still sitting in the back of the room.

He looked up from his work and blinked in surprise. At the very back of the room, a student sat at one of the desks, a cloak pulled over her form.

He was pretty sure that it was a female, judging by the general shape of the body, but it was hard to know for sure. He frowned and climbed to his feet, and she did the same.

And then, without warning, she stepped forward and flitted out the door. It was odd, but Danny might have let it go at that... if not for one thing; the smell of dragon ash in the air.

"Barbara," he murmured as she vanished into the hall.

Without another pause, he bolted after her. The door crashed loudly as he raced into the hall and looked left and right.

There she was, standing almost fifty feet away, at an intersection. She turned and walked to the right, vanishing again, and he ran after her, trying not to look too out of place while he did it.

She was leading him on, that much was obvious, the only question was why. When he reached the intersection and glanced in the direction she had gone, he saw her again, down the hall at a stairwell.

She gave him a nod, then turned and flashed up the stairs. From there, he raced on, just as fast as he could go, catching whiffs of dragon ash here and there, otherwise just following her clues.

It quickly became obvious that she was leading him in circles. They went back through the same intersections multiple times, up flights of stairs and then back down to the same floors they had already passed through.

The minutes turned into almost an hour, but still, Danny didn't stop. He didn't have a clue what she was after, or why she was leading him on, but he assumed that there had to be a reason.

Barbara didn't do much without purpose, the only question was what it might be. Finally, she turned and ducked into the library, and Danny raced inside.

Of course, as he did so, he ran smack into Master Barrydew, who dropped the load of papers he had been carrying. They fluttered everywhere as Danny looked back and forth.

"Where's she go?" he demanded.

"Who?" Master Barrydew snapped his fingers and caused the pages to flutter back up into his hands then tucked them into his inventory. "You saw someone run in here?"

"I did, yes." Danny nodded. "You didn't?"

"No, and I've been standing right here for the last ten minutes." Master Barrydew shrugged then gestured to a table right next to him that was piled high with dozens more papers.

"Routine administration stuff that I've been putting off because of the war. Who did you see? Are you feeling alright?"

Danny scowled. "Come on. You know me better than that. If I say I saw someone-"

"Believe me, I'm aware." Master Barrydew glanced left and right. "My apologies. Perhaps I'm simply trying to make light of a situation."

Danny's eyes narrowed. "What situation?"

Master Barrydew sighed deeply. "Come to my office. I suppose I should have spoken to you earlier today, but I haven't wanted to bother you."

Danny frowned, and followed as Master Barrydew led the way to the office. He kept glancing around for Barbara, but he saw nothing.

If she had vanished, she had vanished, but... Why? Why had she led him here?

When they got into the office and closed the door, Master Barrydew walked over and sat down at his desk. He drummed his fingers against the wood, then nodded to Danny.

"We've just received word, this morning, that a massive attack force is coming this way. It contains the herds of three separate S-ranked dungeons, and they're heading straight for the Imperial City."

"At present, we don't have the faintest idea how we'll defend against it."

"We'll fight." Danny said resolutely, balling his hands into fists. "I can take a lot of them, and-"

"I have no doubt that you can," Master Barrydew said. "That's not the issue. We're relatively confident that with our forces, we can drive the attack back without losing too many civilians, but we're also confident that it'll take out over half of our remaining soldiers and mages."

"And that's a conservative estimate." He shook his head. "In any case, it isn't a hazy grey moral question, to be certain. We aren't debating what to do."

"We're making plans to fight, we simply haven't begun circulating orders yet. The herd won't get here for another three days."

"No use spreading fear. You were going to be told."

Suddenly, the smell of dragon ash filled the room. Danny and Master Barrydew both looked up sharply and found Barbara standing just behind him.

"She's the one I saw almost run you over," Danny commented casually.

"Ahh. I see." Master Barrydew folded his hands and leaned back in his chair. "I don't believe that we've had the pleasure?"

"The name's Barbara." She slowly sat down in an empty chair, pulling her hood back. Her face had a long cut running from her left eye, down across her nose and through the right cheek, but otherwise, she seemed to have fared far better than Nicodemus.

"I tried to kill Danny half a dozen times, and he tried to kill me just as many times. Also, Anne is my sister."

"Ahh! So you're the one they thought was killed by the dragon." Master Barrydew nodded.

"That would be me." Barbara flashed a small smile and nodded.

"Well, I'm glad to see that you're still on this side of the dirt. I do have to admit that I'm rather curious about your... Ahh... Survival." Master Barrydew folded his hands, and Danny had to laugh.

For all Master Barrydew's posturing about curiosity and dealing with the fact that you didn't need to know everything, he was the worst about wanting to know everything that was going on at any given time. "I've been hearing some odd rumors about the survival of Nicodemus. I don't suppose-"

"I didn't come here to gossip." Barbara folded her hands and grimaced. "I know you both have questions, and assuming that we don't all die over the next several months, I'm sure you'll get your answers."

"For the time being, we need to stick to business. I have about two more hours to get back to the place where I'm staying, and it's an hour and a half journey, so... We should be quick."

"You're the one who led me on a wild goose chase," Danny muttered.

"I needed to get the two of you together, and he was busy in a meeting." Barbara folded her hands together. "The very simple answer to why I'm here is that the attack on its way is far more than just a herd."

"It was carefully curated by the Deepcorp Lord."

"How so?" Master Barrydew asked. He took out a sheet of paper to start writing, and Barbara spoke quickly.

"There were three dungeons which, over a year ago, he carefully manipulated and timed to overflow at this moment." Barbara answered.

"One of them is an undead dungeon, one is a beast dungeon, and one is a magical dungeon. When they overflowed, which took place despite your patrols because he was able to misdirect even the minds of your own commanders, he was able to direct them together into one herd."

"The combination of the three groups has created... The point is that any attack that one monster is weak to, the other monsters will be resistant to. It sounds simple, but it means that up and down the battlefield, you'll need mages and soldiers of all specialties."

"There won't be a bandage fix for this, it'll be a harder fight than you can imagine."

"I see." Master Barrydew thought for a moment. "I can see the issue. Is there more to it?"

"Yes." She confirmed. "The bulk of the herd is coming from the east. You know the landscape well enough, you should be able to direct the monsters to funnel points."

"That said, he secretly split off the three bosses from the dungeons. They're coming up from the south. Their details are here."

She passed a small piece of paper across. Master Barrydew took it and frowned down at the writing.

"A giant... A wyrm... A Treant?"

"None of which are impossible to take down by themselves, but when your forces, weary and weak, suddenly find them coming from the south, miles away, how do you think they'll react?" Barbara sighed and slowly climbed to his feet.

"For what it's worth, he knows that this won't destroy the Imperial City, but he doesn't intend it to. This is but the first attack. He has other herds that he's forming, far to the south and to the west."

"The second herd will hit in two more months, and will consist of five dungeons. The third herd is currently planned for about six months down the line, and will, if all goes according to his plans, almost ten dungeons."

"Wonderful," Master Barrydew muttered.

"How do you know so much about his plans?" Danny asked, balling his hands into fists. She raised an eyebrow. "How do we know you're not trying to trick us?"

"Because I would have no reason to trick you," Barbara answered. "You're already ill-prepared to deal with any of this. As for how I know, I cannot say, but you can rest assured that he has no knowledge of my existence."

"He believes me dead, though he does know of Nicodemus's survival. That much, he tolerates, believing that he can control him."

"Can he?" Danny asked.

"We will find out," Barbara said with a shrug. "Now, I must go."

"Wait." Danny held up a hand. "What of the device that Isa is working on?"

"All I can say of it is that he's interested, and he's watching," Barbara answered. "At present, he wants her to do his work for him. He hadn't realized how old it had become, and wishes her to repair it before he steals it back."

With that, she turned and walked away once more, only for Master Barrydew to interject. "You haven't told us how to stop them."

She paused at the doorway. "Because I don't have those answers. I wish that I did. If I had them, I would lay it out for you."

"At present, all I can do is alert you to the fact of what's coming. If at all possible, make sure that you 'discover' the threat in some other way."

"Make sure that he doesn't know that he has eyes upon him. He grows weak with the amount of mana that he's using, and is missing more and more, but he is still tremendously evil."

"If he learns that someone is watching him, he may grow more cautious, and we lose our advantage."

With that, she turned and vanished, leaving Danny standing there in confusion. Master Barrydew sighed and slowly rose from his desk.

"Well," he murmured. "Do you think you can take on three bosses at once, while also helping shore up the walls against the other attacks?"

Danny took a deep breath and set his jaw.

"I guess we'll see."

Auto save - [Savefile: Information]
Health: 100%
Mana: 100%
Quest: Protect the Imperial City
Location: Library
Inventory: Essential Supplies, Basic Armor, Iron Sword, Sword of the Wasp, Aquamarine Sword, Frostbite Sword
Skills: Monster Summoner (Lv. 43), Flame Combat (Lv. 2), Wind Combat (Lv. 5)
Relationships: Friendly with Master Barrydew, Friendly (enough) with Barbara
Time of Day: 12:14 p.m.

Seventeen

Rally

The next week went by quickly. For several days, Danny did his best to keep himself contained, to keep the horrible news to himself.

He thought through option after option, and while he did produce a handful of them, none of them really seemed all that feasible. A lot of people were going to die, and that was just that.

As the days went on, news spread. It wasn't long before Danny began to hear whispers as he walked down the halls, or as he passed through the streets to his home. A general sense of fear was settling in, that was for sure.

Everyone knew that things were dire, and a great many people were likely to die. The simple question on everyone's mind was: "Will it be me? Will it be my family? And, if I survive this round... How much longer will I be able to keep going on?"

At the end of that week, as Danny returned to his home after a long day of teaching, he dropped wearily into the chair at the kitchen table and sighed. He turned and glanced at the empty cupboard, then at the cold hearth.

He was exhausted and hungry, but he knew it would take him a good hour just to prepare any sort of a meal. Making matters worse, at least in his mind, was the fact that pretty much any meal he could think of would be quite large. You couldn't really make a small batch of stew, for example.

Knock-knock-knock.

"Come in," Danny called without really thinking about it. He looked up as the door swung open and Tess stepped inside, flashing a smile at him.

"Hey, Danny." She walked over and opened her inventory, pulling out a few loaves of bread and some cheese. "It's not much, but you're welcome to it if you want."

Danny blinked a few times. "And you knew I was hungry because..."

"Because you're a bachelor whose father is in the hospital." Tess smiled and sat down across from him, gesturing at the table for some plates. Danny jumped up to grab a couple along with some knives and cups.

"You're teaching a class at the Academy, and you're being called on to defend the walls. I, at least, get meals through the army mess hall. You've got nothing, since the Academy mess hall got taken over by the Corp mess hall."

"Well, I can't argue with you there." Danny sighed as Tess started to cut the loaf of bread. "I sure appreciate it."

"Ahh, it's nothing. You're doing the work of ten other mages, even if you just spawn things in to do your work for you." She flashed an ornery sort of smile at him. "I kid, I kid."

Danny chuckled, put a bit of the cheese on a slice of bread, then leaned back in his chair. "So, how are things going with you? What with all the news afloat?"

Tess just shook her head. "Right now, I'm not involved in any of those discussions. I'm in charge of keeping the walls safe, and that's what I'm doing."

"I have a thousand soldiers under my command, and those soldiers defend the walls against the rogue monsters that we're fighting as a matter of course. I don't have the time or energy to think about anything more than that."

She paused, then poked a fork at him. "That said, I did hear an interesting rumor today. High command send out some scouts, and-"

Knock-knock-knock.

"Come in!" Danny called out once more. The door swung open, and a soldier dressed in the garb of the Imperial Palace poked his head inside. Danny frowned and stood as the man nodded to him.

"Your presence is being requested in the Imperial Palace."

"When?" Danny asked.

"I'd eat your meal on the way," the guard answered simply.

With that, Danny and Tess stopped eating and left, making their way along as quickly as possible. Neither of them ate anything on the walk, though that was because the masses along the way were starving and displaying any sort of open food was a recipe for disaster.

Food supplies were low and not moving quickly, which didn't exactly make for a population with full bellies. Danny and Tess made it to the Imperial Palace without incident, and soon stood in the throne room with Emperor Ezra.

The Emperor looked quite haggard with deep bags underneath his eyes and worry marks drawn across his young face. His robes were a bit more tattered than an Emperor's robes should have been, and the crown on his head (just a working crown, not the full Imperial Jewels) sat crooked.

He sighed and crossed his arms as everyone slowly approached, and he gestured down at the table, which displayed a map of the city.

"Thank you, all, for coming," Emperor Ezra began. An aide passed him a goblet filled with a steaming black liquid, which he gratefully drank. "Please, I'll do my best to keep this short, though of course I make no promises."

Danny nodded and glanced around the table. A number of Corp commanders were there along with several high-level mages. Master Barrydew was just walking up while Obadiah and Margot stood across the table from him.

Danny nodded to them, and they nodded back, but otherwise, no words were exchanged.

"I'm sure you've heard the rumors about the herd of monsters heading our way," Emperor Ezra continued. "We've sent out scouts to examine the herd, and have been able to put together a list of the monsters, or at least the largest ones."

"There are one thousand total, each of them ranked at Level 90 or above. None of them are going to be easy to take down, and any one of them would have the potential to deal serious damage to this city."

One of the commanders nodded and started to speak up, but Emperor Ezra held up a hand.

"Now, there's one more thing that you all should know." His voice became grave. "When we were examining the herd, one of our scouts noticed that all three of the dungeon bosses were missing."

"If just one had become separated, I would have thought it was unusual, but nothing implausible. The fact that all three were gone... In any case, what you need to know is that we sent scouts further, and have discovered a secondary herd, formed of remnants of the first one, which contains all three bosses."

"Is there any chance that it isn't headed toward the city?" Obadiah asked.

"No." Ezra pointed down at the map on the table where several markers sat on the eastern and southern side. "The main herd will strike in three days' time and will come from the east. The secondary herd, based on our best estimates, will hit about twelve hours after the first and will come from the south."

The table was quiet for quite some time. Emperor Ezra clearly had more to say, but wanted to allow everyone time to soak it in. When heads began to nod all around, the emperor continued.

"I don't think I need to tell you how dire the situation has become. I don't think I need to tell you just how deadly things will be when the assorted herds arrive."

"I don't think I need to tell you that a lot of good men are going to die." He sighed and crossed his arms. "What I do need to tell you is that, as your Emperor, I've never been prouder of you."

Danny felt a lump grow in his throat as Emperor Ezra continued.

"For years, I've sat on the Imperial Throne as a puppet, controlled by dark minions who sought nothing more than to perform their own will. When I was freed from those influences, I came out, more than expecting to be mocked by you."

"I expected my new level of command to be met with resistance, since, after all, I had never made myself available before. Instead, I found your welcoming arms, and I found an army, nay, an Empire, willing to lay down their lives to protect what this great nation stands for."

"I found a population willing to do anything to protect the little people, who opened up their city and their homes to accept refugees from across the nation, and who have given everything to build walls and provide food and keep them sheltered."

He paused for a moment. "With this attack, I don't know what will happen. I don't know if we'll be able to survive it, or what will come after the fact, but I do know that you all will give every last ounce of breath in your body, every last drop of blood in your veins, to fight against the evil that rages against us."

"For that, I thank you, from the bottom of my heart." He paused. "And, because of that, I'll be on the front lines with you when the monsters arrive."

There was a long pause as everyone digested the news. Finally, Obadiah nodded and stepped forward, raising a hand.

"I know there will be no chance of dissuading you, my Emperor. Know that if you come to the front lines, you'll rally every soldier that we have behind you." He flashed a genuine smile. "You'll be an inspiration to us all."

"I hope so." Emperor Ezra smiled back. "Now, we need to discuss plans for battle. My own tacticians have put together some plans, but I'd like you, the frontline commanders, to look over them."

"I know it's late at night, but I just got these plans back, and I believe we need to start putting things in motion tomorrow if we're to be ready."

With that, sheets of paper were passed out to each person. At that point, Obadiah more or less took the lead as he stepped slightly forward.

"This looks more or less good to me," he said. "You're wanting to put outposts out here, along the ravines. Tess, how many men do you think you could put on an emplacement like this?"

Tess frowned. "That would fit about a hundred, I'd say."

"Good. And Danny, realistically, how many monsters do you think you could take down?" Obadiah paused. "Also, how quickly do you think you could get from this side of the city to the southern side? I think we both know that you're going to be needed in both places."

The discussion picked up in earnest. Emperor Ezra joined right in, writing down troop numbers across the map, and drawing arrows to indicate troop movements.

"We'll need to hit them as hard as possible when they reach this point," Obadiah stated, running his hand along the base of a cliff. "Then retreat to the city before they can counter-attack."

"What about traps?" Tess asked. "Do we have time to prepare any traps?"

"I can't imagine that we do." Another commander spoke up. "The only type of trap that would do any good would be a pit-spike trap, and to get one that would be large enough to use against these things..."

"Danny might be able to have some of his monsters dig a pit," Tess offered. "Danny, you've seen these S-ranked herds. You think you could build something like that?"

Danny thought for a moment then nodded. "It's possible. I suppose it depends on whether or not you can find shovels large enough for my golems."

When the Emperor opened his mouth to respond, Danny grinned. A second later, the Emperor grinned as well.

"A joke! Ahh, we need that all too much right now." The emperor sighed. "Come, keep working."

The planning lasted until the early hours of the morning. As they wrapped up, the Emperor rolled up the map, which now had a great many notations, and put it in his inventory.

"I'll have this report copied and sent out to all the commanders."

"Ahh, Emperor?" Danny held up a hand. "Might it be prudent not to let the battle plans become wildly known?"

Obadiah looked over at him sharply, and several other commanders frowned in confusion. Emperor Ezra gave him a small nod, then sighed.

"I know your concern, Master Youngblood. Simply put, if a certain spy wants to know our moves, he'll be able to do so no matter how widely or narrowly these plans are disseminated. I'd rather have all our soldiers know the plan."

Danny gave a small nod, and with that, everyone more or less began to break away from the table to walk away. As Danny started walking toward the doors, Margot slipped up next to him.

"Hey. I haven't seen you in a while, not really since our last tour together." She frowned. "You okay? You look exhausted."

"Just a lot on my plate at the moment," Danny replied, trying to sound reassuring.

"Yeah, you sorta look like you got trampled by a water buffalo."

"Margot." Obadiah walked up and placed his hand on her shoulder. "It's not polite to say things like that."

"Even when it's true?" Margot scowled.

"Especially when it's true." Obadiah nodded then glanced at Danny. "But seriously, have you been sleeping at all? Or eating?"

"When I get the time." Danny sighed and shrugged. "It sounds like I need to start digging pit traps tomorrow morning... No. This morning, so... I don't know that I'm getting anything right now, either."

Obadiah held out a hand.

"Come to my house tonight. We have a guest bedroom, and we're closer to the wall than your home. You can sleep later, and I'll have a fresh meal prepared for you in the morning."

Danny was so exhausted that he didn't think he could have argued if his life had depended upon it. "You got it."

A few minutes later, he was out in the city, following Obadiah and Margot as they made their way toward the distant home. He felt like he was going to drop, but he knew he couldn't show any weakness over the coming days. They were in the battle for their lives...

And, like it or not, he was a key figure in that battle.

Auto save - [Savefile: Information]
Health: 100%
Mana: 100%
[Quest Update] Get a few hours of rest!
Location: Imperial Palace, Entry Hall
Inventory: Essential Supplies, Basic Armor, Iron Sword, Sword of the Wasp, Aquamarine Sword, Frostbite Sword
Skills: Monster Summoner (Lv. 43), Flame Combat (Lv. 2), Wind Combat (Lv. 5)
Relationships: Friendly with Tess, Friendly with Margot, Speaking Terms with Emperor Ezra the Fifth
Time of Day: 2:14 a.m.

Eighteen

Touch of Healing

"And so, we move into our study of incorporeal monsters," Danny began. He yawned greatly, then shook his head and took a sip of the coffee on his desk.

It wasn't helping him as much as he might have liked, but it was what he had, and he was desperate. "These sorts of monsters are usually magical, though there are a few that fall into other categories."

"Strictly speaking, there's no official category covering incorporeal, and they show up in almost every single other major category of creature, but as they all incorporate unique attacks and can only be fought using certain skills and tactics, I thought it prudent to-"

He paused as he yawned again. The class stared up at him, many of them frowning in confusion. He took another drink of the coffee, then shook his head and slapped his cheeks a few times.

"Sorry, everyone. I've been a bit busy with things lately. I know I'm not on top of my game."

"None of the professors are," a boy near the back complained. "We're not really learning anything. We're either going to fail our exams to move on to the next year, or we're going to have to redo it, all because of you."

"In all due fairness-" Danny began, but Trish snapped around and glared at the naysayer.

"Hey! If you were trying to teach a class while also fighting off hordes of monsters while also trying to keep the last vestiges of civilization from utterly collapsing, you'd be tired, too."

Danny smiled and held out his hand to her. "Thank you."

"Teacher's pet," another student muttered.

"No, this is my pet." Danny snapped his fingers, making a large fox appear next to him. It flicked its tail back and forth then vanished again. "I don't have pets otherwise. Now, where were we?"

Thump-thump-thump.

Something rumbled down the hallway, and a moment later, a figure appeared in the doorway. The person knocked on the doorframe then poked his head inside. He was dressed in little more than rags and had a suitcase that rattled and bumped along the ground and walls.

"Is this where I'm supposed to be going?" he asked in a raspy voice. "They said that we're to-"

Danny shook his head. "No, it's not where you're supposed to be. Go back down the hall the way you came."

"There's a stairwell, it will be on your left. Head down the stairs, and when you get all the way to the bottom, there will be guards who can escort you."

"Ahh! Thanks." The man nodded with a small smile. "I sure appreciate it."

With that, he turned and walked away, and Danny turned back to the class.

"Alright, then. So, incorporeal monsters. There are a few of them that you'll see more often than others."

"The most common are elementals. Now, Elementals will occur most often in low-level dungeons, and can usually be attacked using the inverse of whatever element they happen to take their form from."

He snapped his fingers, and summoned a fire elemental in the air just next to him. It crackled and danced through the air, and he smiled softly. "This was actually one of the first monsters I ever-"

Knock-knock-knock.

Danny turned to see a woman with several small children stepping into the classroom. She looked as exhausted as he felt as her weary eyes settled upon him.

"Is this where I'm-" She paused as she suddenly took in the elemental.

It took a few long moments for her to process what she was seeing, and with that, she let out a powerful scream. It took her almost no time whatsoever to get her children out of there, and they ran off down the hall as fast as they could go.

Danny chuckled softly and shook his head, then wearily walked over and sat down at his desk. "I think we'd be better served if we just put this lesson down and picked it up again in a week."

"After the monster attack." The same naysayer from earlier stood up. "If we're still here, that is, and we're not just a smoking crater."

"Hey!" Trish stood up and spun around to glare at him. "Don't talk to him like that!"

"No, it's okay." Danny shook his head and straightened up. "I remember how I was when I was a first-year. Got myself in a whole lot of trouble, and if I were in your shoes, I'd probably be trying to figure out how to go off to the frontlines myself."

He slowly folded his hands and leaned forward onto the desk. "Look at it this way, if none other. Right now, I can hardly think straight because I'm so tired."

"If we do survive and make it through to the other side, you'll get a better lecture, and you'll be better prepared for the future. On the other hand, if we all die... Well, you won't need a new lecture."

"What if this one might help us?" the boy snapped.

"You know what? If you encounter an elemental or a sprite or a ghost or something in the next week, come to me and yell at me for it, and I'll owe you a good dinner or something." Danny shook his head. "Deal?"

The students all nodded, and soon, they had slipped out into the hall. Danny sighed and leaned back in his chair, feeling every ounce of weight that now rested upon his shoulders.

Knock-knock-knock.

"Turn around, stairway's on your left," Danny answered without opening his eyes. "Head down to the lowest level, you'll find your place there."

A low chuckle echoed through the room, and Danny sat bolt upright. Master Barrydew stood there, arms crossed, a small smile upon his face.

"You look like you've already faced the horde that's coming for us." Master Barrydew walked over and sat down on the corner of the desk. "Want to talk about it?"

"Nah." Danny shook his head and leaned back into his chair once more. Sleep tugged at his eyelids, and he sighed. "That big meeting with the Emperor? I went over to the Flamekeeper's house afterward, got four hours of rest, and then went out to start digging traps."

"I stayed there all day, then came back into town, slept for another four hours, and then got taken back out to the traps. That was this morning."

"I spawned in a few golems and did my best to bond them to the workers so they'd keep going throughout the day. My interface still shows them out there, working, so I'm going to assume that everything's good." He sighed. "I'm just beat."

"As are we all." Master Barrydew folded his hands. "Is there anything that I can do for you to assist? I know you're bearing an immense burden right now."

"No, I'm alright." Danny shook his head. "My plan at the moment is to head over to the hospital to see my dad, and then head home to get some rest before I have to start getting ready for the battle itself."

"Tess was saying that the herd is moving faster than they anticipated, it'll be here tomorrow morning."

"That's what I've heard, myself," Master Barrydew said. "Well, you have my blessing. The only alteration that I might make is asking you to please go to my office, and sleep there."

"Someone will come to get you for something if you go back to your own home. If you look at the bookshelf with the encyclopedias, just pull on the book for the letter Z. There's a secret bedroom there, I use it sometimes during finals."

A grin split Danny's face. "You're joking."

"Nah. Trust me, it'll be great," Master Barrydew said. "And you need some sleep if you're going to be able to fight tomorrow."

Danny nodded wearily then quickly strode off through the halls of the Academy. It didn't take him long to arrive at the hospital ward where he found several nurses bustling about, taking care of some soldiers that had just arrived.

They looked pretty banged-up as Danny stepped to the side while they were taken into the emergency rooms.

"Master Youngblood." One of the nurses recognized him. "You're here to see your father, I assume?"

Danny gave a nod. "Is he okay?"

"I think he might be sleeping, but in any case, he's over there." The nurse pointed off down one of the side hallways. "He was moved out of intensive care."

"Frankly, he still needs to be in it, but we have other people who are injured worse."

"Thanks." Danny flashed a smile at her then slipped down in the direction she had indicated. "I hope everything goes well for... Everyone."

The nurse nodded at the awkward wish then disappeared. A few minutes later, Danny walked down a smaller hallway, glancing into each of the rooms. It didn't take him long to find his father who was sprawled out across one of the beds, his arms and legs secured to keep him from moving too much.

His eyes were indeed closed as Danny entered, and he sighed deeply.

"I won't wake you, dad," he murmured softly, taking a seat next to the bed. "I just want to be with you for a bit."

As he leaned back in the chair, the waves of exhaustion crept up on him, and before he knew it, the darkness had taken him.

When his eyes flickered back open again, he had a crick in his neck that hurt more than some battle injuries he had taken over the years. He groaned and sat upright, hearing Zechariah cough faintly next to him.

"You keep that up, and you'll be in here with me."

"Dad?" Danny spun slightly, his pain forgotten. "How long have you been... How long have I..."

"I don't know what time you got here, but they just brought my dinner by," Zechariah answered weakly. He flashed a thin smile, and shifted slightly in the bed. "The next time they come through, I'll ask them to bring you something."

"No need. I have a bit here." Danny pulled some of the leftover bread and cheese out of his inventory. The bread was a bit stale, and the cheese had the faintest odd odor, but that wasn't too bad a condition in the present climate.

"How are you?"

"Hanging in there. Death keeps knocking at the door, but I keep refusing to open." Zechariah joked. He coughed again, then sighed.

"I took a total of ten arrows. Eight of them punctured the skin, but didn't fully enter my body. They were able to remove all of those."

"The other two were lodged deeper. Are lodged deeper. One of them is slipping down right next to my lungs, hurts like you wouldn't believe just to breathe, and they say if I move much, it'll probably punch straight through into my lung and kill me."

He groaned softly, then shrugged a bit. "And the other one is right next to my tailbone, so laying around here on my back is just about to kill me, but it's not harming me at all."

Danny laughed and held up his hand. "TMI, dad."

Zechariah laughed once more then slowly lifted a hand. He could only raise it a few inches, but Danny caught the gesture and grasped his father's hand.

"If something should happen to me-"

"Nothing is going to happen to you." Danny shook his head.

"If something happens to me," Zechariah pressed, "I want you to know that you've been an incredible son to me. You have no idea how much I wish your mother could be here right now."

"She'd be so proud of you, of our little monster summoner. She'd... She'd love you more than I ever could." He paused. "I hope I've been a good father to you."

"The best," Danny confirmed.

"You know..." Zechariah pressed forward. "It's times like this where you start thinking back on your life. You start analyzing everything."

"Every little slip-up comes to mind. When I yelled at you for something that wasn't your fault, but I was overstressed because of work."

"When I spent too much time working when I should have been with you. When I-"

"Dad." Danny gave his father's hand a squeeze. "I couldn't have asked for a better father. I mean, you have Nicodemus's respect, and I get the feeling that he gives that away about as often as snow falls in the wasteland."

Zechariah flashed a thin smile. "True." He sighed. "I just... I don't know, Danny. I always imagined that my end would be on the battlefield, not laying here on a bed."

"Well, if you do die here, it'll be because you fell on the battlefield," Danny pointed out. He frowned after a moment. "Will they be removing the arrowheads?"

"That's the plan." Zechariah coughed slightly. "Just as soon as bodies slow down just enough for the surgeon to have a free moment. We've had it on the schedule twice now, but every time we're about to go in, someone shows up who's bleeding out, or dying from a venomous bite, or... Something like that."

Danny frowned. "I might be able to help."

"You?" Zechariah laughed. "And when did you take surgeon classes at the Academy? One slip, Danny, and I'm a dead man."

"I just mean..." Danny paused. "My summoning allows me to feel out your body. I might be able to locate the wound and help the surgeon. Just a second."

A few minutes later, Danny stood in the room with said surgeon, who looked irritated at being drug away from whatever he had been preparing to do. He sighed and shook his head as Danny held out his hands over his father.

"Look, you've got thirty seconds to show me what you're talking about," the surgeon snapped. "I've got a man in there who probably has an hour left to live unless I can pull a fang out of his stomach."

"It'll only take a second." Danny stretched out with his senses and connected with his father.

In that moment, he found that he could sense every nerve, every tendon, every muscle, every blood vessel. He could see clearly the arrowhead that was lodged within a millimeter of his father's lung, and noticed that it was still slipping downward (albeit slowly).

The moment he had it, he turned and connected to the surgeon. The surgeon's eyes snapped open, and his jaw dropped.

"I've had healing mages work for me who haven't been able to do this." He bit his lip. "Bring me my tools. This will take two minutes."

Zechariah's eyes went wide. "Really?"

"The only condition is that you stick around and help me clear out the emergency room." The surgeon glanced over at Danny. "Deal?"

For Danny, it wasn't even a question. Sure, he was still tired, and he wanted to sleep and he needed to prepare for battle, but if he wasn't willing to protect everyone, to fight for everyone, what sort of a mage was he?

"Deal," Danny said, ready for anything.

Auto save - [Savefile: Information]
Health: 100%
Mana: 99%
[Quest Update] Assist with Surgeries (1/7)
Location: Infirmary, Research Wing
Inventory: Essential Supplies, Basic Armor, Iron Sword, Sword of the Wasp, Aquamarine Sword, Frostbite Sword
Skills: Monster Summoner (Lv. 43), Flame Combat (Lv. 2), Wind Combat (Lv. 5)
Relationships: Friendly with Master Barrydew, Family Bond with Zechariah, Ascended Fire Mage
Time of Day: 7:45 p.m.

Nineteen

Finest Hour

"Danny!" As a gauntleted hand pounded on the door of the Youngblood home, Danny sat bolt upright on his couch. "Danny! Open now!"

Danny practically flew to the door and threw it open. Tess stood there, concern etched across her face.

Margot stood just behind her, worry and anxiety written all over hers. All around, civilians were slowly starting to surge toward the Academy, to hopefully secure a place in the depths of the catacombs.

The doors had opened days earlier, but few people had bothered to attempt to take advantage of the situation. Now... Well, now that doom was imminent, they looked more than ready to flee in that direction.

"What's going on?" Danny asked, worried.

"It's the herd," Tess answered quickly. "It's here."

"Here?" Danny frowned and looked up at the sky. The stars were just starting to fade, it was only 4:00 in the morning.

"Last night, the scouts said that they weren't expecting the herd to arrive until at least 6:00 in the morning." Suddenly, he paused, and Tess gave a knowing nod.

"That was an oversight on our part. We should have been expecting something like this, but... We were all exhausted and not thinking clearly."

Tess turned and waved down the street. "Now come on! Things are getting started, we need to be there."

Danny nodded and raced after her. Margot took up the rear, flames flickering from her palms as she prepared for the battle ahead.

All around them, soldiers pushed through the crowds toward the walls, and civilians pushed against the soldiers as they fled to safety... Or at least to what they perceived to be safe.

Rrrrrrrrrrrrrrrrrrrrrrargh!

As the roar echoed over the city, loud and long, Danny's heart clenched. In the distance, he thought he heard screams and muffled booms.

It took far too long for them to arrive at the outer wall of the city, when they did, Danny's heart sank.

The monsters were swarming up out of the darkness, marching through the ravines and the valleys. There were trolls, giants, undead, liches, wargs and wolves and orcish lords and a great many more horrid things.

Scorpions the size of buildings, spiders large and lithe, a thousand evil creatures all of which were headed straight for the City.

Danny balled his hands into fists as soldiers rushed out through the walls and formed up in ranks. A few mages, out on the plains, launched fireballs and lighting and other attacks up at the monsters.

They were in retreat at that moment, but Danny could see several bodies of the monsters scattered across the fields, a testament to their skill.

"Who's that?" Danny asked as he took his place near the front of the assembly.

"Master Flamekeeper," a soldier answered. "And, with him... I'm not sure. An earth mage, I think."

Danny frowned and leaned forward, but before he could determine the identity of the mage, a scorpion lunged forward and speared the mage through the chest. The man went limp, and with a sharp flick of the tail, the scorpion threw the man high into the air.

All hope for his survival vanished when a massive drake snapped him up, swallowing him whole in the blink of an eye.

"Alright." Danny took a step forward, but Tess put a hand on his shoulder.

"No." She shook her head. "Wait for your moment. You know the plans."

"That doesn't mean I have to like them." Danny gritted his teeth. "I can start taking them out now."

"And if you do, you'll probably make the back half of the herd scatter," Tess said. "We stick to the plan."

"If we don't, I don't know how many people will die. You're powerful, Danny, but you can't control everything."

Danny set his jaw, knowing she was right but hating it all the same. He watched, gritting his teeth, as several more mages joined Obadiah.

A wide assortment of attacks lanced upward, hitting the monsters and sometimes knocking them down.

And then, with one final roar, the drake lunged just a bit too close, crossing over a boulder that had been painted red to serve as a marker. Tess patted Danny on the shoulder, and he rushed forward.

"Time to find out what we're made of!" He raised his hands and smiled. "Two stone golems, summon with all available mana."

Two brilliant flashes of light flared across the ground, and the huge stone golems rushed into battle. Obadiah glanced over his shoulder and dove out of the way, and the drake opened its mouth wide and lunged forward.

One of the golems, in that moment, smashed a foot into the top of the drake's head, flattening it to the ground.

The massive creature thrashed around, pulled its head back, and spun, trying to use its tail as a whip. The golem caught the tail in its palm, braced itself, and pulled.

It lifted the drake clean off the ground and spun in a circle, now using the drake like a whip, and threw it straight into two trolls. All three monsters went down in a heap, and the golem lunged forward and threw a powerful punch that crushed the head of one of the trolls.

The second golem threw itself into battle, snatching up limestone boulders and throwing them into the heads of the creatures. Most of the time, the limestone just exploded into gravel, but in the process, they dealt quite a damaging blow to the larger creatures.

Obadiah formed a flaming bow in his hand and threw himself into the battle, stinging the monsters with flaming arrows stronger than most mages could ever hope to create. More and more of the monsters fell, building a pile of corpses that sprawled up and over the landscape.

And then, with a powerful roar, the smaller monsters came blasting through.

There were dozens of them; powerful undead, beasts like lions and tigers, and elementals that shot straight through the bodies of the fallen monsters. Danny's stone golems stomped on several as they came past as Tess shook her head.

"Focus on the larger ones! If one of those gets through, it'll tear this whole unit to bits."

Danny nodded and turned the attention of the golems back to the larger creatures in the herd. The battle raged.

With a loud crash, the smaller monsters struck the waiting army.

Swords flew fast, shields were raised, and blood and fur filled the air. A thousand swords lashed out at the monsters, a thousand claws cut right back.

Danny watched in horror as a rhino charged the crowd, lowering its head and tearing straight through the ranks. Soldiers were sent flying, until Tess flashed forward, leapt up, and drove the blade into the monster right behind its ear.

It fell headlong, knocking over more people, and she drew out her sword and charged right back into battle.

Cheers, screams, and roared filled the air. Danny watched as monsters flashed this way and that.

He felt mostly helpless as his stone golems punched their way through the larger monsters, that was for sure. Suddenly, he heard a low growl, and spun to find a goblin lord slowly approaching him.

"So, you're the one the dungeon cores fear." The goblin chuckled, drawing a sword.

Another soldier rushed up, and the goblin spun, casually batted the man's sword aside, and drove his own sword straight through the breastplate of the soldier.

The soldier groaned and collapsed, and the goblin started forward once more. "You're the one they're all talking about."

Danny opened his inventory and drew out his Frostbite Sword. It felt heavy in his hands as he set his jaw.

He had taken plenty of classes on swordplay during his time in the academy, but he was certainly far from exceptional at it. The goblin just chuckled as it raced forward at him.

The goblin struck high, then low, then across the middle. Danny blocked several of the attacks then leapt backward to avoid another strike.

The goblin laughed and twirled his sword.

"See? You're nothing without your little friends." He snorted and nodded toward the stone golems. "When I claim you as a my own, when I can notch you as my kill, I'll be famous."

"Do you know what I think?" Danny raised an eyebrow. "I think you're just a projection of a dungeon core, doomed to respawn the moment I kill you."

"And how exactly do you plan on killing me?" The goblin snorted.

Danny snapped his fingers. He'd only managed to regenerate a few mana points over the previous several minutes, but it was enough.

A flash of light flickered within the goblin's mouth, and he snarled and tried to spit out the monster that Danny had just summoned. A moment later, he screamed in pain... And then froze.

Blood trickled out his mouth, and he toppled over, dead before he hit the ground.

"What..." Tess came running up, but paused as Danny snapped his fingers and re-absorbed the rockworm that he had spawned inside the goblin's body. "You..."

"I can take care of myself." Danny shrugged and turned back to the golems. "I just need to-"

With a single, mighty blow, one of the golems threw a massive punch that smashed the face of a huge troll. The troll, now missing a face, fell over backward and crushed a dozen smaller monsters hiding behind it.

[Notification: Monster Summoning has increased to Lv. 44!][Reward: Mana Increase: 1720 -> 1810]

His mana automatically refilled, and Danny beamed. He quickly raised his hands and added two more stone golems to the mix, and the four of them plowed forward, punching and clawing their way through the swarm of creatures.

Tess gave him a nod then turned and rushed off, cutting the heads off two more goblins who were rapidly approaching.

Ahead, the smaller monsters began to wane slightly, and the Imperial Corp, along with the mages, began to charge forward, pushing the monsters back. Tess tried to call out above the crowd, but few people heard her.

"No!" she shouted. "The plan is to wait! We have to hold back!"

Out on the front, Obadiah, who had indeed pressed forward along with the golems and who was doing everything he could to help, looked up suddenly as the soldiers and other mages came running past him. A few skeletons came racing up, which were quickly cut down, and then...

And then, a low rumble began to shake the ground.

"Danny?" Tess asked, racing up to him. "What's going on?"

"I don't know," Danny muttered. "I-"

FOOM!

Massive rockworms burst out of the ground, behind the lines of the soldiers, hissing and screaming. Tess spun and chopped one clean in two, and it fell dead, but most of them spun and dove back into the ground.

As Danny rushed forward and prepared his sword to assist, he heard something chittering from down within the holes. He paused and slowly looked down... And found two beady eyes looking back up at him.

"Skreeeeeeee-ya!"

Goblins burst up from the holes and began to fly toward the city, racing over the uneven ground. Archers on top of the wall let fly, showering the oncoming goblins, and succeeded in taking out quite a few of them.

That said, more were coming, and Danny saw flashes of gold in their hands.

As they reached the walls, the goblins threw grappling hooks that sailed up and caught hold of the top of the stone. They began to clamber up just as fast as they could go, snarling and snapping loudly.

On the top, the soldiers tried to cut the ropes, but found them to be made of metal, unable to be cut so easily. They resorted to shooting down at them again, but there were just too many.

Out on the field of battle, the soldiers turned to rush back to shore up their lines, but it was just too late.

Tess was a whirlwind of energy, spinning this way and that, striking the creatures down with every second. Danny waded in as well, snapping his fingers and spawning rockworms inside of every single one he could focus on.

They stumbled and collapsed, but once again, not nearly enough were dying. Suddenly, Danny turned, looked at the stone golems, and stretched out a hand.

"Recall!" he shouted.

With a flash, one of the golems vanished and Danny's mana refilled to about halfway. At the same time, he spun and summoned a flock of cave crows which immediately swooped down into the city.

As the goblins raced through the tents, snarling and slashing at whatever they came across, the cave crows dropped from the sky, snatching up the grubby little monsters with their claws and carrying them high into the air.

The cave crows didn't have enough strength to slay the goblins... But gravity, which was provided to the birds for a rather reasonable cost of zero mana, was more than strong enough. Goblins rained down upon the battlefield (back outside the walls), splattering into goop as they struck rocks or fallen soldiers.

One of them landed upon a standard that had become lodged in the ground, which was both gruesome and effective.

"Master Youngblood!"

Hooves pounded across the battlefield, and Danny spun as a horse came riding up. The rider looked to have taken several injuries, but was still upright.

He swung down from his saddle and motioned for Danny to climb up.

"The second wave! It's here!"

"Already?" Danny's jaw dropped. "You're sure?"

"Very!" The man nodded rapidly. "Please, hurry! You don't have much-"

A goblish arrow flashed through the air and slammed into the man's shoulder. He went down hard but waved at Danny.

"Go now! The world is depending on you!"

Danny gritted his teeth, then nodded, turned around, and swung up into the saddle. A moment later, he flashed away across the field, racing across the length of bodies and the growing carnage.

He saw Tess salute him as he raced away, and he let out a long breath.

This first battle had just been the warm-up. Now, it was truly time to see what he was made of.

Auto save - [Savefile: Information]
Health: 81%
Mana: 1%
[Quest Update] Stop the Second Wave
Location: Imperial City Agricultural Area, Southern Side
Inventory: Essential Supplies, Basic Armor, Iron Sword, Sword of the Wasp, Aquamarine Sword, Frostbite Sword
Skills: Monster Summoner (Lv. 44), Flame Combat (Lv. 2), Wind Combat (Lv. 5)
Relationships: Friendly with Tess, Friendly with Margot
Time of Day: 7:46 a.m.

Twenty

Price Divided

The sounds of battle faded behind him as he swept around the southern side of the city and ran out over the rolling hills. He flew past the second wall that his bees had helped put back together, and saw civilians sitting on the top, watching and waiting.

And there... There, he saw them.

The first was another Dragonscale Troll, huge and foreboding, thumping across the wilderness with extraordinary force. Next to it walked a drake that was practically a dragon in its own right.

It snarled and snapped, advancing along toward the city. The final creature looked to be a phantom, floating along the next two.

It was humanoid and huge, a good twenty or thirty feet tall, and carried a great scythe. Danny came to a stop in front of the southern gate, and slowly looked out at the creatures.

They were approaching, slowly and surely, and he gritted his teeth together.

"What's it going to be?" Danny murmured. "How do I stop them?"

He checked his mana. It was now up to 2%, and he sighed.

He couldn't unsummon any of the creatures who were helping with the other side of the battle. Doing so would be tantamount to allowing that side of the army to die.

He opened his inventory and scrolled though his mana stones, and he slowly set his jaw.

Even summoning in his dragon hatchling wasn't going to be enough. It had been able to take down a Dragonscale troll, but even then, it had taken quite a while, and had nearly killed it.

Danny needed to stop the creatures, and to stop them quickly. To do that, he really only had one option, and he knew it.

"Alright." He slowly pulled out his enormous mana stone.

It dropped into his lap, making the horse twist about from the extra weight. Quickly, Danny climbed down and slapped it on the rump, making it run back into the city.

A few soldiers came out from the city to watch him, but he waved them back inside. After a moment, they even closed the gates, leaving him alone.

He took a deep breath then looked out at the creatures. Once more, he sought for any other option, but knew that there simply wasn't one.

It wasn't that he didn't want to use the larger mana stone, but... Once he used it, that was that. He had received it as a token of victory, but once he used it, there was no guarantee that he would be able to get another one back.

"I've just got to use it," he murmured. "If I don't use it now, I'll be dead, and won't have a chance to use it again."

Resolve flowed through him, and he raised it above his head. He glared out at the monsters and activated the stone.

"Green Dragon Scorcher!"

The stone vanished in a brilliant burst of light, leaving Danny standing there alone. He let out a long breath and lowered his arms again, and frowned.

Flap.

Flap.

Flap.

Behind him, he heard screams echoing from the city, and a smile spread across his face. Suddenly, the beast shot overhead, hitting him with a blast of air that blew the doors of the city wide open.

He stumbled and nearly fell, and the dragon swooped low.

It was just as large and grand as when it had attacked him. As it flashed along, it flew lower and lower until it let its claws drag against the road, sending up sparks and dust.

It was huge, and let out a roar that sent a shockwave rolling over the landscape, blasting stones to rubble and flattening trees and the few remaining homesteads. In the distance, the three monsters came to a stop, and the dragon opened its mouth wide.

Danny saw the blast of light long before he heard the noise. Flame washed out from the dragon's mouth, flooding over the ground.

Rivers of magma were left in its wake as it continued forward, and the three monsters simply vanished. It was so brilliant that it hurt to look at, and the dragon crashed full-on into the dragonscale troll.

RRRRRRRRRRRRRRRRRRRRRRRRRARGH!

The blast was so strong that it almost knocked Danny in the opposite direction as the wind had done. The true might of the dragon's roar could be felt in his chest, and the wall quaked.

Several cracks spread up and down its length, which would need to be repaired. The mighty dragon's fire crackled and roared with a fury unlike anything Danny had ever heard before, and he gasped.

The dragon slammed the Dragonscale Troll to the ground, lifted a claw, and slashed it across the troll's chest. Black blood exploded into the air, and it bit down onto the troll's face.

Hard. Black liquid sprayed high into the sky, and Danny suddenly found himself happy that he wasn't up close and personal.

A moment later, the dragon tossed the troll's head off to one side, where it rolled down into a ravine.

The drake snarled and reared up, and the dragon took a step back and blasted it with fire. When the flame died away, the drake looked a little worse for wear, but was still mostly unaffected.

It was probably immune to flame, at least mostly. The dragon took a step back and flexed its claws, and Danny winced.

Then it tore into the drake, tearing off massive chunks of skin and ripping the thing from end to end. More blood poured down across the landscape, and within seconds, the dragon had reduced the drake to little more than pulp upon the ground.

It then spun around, seeking the third target.

And, right about that moment, Danny felt the air grow cold around him.

He leapt backward just as a scythe carved through the place where he had been standing. The reaper flashed forward, staring at him as it let its misty robe spread outward.

Suddenly visible, it stood just higher than the wall of the city, and hissed down upon him with vengeance. It slashed at him again, and once more, Danny dove out of the way.

"You are foolish, Master Youngblood!" It laughed. "You hide behind your monsters, yet you cannot fight at all."

"A classic example of someone too powerful for their own good." It raised its scythe once more. "Where is the beast that you wish to protect you?"

In answer, a jet of dragon fire exploded through the monsters. It was blasted into nothing but mist, which evaporated under the heat of the flame.

A moment later, the dragon landed on the ground in front of Danny and snarled softly.

[Notification: Monster Summoning has increased to Lv. 45!]

[Reward: Mana Increase: 1810 -> 1910]

"I can live with that," Danny nodded in approval.

The dragon bent its neck down, and Danny rushed forward.

This was going to be fun.

Danny had long read stories of flying on a dragon's back, but even in his wildest dreams about what he would do as a summoner, he had never really thought about the possibility. Now, as he swooped through the sky, he found a smile splitting his face as he glanced down on the landscape below.

The herd was still waging war against the army, with countless more monsters lined up throughout the ravines. He could see people on the ground pointing up at him, and he patted the dragon's neck.

"Don't get so close that you kill any of the soldiers."

The dragon nodded, then folded its wings and dove. Danny held on for dear life, shrieking in delight as they flashed down toward the ground below.

The dragon unfolded its wings only feet above the ground and flashed off across the battle, cutting loose with a great gout of flame the moment that they had passed beyond the edge of the battlefield. Massive, S-ranked monsters simple evaporated under the deluge, and within seconds, the battlefield was mostly cleared.

With that, Danny flew back to the main battlefield and landed, then hopped down as the fight against the last remaining creatures lived on. He patted the dragon's neck, but it snarled and snapped at him.

"Alright, alright." He laughed and waved his hand. "Off you go."

With that, the dragon vanished into nothing but light, and Danny charged forward. His mana had been refilled once more, and with a flash, a horde of goblins, perfect for clearing up the smaller monsters, appeared around him.

They raced headlong into the fray, and Danny beamed.

Now this was how to fight.

All told, the rest of the battle took another thirty minutes, though the last twenty were spent systematically hunting down and slaying the last of the stragglers. When it finally came to an end, Danny found himself standing on the desolate battlefield, utterly spent.

Tess slowly walked up to him, threading her way between the bodies and the filth.

"Danny." She nodded to him gratefully. "How are you holding up?"

"Alright, I suppose," he said as a few notifications flickered across his vision and a small smile came across his face. Before he could check any of them, though, he noticed the downcast look on Tess's face, and he frowned.

"What?"

"Just... This." She sighed and slowly turned to gesture about the battlefield. There were dead bodies everywhere, monster and human alike.

"I just spoke to Commander Johnson. We'll need a few days to count, but it looks to me like we're looking at almost twenty-five percent of our forces dead."

"That's not as bad as it could be," Danny said.

"No, but it's not as good as it could be, either." Tess sighed and knelt down, picking up a helmet that lay on the ground.

"Did you know that every helmet in the Corp is personalized? It has the person's name, and house crest if they have one, stamped into the metal inside the rear band."

"That way, if the person themself can't be identified, we still know who was killed."

"Hmm." Danny shook his head. "I'm so sorry."

"Don't just be sorry for me. This is our loss, too."

"The differences between the Corp and the mages are null and void anymore. You should know that as well as I do."

Danny crossed his arms. "What's gotten into you? You sound like you're angry at me."

"No, no. No." Tess sighed. "You did a good job. You probably killed as many monsters as everyone else put together, and when you consider the fact that you took out the bosses, I'm sure it's not even remotely comparable."

"I just hate seeing this much death. I also..." She paused. "There's talk that I've already heard among the ranks, as people are filing back into the city."

"They're wondering why you didn't pull your dragon out earlier."

Danny shook his head. "I kept it in reserve because-"

"Danny, you don't have to justify yourself to me." Tess held up a hand. "If I'm being completely honest, I wish you had saved it for the next wave against the city."

"This was the little wave, the next ones are only going to get bigger, and now, the Deepcorp Lord knows that you have a dragon summons. That isn't going to go over well."

She sighed. "I'm just saying what I'm hearing. A lot of people are saying that you should have pulled it out at the beginning of the fight, not the end."

"They're saying that you only held it back so it would look more epic when you finally came swooping in. They're saying that it looked like you were having fun, when they were sweating and dying for their city."

She paused. "There's actually a whole lot more that they're saying, and I don't plan to sit here and blast you with it right this second. I'm just saying that when you get back into the city, you're probably going to face a proverbial firing squad."

Danny took a deep breath, trying to remain calm. "Because I saved the city," he said evenly.

"Because these men just lost their friends, their brothers, their fathers," Tess snapped. "They're angry and they feel hopeless, so they're looking for something to lash out at."

"You're going to be an easy target." She paused, and drew in a deep breath. "I'm just trying to warn you."

"Sorry, I'm a little wound-up, too. This was brutal, and I can't even begin to imagine what this is going to look like as it gets more and more intense."

She paused, and a tear trickled down her cheek. "Danny, I honestly don't know how we're going to survive this."

Danny sighed then slowly looked down at the ground. It was a victory, but as Tess's words sank in, it almost felt like an empty one.

It felt as though they had won only to delay the inevitable. They were all expecting to lose at some point.

The only question was when it would happen.

"No." He slowly balled his hands into fists. "We won here, today. The blood of those who died helped ensure that we would keep living."

"I'm not going to sully their memory by pretending that everything is doom and gloom."

Tess flashed a small smile and slowly turned away. "I hope the rest of the city can come to see it like you."

Danny watched her go then slowly looked across the battlefield. Crews were coming out of the city to pick up the bodies to be taken back for burial.

A stack of helmets was growing by the city gate, and Danny sighed. It had been a victory, but a costly one.

Perhaps he should have tried to find some other way to slay the monsters. Perhaps there simply had been no other way, in which case, perhaps he should have led with the dragon.

He didn't know, and it wasn't worth asking questions about it then. All they could do was pick up the pieces and brace for the next impact.

Hopefully, they would have a better plan in place by the time that happened, or else... Or else, it was highly likely that the Imperial City would soon be nothing more than rubble.

Auto save - [Savefile: Information]
Health: 74%
Mana: 12%

[Quest Update] Return to the City

Location: Imperial City Agricultural Area, Eastern Side

Inventory: Essential Supplies, Basic Armor, Iron Sword, Sword of the Wasp, Aquamarine Sword, Frostbite Sword

Skills: Monster Summoner (Lv. 45), Flame Combat (Lv. 2), Wind Combat (Lv. 5)

Relationships: Friendly with Tess

Time of Day: 9:27 a.m.

Twenty-One

Unknown Device

The next several days were solemn ones, indeed. As everyone returned to the city, the dead were counted, and repairs made.

Danny helped out where he could, supplying his giant bees to patch up the walls, or using his goblins or golems to serve as extra manpower. Through it all, he wound up getting more than a few ugly looks, but could do nothing but push forward and keep working through it all.

The days turned into weeks, and soon, cold air began to blow across the landscape. Winter was coming soon, and with it, the city began to tremble with a sense of dread.

"What's going to happen to us?" Danny asked one day as he stood in the great library, looking out across the city.

Rain splattered down across the rooftops, running like rivers through the streets. He could see people packing into their tents and into what buildings would allow them, but it was far too overcrowded.

Outside the city, the world seemed to keep growing darker, and that was just the reality of it.

"I don't know," Master Barrydew answered softly. The old master folded his hands behind his back, and shook his head.

"When winter comes fully, all sources of food will dry up. The Empire has long had storage units full of food that will be opened at that time, but will it get us through to spring?"

"I don't have the faintest idea."

Danny nodded slowly. "And when is the next horde due to arrive?"

"Two months. Smack in the middle of the coldest part of the year," Master Barrydew answered grimly.

"I'm not going to lie to you, Danny, it doesn't look good, but I have faith at that least some of us will make it through."

"Yeah, that's the sort of thing that everyone on a sinking ship wants to hear," Danny said. "I'm confident that at least some of the countless passengers on board will manage to survive."

"Well..." Master Barrydew flashed a thin smile. "It sounded better in my head."

Danny nodded, then slowly turned to walk away. Master Barrydew turned after him, frowning.

"And where are you off to?"

"For the moment, I'm going to go talk to Isa," Danny answered. "After that... I don't know. Play a game of Daggers with Tess to see if it gives me any ideas for getting us out of this mess."

"Well, if you have any thoughts, please do tell them to me," Master Barrydew joked.

Danny smiled then swept out of the room. As he made his way through the long and winding hallways, he did his best to stay optimistic, but it was hard.

He had hoped, rather idly, that taking out the three bosses in the horde would have netted him another reward, but no such luck. Likely, the Deepcorp Lord had wounded them slightly when he turned them aside, thus negating any reward that Danny might have received (since he didn't defeat them entirely himself).

The next horde was expected to be even stronger than the last one, and he had far fewer weapons. How could he possibly win?

How could the city win? As much as they were standing up against the fury of the dungeons, as much as they were raging against what the Deepcorp had thrown at them, Danny felt as though they were fighting a losing battle.

He didn't see any way they were going to come out on top, and he didn't see any way they could possibly pull through.

Then again, he had felt that way in the past and things had always worked out.

When he knocked on Isa's door, there was a soft scramble inside, and the door popped open just a crack. Isa gazed out and saw him, a smile spreading across her face.

"Danny! Just a second."

She closed the door, and Danny heard some bolts and chains being rearranged before she opened the door wider to allow Danny to step through. After he stepped in, she closed it again.

Danny frowned as she quickly locked and bolted the door.

As she did so, he looked around and saw what she was working with.

Every single table in the place, along with several of the chairs and most of the floor, was covered with carefully-arranged gears, cogs, rods, pistons, and more. There were springs and pulleys, chains, mana crystal fittings, and a great deal more.

Danny's jaw dropped, and Isa beamed.

"It's taken me just close to forever, but I've almost got the thing completely disassembled."

She carefully led Danny through a single path that ran down the middle of the chaos and over to the shell of the old globe. There, just about the only thing still inside the casing was the central sphere, now visible as a bronze, tarnished sort of object.

It had a clasp that allowed it to open, though when all the gears and other parts were clustered around it, Danny was certain that it couldn't have properly opened at all. It was very strange, there was no doubt about it.

"Any idea what it does, yet?" Danny asked, stroking his chin.

"Not a bit!" Isa laughed as she turned and picked up a clipboard that had a massive pile of papers covered in countless calculations. Next to it, on the table, was another pile of papers that seemed to notate how all the assorted pieces went back together.

"That said, I do think I've been able to deduce what all the mana stones happen to be. I've put in an order with Master Barrydew, he's in the process of getting them all to me."

Danny shook his head in amazement. "If you're getting mana stone priority in this war, you know this thing is important."

"True," Isa said. "I just wish I knew what it did. For all I know, it could just be a really fancy map."

"Well, right now, we're desperate enough that I imagine most people are willing to make that gamble," Danny murmured. "Not even my own magic is enough to stop the advance of the monsters, so we're not really left with many options."

"Ahh, we'll make it through." Isa clapped him on the shoulder then pointed at the central orb. "Now, this thing is really interesting. I actually do have somewhat of an idea what it does."

"Really?" Danny asked. "How?"

"Well, I think it serves as the brain of the thing." Isa reached out and flipped it open, revealing a hollow about the size of her fist.

"You know those things I showed you earlier? That can control the flow of mana throughout this machine?"

Danny nodded. "You called them circuits, I think?"

"Exactly. Well, the ultimate source of them seems to come from here." She pointed at the orb.

"Every single one of the circuit patterns, the way they move and connect throughout the machine, ties back to here. Only thing I can figure is that this thing is what ultimately decides which paths to direct mana down, which then gets parsed out through the rest of the machine."

She sighed. "It's far beyond its time. I think I said this before, but I feel like I'm looking at something that shouldn't be invented for another thousand years."

"Maybe you are," Danny said.

"No." Isa shook her head. "Time travel violates the laws of physics on something like twenty different points. A single speck of dust traveling through time would cause a collapse of our entire reality."

Danny wrinkled his brow. "What?"

"Sorry. There was a mage about fifty years ago who wrote a really interesting paper about it," Isa answered.

"I don't have much free time, but I try to make sure I use it doing productive things, like reading."

"Sounds like just the sort of thing to kick up your feet and relax with." Danny shook his head in amazement. "Alright, alright. So you're confident that this is something that was created in our own time."

"Several hundred years ago, but yes," Isa said. "I'm pretty confident that it was created by a mage, not pulled out of the dungeons like this. As to how they did it..."

She tapped the hollow. "I think this thing holds a Pearl of Wisdom."

Danny blinked a few times. Pearls of Wisdom were incredibly rare items that granted a user access to a vast ocean of knowledge and information.

At least in theory, if a person were to use one, they would almost instantly become the most intelligent person in the land, and would be functionally incapable of making a bad decision until it ran out.

"That would actually make some sense." Danny opened his inventory and started to scroll through it.

"I asked Master Barrydew for one, and he turned me down," Isa said. "He told me that they're just too expensive. Anyone who already has one isn't going to give it up, and while the

Empire has a few, they're currently being saved for use in figuring a way out of this situation."

"Here." Danny pulled out his own Pearl of Wisdom.

The rare magic item gleamed in the light as it rested in his palm, and Isa's jaw dropped.

"You still have that thing?" she gasped. "I thought you used it already!"

"Nope." Danny passed it over to her. "I mean, I did use it to distract Marshal when he was trying to destroy the city, but I didn't activate it. It's all yours."

Isa slowly took the pearl and gazed down into its depths for a moment. It was about three inches across, just the same as it had always been, and she slowly held it out and dropped it into the hollow.

The moment it entered the space, beams of light shot out of the item, connecting it to the shell, and lights began to radiate throughout the machine.

The pearl hovered at the exact center of the hollow, and without any input from either human, the lid of the inner casing slammed closed. At that moment, rivers of energy flowed across that inner shell, sparking and flickering where it wanted to flow up and into the missing gears and rods and levers.

"Ahh... Huh!" Isa blinked a few times. "I guess I'd better start putting this back together."

"I guess so." Danny chuckled and crossed his arms. "You're welcome."

Isa turned to him and gave him a hug, then turned and gestured at the far table. "Can you go bring me the gear that I have labeled as Z-27?"

Danny frowned then nodded and walked over to the table. It took him a moment to locate it, but quickly enough, he was able to find the thing.

He picked it up and brought it back to Isa, who reached down into the shell and began re-attaching it.

"Great! Now I need the rod that goes through it. I think it's also labeled Z-27. No!" she called out as she glanced over at her notes.

"Z-26!"

Danny laughed, and with that, the two of them got to work. Over the course of the next hour, they were able to put a good portion of the thing back together.

They could have kept going, but they reached a casing where a missing mana stone halted their progress. Isa sighed as she bolted the casing into place, then crossed her arms.

"I'll have to get an actual stone in this thing before I can go any further." She pointed at the next set of gears.

"Those will block it in, and I won't be able to touch it."

"Wow." Danny shook his head as lights flickered through the machine. "Now do you have any idea what it does?"

"Please believe me when I say that I'm still at a loss." Isa walked over and sat down on a nearby chair, gazing at the object.

"You brought me all those lovely books about the Dead Mountains, but I just couldn't find anything about them that connects to this. Nothing in the dungeons, nothing that grows or lives on the slopes..."

"I'm at an utter loss. All I can do is try to put it back together and hope that it works right."

"Well, if you need me for anything else, just let me know." Danny waved as he walked up to the door.

"Lean on Master Barrydew and see if he can get me those mana stones faster," Isa said.

"I'll see what I can do!" Danny turned and strode through the halls, sweeping away from Isa's room and angling back up toward the library.

It didn't take him long to get there, where, as he walked in through the door, he found Master Barrydew looking down at a large roll of paper with an envoy from the Emperor. The envoy looked up, gave a nod, rolled the paper back up, and left.

Danny frowned after him, and Master Barrydew shrugged.

"There are some rumors of revolt running around through the city," Master Barrydew said. "We're just trying to get ahead of it. We don't want to start crushing civil liberties, but also, having a population that's rioting against us isn't going to do us any good."

"Right." Danny frowned. "Want some good news?"

He quickly explained how things were going with Isa. When he finished, Master Barrydew slowly sat down.

"Interesting. Very interesting."

"You don't sound pleased." Danny sat across from him.

"I am, I am." Master Barrydew sighed. "I'm simply nervous. Arming something that you don't understand is an easy way to kill a lot of people."

"I only hope that this thing she's building is actually helpful."

"Do we have a choice?" Danny asked.

"There's always a choice." Master Barrydew slowly turned and looked Danny in the eyes.

"Do you remember Master... What was his name again? Taught up in the tower, everyone hated him?"

"Right!" Danny nodded. "Ahh... Thornwood. Master Thornwood."

"Yes, that's it." Master Barrydew flashed a thin smile. "Believe it or not, he actually vanished as soon as this crisis reared its head. Went running right back to the tribes where he had spent so much time."

"I digress, though. The point is that he was always posing moral questions, and trying to get you to choose a grey area."

"Neither you, nor many of the other students, ever really accepted his philosophy. The point that you showed him was that there always was a choice, even when it was painful."

"Sometimes... Sometimes, the best choices are the ones that hurt the most." He slapped his thigh, then slowly pushed himself to his feet.

"I'll get her the mana stones. That much isn't a question. I only wish that we had a better idea of what it did, so we knew that we weren't signing our own death warrants."

With that, he strode off, and Danny sighed. He couldn't argue with the master, much as he wanted to.

It was a simple truth; they were messing with something that they simply didn't understand.

And, unfortunately, only time would tell if it wound up helping them or hurting them.

Auto save - [Savefile: Information]
Health: 100%
Mana: 100%
[Quest Update] Keep morale as high as possible
Location: Library
Inventory: Essential Supplies, Basic Armor, Iron Sword, Sword of the Wasp, Aquamarine Sword, Frostbite Sword
Skills: Monster Summoner (Lv. 45), Flame Combat (Lv. 2), Wind Combat (Lv. 5)
Relationships: Friendly with Master Barrydew, Friendly with Isa
Time of Day: 11:38 a.m.

Twenty-Two

—·—

Lessons With Daggers

"And... I think that should more or less wrap things up when discussing the merits of battling fire creatures in a snowy environment," Danny said confidently as the class frantically scribbled on their notepads. "Any questions?"

Unsurprisingly, Trish raised her hand. "Yes, actually! Obviously, as you indicated, environment is useful in defeating these creatures, but I was wondering if it would be helpful to use water spells. I'm a natural water mage, is there any way that you could combine the freezing air of the colder environment to create impromptu ice spells?"

Danny paused thoughtfully. "Ahh... maybe. I'd have to look into that further to give you a definitive answer."

"The short answer is no." A deep voice came from the doorway.

Danny looked over and smiled broadly as his father slowly hobbled into the room, leaning heavily on a cane. Seeing him walking, even with difficulty, warmed Danny's heart.

"No?" Trish asked. "Why's that?"

"The very simple answer is because the magic of a water mage helps keep water stable in environments that would otherwise be hostile to such a thing," Zechariah explained as he made his way to the front of the classroom.

"And who are you?" a student called out from the back.

"Zechariah Youngblood, Ascended Fire Mage," Zechariah replied softly. "Ten-year veteran of the northern front."

The class fell silent as Zechariah took a deep breath before continuing. "Water spells work even when the air is too hot or cold for water to naturally exist in liquid form. While it can sometimes be a hindrance, the idea is you can preserve your natural fighting style without the environment interfering."

He smiled wistfully. "I should know, my best friend was a water mage who struggled in the northern plains. That said, as you'll learn in your water-specific environmental studies, there are many ways to use an icy setting to your advantage."

"Water spells can easily pick up particles and objects from the area, far more than most spell types. You could potentially hit the ground with a jet of water, harvest the shards from the air, and use that to amplify the force and chill of your next water attack. But that's just one small example, as I'm not qualified to teach water theory in depth."

"What's the strongest monster you've ever killed?" another student shouted.

"A red dragon," Zechariah replied, "in the S-ranked **[Double Flame Dungeon]** down in the southern wastes. My unit got pinned down on a routine mission and accidentally discovered a shortcut to the boss chamber. Believe it or not, we all made it out alive." He crossed his arms. "Any other questions?"

The class asked several more, which Zechariah happily answered. When finished, they all filed out, leaving Danny and Zechariah alone.

Danny sat at his desk and began looking through papers the students had handed in that day. Zechariah smiled and perched on the corner of a desk nearby. "You're a natural, you know that?"

"I think I prefer teaching to fighting," Danny admitted, glancing up from the papers. "Maybe that sounds crazy, but..."

"No," Zechariah said, shaking his head. "It took me almost twenty years to reach the same conclusion. Nicodemus would say it took him even longer. Out of all of us, only Barrydew figured it out early on. He just turned around and entered the Academy straightaway."

Zechariah held up a finger. "The trick is to want to teach and detest battle, but still go when called."

"Trust me, I'll be there," Danny assured him. "I just wish we had a better chance of winning."

Zechariah puffed out his cheeks and nodded. "Me too."

Danny turned his focus to grading the papers as Zechariah slowly walked around the classroom. When Danny finished, they left the Academy and headed home through the grey streets.

Thick clouds blanketed the sun overhead, but fortunately no rain fell. The air felt thick and humid, though cold instead of warm. As they passed, the townspeople either sneered at them with hatred or drew back in fear.

Danny sighed, knowing there was nothing to be done about it. In their shoes, he understood he'd likely feel just as upset - powerless under the looming threat of a crushing boot. He could only imagine how he'd feel if their situations were reversed.

They soon arrived home, unlocked the door and slipped inside. Zechariah pulled some vegetables from his inventory and ignited flames in the hearth with a flick of his wrist. Before long, a thin stew bubbled on the stove.

They both sat back in their chairs, a heavy silence hanging between them. When the stew was ready, they ate quickly, then pulled out their **[Daggers]** board as night began to fall. Just as they were setting up their pieces, a sharp knock sounded at the door.

"Come in!" Zechariah called without looking up.

The door swung open and Tess stepped inside, a small smile on her face. She sighed, closed the door behind her, pulled off her cold gauntlets and approached the fire.

"What's up?" Danny leaned back in his chair and nodded at the board. "Want to try and beat my dad?"

"She could try," Zechariah said confidently.

Tess raised an eyebrow as she grabbed a bowl from the counter and helped herself to some soup. "You sound sure of yourself."

"Dad, I've never seen her lose a game of **[Daggers]**," Danny commented, scooting his chair to the side of the table.

Tess pulled up a chair, sat down, and began eating while rearranging the pieces Danny had carefully set up.

"And I've been watching her play for ages," Danny added. "I didn't know you played **[Daggers]** much at all."

"Ah, this was the game to play when I was in the Academy," Zechariah recalled, finishing his own board setup. He respectfully closed his eyes and leaned back as Tess completed hers.

"Master Barrydew dominated the first three years, so I checked out a book on it from the library. I studied all of fourth year, and since then, in my fifth year, I've never lost a game."

Tess chuckled and finished arranging her board. "Your move, old man. You're white."

"Fair enough." Eyes still closed, Zechariah commanded, "Take the pawn in front of the right bishop. Forward two spaces."

Danny reached out and moved the piece as instructed. Tess frowned, then countered by advancing a pawn in front of one of her knights.

For the next several turns, Zechariah kept his eyes shut, moving pieces into a defensive formation. Tess did much the same, until finally, Zechariah opened his eyes.

"Alright! Now we're cooking." He studied the board intently.

His own side had his bishops primed to flash across the board, two knights just behind them, and his queen exposed. Meanwhile, Tess's side had one bishop in front, the second in reserve but ready to withdraw, and pawns staggered to cover each other.

After a few moments, Zechariah nodded. "Your front bishop is empty. Hidden bishop has a dagger, along with both knights. All swords are held by pawns and rooks, queen has the poison."

Tess's jaw dropped. Zechariah winked at her. The rest of the game took mere minutes, with Zechariah seeming to know Tess's every move. She pushed a piece forward and he tore her defenses apart.

Within seconds, her king was captured. Zechariah crossed his arms and leaned back. "The master maintains his throne."

"How did you do that?" Tess leaned in, eyes hungry. "I have to know!"

"Go to the library, check out 'Daggers: A Complete Guide,'" Zechariah advised. "If for some reason it no longer exists, I'll write down everything I remember. Here, set your board back up as it was."

Tess frowned but nodded. Within moments, the board was reset to its post-staging state. Zechariah folded his hands and began to explain.

"In ordinary Chess, the Staging segment often lasts two or three turns, sometimes only one if you're skilled and your opponent is careless. In **[Daggers]**, Staging usually takes four to five turns, mimicking court politics. You don't want to attack too early and expose your own hand."

"While there are technically near-infinite ways to arrange your pieces, people tend to follow certain patterns. You're a soldier, which means you think in hard, concrete terms. You play aggressively, as if trying to kill everyone in the court outside your own faction."

"The way you stagger your pieces, making sure everything is open and ready to strike... No matter how you try to hide it, I could see exactly what you were doing and why. I, on the other hand, used a Mage setup - ready to attack from a distance."

"As you can see, I have three long-range pieces here. Likely one of them has a sword, but you faced the question of which one. And because you're a soldier, you tried to defend against all three."

Tess frowned and slowly nodded. "How many setups have you memorized?"

"I've more or less memorized ten of them," Zechariah replied. "Come on, I'll teach you a few."

Outside, the night sky darkened as the small group huddled by the meager hearth inside the house. Danny felt bad for those left out in the cold, but what could they do? Their home wasn't big enough for the whole city.

Finally, Tess leaned back and shook her head in amazement. "I have to admit, you're a master."

"Well, I look forward to the day when you, or someone else, can give me a real challenge." Zechariah flashed a small smile. "Now Tess, why did you stop by?"

Tess sighed as she pulled on her gauntlets and headed for the door. "Honestly? I'm not sure. I saw the fire walking by and thought it would be nice to spend a moment in good company."

She bit her lip. "Things are getting dark out there, and I don't just mean the cloudy night. People are losing hope. My own soldiers are quaking in their boots. I heard we're seeing about fifty defections a day."

"I know most are just throwing down their armor and living in the city, not even running off into the wilderness like deserters used to. It sickens me. I just... I don't know. I needed a morale boost myself, and I got one, even if I did get soundly beaten. So... thanks for that."

With that, she turned and walked out, the door slamming shut behind her. Danny frowned and crossed his arms as she left. Zechariah glanced over at him.

"What are you thinking?"

Danny shrugged. "I wish life were as simple as a game of **[Daggers]**. That we could just figure out what's going on with this Deepcorp guy and go from there."

"That would be handy," Zechariah agreed, climbing to his feet, "and then again, it wouldn't. If it were really that simple, it wouldn't take much for him to outsmart us, and then we're dead."

"The reality of the situation is enough to keep us afloat a bit longer, and that's good enough for me." He smiled and started hobbling off to bed. "I'll see you in the morning. I have an early meeting with the Emperor, so I need some rest. Goodnight, son."

Danny watched him go, then sighed and nodded. He slowly headed to bed as well. It was hard not to succumb to the same despair pulling everyone else down... but in that moment, he vowed not to give in.

There was always a way, they just had to find it. They weren't going to fall... and one way or another, they would retake their land.

[Auto save] - [Savefile: Information]
Health: 100%
Mana: 100%
[Quest]: Find a way to survive
Location: Youngblood Residence
Inventory: Essential Supplies, Basic Armor, Iron Sword, [Sword of the Wasp], [Aquamarine Sword], [Frostbite Sword]
Skills: [Monster Summoner] (Lv. 45), [Flame Combat] (Lv. 2), [Wind Combat] (Lv. 5)
Relationships: Friendly with Tess, Family Bond with Zechariah, Ascended Fire Mage

Time of Day: 8:58 p.m.

Twenty-Three

Estate Survivors

The wind howled through the city streets as Danny and Zechariah made their way to the Imperial Palace the next morning. The humidity was largely gone, but the cold weather had only settled in all the more, forcing the refugees to cower under their shelter all the more.

When they arrived at the Imperial Palace, they were granted entrance, and soon arrived in the throne room where Emperor Ezra was waiting.

On that day, he wore tan robes drawn by a simple belt, while his crown appeared to have been dented slightly. He looked more gaunt than usual, as if even he wasn't eating terribly well.

As the two mages approached, the emperor folded his hands behind his back.

"I don't recall Master Youngblood being invited to this meeting."

"My apologies," Zechariah answered. "I'm still not terribly sure of foot, so he helped me here, and on the way, he had an idea. I thought it would be worth it for his proposal to reach your ears."

Emperor Ezra gave a small nod. "Tell me. Then, I'm afraid, I'll have to ask you to leave. One of my aides can escort your father to the Academy."

Danny took a deep breath and nodded, then folded his hands behind his back. "I was just thinking about these herds of monsters that are heading our way, and I was thinking... I don't know, what if we could turn them aside?"

"What if we send someone out now, while they're still a month or two away, and have them attack the things, lead them out of the way? Direct them to the south, or to the ocean, or something?"

The Emperor flashed a thin smile. "I'm terribly sorry, Master Youngblood, to disappoint you, but we have already thought of that possibility."

"Really?" Danny paused then crossed his arms. "Why'd you decide against it?"

"Because, quite frankly, there's only one mage powerful enough to do what you're proposing," the Emperor said. "I think we both know that I'm looking at him."

Danny set his jaw. "Okay, so... Why not send me?"

"Let's say that you do go." Emperor Ezra gestured out at the door. "You march to the herd, and you attack. For starters, you risk dying, and if you're taken down so far away from help, the rest of the world isn't going to fare well."

"To continue, let's suppose that you do turn it aside. Right now, the Deepcorp Lord has placed the monsters on a path that avoids most other herds, likely to eliminate the possibility of their being turned aside."

"If they divert from their current path, they'll only run into other herds, combining and growing, snowballing into an avalanche that I fear will be unstoppable."

"Then I can just go destroy them," Danny offered.

"And then you'd have to go fight the next herd, and the next, and the next," Emperor Ezra said. "You'd spend the rest of your life fighting against every new herd that the Deepcorp Lord puts together, desperately fighting to protect an ungrateful city, until, finally, you perish."

"It's a nice thought that you could just go and knock out the one heading our way, but the Deepcorp Lord would, quite simply, put together another herd. The same would happen if you did successfully turn the herd aside into a path that didn't cause it to snowball."

"The Deepcorp Lord could simply make a course-correction when he realized what you had done. With his influence on the table, we can't be too careful."

"We can't just do nothing!" Danny exclaimed, trying to keep his frustration in check.

"And we're not doing nothing," the emperor answered. "Now, please, Danny. I have the finest minds in the Empire working on this problem, and evaluating the solution."

"We do have some thoughts and theories, but it's going to take some time to work through the possibilities. This isn't the sort of decision that can be made overnight."

As the Emperor finished, he bowed his head to Danny in a mock sign of respect. In that moment, Danny thought he saw a bit of smoke trailing out of the corner of the Emperor's eye.

It wasn't much, only a brief flicker, but... there it was. Danny's hands balled into fists, and he did his best to bow in return.

With that, he turned and walked away, trying to look frustrated but determined.

In all reality, though, he was livid. Furious, angry... It seemed that the lord really did have everything under control.

He could take over the mind of (almost) anyone he desired, he could manipulate the very monsters that surged through the landscape as they ground civilization into dust. It seemed that there was nothing he would be unable to do, and that, more than anything else, made Danny terrified.

How were they to fight an enemy who knew their every move, who could pop into their command rooms and issue orders that played right into the hands of said enemy? It seemed a hopeless task, and as he stepped back out onto the street, he sighed, glanced up at the Academy overhead... And then turned and marched out to the wall.

When he reached the outer wall and stepped through the gate, he found the wind howling all the stronger across the barren landscape. Tess was just mounting up on a horse, and she glanced over at him.

"What are you up to?" she asked. "Don't you have a class to teach today?"

"Nah. It's my day off." Danny shook his head then stretched out a hand toward the horse she was riding. A moment later, he had absorbed its attributes, and snapped his fingers to create one with a flash of light.

Quickly, he climbed up onto the thing, then shrugged. "You came to my house last night to play games to destress. I'd kinda like to head out to punch something. Might make me feel a little better."

"Well, I can't argue with that logic. Done it a few times myself over the years." Tess glanced back and forth then nodded out across the rolling hills.

A few springs of grass grew here and there, but most of it was just black. The last attack had taken place so late in the year that there hadn't been time for the grass to regrow before the colder seasons struck.

"There's a family of trolls that moved into a cave just over the hill. Used to be used by shepherds to shelter their sheep in storms."

"I've been thinking about clearing it out. Want to come with?"

"Yeah." Danny drew in a deep breath. "Let's do this."

They shot off across the barren wasteland, flashing over the countless bones and half-decayed carcasses that lay scattered. Here and there, some of the skulls, particularly goblin skulls, had been mounted on poles made from leg bones, probably the somewhat warped humor of soldiers too long on patrol.

As they passed down into the ravines, they went past the singularly enormous bones of the massive trolls and other creatures, bones as thick as tree trunks. When the war was over, it was likely that they would be used in rebuilding the town.

In any case, they soon passed them by, and went down along a low lake stained black, then along a ravine that stretched away from it, heading southeast.

"It's right at the end of this place," Tess called, pointing ahead. "At the very end. They've been mostly quiet, so we haven't been too worried about it. Bigger issues, you know?"

"Yeah." Danny gritted his teeth. "Let's do this."

With that, they flashed around a corner in the ravine and came into sight of the cave. It was huge, forty feet high, and seemed to sink deep into the hillside.

Truly, it did appear to be a magnificent location to herd sheep. Beady eyes now looked out from it at a height of thirty feet, and Danny heard a muffled grunt.

"Watch out... Now!" Tess swerved to the left, and Danny went to the right. A boulder flashed out of the cave and hit the ground between them, churning up the soil and shattering the boulder into bits.

Several more came out mere instants later, and Tess swerved up behind a small outcropping. Danny, though, charged forward, racing for the darkened entrance.

"Danny!" Tess called out. "Be careful!"

Danny set his jaw. He would be careful, alright. Careful not to leave a single troll alive.

He stood up in the saddle as he approached, and another boulder came flashing out. It arced through the air, aiming straight toward him.

Down, down it came, and he drew in a deep breath.

"Stone Golem!"

With a flash, the creature appeared. It snatched the rock out of the air just before it hit him, spun, and threw it back into the cave with all its might.

A resounding boom filled the air, and dust came billowing out. With a startled roar, two huge trolls came stomping out, clubs at the ready.

Neither one was really a match for Danny, but he didn't really care at that moment. He just wanted something to beat up, and they were a handy target.

With a roar, the golem went charging forward, and Danny pulled up short, watching as the golem threw a punch into the gut of one of the trolls then snatched the club out of the hands of the second one. It spun and smashed the club over the head of the first troll, breaking it into splinters, then cast the pieces aside and punched the second one again.

A third troll, then a fourth, came out, and Danny drew up short to watch the fight. Tess rode up next to him as well, and together, they just watched the proceedings.

It was brutal in every sense of the word, as the golem simply beat its way through the four trolls. Finally, it picked up a large boulder and smashed it over the head of one of the beasts, caving in the skull of the thing.

It collapsed, and the golem snarled in victory, spun, and smashed its fist through the face of a second troll.

It wasn't long before the creatures had been defeated. As the last one fell, Tess rode forward, up toward the cave.

Danny followed, a bit confused, and she came to a stop at the mouth. Wordlessly, she climbed down and drew out a torch, slowly pressing forward.

Danny dissolved his horse and followed, a bit confused as to what she was doing.

"Look at this," she murmured after a moment, gesturing at the pens and the corals that had been meticulously built into the cave ages earlier by the shepherds. Now, they were little more than splinters, smashed to bits by the huge creatures.

"Just sad."

"Yeah," Danny said. "When we get the monsters kicked to the wind, we're going to have a time rebuilding."

"Do you think we can?" Tess asked, turning slightly to him.

Danny drew in a deep breath. "I think they built this Empire from scratch once. I think we can probably do it again."

Tess flashed a small smile at him then turned and forged forward once more. "That's what I love about you, Danny. You can summon optimism just as easily as all your monsters, even when I know you don't feel it personally."

Danny flashed a small smile, then nodded to her. "What are you looking for?"

"I'd rather not say unless I find it." Tess frowned as they reached a fork in the tunnel. The cave truly was a deep one.

She moved her torch between the two, then pointed at the left tunnel. "This is the larger of the two, and if you look there, there are scuff marks on the wall. They've been using this passage."

As she started walking down the path, she nodded to Danny. "If you see a monster, kill it. Nothing fancy, just kill it."

Danny frowned, but nodded. Suddenly, as they came to an opening, a monster did, indeed, come bursting out of the darkness.

It was yet another troll, this one smaller and lither, with a great deal less belly and a great many more teeth than the majority of its race. Its skin was white, as if it had never seen the sun, and it wielded a white staff that looked more like it belonged in the hand of a wizard than the hands of a troll.

[Monster Identified: White Troll. Level 27. Hp: 1,941]

Danny snapped his fingers, and a swarm of rockworms swam through its vital organs. The troll gulped and gurgled as it staggered toward them then fell headlong across the rocks.

The worms burst out through the skin a moment later, and Danny unsummoned them just as quickly as he could.

"Ugh." Tess gulped as they stepped past the troll. "You didn't have to kill him quite like that."

"Sorry," Danny said. "You said to do it quick. Any reason why?"

"Yeah." Tess turned and raised the torch slightly. "That's why."

Danny frowned then blinked in surprise. Over in the corner of the room, a handful of hostages were tied and bound, tossed there like a pile of potatoes.

They wriggled about and tried to call out through their gags, and the two warriors quickly ran over and started untying them. As they did, Danny blinked in surprise.

He recognized them.

"You're all from the Silver Estate," he gasped as he recognized the butler who had helped him so much, as well as a handful of lords and ladies. "Boniface, right?"

"The one and only." The man straightened up and dusted off his uniform. "Apologies for the rough appearance. I'm afraid we got into a bit of a scrap on the way here."

Danny chuckled and flashed a small smile. "I'd ask how the other guy looks, but I think I just killed him."

"And in a stunning display, one that I must say, from my side of things, was extremely gratifying." Boniface sighed and folded his hands neatly behind his back.

"That said, I'm afraid that they're not the main culprits I'm concerned about. My master's brother, Lot Silver, betrayed us on our journey in."

"When the trolls appeared, he turned and killed one of our horses, making us easy prey. The last thing I saw, as we fell behind, was Abraham being clubbed over the head."

"I'm afraid that he's either dead, or being held as a captive in the city."

"We'll find him," Tess promised.

"He wouldn't want you to waste the resources, not when so many other people are in such need." Boniface shook his head. "That said, with your permission, I'll be conducting my own search."

"It was three days ago when we were captured, I have little doubt that Lot won't have simply huddled down in the first tent he found upon entering the Imperial City."

"Why'd you come down here, anyway?" Danny asked. He winced as he realized the likely answer, and Boniface sighed as they walked up and out of the cave.

"I'm afraid that the Silver Estate is no more." His voice was sad. "An ice dragon came down from the north not a week ago. It laid waste to almost the entire kingdom."

"Master Abraham and Lot, working together, managed to use their powers to drive it off, but it killed... I don't even begin to know. Tens of thousands."

"Most of the survivors decided that they would stay, but some of us set off for the Imperial City."

"You're a good man. We'll see what we can do," Danny promised him. Tess nodded as well, and Boniface sighed.

Danny had quite a few questions as they started back toward the city. First off, had Tess known about the captives?

It certainly seemed that way. If so, why had she been so casual about maybe going off and attacking the cave at some point?

It didn't make a lot of sense in Danny's mind, but... Whatever the case, they had rescued the survivors of the Silver Estate, and that was good enough in Danny's mind.

He only hoped that justice could be done for Abraham, and that all things, in the end, could be set right.

Auto save - [Savefile: Information]
Health: 100%
Mana: 71%
[Quest Update] Get the survivors back to town
Location: Shepherd's Cave, Imperial City Agricultural Area, East Side
Inventory: Essential Supplies, Basic Armor, Iron Sword, Sword of the Wasp, Aquamarine Sword, Frostbite Sword

Skills: Monster Summoner (Lv. 45), Flame Combat (Lv. 2), Wind Combat (Lv. 5)

Relationships: Friendly with Tess, Speaking terms with Boniface

Time of Day: 9:21 a.m

Twenty-Four

Temple Price

Upon returning to the city, Danny continued his patrol with Tess while the Silver survivors slipped into the city and vanished. That evening, as he and his father sat down to eat dinner, Danny recounted the story.

When he finished, Zechariah folded his hands, frowning in deep concern. "Interesting. Very curious, indeed."

"Something I missed?" Danny asked, perplexed but determined to understand.

Zechariah shook his head. "No, I don't think so. I simply find it odd that Abraham could be taken advantage of so easily."

He paused thoughtfully. "That said, if your own brother turns against you in a dire moment, the best of us could be taken aback. It took me a good thirty minutes to process the news that Nicodemus had attacked the Imperial City."

Zechariah smiled slightly. "You know, now that I think back on it, I feel so foolish. When Nicodemus attacked the Imperial City, he used a red dragon. Precision blasts, targeting the Imperial Palace."

"When he fought the Deepcorp Lords out on the southern hills, he used a black dragon. Widespread destruction. If that same dragon had used the same attack in the middle of the Imperial City, it would have melted the entire city into slag and left survivors you could count on a single hand."

He shook his head. "He obviously wasn't trying to destroy the place. Not that it's important, anyway. He's gone, now. Strange how so many things can be forgiven when you sacrifice yourself."

Danny smiled at that. He opened his mouth to respond, but was interrupted by a sharp knock on the door. Before he could say a word, it burst open, and Isa ran inside.

She looked freezing cold, wearing only a light garment suited for the interior of the Academy, hardly adequate for the cold streets. Her eyes were wide, and Zechariah waved his hand to close the door behind her.

"What's going on?" Danny leapt to his feet and rushed to her side. "Are you alright?"

"Yes!" She gasped, barely able to talk. She turned and pointed at the door. "The sphere was just taken! Right from my laboratory."

Danny bolted for the door, but Zechariah held up a hand. "Wait! We need the details. Ten seconds more won't make a difference, not when they've had so long."

Isa nodded. "I took... I put the top of the sphere on. It clicked. Lights started to appear on the surface."

"It started to turn by itself. Then, I heard a crash behind me. I turned around, and heard something grab the sphere."

"When I turned back, it was just disappearing, and there was one of those knight things standing there. It shoved me down and ran."

"So, whoever it was pulled the sphere into its inventory," Zechariah mused. "Interesting."

"And it takes up a lot of inventory space, so they must have been waiting for it," Danny added.

"I was thinking the same thing." Zechariah crossed his arms. "Did you see anything more? Did you see which way he went?"

"Out through the window in the hall," Isa answered. "It faces to the east, I think."

"I know the part of the city," Zechariah said. "Come on, Danny. Let's go."

"You're coming?" Danny asked, surprised but grateful for his father's support.

Zechariah sighed as he forced himself to his feet. He lifted his cane then stuck it into his inventory. "I'll manage."

With that, father and son flew from the building, instructing Isa to enjoy the fire. As they flashed through the streets, Zechariah gritted his teeth.

"We need to get higher. Any chance you can give us a lift?"

Danny nodded, and with a flash, a stone golem appeared in the street in front of them. Refugees screamed as the great monster bent down and held out its palms.

Danny and Zechariah leapt upward, and with a practiced flick of the wrist, it tossed them onto the roofs. With that, it vanished, and Danny and Zechariah put on a burst of speed.

Zechariah, even with his injury, could move quite fast. Danny could still see him limping, magic flaring through the wounded leg, but Zechariah didn't stop.

When he reached a street, he leapt into the air, sailing across on his magic. Danny gritted his teeth then leapt out as well, summoning a swarm of cave crows.

Carefully placing them as stepping stones, he re-absorbed them the moment he was across. He re-absorbed the stone golem as well, ensuring he had plenty of mana.

The two mages flew across the city, far faster than they ever could have done below. Zechariah held out his hand, sensing the area as best he could.

Danny wished he could have done the same, but regardless of his summons' power, he was still only a Level 45 mage, while Zechariah was somewhere around 80 or 90. Suddenly, Zechariah called out.

"I've got him! This way!"

Danny nodded, and they shifted direction, running slightly more north. Suddenly, a building loomed ahead, an old temple, and Danny had the feeling it was their destination.

As they approached, Zechariah leapt high into the air, forming a fiery spear in his hand. He launched it down at the roof, smashing straight through and falling into the hole.

Danny followed a second later, summoning a stone golem around himself as he fell. It allowed him to land without assistance, and he slowly looked around.

The temple was old, abandoned for years. Temples were uncommon in the Imperial City, due largely to the fact that Temple Dungeons made people inherently wary of them.

That said, every now and then a few of them went up. This one looked to be for a deity native to the jungle, judging by the carvings spread around the exterior of the room.

There was an altar at one end, just in front of an empty pedestal where an idol had once been placed. There were other details as well - columns, statues, and paintings - but Danny didn't have time to take them all in.

No, he was focused on the cloaked figure standing on the pedestal where the idol had once been.

"So, you found me." The dark voice hissed.

"Have to say, it wasn't your best escape job." Zechariah answered with a shrug. "Now, take off that hood and let's see who we're really dealing with. You led us here for a reason, and I'd like to know what that reason is."

The dark lord simply chuckled and slowly raised his hands. "I am here because I am here. Now... Die!"

The Deepcorp Lord launched several fireballs, white ones, that exploded throughout the room and melted pillars of stone into slag. Danny winced, then leapt backward out of his stone golem and sent it flashing forward.

The lord snarled and threw another fireball which punched straight through it without a second thought.

[Notice: Stone Golem has been destroyed]

"Yeah, got that," Danny muttered. He balled his hands into fists and waited, biding his time, as Zechariah engaged the man.

Truly, seeing two masters battle was something that would haunt Danny's mind for the rest of his life. Flames trailed off Zechariah's body, and he launched a fireball straight into the dark lord's face.

The dark lord snarled and absorbed it, then threw another of the white fireballs at Zechariah. Zechariah, without missing a beat, simply snatched the fire out of the air, spun, and returned it to the sender.

Powerful explosions shook the ground as both unleashed powerful firestorms against the other. Bolts of flaming lightning fell from the sky and broke down the walls, blasting the ceiling into ash.

The wind picked up, howling about the battlefield to form a flaming curtain. Danny gasped in awe as the two launched bolt after bolt of fire at one another, desperately vying for the upper hand.

He wanted to help, but knew the slightest misstep could cause his father's demise. The Deepcorp Lord laughed as they fought, even as strain stood out on Zechariah's face.

"There! You are weak. You are nothing before me. You cower, you shrink back."

"Yes, you're powerful, but that power will not get you all the way. You will fall before me, for I am far more ancient than either of you."

"I saw the rise of the Empire, and I will see it rise again. I am-"

The dark lord's tirade was interrupted as a new figure leapt into the battle, breaking clean through the fiery wall and landing next to Zechariah. Flames trailed off Obadiah Flamekeeper's own clothing, and he formed a fiery bow in his hand.

Zechariah gave a single nod, and they both pressed the attack, driving the Deepcorp Lord steadily backward. Blast after blast broke through his defenses, until, finally, he was slammed into the altar hard enough to drop to the ground.

The wind around the battlefield died down to a whisper, leaving the two mages standing victorious over their foe. Obadiah strode forward and kicked the shoulder of the Deepcorp Mage, flipping him onto his back.

His face twisted in shock and surprise... With a flash of light, the figure changed. Suddenly, still cloaked in black, Barbara lay there, groaning softly.

Her eyes flickered open and she sat up, rubbing her head. "You... Here..." She glanced around and climbed to her feet. "You managed to knock him out?"

Zechariah glanced over at Obadiah who stepped back, horror on his face. "Yes," Zechariah finally answered. "Yes."

"Then you have to kill me," she snapped. "Kill me, quickly. He'll reappear, still unconscious, and then you can kill him."

"What are you talking about?" Danny demanded, determination in his voice.

"Come on, you should be able to figure it out," Barbara said. "When the fire hit, I absorbed some of the magic to bond myself with him, just like I'd once been bonded with Anne."

"When he's asleep, I appear. Same way that things used to work with Anne. Now, kill me so he comes back, and then end this."

"We can't just kill an innocent person." Danny held up his hand. "We'll separate you again."

"No!" Barbara screamed. "You only have one summoner, not two. Now do it, quickly, before he wakes up. I can feel him stirring, you have seconds."

"If that's true, then why haven't you asked us to kill you before?" Zechariah demanded.

"Because he's always been asleep, not beaten in combat." Barbara almost seemed beside herself. "Seriously, you can end this, here and now. When he's gone, almost all of this goes away, and it becomes just a simple fight for survival instead of a losing battle."

"What else do I have to give you?"

Zechariah grimaced, and her eyes went wide. "He's coming back!"

She opened her inventory and pulled out two items. The first was the globe, which she cast onto the ground in front of them. It slammed down as it appeared once more.

She then lifted a dagger and drove it straight at her heart. The instant the blade touched her there was another flash, and the Deepcorp Lord appeared once more.

He gasped as his own blade plunged into his heart, and he staggered backward and collapsed on the steps leading up to the altar. Zechariah raced toward him to finish the job, but as he drew his sword and leapt at the fallen man, a blast of darkness lanced upward, hitting Zechariah and knocking him backward across the battlefield.

Danny rushed forward and transferred the globe into his own inventory, and the Deepcorp Lord slowly staggered to his feet.

"You opened my inventory?" He groaned softly, his face still hidden beneath his cowl. "And you tried... To kill me with my own knife? Bold."

He spat out black blood, pulled out the knife, and turned. As he twirled around, his cloak swirled, and with that, he was gone.

Danny and Obadiah stared at the place where he had just been, and Danny slowly balled his hands into fists.

"There must be a better way." Obadiah turned around and placed his hand on Danny's shoulder. "There must have been."

"You don't know that," Danny said, his voice heavy but resolute.

"True, but..." Obadiah shrugged. "I also know that my own daughter would have done the same thing in that situation, and I know that I'd fight through every dungeon in the entire world to make sure that she didn't have to sacrifice herself in such a way."

He sighed, then walked over and helped Zechariah back to his feet. "Come on." He murmured. "What's done is done. Let's get that sphere back, and this time... Let's make sure it's placed under a far more secure lock and key."

Auto save - [Savefile: Information]
Health: 100%
Mana: 91%
[Quest]: Find a safe place for the Globe
Location: Shepherd's Cave, Imperial City Agricultural Area, East Side
Inventory: Essential Supplies, Basic Armor, Iron Sword, [Sword of the Wasp], [Aquamarine Sword], [Frostbite Sword]
Skills: [Monster Summoner] (Lv. 45), [Flame Combat] (Lv. 2), [Wind Combat] (Lv. 5)
Relationships: Friendly with Isa, Friendly with Obadiah Flamekeeper, Ascended Fire Mage, Family Bond with Zechariah, Ascended Fire Mage
Time of Day: 10:22 p.m.

Twenty-Five

Discovery

"And... Here it is." Danny opened his inventory and dropped the globe onto the floor of Isa's laboratory.

For a long moment, everyone in the room just stared at it. Then Master Barrydew frowned deeply.

"I don't mean to be a terribly wet blanket, but..." Isa held up a hand. "I do feel that I should point out that the globe was stolen from this exact room only a few hours ago."

"True." Master Barrydew mopped his forehead with a cloth then turned to Zechariah and Obadiah, both of whom stared at the globe with interest, concern, and confusion. "That said, I'm not sure where else in the Academy we could possibly put it where it would be under a tighter lock and key."

"The forbidden archives," Isa suggested. "Or one of the training dungeons down in the basement."

"Alright, alright," Master Barrydew said. "There are, technically, places that are more secure than this room. I'm simply wondering if they're secure enough."

"He is, after all, quite ancient, and easily more powerful than any of us," Obadiah mused.

"And yet..." Zechariah held up a finger. "We managed to knock him down. We didn't kill him, perhaps, and it took two Ascended Mages to do it, but we did manage to knock him down."

"That has to count for something. He's not immortal, and he's not all-powerful."

"He's also being weakened by the source of magic that he's using," Danny said confidently. "Isa and I saw this mana stone that provides a more or less infinite amount of mana."

"He has Black Mana stones?" Master Barrydew turned white.

"Yes, but that could help us," Isa said. "Black Mana Stones are notorious about killing the people wielding them, since you're using so much more mana than you're used to wielding."

"He's a lot weaker than he wants us to believe, and that's just a fact. That's the point with all of this. He wants us to believe that he's unstoppable, and frankly, he's close to it, but he's not completely invincible."

"He has weaknesses, and we can exploit them if we can just deduce what they are."

Danny frowned and raised a hand.

"You're a Master, Danny," Master Barrydew said. "This isn't a class where you need to be acknowledged."

"Maybe not, but I don't like to just butt in," Danny said. "I was just wondering if we knew how he had concealed himself in here. When he attacked and stole the globe, do we know how he was hiding himself? What spell he used, or what level of power it was drawing at the time?"

Zechariah shook his head. "I'm not sure it's possible to know that sort of information. Maybe if we had scanned him or something at the time, but by now—"

"Actually..." Master Barrydew snapped his fingers. "It just might be possible to figure that out."

"You have a time machine?" Obadiah raised an eyebrow.

"No." Danny held up a finger. "Apparently even a single particle of dust traveling through time would cause the universe to collapse."

"You were listening!" Isa beamed.

"Please." Master Barrydew held up a hand.

Everyone in the room grew quiet, and he held out his palm toward the door. Red lines pulsed from his fingertips and traced their way through the air, and, after a moment, a vague form appeared.

It was about the same height and size as the Deepcorp Mage, and might have been wearing a cloak, but the details were too fuzzy to tell for certain. Everyone stepped back as Master Barrydew approached the apparition, and the old master slowly nodded.

"Seems like we're in luck."

"Care to explain how this is possible?" Zechariah asked.

"It's actually fairly simple." Master Barrydew paused. "You all are familiar with the concept of a magical trace, right? We used one ages ago to try and figure out who was behind the attacks, I think in Danny's second year."

"Well, it's a little-known fact, but most cloaking spells will leave behind a magical trace as well. Now, it doesn't completely nullify the effects of the cloaking spell, since you both have to know to look for it and have to be powerful enough to read it, but that's the reason why more higher-level mages don't employ it more often."

"The things you learn." Zechariah frowned. As the adrenaline of the fight wore off, he pulled out his cane and leaned upon it, and Danny stepped up to the specter.

Master Barrydew examined it for a moment longer, then let it fade away.

"He was using a Level 86 simple cloaking spell. Powerful enough to conceal entirely from sight, and removes almost one hundred percent of sound," Master Barrydew said.

"Still, it uses a fairly low mana drain, and doesn't allow a user to pass through any solid objects or invisible barriers that they wouldn't otherwise be able to pass through."

"Then we really would be better off putting it somewhere more secure?" Isa asked.

Master Barrydew nodded. "We would need some safety precautions. I think the forbidden archives would work well, provided that someone can only access it with multiple people present, and after trace scans are performed to ensure that no one is cloaked in the room at the time."

"Deal." Isa held out a hand. "How do we get started?"

It took the small procession little time to make their way up to the library then the forbidden archives. Danny didn't know if he was really supposed to be tagging along, but no one told him to leave, and he wasn't about to start questioning it.

They stepped out of the main classroom and into a smaller room, where Master Barrydew performed another scan (and found evidence that someone cloaked had been in the room almost a week earlier, though it was too distorted to know who), and taught both Zechariah and Obadiah how to do the same.

That done, they stepped through the final door and into the forbidden archives... A place that Danny had long desired to see with his own eyes.

As he walked through, his jaw slowly dropped. It was about half the size as the main library, which was a good deal bigger than he had imagined.

There was one table at the exact center, with shelves of books and tomes extending outward in all directions. The books themselves... It was hard to explain exactly how, but they just felt evil.

Several of them seemed to quake on the shelf as he walked past, and he shuddered.

When they reached the center, Master Barrydew moved the table to the side, and the globe was placed where it had once been. Once again, they performed another scan of the room, but this time, found nothing.

Whoever had been cloaked in the entry room hadn't been able to make it all the way inside. There was a long pause, and Master Barrydew gestured at the globe.

"Isa? This is your project. I'd say you have the right to see it through."

Isa let out a long breath and slowly approached the globe. She placed her hands on the outer ring, the wooden rim that ran around the whole thing, and lights flared across the surface.

For a moment, they simply danced this way and that, and then the globe began to spin.

It whirled first one way and then the next, turning over and around and about. Lights continued to sparkle upon the surface, though they took no particular pattern nor did they settle down.

"I think it's getting itself ready," Isa commented. "Almost like it's stretching itself out before it starts exercising, you know?"

Danny nodded. "I just want to know what this thing does."

The other heads in the room nodded. Would it prove to be a weapon so powerful that they shuddered to even contemplate its destructive power? Or would it be something absolutely useless?

It seemed impossible that it would be something in the middle. Finally, the spinning slowed, and the globe whirled around to place the Empire itself in front of Isa so she could see it clearly.

An interface appeared, though it was blurred for Danny's vision. Isa frowned then tapped a button.

"Welcome, all of you." A ghostly image appeared above the globe, depicting a mage in an ancient style of combat robe. It turned to look at all of them then gestured down at the object.

"This is my creation. Well, the creation of myself and my students. We've worked for years to bring this dream to reality, and now... Well, you can see for yourself."

"It's truly a wonder to behold, and I say that on behalf of the countless hours that my students poured into it, not as an attempt to blow my own horn."

"If this is your first time activating the globe, I'm sure you're wondering what exactly it is. In short, this is the culmination of, ultimately, several hundred years of work performed by generations of mages, working quietly and laboriously."

The specter smiled softly. "In the early days of the Empire, as our borders were being settled, a question often asked was what lay beyond. In an attempt to discover this information, a small group was founded. Known then as the Explorers, they struck off into the distant wilderness."

"They brought with them relay crystals, which they then began to set up across the world."

"What are relay crystals?" Isa asked, pausing the ghost. "I've never heard of them before."

"They're a specialized sort of mana crystal that can be used to bounce magic further than you'd ordinarily be able to cast it," Master Barrydew answered. "They're actually quite easy to manufacture, we used to have a class at the academy that did it regularly, but they're not ordinarily deemed to have much real use outside of setting up traps."

Isa frowned then nodded as the ghost continued.

"This group of explorers traveled across the world for several hundred years. Their children, born on the journey, picked up where their parents had left off, until, countless years later, having placed relay crystals across the globe, they returned to the Empire."

"There, atop the Dead Mountains, they placed one final relay crystal, which was able to tap into what had become a global network. This is where my own work began."

"I, a direct descendant of the founders of this great expedition, began the work of translating their data into exact science, into something useful. To do so, I was forced to delve heavily into the research previously drawn up by a man who has little esteem in the community of mages, which may have tarnished my reputation somewhat, but I truly hope that such a stigma hasn't carried along down to my students, or to this globe."

"In any case, with the groundwork laid, this globe can show you nearly anything that is happening on the surface of the world, which is, indeed, round. It can show you settlements, civilizations, dungeons, monsters, and more."

"Ask it a question, and if it is within the realm of what the sensory crystals placed across the globe can sense, it will be able to answer. I do hope that you find this tool as helpful as I intend it to be, and hope that it truly can move our world steadily onward. Farewell."

After the ghost vanished, Danny bit his lip.

"So... It really is just a fancy map?" Obadiah asked. "Have we really wasted all this time?"

"Perhaps." Master Barrydew frowned and walked over to the globe where he placed a hand on top of it then stepped back. "Then again, perhaps not. Globe, could you please show us all centers of civilization throughout the world?"

With a flicker, the globe spun around and white lights appeared across the surface. There was one, brilliant white one in the middle of the Empire, smack where the Imperial City was located.

Beyond that, only a few small specks dotted the rest of the Empire's map, likely the enclaves where the Deepcorp Lord had set things up.

Outside the Empire's boundary and stretching across the continents to the south, the islands to the east and west, across dozens of other landmasses spread out over the face of the world, lights burned brilliantly. Some of them were even brighter than the Imperial City, causing Danny to whistle softly.

"So, we really aren't alone," Master Barrydew murmured.

"Fascinating!" Obadiah commented. "Can I-"

"Wait." Master Barrydew held up a hand. "Now, please show us all dungeon activity throughout the world."

With a flicker, all the white light vanished, replaced by red light. The Empire now became a seething mass of red specks, making it appear as if the whole continent were on fire.

To the immediate south, the landscape burned as well, but, as the map moved on to the lands that were more settled, it became little more than... Well, what might be expected.

Clusters of dungeons here and there, usually close to the places that Danny remembered as being centers of population, but that was it.

"Sometimes I like being unique, and other times, I wouldn't mind just blending in with the rest of the crowd," Zechariah commented.

"You can say that again," Danny muttered then crossed his arms.

Master Barrydew had one more inquiry.

"Please show me where the Deepcorp Lord is located. I imagine you know the one."

The map spun back to show the Empire, and a stab of light rose from the far eastern side. It glimmered then jumped to the south where it seemed to stay.

Danny crossed his arms, and Master Barrydew smiled.

"And that's how we weaponize this." Master Barrydew turned to the others. "We know our enemy, and now, we can track him. We can track the herds without the need of scouts. We can keep track of our own people when we send them out onto missions."

"This isn't a weapon that can just kill everything that crosses our path, but it is something that will likely change the game for us."

"So, what do we do with it from here?" Danny asked.

"We must keep this secret. We must keep it safe," Master Barrydew said. "I want someone watching the Deepcorp Mage at all times. We'll find guards we trust, and put them on a rotation."

"Tess will be able to give a list, I'm sure of it," Danny commented.

"Good." Master Barrydew let out a long breath, and a smile flickered across his face. "We're going to win this, in the end. We're going to come out on top."

He leaned forward, and gazed down at the globe. "And now, we have the weapon we need to do it."

Auto save - [Savefile: Information]
Health: 100%
Mana: 100%
[Quest]: Protect the Globe, make plans for the future
Location: Forbidden Archives
Inventory: Essential Supplies, Basic Armor, Iron Sword, [Sword of the Wasp], [Aquamarine Sword], [Frostbite Sword]
Skills: [Monster Summoner] (Lv. 45), [Flame Combat] (Lv. 2), [Wind Combat] (Lv. 5)
Relationships: Friendly with Isa, Friendly with Obadiah Flamekeeper, Ascended Fire Mage, Family Bond with Zechariah, Ascended Fire Mage, Friendly with Master Barrydew
Time of Day: 12:02 a.m.

Twenty-Six

Reckoning Loss

The next morning, Danny didn't wake up anywhere close to on-time. In fact, it wasn't until he felt someone shoving him out of bed that he opened his eyes.

"What- Ahh!"

With a rather loud thump, he hit the floor, just soft enough not to completely smash his nose into his face. He groaned and slowly climbed back to his feet, where he found Tess glaring down at him.

"You guys tag-teamed the Deepcorp Mage last night and you didn't think to call me?"

"Sorry." Danny rubbed his head. "It was sorta impromptu. Yell at Isa, not at me."

"Oh, she's already heard it from me," Tess scowled, then shrugged. "And, yeah, I got her the list of trustworthy guards. She told me all about the globe, that's so cool!"

"There are really other nations out there?"

"That's what it looks like to us." Danny shrugged. "Don't know anything about them, of course, but it sure made the Empire look pretty sparse by comparison."

"Makes me curious just to think about it." Tess shook her head. "I wonder if we'll be dispatching any exploratory parties when this is all said and done."

"If we wind up surviving this, my guess is that anyone who wants to go check it out will be more than allowed to do so." Danny chuckled.

He sighed and started walking toward the kitchen, yawning loudly. "I'm just glad we have the thing safe and sound, and that all the business with the Deepcorp mage should be taken care of."

"Fool!" The voice was distant but obviously loud enough to echo quite a distance. "Get out of here! You've no business meddling with the Silver Estate!"

Danny sighed as he walked over to his window and pulled it open. There, Boniface came stalking by, chasing after a large, burly man who looked quite like Abraham Silver.

Danny pulled his head back inside.

"What do you need me to do?" Tess asked as he turned around to look at her.

"Go get Radiance," Danny said. "I have a feeling that we're going to need some backup."

"You think it was coincidence that they came by here just now?" Tess asked as they started for the door.

"Nah. It's a big city," Danny replied. "If I had to make a guess, Boniface managed to make sure that they walked this way, and then made sure that one of them hollered loudly enough to get my attention."

"There's going to be trouble, I'd just like to get ahead of it."

"Then I'll head out and get Radiance just as quick as I can."

Tess jogged out of the house and out down the street toward the Academy while Danny strode out and looked down the street in the direction that Boniface and Lot had gone.

He paused, trying to decide if he should wait for backup before deciding to go ahead and follow after them anyway.

As quickly as he could, he dashed down the streets, threading his way through the throngs of people. Ahead, he caught sight of the man he thought was Lot.

He stood almost a head taller than some of the people around and shoved through the crowd with a pompous arrogance that made it clear he was 'someone important.' Danny followed as quickly as he could and caught up with them as they passed through the eastern gate and into the camps beyond.

The outer wall rose in the distance, and Boniface turned slightly to catch Danny's eye. He gave a small nod, and Danny jogged toward Lot.

The huge, former noble caught sight of him and slowly turned.

"What do you want, Academy brat?" he snorted, his eyes opened slightly. "Not just any Academy brat. You're the Academy Brat."

"Youngblood, right? I saw you back at the Silver Estate last year."

Danny gave a small nod. "That's me."

"Then you'll know that I'm no one to be trifled with," Lot snarled, and drew himself up slightly. "Run along, little mage. Run along and leave me alone."

"Do that, and I might just let you live."

"No one to be trifled with." Danny frowned in approval. "That's quite the title, but... See, I'm also no one to be trifled with."

"Yeah?" Lot laughed. "You're what, the same year as little Rad?"

"I am, yes." Danny nodded slowly, then shrugged. "And, in those same five years, I've risen to the rank of Master and currently sit as a Level 45 mage."

"I also more or less single-handedly took down the trolls that were chasing you into the city, freeing Boniface at the same time, which is why I know you have your brother contained somewhere within the city."

"You don't know anything." Lot snarled, though he suddenly looked a lot less confident. Ice crystals began to form across his fingers, and Danny braced himself.

He snapped his fingers, and a stone golem appeared behind him, snarling down at the interloper. Lot looked up at the monster and turned somewhat pale, and Danny gave him a nod.

"Now, where's your brother?"

Lot shook his head. "Like I said, you don't know what you're asking. Lay off it, summoner."

"I'm asking you, once more," Danny pressed.

By now, a small crowd was gathering. With a flash, a second golem appeared right behind Lot and placed its hands on his shoulders.

Lot suddenly looked rather sick.

"Where is your brother?" Danny repeated.

With a crash, Lot Silver kicked open a door leading down into a basement apartment. As he sighed and gestured for them to enter, Danny raised an eyebrow.

After a moment, Lot gave in and went inside first, grumbling and grunting all the way. Danny followed, finding himself in what amounted to a little studio apartment.

Whoever had once owned it was long gone, as the cobwebs strung up through the corners of the room made it clear that no one had lived there for a good, long while. Abraham Silver sat in the corner on a chair, bound tightly with a magical cable.

His eyes went wide as the party stomped inside, and Lot reluctantly walked over and unbound him.

"Ahh!" Abraham slowly climbed to his feet and rubbed his wrists then his jaw. "Many thanks, Youngblood. Ahh... Master Youngblood?"

"Are those master stripes on your robes?"

Danny bowed his head. "I'm told I was promoted, yes."

"Well, from what I've seen, it was certainly well-earned!" Abraham sighed then glanced at his brother. "As for you, you should rot in the darkest jail cell that's been forged in this city!"

"You should hang, you should-"

"I think a more fitting punishment might be a tour of duty with the Imperial Corp?" Danny suggested with a small smile. "A way to really work off his infraction?"

Lot turned pale. "How dare you suggest that I-"

"I think it an excellent suggestion!" Abraham clapped Lot on the shoulder. "I don't suppose you know someone who would be able to facilitate such a thing?"

"As a matter of fact, I do." Danny gave a small nod. "A commander who knows how to keep mages in mind. Shall we get moving?"

From that point, it took a little while to get everyone back together. They had to actually find Tess and Radiance, who had made their way back to Danny's house, since, of course, they didn't know where to go.

From there, it took some time to find a place to meet. Eventually, though, they wound up back in the Academy, with Lot being led away by a handful of soldiers to begin his punishment.

He looked angry, but he also knew that there was nowhere else in the country to run, and Danny would find him if he tried to shirk his duty. The rest of them, Tess, Radiance, Danny, Abraham, along with Master Barrydew and Zechariah, all sat down in the library where they could see the city out through the immense windows.

"I have to say, I never thought I would abandon the Silver Estate for anything," Abraham murmured, tapping his hands against the table where they sat.

"I'm just glad you're alive, dad." Radiance leaned into him then paused. "So, where's everyone else? Surely two carriages weren't the only people who made it to the city?"

"I can't speak for everyone else." Abraham shook his head. "Lot and I were the last ones to leave. After the dragon struck, we urged everyone to evacuate."

"Most people did, though a few people decided to stay. We stuck around to make sure that we helped everyone who was staying get settled in, and to make sure that everyone leaving was able to get on the road quickly and efficiently."

He shook his head. "If they made it into the city, they made it ahead of us. Some of them left a good week before we did."

"I have no idea how many of them made it, and how many of them didn't."

Zechariah grimaced. "I'm so sorry to hear that. I've always had a fondness for the Silver Estate."

"When I was fighting on the northern fronts, we would sometimes have to go over to your land for one reason or another. It was always a good time, if for no other reason than to see what you had managed to do over there."

"It was stunning to behold."

"Don't remind me." Abraham grumbled, then shook his head. "But I'm getting ahead of myself. My ancestors carved that estate from the ice and the mountains with their bare hands, and I'll do the same again."

"Sure, it'll take a few years, maybe a few generations, but the Silver Family will be proud of it once again."

"I'm sure they will." Zechariah flashed a thin smile.

"Pardon me." Master Barrydew spoke up. "I was, however, curious about the dragon that attacked your estate."

"Mm. Yes." Abraham nodded. "It was a frost dragon, very rare but very dangerous. I have reason to believe that it came from a dungeon far to the north, the Rolling Snow dungeon."

"I've heard of it," Zechariah said. "We never had to clean it out, your own mages always took care of it."

"It's been one of the hidden gems of the Silver Estate for years," Abraham said. "It holds dozens of treasures within its depths, we carefully maintained it to ensure that it would never overflow while we harvested its many treasures."

"What I can't figure, though, is... Well, exactly that! The dragon should only have spawned if it had been abandoned for a good six months, and I know we cleaned it out only three months ago."

"We made sure the beast would never spawn, as it provided an immense hazard without actually providing any loot. The nest of dragon eggs spawned independently of the dragon, so... There was no need of it."

Master Barrydew grimaced. "Unfortunately, on our journeys, we've been encountering more and more dungeons that have upgraded in rank. It's possible that it was uplifted to an S-rank, or something like that."

"I suppose." Abraham shrugged. "In any case, the dragon got away. I can give you the flight pattern, if you like."

"Flight pattern?" Zechariah asked.

"Yes." Abraham nodded. "Dragons, when they escape their dungeons, will always fly in a set pattern, usually a figure-eight spread out over a hundred miles or so."

"You knew that, didn't you?"

There was an uncomfortable silence as the mages all looked at one another. Finally, Danny held up his hand.

"As the current Monster Theory professor here, I can confirm that no, we didn't have a clue that dragons did that."

"Ahh! Well, then it'll please you to know that it's a fact," Abraham said. "And, when the dragon came down from the dungeon, it was following the pattern to the letter."

"That much, at least, hasn't changed even if other things have. You wouldn't happen to have a map, would you?"

A smile came over Master Barrydew's face. "As a matter of fact, we would."

It took them almost no time to make their way into the Forbidden Archives where a guard stood next to the magical globe. A beam of light clearly showed the location of the Deepcorp Mage down in the southern reaches of the Empire.

As the guard stepped back respectfully, Abraham whistled sharply.

"Now this is a machine. What dungeon did you pull this from?"

"Now that's a long story," Danny said.

"Just step up to the globe and... Well, it ought to be pretty self-explanatory," Master Barrydew said.

Abraham nodded and approached the globe. "Ahh... There's an interface here... Let's see... Alright... Transferring the flight pattern from my mind to the globe..."

With a flash, a brilliant figure-eight appeared on the northern portion of the Empire. It ran from the Silver Estate to a position due north of the Imperial City then back around to cross over the Silver Estate only to loop far to the east before returning again.

The mages stared at it for a moment.

"Will the dragon pursue things it finds intriguing?" Danny asked. "How far will it deviate from its flight path?"

"At least in theory, it might go across the whole of the Empire," Abraham said. "Why?"

"Because not too long ago, a dragon attacked me, one that had come from thousands of miles away," Danny murmured. "I was just wondering what it might take to return the favor."

"You want to use the dragon?" Master Barrydew spun to face Danny.

"Not necessarily this dragon, but a dragon. I don't know." Danny shook his head. "I'm just thinking through options."

"We have this guy on the ropes, and I'd like to keep him there. If we sent him a little present down at his hidden refuge... Wouldn't be the end of the world, in my mind."

"Maybe not, but that's a slippery slope, in my mind," Master Barrydew said. "Let's sleep on it, and we can decide in a few days. Or even a few weeks."

Danny flashed a thin smile. They soon left the Forbidden Archives, though not without returning the globe to display the location of the Deepcorp Mage.

He certainly wasn't moving much anymore, which Danny hoped meant that he was wounded far more than they realized. As they made their way through the halls, Abraham continued to speak of the Silver Estate and how he hoped he could help the city, while Danny's mind turned only to the matter at hand.

He was desperate to put things to end, for good.

He only wished that he knew, for sure, that trying to use a dragon would work.

Auto save - [Savefile: Information]
Health: 100%
Mana: 100%
[Quest Update] Figure out how to weaponize... Pretty much anything
Location: Forbidden Archives
Inventory: Essential Supplies, Basic Armor, Iron Sword, Sword of the Wasp, Aquamarine Sword, Frostbite Sword
Skills: Monster Summoner (Lv. 45), Flame Combat (Lv. 2), Wind Combat (Lv. 5)
Relationships: Family Bond with Zechariah, Ascended Fire Mage, Friendly with Master Barrydew, Friendly with Tess, Friendly with Abraham Silver, Ascended Ice Mage
Time of Day: 11:14 a.m.

Twenty-Seven

Hunger

"Hey, Danny." A knock echoed on the door of Danny's classroom, and he looked up to see Tess poking her head inside. "You got a minute?"

"Yeah, for sure." Danny set down his pen. "I'm just grading some papers, come on in."

"Danny the professor." Tess shook her head as she walked over and sat on the corner of a desk. "I pegged you for it back when we were first-years, but I did sorta think you'd wait until you graduated."

"I think a lot of us thought we'd wait to do a whole lot of things until after graduation," Danny murmured. "I think Master Barrydew mostly has me doing this to keep me busy, but-"

"But, in all fairness, most of the qualified mages are on patrol around the city," Tess said. "Which means it's either you, or the students go without classes."

"Exactly." Danny grimaced and leaned back in his chair.

He glanced at the door, almost getting up to close it, but Tess stopped him.

"If you're looking to complain about something, you might as well wait until we're outside city limits, where no one can really hear you."

Danny frowned and straightened in his chair. "What are you talking about?"

"Right! I'm supposed to ask you before just assuming you'll help." Tess shook her head. "Silly me. Obadiah came to me, said he got a tip about a cache of food to the south of the city."

"Like a lot of food?" Danny raised an eyebrow.

"Enough to give us another week or so before people start dying of starvation," Tess answered. "I'd say that's enough for me."

Danny frowned, then shrugged and climbed to his feet. "How many people are going?"

"Just us. And Margot." Tess paused and scratched the back of her head. "This hasn't exactly gone through official channels."

"What do you mean by 'exactly'?" Danny asked.

"It means he brought this to the Emperor's attention and was told to forget about it, that it was too risky," Tess said. "So... He decided to take matters into his own hands. Forgiveness, permission, and all that."

"Yeah, but it's harder to ask forgiveness when permission has been clearly denied." Danny shrugged and started for the door. "Thankfully, I at least have plausible deniability. Where are we heading?"

Tess and Danny soon made their way back out through the Academy, the city, and all the way to the southern gate of the outer wall. There, soldiers patrolled while several of them fought a large cat.

Obadiah was with them and threw a flaming spear through the beast right as it charged at Margot, who stood nearby. The beast fell dead, and the two mages walked over to Danny and Tess as the soldiers continued on their way.

"Thanks for coming." He flashed a smile at them. "I... I don't have any horses, due to the irregular nature of this mission."

"You were denied your request, so there was no reason for them to provide horses," Danny surmised. He shrugged and snapped his fingers, summoning his own horses. "You'll have to ride bareback, but I promise they won't buck you off unless you annoy me."

Obadiah laughed and quickly mounted one of them. Tess took another horse, Margot mounted just next to Tess, and Danny took the last one.

With that, they shot off across the prairie, racing south across the rolling hills. They flew over the burned and scorched area, and Danny glanced to the side toward where Nicodemus and Barbara had faced off against the Deepcorp Lords.

It made his heart ache, but he swallowed it down and forced his way onward.

"So where are we going?" Danny asked as they swept along.

"There's an estate about six miles south," Obadiah called out. "I've known about it for some time, but I happened to meet with the owner. They've been in town for a while, managed to secure one of the nicer apartments."

"He told me he had these vaults where he'd been storing food and other supplies for emergencies. He'd been hoarding it while hope held out that all this would end, but now he wants to turn it over to the city, to do at least a little good before it all comes crashing down."

"He sounds like a good man," Danny commented.

"He is," Obadiah confirmed, then snarled softly. "Our Emperor, on the other hand... When he came out of hiding, he really sounded like he had a good head on his shoulders, but now all I hear is garbage."

"He's given up on our survival, he just wants to rule the roost while it all comes crashing down around us."

"Danny has a beef with him, too," Tess commented.

Danny grimaced. He didn't have a beef with the Emperor so much as the Deepcorp Lord manipulating the Emperor's mind, but that was something he wanted to keep close to his chest.

"I'm just frustrated that I'm not allowed to go out and do anything. I'm rarely allowed on patrol, and I'm not allowed to do anything about the monsters stampeding toward our city."

"I just want to... You know..." He sighed. "Do something. They want me in reserve in case they need me, but if they'd just use my talents, they wouldn't need me in reserve, you know?"

"Strange as it sounds, yes, I understand completely," Obadiah laughed. They raced out the southern side of the burned area, and Danny glimpsed stone walls running across the hills to his left.

"I wish I had a better answer for you. Part of me wants to tell you to just trust the Emperor, to stick to orders and everything will be okay. The other part wants you to run off and become a lone ranger, just do what needs doing and let the chips fall where they may."

"That's probably not the right thing, if everyone did that we'd have anarchy, but... Still. It does sound nice."

They soon came to a small road that turned off to the side, and Obadiah led the way as they left the main path and went down through the rolling hills. It dropped sharply into a ravine, mostly keeping to the low paths after that.

After a quarter-mile or so it came up once more, fully into view of the walls Danny had glimpsed earlier.

A gate stood across the path, held up by two immense columns at the ends of a large, stone wall that stood about twenty feet high and wrapped across the prairie. There were quite a few large gaps in the wall now, likely due to monsters smashing through.

But the parts still standing were impressive. Instead of opening the gate, they rode to one of the openings and slipped through, where once more Danny found himself more than a little amazed.

The estate was nowhere near as large as the Silver Estate, but it still covered many square miles. From where they stood, the ground fell away, allowing them to see the vast majority of it in a single glimpse.

A lovely, tree-lined drive ran along to an immense home made of limestone and built in a wonderful, castle-like style. Beyond that were gardens, large fountains, and several ponds connected by little rivulets.

It was wonderful to behold, and Danny whistled.

"Come on," Obadiah ordered. "We need to get moving."

They swept down the drive and through the trees, up to the large, iron doors of the home. As was the case with so much these days, the windows were all broken, the door was ajar, and the walls were covered in claw marks.

It was sad to see such a great estate in such disrepair. Obadiah walked forward and pulled the door open, then carefully stepped inside.

The entry hall was in utter ruin. Priceless porcelain lay scattered and broken, paintings were clawed and slashed, tapestries hung in tatters.

Somewhere else in the house, something fell, and Obadiah let a few flames trickle down from his fingers.

"Tread lightly," he murmured. "I doubt we're alone here."

Danny nodded, and Obadiah set off through the home. He seemed to know the way, likely having been given a description from the owner.

They moved to the kitchen which had three separate hearths and an immense array of cookery (which was now scattered over just about everything). There, Obadiah pulled open a closet where he bent down and pulled up a trap door.

Soon, they were down in a hidden basement with Obadiah creating floating balls of flame to light the way.

"This was his secret cellar," Obadiah murmured as they walked along a narrow, arched tunnel made from cobblestone. A few doors opened off to the sides, but he paid them little mind and simply pressed forward.

"Most of these rooms hold statues or documents. One of them holds some particularly fine vintages of wine, I'm told. Down here... Ahh."

The little balls of flame ahead revealed an iron door that sat in the wall. It had a handful of locking mechanisms across the front.

Obadiah whistled as he approached it. "Now this is a beauty. Probably costs as much as the rest of the estate."

He leaned forward and took hold of a little knob in the exact center which was covered in little markings. "I've only seen one of these once before, and-"

"Stop!" a harsh voice commanded.

Obadiah turned. Danny did the same while Tess drew her sword.

Emerging from the darkness by stepping out of one of the side rooms was an older woman. She wasn't so old as to be infirm, but she certainly looked to be at least sixty years old.

She held a crossbow in her hands which she had pointed squarely at Obadiah.

"I may not be much to look at anymore, but I swore to protect the belongings of my master, and I'll do that until my dying day," she snapped.

"Ahh..." Danny blinked a few times. "You would be-"

"Madame Laforte," Obadiah said. "Your master mentioned you when I spoke to him."

"He... He did." She blinked a few times. "How so?"

"He... he believes that you're most likely dead," Obadiah said. "He told me to look for your remains and bring them back with us when we returned, if we could find them."

"The old goat." The woman lowered the crossbow and snorted. "I told him we should have left weeks before he finally did. I told him it was getting too dangerous, but no!"

"No, he wanted to stick around, to make his claim on the land, and then when that horde of orcs came through in the middle of the night, he fled, and I was left behind."

She sighed and set down the crossbow. "I'd wondered why no one came back for me, but I knew I couldn't make the journey on my own."

"Well, we can take you back with us," Obadiah answered. "He asked me to transfer his food supplies to the city. Things are bad there, we could really use it."

Madame Laforte sighed then shrugged. "Well, if he gave you permission... You knew my name, so you obviously either spoke to him or really did your research. Go ahead and take it. Won't do me any good here, nor him there."

Obadiah nodded and turned back to the lock. Suddenly, a low growl echoed through the air.

Danny frowned.

Madame Laforte gasped, and she snatched up her crossbow once more. "You brought them down here!"

As she spun and fired, an orcish scream of pain echoed through the air. With that, Danny grabbed her and pulled her back, putting himself between her and the oncoming monster.

Well... Monsters. Plural. Half a dozen of the ugly humanoids were racing down the hall, weapons drawn, snarling and snapping.

The lead one had an arrow sticking out of his chest, but it didn't seem to be slowing him down all that much.

"All lined up for me," Danny said. "Too easy."

With a flash, a stone golem suddenly filled the tunnel between the two groups. The orcs let out a scream of fear as the golem lunged forward, crushing them into a pulp, but there was very little they could do.

A moment later, the way out was clear, though Danny could sense a great many more monsters rumbling around through the building above.

"Sounds like we attracted some trouble." He glanced at Obadiah. "You almost done? We're going to have to get out of here pretty fast, I think."

"Almost... Got it!"

With a sharp ping, the door swung open, and they quickly rushed inside. As Danny ran into the vault, which was a massive room packed full of crates, he felt a glimmer of hope.

Things were dire, but people were beginning to fight back. It wasn't completely hopeless.

It couldn't be. Not if the world was going to survive.

With this, the citizens of the Imperial City were going to keep kicking just a little bit longer.

Auto save - [Savefile: Information]
Health: 100%
Mana: 67%
[Quest]: Transfer the food back to the Imperial City
Location: Hidden Vault, Auclair Estate
Inventory: Essential Supplies, Basic Armor, Iron Sword, [Sword of the Wasp], [Aquamarine Sword], [Frostbite Sword]
Skills: [Monster Summoner] (Lv. 45), [Flame Combat] (Lv. 2), [Wind Combat] (Lv. 5)
Relationships: Friendly with Obadiah, Ascended Fire Mage, Friendly with Margot, Friendly with Tess, Speaking Terms with Madame Laforte
Time of Day: 3:48 p.m.

Twenty-Eight

Dragonrider

"Your actions are nothing less than complete and utter insubordination!" Emperor Ezra was furious as he stalked back and forth across the front of the throne room.

Danny, Obadiah, Tess, and Margot stood there, heads high, while a handful of attendants and other mages busied themselves and tried not to look like they were listening.

"I gave you very specific instructions, Obadiah. Very specific," the emperor continued.

Obadiah kept his head high. "The people will eat because of what I did."

"And I don't deny that." Emperor Ezra sighed and pressed his fingers to his temples. "Look, I realize now that I should have given you permission. It was a lapse in judgement, and I'll own that."

"However, what I expect you to own is the fact that you clearly disregarded an Emperor's orders, went behind my back, and journeyed into enemy territory without any of the proper safeguards that we have in place for that very thing."

Obadiah bowed his head slightly. "I'll own that."

"Good." Emperor Ezra sighed. Danny could practically see the weight of the young man's office pressing down upon him, crushing him into the floor.

"For what it's worth, I'm sorry I denied your initial request. You did good work, Obadiah."

"Thank you, sir," Obadiah said.

"As punishment for your insubordination, you're consigned to work night patrol on the wall for the next week before returning to your normal duties," Emperor Ezra ordered. "And, in the future, if you think I'm off my rocker, come and express it to my face, personally."

"If a second incident like this happens, the consequences will be more severe. I don't want to appear too harsh, but in times like this, the moment that order starts to break down, society itself crumbles."

"At the moment, this city is being held on a thread. One wrong move, and we plunge into looting and anarchy."

"I can't have that wrong move coming from some of my most trusted warriors." He sighed. "Dismissed."

The group left the throne room as the emperor called in several soldiers to begin discussing tactics. Danny grimaced as he looked over his shoulder, but he was shooed out by several guards.

Soon, the small group was walking through the city streets, angling back toward the Academy. A cold wind blew through the streets, while clouds seemed to be darkening the southern horizon.

A storm was likely on its way; a big one from the feel of the wind.

"Well, that could have been worse," Tess commented as they walked along. "You got off pretty good."

"I agree." Obadiah paused for a moment. "What he said was good, though. I should have come back to him instead of simply taking matters into my own hand."

"We still have food reserves in the city, we weren't at the point of total starvation, which means that I had the time to approach him. I didn't take that time."

He turned to the younger mages, and flashed a thin smile. "Take that for what it's worth."

Danny gave a nod while Tess just shrugged. With that, he and Margot struck off toward their home while Danny and Tess made their way back up toward the Academy.

They were nearly there when a messenger came running up to Tess, a piece of paper in her hands.

"Tess! You're needed out on the wall. A fight just broke out between some of your soldiers."

Tess nodded. "I'll be right there. Thanks for the heads-up."

With that, she was gone, leaving Danny alone. He made his way up and into the Academy.

At the library, he sat down at a table looking out across the city and drummed his fingers on the table.

"Copper for your thoughts?" Master Barrydew walked up and sat down next to him, looking more haggard than usual. "I heard about what you did. Good move, if you ask me."

"The Emperor chewed us out pretty good, but I think he did make some good points," Danny muttered. "Obadiah took it well, in any case."

"Good, good," Master Barrydew said. "The Auclair Estate is a family I've known for some time. They're similar to the Silver Family, former nobles who had their royalty credentials removed when the Corp formed."

"Instead of maintaining a vast estate, they withdrew into the estate that you saw, where they've really been quite content. They've produced a handful of mages that have served in the dungeons, I have very little but respect for them."

"Madam Laforte was still guarding her master's goods even though he had left her alone... Months ago, now," Danny said. "It's some level of dedication."

He paused, then turned to Master Barrydew. "Can I change the subject? Like... Immensely change the subject?"

"Go for it," Master Barrydew said. "What's in your mind?"

"The Deepcorp Lord," Danny answered. "I've been thinking about him a lot."

"We all have been." Master Barrydew's voice was quiet. "Mostly, I keep thinking over his attacks. He seems to be a fire mage, he was quite proficient with-"

"I think he's a summoner."

Master Barrydew paused, then folded his hands. "What makes you say that? You saw his flame attacks."

"I did, but I also know that he said that he saw the Empire rise the first time." Danny shrugged.

"Maybe true, maybe not, but we already know that they can keep themselves alive longer than normal. If he somehow is that old, it's plausible that he's leveled up other skills as well."

"Plus..." Danny shrugged. "If you'll remember my research from a year ago or so, the original summoners had other skills as well. It wasn't until later on that summoning was substantially disconnected from things like fire magic or wind magic."

"Mm, right." Master Barrydew paused and shook his head. "You really think that could be the case?"

"I do. The way he can manipulate minds... I don't know. It reminds me of the way that I can reach out with my summoning to affect people," Danny answered.

"I've never tried to make someone do something they didn't want to do, but I've been able to separate magically conjoined twins, I've been able to naturalize dungeon monsters, I've been able to do a handful of such things. It doesn't seem to me to be out of the question, and it lines up well with what I already know."

"Hmm." Master Barrydew shrugged. "I don't know. It's certainly worth some thought."

He sighed and climbed to his feet. "I have to be getting along, I have a meeting with Headmaster Bluestream. Good talking to you, Danny."

Danny nodded, then paused. "Hey! Real fast, is there any chance I can see the globe?"

Master Barrydew hesitated. "You have something specific you're wanting to do with it?"

"Yeah," Danny confirmed. "It's hard to explain, but there's been a bug crawling around in the back of my mind for a few days now. I'd just like to see what it's capable of."

"Well... Sure. My meeting isn't for another half hour, and the headmaster is always late, anyway." Master Barrydew gestured at the door. "Come."

They soon performed all the necessary scans and checks to ensure that no one else was there as the two mages stood before the globe. The guard stepped back, nodding to the object which still showed the Deepcorp Lord as hiding in the south of the Empire, though in a slightly different location than before.

Danny frowned and leaned over it, placing his hands on the rim of the globe.

[Welcome to the Explorer Globe. What can I do for you? Please select from the following list of options, or simply think or say what you'd like me to do.][Show all dungeons in the world][Show all settlements in the world][Show all monsters outside of dungeons in the world][Display safe travel routes][...]

Danny glanced through the options. "Show me if there's any civilization near the Deepcorp Lord right now."

The globe adjusted itself slightly. The Deepcorp Lord himself turned red while several small specks of white light appeared nearby.

[There are no settlements nearby. The Deepcorp Lord is hiding in a large spire of rock, the closest living human is fifty-three miles away]

"Sounds like he's in Castle Rock." Danny chuckled as he thought over his next move. "Obadiah will be pleased."

Master Barrydew chuckled, and Danny pressed forward. "Now... Show me all dragon flight patterns that cross within one hundred miles of that location, as well as the current location of said dragons."

Master Barrydew shifted slightly, but Danny didn't stop. Glowing lines appeared across the globe, depicting no fewer than four in the area.

One of them actually made a large circle that more or less had Castle Rock as the center. Another had an elaborate, bow-tie route that passed not terribly far from the rock, while the other two were, essentially, three-loop figure-eights.

Danny paused as he looked it over, noting the locations of the dragons themselves, which were shown as slightly brighter points of light on the routes. He leaned forward, noticing two of them were quite close.

Now, I need to connect to them.

He didn't know whether the globe could do that or not. Suddenly, though, as he reached out into the globe with his monster summoning powers, he felt himself drawn up and away, out across the Imperial City, out across the city.

In the blink of an eye, he could see in his mind's eye the two dragons, flying along through the air. Both of them twitched their heads as Danny's mind was detected, and he balled his hands into fists.

One of the dragons was a blue dragon, two hundred feet long. The other was a red and black dragon and looked to be a good five hundred feet in length.

Danny let out a deep breath at the sight of the beast. He slowly closed his eyes then focused entirely upon the black and red dragon.

I order you to attack castle rock.

The dragon roared loudly, and suddenly it was as if Danny was sitting on the back of the beast. It raged and began to buck about.

He could see the ground, far below, and he could feel the air rushing past him. He could feel every bone and muscle in the great beast, and he could feel the overwhelming fire brewing up within its heart, raging against him with every ounce of power it had.

Truly, it had a lot of power.

You will obey me! Danny ordered. Now!

The dragon spun its head around and looked Danny in the eye. It was huge and oppressive, punching straight through his soul.

Danny felt flames flickering around his fingertips, burning through his body, and he let out a muffled cry. It was going to burn him to death.

He heard Master Barrydew and the guard charge forward, and he knew he only had seconds.

"Fine," he muttered. "Have it your way. Green... Dragon... Scorcher."

He didn't properly summon the monster, but he pulled it firmly into his mind, into that mental battle of wills that spanned a thousand miles. In his mind's eye, he felt the resolve of the red and black dragon suddenly facing off with another dragon, another beast of its own might and mind.

Suddenly, dragon fire surged back into the heart of the black and red dragon, and Danny gritted his teeth.

Wham!

He suddenly saw the two dragons tumbling through the air, fighting and clawing with one another. It was a battle of will, a sheer contest of might and mind.

The green dragon blasted the other with fire, and the gesture was returned in kind. Danny kept his own mind focused upon the great beast and sent one final message.

You will attack the castle rock. Then, you will be free.

The red and black dragon let out a roar that shook the ground far below, then spun and flew away. Danny followed it, the magic of the globe as his power, and watched as castle rock appeared on the horizon.

The red dragon flapped faster and faster, likely eager to get Danny out of his mind, and opened his mouth wide.

The beast had to have been moving at at a good two hundred miles per hour when it struck the stone. Instead of simply performing a strafing run, it swooped down low, flying only feet above the ground, then launched three fireballs in rapid succession.

They struck the base of the immense spire, blasting a hole clean through and melting the stone up to an immense height. A second later, the dragon flew straight through the thing, blasting it into nothing more than slag.

As it came out the other side, perhaps simply to humor Danny, it roared again, launching one final flame attack that melted the entire area. Hundreds of feet in all directions were covered with flowing rivers of magma.

Danny gave a nod.

Thank you.

The dragon glared at him once more. If I ever meet you in the flesh, I will destroy you.

The threat echoed through Danny's mind, and the connection was broken. With that, Danny snapped back to the forbidden archives where he found Master Barrydew and the guard trying desperately to pry his hands off the rim of the globe.

He gasped and let go, falling backward and landing on the ground. Smoke drifted up from his clothes, and he suddenly found it difficult to move.

It looked as though his fingers had burned marks into the wood of the globe's table. He groaned and slowly rolled over onto his side.

"What... Why..." Master Barrydew gasped. "What just happened?"

"Forgiveness, permission, and all that," Danny groaned and slowly sat up. Every part of him hurt.

"Well, you're suffering from severe mana burns," Master Barrydew grumbled. "We've got to get you to an infirmary."

"Wait." Danny gestured at the globe. "Where's... Where's the lord?"

Master Barrydew shrugged and stood up. A moment later, a pinpoint of white light appeared on the globe.

It had moved to the east and was far weaker.

"It says that his life force is so diminished that it can barely sense him at all." Master Barrydew shrugged. "Looks like you did some good."

Danny sighed, and allowed the guard to help him to his feet. "Good," he whispered as he allowed himself to be led away, on down toward the hospital.

Whether or not he got a proper ripping for it, like Obadiah, he had done some good. And, unlike Obadiah, he hadn't been told no beforehand.

All things considered, he counted it as a win.

He only hoped that, in the long run, it would help.

Auto save - [Savefile: Information]
Health: 30% (capped)
Mana: 1% (capped)
[Quest Update] Proceed to the infirmary
Location: Forbidden Archives, Library
Inventory: Essential Supplies, Basic Armor, Iron Sword, Sword of the Wasp, Aquamarine Sword, Frostbite Sword
Skills: Monster Summoner (Lv. 45), Flame Combat (Lv. 2), Wind Combat (Lv. 5)
Relationships: Friendly with Master Barrydew
Time of Day: 8:56 a.m.

Twenty-Nine

Orders

Danny spent the next week in the hospital. He was certain he could have gotten up and about by the second day or so, but judging from the nurses' looks, he was basically being placed on house arrest for his actions.

Still, he had a hard time feeling bad about them. He had done some good, hopefully a lot of good, and that was something that hadn't happened for a long time.

In any case, when he was finally released, he was sore from laying in bed so long, but all his wounds were healed and everything seemed to be forgiven. Zechariah escorted him out of the Research Wing and put his arm around him as they started up the stairs.

"I'm glad you're feeling better," Zechariah commented then laughed softly. "The two of us need to stop getting put in there!"

"I don't disagree." Danny laughed as well then sighed deeply and nodded upward. "Where are we heading?"

"The Headmaster's office," Zechariah answered. "He asked to see you, the moment you were allowed out and about."

Danny's gut twisted, but he nodded. They climbed flight after flight of stairs, soon reaching the Headmaster's office located in the Academy's highest spire.

There, the door opened as soon as they knocked, and they stepped through to find Headmaster Bluestream sitting at his desk, with Master Barrydew just across from him. Danny flashed a small smile as they approached, and the Headmaster slowly climbed to his feet.

"Master Youngblood." Headmaster Bluestream inclined his head. "I'm glad to see you're on your feet again."

"So he can go get into more trouble, I suppose," Master Barrydew commented wryly.

"I'm sorry I didn't tell you what I was about to do." Danny sighed and walked over next to his old master.

As everyone took a seat, Danny folded his hands. "I should have said something."

"No, you probably did the right thing. No way I would have let you try something so foolish." Master Barrydew could only shrug. "He hasn't moved from his new location in a week. Still seems pretty badly injured, as far as the globe can tell."

"We've had the device look in on him, and it seems he's buried pretty deep underground, some sort of bunker beneath an old lava flow, out on the southern coastline."

Danny frowned and nodded. "If we hit him again-"

"Absolutely not." Headmaster Bluestream shook his head. "It's utterly out of the question."

Danny gave a small nod, and the headmaster rose and turned to look out the window. Dark clouds were starting to blow across the city, heralding the fast approaching winter.

"Have you met with the Emperor recently?"

Danny shook his head. "Not since I got chewed out for getting food from the old estate. Why?"

"Because, since you attacked the dark lord, he's been even more erratic than usual." Headmaster Bluestream turned back around and raised an eyebrow. "His orders are chaotic, changing on a dime."

"I know there were rumors that the dark lord had influenced him even before this, but I can only assume that the dark lord somehow cursed him from a distance. I truly don't believe he's actively influencing the Emperor, but I do suspect he did something out of retribution, and it's making life rather difficult."

"I can go try to drive out-"

"I have healers working on the issue." Headmaster Bluestream turned sharply. "Curses are not the same as possessions, and dark lords are not the same as evil spirits."

"I suppose so." Danny crossed his arms. "So what's going on here? Why have I been asked here?"

"Because, Master Youngblood, we stand on the precipice of disaster," Headmaster Bluestream answered. "Our city is balanced on the edge of a knife, as they say. If we tip in either direction, or if our weight simply causes us to be cut in two, we will all die."

"We must survive the winter, and come spring, we need to have hope. If that doesn't happen, I'm afraid the last remnants of this Empire will dissolve."

"You sound like an Emperor yourself," Danny commented.

"If our real Emperor won't be, then someone must step in." Headmaster Bluestream turned back to the windows. "Please don't mistake me. I'm not making a power grab, but something must be done or the death toll will be catastrophic."

"As such, several others and myself are laying plans."

Danny frowned. "What sort of plans?"

"Nothing that you need to concern yourself with. Yet..." Headmaster Bluestream sighed. "The second herd of monsters will arrive in about one month's time. I want you to make yourself stronger, do everything you can to prepare for it."

"Go on patrol, fight monsters, just make sure it falls within any existing guidelines you have, so the Emperor doesn't become suspicious and grow angry. If he was cursed, it's likely the dark lord added some part to the curse making him do things that will hurt us, and that will almost certainly involve impeding your efforts to become stronger."

"Make sure you don't cross any lines that will draw his ire."

"I... I see." Danny frowned and slowly climbed to his feet.

As he did so, Master Barrydew shifted and glanced at Zechariah, who gave a nod.

"What?" Danny asked, confused. "Something I'm missing?"

Master Barrydew sighed, then nodded. "Even though we've done what we can to keep things under wraps, word of the globe has leaked out. No one outside our circle knows precisely what it does, but word on the street is that there are countries out there which haven't been taken down by these hordes of monsters."

"There's a growing movement among the civilians to try and make a run for one of those. To form a caravan, or an army, or something like that, and to just abandon ship, so to speak."

Danny frowned. "Would that even be possible, on such a large scale?"

"Depends on what you define as possible, and how you rate the risks of staying here." Zechariah answered. "If you're convinced we're all going to die here anyway, might be worth the risk to get out of here to make a run at heading south. Punch across the desert, it's only about a thousand miles to our closest neighbor."

"And how would they respond to an entire nation suddenly trying to pile into their borders?" Danny asked with a small laugh.

"That much... I don't have a clue. Likely not well, though," Headmaster Bluestream answered. "There are many issues with the plan, though I suppose I don't need to tell you that. We need to get this situation under control, and we need to do it quickly."

"Danny, you have your orders." He put his hands behind his back. "Get to it. Now."

Danny nodded and slowly rose and walked out of the meeting. As the darkened clouds rolled over the city, he couldn't help but feel that, even in defeat, the dark lord had somehow managed to secure a victory.

The real question was exactly how cursed the Emperor was and whether or not it would have long-lasting effects.

Danny hurled himself into his work with relentless intensity. He continued teaching his class, alternating days with Zechariah, but every free moment was spent on the frontlines.

There, he battled monstrous hordes, fighting tooth and nail for every scrap of experience he could glean. His fervor was such that he would have been out there every waking hour, but strict military orders enforced rest days between rotations to prevent exhaustion.

Remembering his pledge not to upset the Emperor, Danny adhered to these orders with begrudging precision, though not always in spirit. He was invariably the first to charge into battle and the last to retreat, often spending his teaching days in a haze of fatigue, barely keeping his eyes open.

As the month drew to a close, Danny's relentless efforts bore fruit—he leveled up. This small victory was a welcome spark of hope as winter's icy fingers clawed at the city.

Refugees huddled closer, their makeshift shelters pressed against the city walls like frightened children. They clustered in every nook and cranny, desperate to shield themselves from the merciless elements.

The air grew heavy with foreboding as the monstrous horde's distant rumble became a constant, terrifying reminder of impending doom. It was in this atmosphere of creeping dread that Danny awoke one morning to a summons from the Emperor himself.

The throne room Danny entered was a study in somber grandeur. As the doors sealed shut behind him with an ominous boom, the howling wind outside seemed to mock their fragile safety.

Despite the numerous blazing hearths throughout the palace, an insidious chill wormed its way into Danny's bones. At the far end of the chamber stood Emperor Ezra, a solitary figure of authority amidst the encroaching chaos.

He stood motionless before his war table, eyes fixed on the map of his beleaguered Empire, fingers absently stroking his chin as if trying to conjure solutions from thin air.

"Something I can do for you, your majesty?" Danny knelt briefly before the Emperor.

He glanced around, confused. There were no other people in the room, no aides, no guards, nothing.

Emperor Ezra paused, then slowly turned to look at Danny. "Some people are saying that I've been cursed."

The emperor sighed and folded his hands behind his back. "Some people are saying that I'm suffering from the stress of ruling an entire Empire at such a young age. Some people say that I'm just crazy. What, pray tell, do you think?"

Danny shrugged. "I think that if I was in your shoes, I'd have a hard time sitting on my throne and not charging off into battle."

Emperor Ezra flashed a small smile at him. "I have absolutely no skill in combat. I'm not even sure I'd be able to hold a sword properly if I were to try, and yet... Yes. I feel absolutely powerless."

"Strange, how the most powerful man in the nation can feel weak and pathetic, shaking in his boots as he watches so many forces, far more powerful than himself, bowing to him for orders."

Danny paused. "Well, that's kind of the point of it. If you were the strongest person in the nation, we'd need you out on the front, but then... The person on the frontlines can't see the whole picture. That's why we need you here."

"I suppose so." Emperor Ezra chuckled and shook his head. "Strange words from the person known to disobey orders at the drop of a hat."

"Oh, I don't think of it like that." Danny shook his head. "I always obey orders, I just sometimes put a personal touch on it."

"Perhaps." Emperor Ezra nodded down at the map of the Empire which had a great many little tokens spread across it. "Now, tell me something, Master Youngblood. If I gave you the order to protect this nation, to protect this city, and left the rest up to you, what exactly would you do? How would you go about doing it?"

Danny thought for a moment. The Emperor certainly seemed more lucid than he had seemed as of late. Had the curse finally been kicked, or was the Deepcorp Lord trying to glean insight into their response so he could counter it?

Danny didn't know, nor did he rightly know how to judge such a thing. Finally, he sighed and decided to (more or less) just tell it straight.

"I'd go down to the herd that's approaching the city." He pointed at it. "Right now, it's just following geographic lines, right? From my understanding, it won't actually be able to detect the Imperial City for a few more days."

"If we send someone south, right now, we might be able to turn it aside, send it off this way." He shrugged. "It's not a final solution, but it gives us more time. The bosses haven't been separated from the herd like before, which tells me that the Deepcorp Lord is still injured."

"I think I got him pretty badly, I just wish he'd actually go and die."

"You and I, both." Emperor Ezra paused for a long moment then slowly folded his hands behind his back. "You have permission to do exactly what you've just proposed."

"I do?" Danny was surprised. "You're sure?"

"I am," the emperor confirmed. "Just yourself, no one else. Go south, and go south quickly. I want it turned aside, and I want it done quickly."

"No heroics. The moment you're done, get back here. Understand me?"

"Got it." Danny nodded. "Thank you for the chance."

"Thank you, for all that you do," Emperor Ezra said. "I've heard the reports. You're putting in overtime, and I can't tell you how much I appreciate it. Now, get moving. The herd is getting closer, and... I'm only sorry that it took me so long to realize that this was the course that we needed to take."

Danny nodded once more then turned and left the room. As the door boomed shut behind him, he let out a long breath.

Half of him wanted to head for the monsters that instant, but something told him that things were off.

Ten minutes later, he reached his family home. Zechariah was missing, but that was hardly surprising. His father was working later and later each day.

Quickly, Danny grabbed some supplies out of the cabinet to make it look like he had gone there for a reason, then pulled out a sheet of paper and wrote down what had just happened. As he finished the description of the scene, he added a few more words.

"I think something's up. There's likely a reason that he wants me out of the city. Stay safe, stay alert."

With that, he placed the letter in the cabinet, where his father was likely to check. He then wrote a second copy of the letter, which he sealed in an envelope.

He would hand it to one of the soldiers on the way out of town. With luck, he'd even meet Tess on the way, which would ensure that the letter reached the ears of his father.

There was no telling exactly what was happening or why things were so strange. All he could do was follow orders...

And, of course, add his own personal touch to it.

Auto save - [Savefile: Information]
Health: 100%
Mana: 100%
[Quest]: Stop the oncoming attack

Location: Youngblood Residence

Inventory: Essential Supplies, Basic Armor, Iron Sword, [Sword of the Wasp], [Aquamarine Sword], [Frostbite Sword]

Skills: [Monster Summoner] (Lv. 46), [Flame Combat] (Lv. 2), [Wind Combat] (Lv. 5)

Relationships: Friendly with Master Barrydew, Speaking Terms with Emperor Ezra the Fifth, Family Bond with Zechariah, Ascended Fire Mage

Time of Day: 12:57 p.m.

Thirty

Things Known

Danny encountered Tess on the way out of town. He passed her the note, causing her to raise an eyebrow in confusion, and with that, he set off.

He spawned in a horse, climbed up, and flew south just as fast as he could go.

The horde, to his knowledge, was south of the central mountains and moving slowly. They weren't in any great hurry, just wandering along as herds of creatures were likely to do.

Danny needed to come at them from the side, hit them hard, then withdraw to force them to follow. For that, he needed to get around to the far side of them, and for that, he was going to need to take a detour.

He didn't know exactly how to do that, but as the cold wind blew across the prairie, he went south by the main road, and then, as night began to fall, he took a road that branched off to the west, hopefully wrapping around the side of the Central Mountains.

Night soon fell, and the stars sparkled overhead. He could see storm clouds on the horizon and hoped beyond hope it wouldn't bring snow.

There hadn't yet been a snow that winter, but that fact could change at any moment, and right in the middle of a monster attack was a terrible time for it.

His summon continued to run long after the sun dipped below the horizon. Though exhaustion tugged at him, the cold air stung Danny's face, making sleep impossible.

Near midnight, with the moon high above, he spotted a small cottage off the path. Gratefully, he sought shelter there, collapsing wearily in a corner.

The building, likely abandoned months ago, was empty but warmer than the bitter outdoors.

At dawn, Danny rose and resumed his journey, surprised to find the mountains closer than expected. What should have been a two-day trek had brought him to their shadow by noon, racing down secluded roads that twisted through the rocky foothills.

The central mountains stretched for a hundred miles across the country, with the main road cutting through the middle of the range. Danny's path had veered somewhere between the midpoint and the range's end, leaving him another twenty-five miles to cover.

His tireless mount sped beneath him, unburdened by the need for food or water. By sunset, he had reached the last mountain in the range—a small peak that might be considered a large hill elsewhere.

He flew around its slope, navigating trails barely wide enough for rabbits, and soon raced along the southern slopes, intent on reaching the herd. There, he found a road sloping south and east, and he took it, glad for the solid footing in the gathering darkness.

Night fell, but Danny pushed onward until sheer exhaustion began to drag him from the horse's back. Cresting a hill, he spotted an old town, its dim light from a single lantern guiding him down to an ancient tavern.

Inside, he gratefully collapsed into a booth, falling asleep before he could fully grasp his surroundings.

The next morning, pale light filtered through the windows, and Danny groaned as he slowly sat up. As he did, a shadow moved across the floor outside, sending a chill through his veins.

He froze, looking out to see that... he was now smack in the middle of the herd. A troll, covered in thick winter hair, slowly walked by, its heavy steps thumping against the ground.

Several wooly mammoths lumbered past as well, trumpeting and snorting, while they in turn were followed by a contingent of orcs led by a dark leader. The leader grunted and snorted, turning this way and that.

He looked straight at Danny, paused, then kept walking onward.

"He can't see you," a voice echoed behind him, and Danny turned slightly to find a man standing there.

He looked rather haggard, but was alive. Danny frowned, and the man nodded at the glass.

"That's been enchanted. Monsters can't see through it."

"Really?" Danny walked up to peer through.

The ground shook as more creatures came through.

"Yeah," the man said. "I had it put in a few years ago, back when we had another big dungeon break. Thing with monsters is that they won't normally smash things unless they have a reason to do so."

Screeeeeeee!

A massive dragon flew down and landed on a store just across the street, smashing it into dust. It was a white dragon with green stripes, and it proceeded to stomp the building to bits, spun and lashed its tail through the building just next to it, then flew up into the air again.

"Of course, there are always exceptions," the man sighed. "Well, let's head downstairs. Probably safer than being up here, and I've got a whole warehouse of bottles that no one else is drinking."

"Might as well get one for you."

"I appreciate the offer, but this herd is actually why I'm here," Danny answered. "We're trying to divert it away from the Imperial City."

"Well, more power to you." The man chuckled and started toward the back of the store. "Do me a solid and give me a few minutes to get underground again."

"And if you felt like doing your fighting a few blocks away, so I'm a little less likely to get crushed, I sure wouldn't mind it."

"I'll see what I can do." Danny flashed a small smile at him.

The man quickly stepped behind the bar of the tavern and vanished down a secret staircase, and Danny leaned against the window. After a few minutes, a bell rang at the register that Danny hoped meant that the man was settled in, and with that, Danny pushed his way out into the street.

A loud screech echoed overhead as a massive drake lumbered by, its thick body and impossibly long neck towering as high as the Academy spires. Several smaller drakes followed, striding on two legs with spindly arms that grasped and clawed at the air, their long tails swaying for balance.

Behind them trailed the usual mix of trolls, goblins, zombies, and other monstrous creatures. Danny cracked his knuckles, then turned and sprinted down the street, leaving the tavern behind.

The town was small, with its edge visible just a few blocks to the north. Beyond that, the road climbed toward the mountains, where a sea of monsters stretched across the plains between the slopes and the town.

Danny couldn't help but smile—this was going to be fun.

An orc shuffled along the sidewalk ahead, oblivious. Danny darted past on the orc's right, casually tapping its left shoulder as he sped by.

The orc grunted, turning left to investigate, only to let out a frustrated snarl when it found nothing there. By then, Danny was already far ahead, racing toward the mountains with a grin.

Moments later, another startled grunt echoed behind him. "Hey! Human!"

Danny turned around and flicked a hand, spawning a rockworm inside the orc. The creature jerked and collapsed, and Danny re-absorbed the monster as he raced along.

Off to his side, he saw several other orcs jerked out of their stupor as they looked around to try and find the source of the problem. Danny felt a grin grow across his face, and ducked into an alley as shouts rang through the air.

"Hey! He's dead!"

"Sound the alert!"

Danny let out a long breath then summoned a troll and allowed himself to be absorbed into it. With that, he stumbled out into the street, squinting his eyes and looking left and right.

Goblins and orcs raced past him, looking for the mysterious warrior, while the drakes around them began to look about. Their less developed brains couldn't quite understand the warnings, but they got the idea that things were wrong.

Danny did his best to make the troll look confused, stomping out into the street where he 'accidentally' crushed another orc underfoot.

"Hey!" he hollered, jumping back away from the corpse. "The human killed another one!"

That sent things wild. Some of the orcs started accusing the others of having fabricated the whole thing in the first place, while others started discussing the prospect of killing the troll outright.

By now, tremors of discontent were spreading throughout the herd. Good.

Danny stomped along, until he was outside the town, and then turned around. He looked up at the drakes, the wooly mammoths, the dragon flying overhead... And slowly lifted a hand.

"Summon as many rockworms as possible."

All around, monsters suddenly began to roar in pain as the worms ate right through their bodies. Two of the really tall drakes stumbled and fell into one another, crashing down and flattening one of the stores on the outer edge of town.

The two-legged drakes fell flat on their faces and didn't move. A whole herd of the mammoths simply collapsed, and, to top it off, the dragon came straight down out of the sky and hit the ground with a powerful crash.

Monsters spun in his direction. High on the slope, sensing blood and battle, they started to return, thumping down the rocky ground as they tried to figure out what was happening.

Meanwhile, from behind, more of the monsters lumbered forward, looking this way and that as they sought for the source of the conflict. More and more of them came forward, and more and more of them died as Danny kept up the attack, absorbing the worms once their job was done, and creating new ones as soon as he had the mana to do so.

Still, for every one he killed, two more joined the search, and soon, the outer edge of the town was crawling with the beasts. He began to prepare for his departure, when...

[Notification: Monster Summoning has increased to Lv. 47!][Reward: Mana Increase: 2020 -> 2140]

A sharp ding ran through the air, and a great many celebratory sparkles appeared over his head. Ordinarily, it was quite fun to have such a thing happen, particularly in a group, as it meant that everyone around you could celebrate the fact that you just got a little bit stronger.

Now, though, a great many eyes turned in his direction, and he felt extremely vulnerable.

"Hey." He raised a hand, then turned. "Sorry to run, but I've got another dungeon to get to. Bye!"

None of them understood what he was saying, he was sure of that, but the banter made him feel better. With that, he bolted away as fast as he could go, running to the south.

There was a pause... And every last beast, monster, zombie, troll, goblin, orc, drake, and more, let out a powerful roar that shook the ground.

The chase was on.

Danny didn't dare look back over his shoulder, but he could hear the monsters tearing along the ground, ripping soil into the air and clawing the ground to ribbons as they fought to get at him. Hot breath flared upon his neck, and he felt claws rake against the flesh of the troll.

"This isn't working." He muttered. "Have to speed up. Spawn my fastest summon."

With a flash, the troll vanished, and Danny fell down through the air. Talons flashed over his head a second later, and Danny landed smack on the back of a large warg.

He blinked in surprise, and it lowered its head and took off at top speed. Which, all things considered, wasn't all that much faster than the other creatures, but it did give him a small advantage over his previous summon.

Now, he was free to glance back over his shoulder, though, admittedly, doing so made him wish that he hadn't. Tens of thousands of monsters stretched out in an immense line behind him, wrapping far beyond the town.

Still, though, they were streaming away from the mountains, and thus, away from the city. A smile came across Danny's face, and he urged the mount onward.

The warg flew south as fast as it could go, keeping off the main road. It leapt across streams and crags here and there, dashing up steep, rocky slopes in others.

Finally, pulling slightly ahead, Danny saw his chance. He spawned a goblin onto the warg right in front of him, and, just as it leapt over a deep crevice, he dropped off.

It likely hadn't been the best place to make such an attempt, but he survived. Barely.

He hit the side of the crevice and slid downward, allowing himself to drop all the way to the bottom, a good thirty feet below. When he struck, he groaned, but pulled himself underneath an overhang that protruded from the side of the rock.

Even so far down, the ground trembled as the beasts all show right over him and kept going, and he held his breath.

It took the better part of two hours for the herd to completely pass overhead. Finally, the noise diminished from a thunderous roar to a gradual tremble and then to an occasional rattle.

Finally, it was entirely quiet, and Danny slowly rolled out and climbed to his feet. It took him a short while to climb out, where to the south, he could see the dust clouds from the receding army.

A sigh of relief swept over him, and he leaned against a nearby boulder, watching it go.

He had redirected the herd. Now, all that was left to do was to head back to the Imperial City where he could only hope all was well and that no mischief had been worked while he was gone.

Auto save - [Savefile: Information]
Health: 98%
Mana: 54%
[Quest Update] Return to the Imperial City
Location: Northern Wasteland District
Inventory: Essential Supplies, Basic Armor, Iron Sword, Sword of the Wasp, Aquamarine Sword, Frostbite Sword
Skills: Monster Summoner (Lv. 47), Flame Combat (Lv. 2), Wind Combat (Lv. 5)
Relationships: Speaking Terms with [Unknown Bartender]

Time of Day: 10:14 a.m.

Thirty-One

New Plan

Danny's trip back up to the capital was, if possible, even faster than his trip there. The storm he had glimpsed on the trip down was just arriving, covering the sky like smoke.

The wind howled, and soon, snow began to blow. When night fell, Danny kept going, trusting the magic of the summon to keep him moving forward.

He knew that if he stopped... Well, there was no way of knowing what he would find the next morning, whether he would be snowed in or not, so he just kept pushing on. The cold air kept him awake, and when the day brightened the next morning, though he couldn't see the sun, he found himself again on the northern side of the mountains.

There, he pressed back north, fighting the wind and the snow as it came faster and faster. Thick flurries blew across his path so hard that sometimes he couldn't see more than two or three hundred feet down the road.

Once, he stumbled right into the path of a lost cave troll which was slowly pressing forward, hand raised against the fury of the storm. Danny drew up short, waiting for a moment until it walked over the path and wandered off into the wilderness once more.

It never saw him, and he had no reason to engage it just for the sake of it.

In any case, the snow was still blowing fiercely when, out of the storm, he suddenly came up against the gates of the city. He drew up short, almost running smack into the wrought iron.

One of the sentries let off an arrow, which, thankfully, was turned by the wind and shot past Danny's head instead. As Danny turned and glared up at him, the sentry waved an apology.

"I don't know whether to be mad at you because you almost shot me, or mad because you missed!" Danny called up to him. "Make sure you can hit any monsters that show up, alright?"

The man flashed him a thumbs-up, and with that, Danny rode on. He flew back along the road that wound through the camp, and in time, came back into the city proper.

His first stop was the Academy, where he trudged into the warm building and felt heat sinking into him for the first time in what felt like days.

"Danny!" Zechariah, who was sitting in the Grand Hall chatting with Master Barrydew, leapt to his feet. "You're back!"

"Guilty as charged," Danny nodded wearily.

He let out a gasp of pain as his frozen limbs began to heat back up, and Zechariah took his arm. They soon had him up in Master Barrydew's office, where they pulled off his winter clothing (leaving him in a tunic, of course), and began to work his limbs back and forth, placing his hands in cold water to ease them back to warmth, and so on.

Finally, after drinking several mugs of hot cider to warm the inner portions of his body, he sighed deeply and nodded to them.

"Thank you."

"You're very welcome," Zechariah nodded then slowly stood up and scowled. "Now that you're alive... What were you thinking? You could have been killed! You could have vanished without a trace, and what was that note all about?"

He took a deep breath and turned around, obviously frustrated.

Danny bit his lip. "I can explain."

He quickly told them about the conversation with the Emperor. When he finished, Zechariah sighed deeply, and Master Barrydew gave a nod.

"You did the right thing, Master Youngblood. Good work."

"Thank you," Danny bowed his head then scowled. "So, why am I in trouble?"

"Because it was unexpected, and as your father, I'm under oath to be worried about such things," Zechariah sighed and pressed his fingers against his temples. "You think something happened while you were gone?"

"It sounded to me like he was trying to get me out of the city," Danny nodded. "Like... I don't know. Maybe the Deepcorp Lord changed his mind about the way he wants to destroy the city. He didn't need the herd anymore, so... He sent me off down there so he could do something else."

"Well, we stayed alert through the whole time you were gone, per your note, and we didn't see anything," Master Barrydew shrugged. "His presence is still weak, and still reading as being in the same location. There aren't any other large monsters in the area, everything is... More or less just like you'd expect it to be."

"Then what's going on?" Danny demanded, determination in his voice. "It doesn't make sense, otherwise. There's something afoot."

"I agree," Zechariah shrugged. "Until we know more, though, I'm just not sure there's all that much we can do. We can speculate, but we can't act unless we know more."

"Mm." Danny nodded, then shrugged. "Well, I'm glad you were able to keep your eyes open. The herd has been diverted, which I'm sure you've confirmed with the globe, and-"

"Masters?"

The voice came from the door, and Danny turned to find a member of the Imperial Guard standing there, at attention. The three masters all climbed to their feet, and the man bowed his head.

"I apologize for interrupting you, but I'm afraid that you're all being summoned to the throne room."

There was little that they could do except obey, and frankly, there was nothing else that Danny wanted to do except obey. He was desperate to catch a glimpse of the Emperor, to see if anything could be confirmed.

When the three mages strode into the throne room, though, it seemed as if everything was business as usual. Aides were carrying documents about here and there, while lords, attendants, mages, soldiers, and all sorts of other people stood at the ready.

Danny frowned as he approached the Emperor's table.

"Welcome, masters!" Emperor Ezra beamed. "I'm so glad you all could make it."

"What can I do for you?" Danny asked, taking the lead. He suspected that his return into town was part of the reason for the summons, and didn't want to put the other two in a position of dealing with his issues. "Any problems with the herd redirection?"

"As I wasn't there, you'd have a better idea of that than me, but two days ago, I was told that the herd was moving to the south via the fancy globe thing you have, so I'm going to assume that everything went according to plan," Emperor Ezra nodded with a smile. "And that, frankly, brings me to the point of today."

"Which is?" Danny frowned, slightly confused and concerned.

There was still something off about the Emperor, though it wasn't the same as usual. There was no smoke, and Danny didn't feel like there was a curse in place. Still, though, he couldn't shake the feeling that something was very wrong.

"Well, as this has been quite successful, I'd like to propose that we do something similar for future herds," Emperor Ezra answered. "I'd like to start reclaiming our territory."

"What exactly do you have in mind?" Danny asked.

"In short, I've been drawing up some plans." The Emperor snapped his fingers, and an aide came forward bearing a scroll. It was unrolled on the table, and Emperor Ezra leaned forward.

There, it displayed the Imperial City, along with a vast space around it, about ten miles out, it appeared. "I believe that if we can reclaim these lands depicted here, and double down on the agriculture production of this area, we can truly rebound."

"You want to... Build farms?" Danny glanced at the Emperor in some confusion.

"Yes and no," Emperor Ezra shrugged. "Right now, the city is about ten miles wide, from one side to the other. If we double that, and run farms out for another five miles in every direction, based on our calculations, we should be able to produce enough food to sustain the city."

"We won't be living in abundance, our homeless won't have the table of a king, but it'll be enough to keep us afloat."

"I see," Danny crossed his arms. "It's not the worst idea in the world, but... That's a lot of ground, and it'll only take a few monsters stomping through to really ruin it."

"And that, I heartily agree with," Emperor Ezra confirmed. "That's why I'd like another wall to be built around it."

"Another wall?" Danny bit his lip. "Are you sure?"

"Yes," Emperor Ezra nodded. "It'll be a huge undertaking, but with your summons, I think we can do it. It's a far cry from retaking the entire Empire, but at this point, I just don't know that we can count on such a thing."

He paused. "Please. I know the plan is odd, and some might even say insane, but we have to start rebuilding, even if it doesn't look like what we'd prefer."

Suddenly, something clicked in Danny's mind. "You're trying to prevent people from just walking off into the wilderness."

"Yes," Emperor Ezra sighed after a long moment of debate. "From what I hear, a lot of people will be preparing to march off the moment that spring arrives. If I let everyone go... It'll kill thousands."

"On the flip side, if we start building farms... I don't know, I just think it might be possible."

"It's far from the worst plan I've heard," Zechariah cut in. "We'll get started on it immediately."

"Thank you," Emperor Ezra bowed his head. "I'll look forward to hearing progress as soon as you have it."

Danny pulled his cloak a little tighter around his shoulders as he marched out into the swirling snow. The storm was letting up, but it was far from done yet.

He had advocated for waiting a mite longer before starting up their work, but the Emperor had been insistent, as had Zechariah. They needed to get to work, and they needed to do it quickly.

Tess came along with him, trudging through the snow as they made their way down the long road.

"Can you... Summon... I don't know. A dragon or something?" Tess asked in frustration. "Something to warm the air and melt the snow."

"You wouldn't want that," Danny shook his head. After a moment of thought, he shrugged. "I suppose I could spawn in something with a fire attribute. Might work to melt a path through the snow, but I think that'd be all the benefit it would give."

"Well, I'd take it," Tess grumbled. She glanced over her shoulder at the receding city. "Where are we heading?"

"Five miles out," Danny answered. "Almost to the old estate. I think that's it, ahead."

Tess nodded, and they pressed on. Soon, they stood right about where the Emperor wanted his new wall to begin.

Danny bit his lip, then snapped his fingers. A handful of giant bees appeared and began to fly down to the nearby estate to remove stones to start the work.

The first part of the job, as it had been formally described in a follow-up visit from several of the emperor's aides, was to go around and build watchtowers. They were to serve as guard posts, as well as to mark the path that the wall would follow.

When workers came back through later, they would draw a line across the landscape from one watchtower to the next. It made for less guesswork when the wall itself was going up, and would ensure that things were built in a more or less proper manner.

Danny didn't know how it would all shape up, or even if it would shape up, but he was willing to give it a shot for the time being.

"So what's your take on all this?" Tess asked as the bees started bringing back chunks of stone and piling them up, sealing them with beeswax and then heading back for more. "This project. Good idea, bad idea, or somewhere in the middle?"

"Honestly, I don't know," Danny answered. "If it was coming from anyone else, I'd say it was a good idea. This is more or less what I've thought we should be doing ever since we gave up trying to maintain the whole continent."

"Fight the monsters as they come, divert what we can't fight, and focus on reclaiming territory inch by inch. Problem is..." He paused and shrugged. "Something just doesn't feel right. The Emperor's heart has changed so dramatically on it that I just can't figure out what's going on."

"I can't decide if it's a ploy of the dark lord, or something we need to be doing."

"I agree," Tess muttered. After a moment, she shrugged. "Well, whatever it is, we're building solid infrastructure again. If the dark lord is the one doing it, you can't really fault him, you know?"

"True," Danny crossed his arms as the tower slowly began to grow. "I just hope we aren't building something that we'll regret, you know? Putting up walls that are supposed to keep monsters out, when they're really just to keep us in."

"I hadn't thought about it that way," Tess scowled and kicked at the ground then turned to Danny. "You know what I wish? I wish we could send one or two people off to these other empires, other nations."

"If we can't just take everyone and head there, why don't we take one or two people, head that way, and beg for help? You know?"

Danny frowned. "That... That actually does sound like a good idea."

Tess paused. "What?"

"What what?" Danny did his best to play innocent.

"You just had an idea," Tess held up a finger. "I know you just did."

"Possibly," Danny grinned.

"So spill it!" Tess snapped.

"Well..." Danny rubbed the back of his neck. "I was just wondering... What if we didn't have to actually have someone go all the way there?"

"You want to write them a letter?" Tess laughed.

"Something like that," Danny confirmed.

Tess laughed again, then paused. She seemed to chew it over for a few moments, then glanced at him.

"I like it. Master Barrydew will never let you do it, though."

"Who said anything about him letting me do anything?" Danny asked. A smile came across his face, and he slowly turned to look up at the growing watchtower. "We'll move tonight."

Auto save - [Savefile: Information]

Health: 100%

Mana: 32%

[Quest]: Build the new watchtower

Location: Imperial City Agricultural Area, South Side

Inventory: Essential Supplies, Basic Armor, Iron Sword, [Sword of the Wasp], [Aquamarine Sword], [Frostbite Sword]

Skills: [Monster Summoner] (Lv. 47), [Flame Combat] (Lv. 2), [Wind Combat] (Lv. 5)

Relationships: Friendly with Tess, Speaking Terms with Emperor Ezra the Fifth, Friendly with Master Barrydew, Family Bond with Zechariah, Ascended Fire Mage

Time of Day: 1:19 p.m.

Thirty-Two

A Reach

Danny and Tess finished building three watchtowers that day. Danny unsummoned his bees as the sun set, and the two of them rode back into town.

It was long after dark by the time they'd made it back to the Imperial City, where Danny paused at the stables. Tess hopped down and started working to turn in her beast, and Danny nodded off across the city.

"I'm going to go get Radiance," he said. "I'll meet you in the Library?"

"See you there."

Danny nodded and rode off as quickly as he could. His horse flashed through the city streets as quickly as possible, and soon came to the little basement apartment that Lot Silver had discovered when he had first arrived.

He swung down from his horse, unsummoned the beast, and knocked on the door. A moment later, it opened, and Abraham beamed.

"Master Youngblood! Would you care to come inside?"

"No. I was wondering if Radiance was here?" Danny asked. "There's some urgent business at the Academy that I could use her help with."

Radiance appeared a second later. She was eating a sweet roll, and she frowned.

"What sort of urgent business?"

"The kind that I need you for, but I can't tell you why I need you for it until we get there," Danny said. "If that makes any sense."

"Believe it or not, it actually does." Radiance glanced at her father.

"Just make sure you don't get arrested," her father said.

"I make no promises, but I don't plan on it." Danny waved as they started off down the street. "Thanks!"

Radiance frowned as they strode down the cobbles. The storm was over now, but a cold wind still blew through the streets, chilling them both to the bone.

When they arrived at the Academy, it was far warmer, but Danny couldn't shake a frigid feeling in his bones. Whether or not it was a good idea, they were going to be in serious trouble.

Plus, they needed someone who would let them into the Forbidden Archives and who could scan for the Deepcorp Lord. There were very few people who would be able to do such a thing.

Master Barrydew was one, Zechariah was another, and...

"Obadiah!" Danny called out. Off to one side, Margot's father turned his head, and Danny felt heat rise to his cheeks.

"I mean... Master Flamekeeper," Danny said in a lower tone.

Obadiah smiled and walked over, bowing his head. "I knew you were made a master, Youngblood, but I didn't realize our battle bonds were so close."

"Sorry." Danny winced and rubbed the back of his neck. "You always appear in my interface as Obadiah Flamekeeper, and I'm tired, so..."

"Ahh, I'm just giving you a hard time." Obadiah laughed. "What do you need?"

"We actually need to see the globe," Danny answered.

Obadiah's eyes narrowed. "You're not trying to manipulate another dragon, are you?"

"No!" Danny laughed and waved his hand. "Nothing like that at all. I'm pretty sure I was told never to do that again, and I'm not going to disobey a direct order."

"But you might disobey an indirect order." Obadiah's eyes narrowed more, but then he shrugged. "Meh. Last time, the way I see it, you did us a favor."

"Sure, I'll come along. Whatever you're about to do is surely for the good of the Empire."

"That's the way I see it, too," Danny confirmed.

They swept along, and quickly mounted the stairs that led them up to the library. When they arrived, Tess was already there, sitting at a table looking over a book about combat.

She looked up as they walked in, and rose to her feet.

"Master Barrydew is gone," she said, answering Danny's unspoken question. "Some sort of emergency that needed his attention."

Once more, Obadiah frowned, but he simply led them to the little room that led into the archives. As they all stepped inside, he initiated another scan.

The door closed and magic swept around the room. There was nothing of any importance, just the fading signature of the student that had appeared the first time they'd ever checked, and with that, they entered the archives.

In the archives, a guard still stood over the thing, watching it intently. The speck of light showing the position of the Deepcorp Mage was still flickering in the southern portion of the Empire.

The guard nodded to them respectfully as they approached.

"I'll step back." He folded his hands and retreated to a safe distance, making sure that he wasn't intruding on anything.

Danny nodded gratefully to him and approached the globe.

"Alright," Obadiah said. "So what are we doing here, so secretly? You owe me that much."

"I'm just here as muscle," Tess answered, crossing her arms. "I was there when he had the idea, and it was sorta also my idea, so here I am. That's about it."

"Right." Obadiah turned to Danny as he stepped up to the globe. "And you?"

Danny placed his hands on the wooden surface, his fingers perfectly matching the burn marks where he had been standing the last time he had done something questionable. "I'm about to try and contact one of these other nations to see if we can get some help."

Radiance's eyes snapped open. "You need me as a diplomat?"

Danny shrugged. "I said you'd know it when you saw it. You know formal stuff better than the rest of us."

"Yeah, that's true, but you're talking about sealing a deal that could save or destroy the entire-"

Danny quit listening as he turned his attention to the globe. "Please show me a map of all nations throughout the world."

Green lines appeared across the assorted continents, carving up nations, states, and empires. To the south of the Empire there were only a few scattered nations, nothing large.

Out to the west, though, across a small ocean, there was a massive continent that seemed to have a large number of very large nations. There was no way of telling exactly how they were all connected together, but it seemed the best choice to Danny.

He glanced at Tess and Obadiah who both frowned.

After a moment, Obadiah stepped forward.

"Contact that nation there," he murmured, pointing at one slightly to the south. "The way it's positioned behind that mountain range, they're more likely to be able to spare soldiers to come and help us."

Danny nodded then tapped the country. "Can you contact the leader of this nation?"

There was a long pause, and the globe whirled about slightly. Radiance stepped forward, still protesting slightly, and put her hands behind her back.

Suddenly, all their minds seemed to be sucked into the globe... And were spat back out halfway around the world.

Danny suddenly found himself standing in a large, open throne room. It was quite unique, with massive arches open to the air on all sides.

Tapestries and banners fluttered in a soft wind that blew through the room, though he could see wooden slats that looked as though they could be pulled across the openings in the case of bad weather. Palm fronds grew in large, ornamental pots, while attendants bustled this way and that.

The throne itself was made of gold and sat upon a large pedestal of sorts, which itself was carved quite elaborately. A man sat upon the throne, dressed in elegant robes that flowed all the way to the floor.

He sat up sharply, and Danny bit his lip.

"Can you hear me?" Radiance stepped forward, taking the lead.

She appeared ghostly, as if made of mist.

"Yes, I can hear you." The king sounded amused. He waved his hand, and several guards came charging forward.

They drew curved swords that they slashed through the apparitions, doing no damage whatsoever. "Who are you, and how do you come to my palace?"

"We represent the Empire," Radiance answered. "And we come here to beg for your mercy and your assistance."

"The Empire?" The king raised an eyebrow. "And which Empire would that be? I do not recognize your clothing."

"Are you from the Middle Ocean Empire? Perhaps the Desert Empire? The Empire of the Foot?"

"Ahh... We only know of it as the Empire," Radiance admitted. "Until just a few months ago, we believed ourselves to be the only nation in the world. We thought we were alone."

"We've been forced to realize that we are anything but alone, in the same moment that we face annihilation."

That seemed to get the king's attention as he leaned forward. "You're from across the sea. From the east!"

"You know of us." Radiance bowed her head.

"We know only of a land besieged by monsters, to a degree unseen in any other part of the world." The king answered. "We have attempted to make contact several times, but great ocean dungeons lining your coast have made it impossible."

"Are you telling me..."

"The dungeons are overflowing." Radiance bowed her head. "Due large in part to the scheming of a dark lord, the beasts are covering the face of our nation."

"At present, we estimate that around half of the Empire's population has been killed, and the other half has crammed themselves into the Imperial City, where we face starvation, along with attacks. We come now, humbly, to implore your assistance."

"I see." The king raised an eyebrow. "And you are? Personally?"

"My name is Radiance Silver, of the esteemed Silver Family." Radiance answered. "This is Master Flamekeeper, Ascended Fire Mage, Tess Stoneflower, Commander in the Imperial Corp, and Master Youngblood, considered by many to be the most powerful mage in the nation."

The king chuckled. "You are skillful with your tongue, madam Silver, but I can see through you. You are contacting me without your Emperor."

"You do not claim to be representatives of him. You are acting independently of his will."

"I, as a fellow sovereign, cannot risk my men for the actions of a commoner when the ruler does not mirror them."

"Forgive us, but asking permission was out of the question." Radiance bowed her head. "We still honor Emperor Ezra the Fifth as our leader, however, he appears to be under the influence of the aforementioned dark lord."

"Telling him something is the same as telling our enemy something."

"Interesting." The king seemed to yield for a moment. "We've had that problem ourselves, in the past. My own grandfather tried to raise a volcano in the middle of our capital city."

He paused. "Give me the details."

"Bring me a map," Radiance ordered.

A map was quickly brought out, along with a scribe. Radiance traced her finger across it, and the scribe followed quickly, marking out the boundaries of the country, the location of the Imperial City, and more.

When she finished, Radiance stepped back, and the king sighed.

"I will consider your request. I will also share it with my allies. I have many friends on this continent, I may just be able to help you."

"That said..." He paused. "Do not think that my help will come for free. If I come and assist you, it's because I see a benefit for my own nation."

"I should also note that my allies will think the same way. Your country has always, as I have said, been unreachable."

"I will risk countless men on this rescue mission."

"I'm sure you'll be given payment." Radiance bowed her head.

"I also... I cannot guarantee I will be able to make it." The king gave one final warning. "I do not know for certain what my allies will say, and even if they agree, we may simply not be able to make it past the sea dungeons."

"We're grateful simply for your consideration." Radiance knelt down before him.

Danny did the same, followed by the others.

"We wouldn't come before you unless we were desperate," Radiance continued.

The king sighed and nodded. "I know. For what it's worth, the only reason I'm considering this is because our own nation once teetered on the brink of collapse, and it was only by the sacrifice of others that I sit here today."

"You'll know my response when soldiers show up, or when they never do. Please, do not contact me again, and I highly recommend against contacting anyone else."

Radiance rose once more. "You'll not hear a peep. I do hope that we can meet, in person, when you arrive in the Imperial City."

With that, Danny pulled them back, and they were sucked away from the throne room. An instant later, they stood once more in the forbidden archive.

Danny gasped and pulled his hand away from the table, seeing where he had burned a second set of fingerprints into the wood. A moment later, the door burst open and Master Barrydew came marching inside.

"What's the meaning of this?" he demanded, looking at them. He strode up to Danny in particular, and crossed his arms.

"I leave for twenty minutes, investigating something that Tess set me on, and you break into my archive?"

Obadiah held up a hand. "They didn't break in. I let them."

"Then you'll tell me what they were up to." Master Barrydew scowled.

"We were just talking about things." Obadiah raised an eyebrow.

Master Barrydew hmphed then turned back to Danny. His eyes flickered down to the burn marks on the wood, and he sighed deeply.

"Whatever it was, when will I see the response to it?"

"You'll either see it, and know exactly what caused it, or you'll never see a thing and always wonder," Danny said.

"Fair enough." Master Barrydew sighed. "Well, get out of here! I have a meeting with the Headmaster I need to get off to. Out! Out!"

As Danny allowed himself to be shuffled out of the room, he cast one last look at the globe. It once more showed the location of the Deepcorp mage.

Would the bid work? Maybe.

Maybe the king would show up with soldiers galore and help free the nation. Maybe he would simply take it over and declare it to be a client state of his own nation.

There was no way of knowing.

No way... except to wait and find out.

Auto save - [Savefile: Information]

Health: 87% (capped)

Mana: 64% (capped)

[Quest Update] Exit the Forbidden Archives

Location: Forbidden Archives

Inventory: Essential Supplies, Basic Armor, Iron Sword, Sword of the Wasp, Aquamarine Sword, Frostbite Sword

Skills: Monster Summoner (Lv. 47), Flame Combat (Lv. 2), Wind Combat (Lv. 5)

Relationships: Friendly with Tess, Friendly with Master Barrydew, Friendly with Radiance, Friendly with Obadiah Flamekeeper, Ascended Fire Mage

Time of Day: 4:37 p.m.

Thirty-Three

Stone Lesson

"And that, class, should sum up everything that we know about stone-based monsters." Zechariah folded his hands behind his back. His cane was leaning against the desk nearby, but more and more, he only used it in absolute emergencies. "I do hope it's been informative."

Trish raised her hand, and Danny, sitting at the desk, nodded to her. "Yes?"

"Master Youngblood... The younger one..." She glanced back and forth between the two for a brief moment. "You fight primarily using a stone golem, correct?"

Danny gave a small nod. "Correct."

"Could you possibly tell us why you do that?" she asked. "We just had a lecture on how to fight against those sorts of monsters, but I'd like to hear your reasoning on why you make use of them. It might give us even a little more insight on how to fight against them."

Zechariah nodded and stepped to the side. "An excellent observation. Master?"

Danny slowly climbed to his feet. His father never referred to him as Master in private, but... In public, where it was more formally required, it felt odd.

Danny folded his hands behind his back, adopting a more professional pose, and stepped out into the middle of the room.

"I use a stone golem because, at least to me, it's the most versatile," Danny answered. "Most summoners throughout the years have made use of one summon primarily, a reflex to pull out before you've been able to properly assess the situation."

"The previous summoner, Nicodemus, used a troll, while others have used goblins, wraiths, or wolves. It's don't know that any two have chosen the same primary summon. In any case, I prefer the stone golem because, as a humanoid, it can adapt to most any situation that a mage or soldier would be able to handle."

"The stone makes for good, natural armor." Danny shrugged. "It stands up well against most elements, it's just... It's very well-rounded."

"Which ties in with what the other Master Youngblood was saying." Trish looked down at her notes. "If you're up against a stone-type monster, unless you can one-shot it, you're probably in for a slog."

"Yup." Danny nodded with a small grin. "That about sums it up. Ahh..." He paused. "One thing that I personally have noticed is that stone pairs very well with attributes like fire or magma. I haven't necessarily seen a correlation out in the wild, but personally, you slap the stone golem with magma, and you're looking at a pert near unstoppable combination."

"I'll keep that in mind." Trish put down her pen. "Thanks!"

Zechariah answered a few more questions, and with that, the class ended. As the students all filed out fairly quickly, Zechariah slowly walked over to stand next to the desk where Danny was looking over some papers.

"You do a good job at this." Zechariah took up his cane and leaned upon it heavily. "You really do. You're a natural."

Danny flashed a smile. "Thanks. I'm enjoying it more now that I'm teaching it alongside you."

Zechariah pulled up a chair, taking a seat just next to Danny. "You know, the very first time I held you, I looked down at you, and I just thought... I'm going to fight next to him."

Danny chuckled. "You did?"

"Yep. I had it all planned out. I was going to start training you in fire magic as soon as the Academy would let me give you powers, and then you'd enter the academy, graduate with honors, and we'd build our family dynasty a little bigger."

Zechariah sighed then shook his head. "I never imagined that we'd be teaching side by side. Frankly, I just never imagined that I'd be teaching, unless maybe once I was elected Headmaster."

Danny laughed at that, and Zechariah shook his head. "I wasn't exactly the least conceited warrior, back in the day."

"We all have to mature sometime," Danny shrugged. "Some of us just happen to do it faster than others."

They both laughed again, and Danny climbed to his feet. "Well, I'd better get going. The Emperor wants me to try to build another guard tower today, if possible."

"How many of those have you put up over the last two weeks?" Zechariah asked.

Danny puffed out his cheeks and shrugged. "I don't even know. I think we have about ten of them raised. I'd have more, my bees are fast workers, but we don't exactly have a quarry in the city."

"I'm having to spawn goblins to mine the stone themselves. It's not the end of the world, but it does take a bit of time."

"Still, ten guard towers in fourteen days, that's not too shabby," Zechariah clapped him on the hand. "And I'm sure the Emperor would understand if you took a day off. Things will get crazy enough in time. Come on back home."

Danny wanted to fight, but... In the end, he relented, and after grading a few more papers, they put down their work and made their way back through the swirling snow to their home. The snow had ceased to fall, but there was a good layer of the stuff over everything, and bursts of wind blew ice crystals up into their faces here and there.

It was downright miserable, and Danny knew that they had it easy compared to most of the population. Eventually, they arrived back in their home where Zechariah set about baking some flatbread for their dinner while Danny chopped a few vegetables.

They didn't have much, but it would be enough to keep them running.

A knock echoed on the door as they sat down to eat. Danny frowned, but Zechariah lifted a hand and gave it a small wave. "Come in!"

The door opened up, and Obadiah and Margot stepped inside. As they kicked the snow off their shoes, Obadiah nodded to them.

"Mind if we sit a spell? I've got food at our house, we'll eat when we get there, no need to go to any trouble for us."

"Please, have a seat." Zechariah gestured at the empty chairs.

The two warriors quickly joined them, and Danny tucked into his food. The bread that Zechariah baked was hard, and was functionally a stiff tortilla shell.

By covering it in chopped carrots, diced onions, and a bit of lettuce, and then drizzling a bit of vinegar over it, it was edible, but it was certainly far from the nicest meal that they had ever eaten.

"You two look cold," Zechariah said.

"Just finished a tour of the western wall." Obadiah rubbed his hands together and nodded to Danny. "I can see some of the towers you're putting up. Good work. You're moving fast."

"I'd be moving faster, but someone convinced me to take the day off." Danny grinned then turned to Zechariah who just shrugged.

"You're welcome to go out there in the cold, I just thought you'd want the evening off," Zechariah said.

"And you've earned it," Obadiah commented. "Trust me." He shivered, then sighed. "Trust me, the idea of getting these fields and things in place sounds like a good one to me, but I don't know how we're going to patrol the walls."

"Right now, we have about thirty miles of walls that we're dealing with, and that's hard. When we get the outer-outer wall up, we'll have a good... What, they're extending it five miles in every direction? Makes it ten miles from the outer wall to the city's center, so... Sixty miles?"

"Just about doubles it?"

"That sounds about right," Danny grimaced. "It's going to be quite a trick."

"And not an impossible one, mind you, but it's going to keep us busy," Obadiah flashed a smile. "Just today, I had to knock some heads together keeping the Corp straight. Old divisions are starting to crop up again, that's for sure."

"How so?" Zechariah asked, taking another large bite of his food.

"Well..." Obadiah sighed, but Margot jumped in before he could finish.

"Basically, the soldiers are feeling like they're little more than monster fodder," Margot explained. "They're being forced to patrol endlessly. I mean, they're on a rotation, about the same as us, but they're getting killed at a much higher rate than we are."

"They think we're just using them, so on and so forth. The tensions are about the same as they were when we all entered the Academy, honestly. Not worse, not as bad as they got, but the feeling of working together is definitely going out the window."

Danny frowned. "That's a bummer to hear."

"But we didn't come by here to talk doom and gloom!" Obadiah thumped the table. "We saw the light on in here, and just wanted to stop by and say hello. They always say that the best time to celebrate is smack in the middle of winter, to shake your fist at the ice and the darkness, and to that, I say yes."

"To that, I say..." He held up his hand, and a fireball formed. "Let's drive back the darkness once and for all. Does anyone have any sort of musical instrument?"

"I played a mean harmonica back in the day," Zechariah said. "It'd probably drive all the mice out of the house, but I imagine that would just about be the only benefit these days!"

Obadiah laughed and clapped his hands. "Well, then, we'll have to resort to singing!"

"No, dad." Margot buried her head in her hands. "Please don't."

"Do you remember that old song we used to sing back in the day?" Obadiah leaned forward, looking at Zechariah. "You know, the one about the dungeons and the zombie?"

Zechariah paused in thought. "It sounds familiar, but I think that one became popular after I'd left the Academy. I was a year or two ahead of you, as I recall."

"Alright. Well, what about the one about the dragon?" Obadiah crossed his arms.

Zechariah's eyes lit up. "The Dragon of Heartstring Pass?"

"That's the one!" Obadiah pounded his fist on the table. "Oh, the greatest-"

"Wait." Zechariah held up a hand then climbed to his feet. He dashed off to the pantry, then returned with several mugs, which he filled with a cider that they had been keeping around.

"I've been saving this for a special occasion. It's not the really good stuff, but you can't sing the Dragon of Heartstring Pass without a drink in your hand, whatever the inebriating powers of that drink happen to be."

Obadiah grinned from ear to ear while Margot and Danny looked at each other, confusion painted all over their faces.

"One of the greatest traditions of the Academy which has sadly been discarded over time as the folly of youth has crept into those great halls was singing contests in the mess hall." Zechariah stood up and placed one foot upon his chair.

Obadiah matched him, and the two warriors stared each other down.

"You ready to face your doom?" Zechariah asked.

"Wouldn't be the first time I managed to take down someone more powerful than myself." Obadiah drew in a deep breath, and, in unison with each other, they both began to sing at the top of their lungs.

"Oh, the greatest warrior in the land, his name was Donald Dent! He fought the beast of Heartstring Pass, and here is how it went!"

Danny and Margot both tried to sink as deep into their chairs as they could as their fathers engaged in one of the oddest battles that Danny had ever seen. Audience or not, Danny knew he was going to be embarrassed just by the thought of it, though... He did have to admit that they looked like they were having a great deal of fun.

They sang the chorus together, and then alternated verses. The verses, of course, were entirely ad-libbed, and described the assorted ways that the aforementioned warrior battled the dragon.

In the end, Zechariah wound up stumbling over a few words and allowed the verse to die out, and Obadiah laughed.

"And that was how it went!" He finished the cider with a single gulp then slammed the mug down onto the table. "Ahh, I've still got it!"

Zechariah shook his head. "You're not bad, not bad, but..." A sparkle came to his eye. "How good are you at Daggers?"

The next hour proved that not only was Obadiah an excellent singer, but he also happened to be a master at Daggers who squarely put Zechariah in his place. Following that, they just sat and talked for some time then parted company as night fell over the city and the cold wind blew all the harder.

As the door closed behind them, Zechariah sighed deeply.

"And that's the hope that will keep this nation going, one way or another," he said.

"I sure hope so," Danny grimaced as he cleared off the table and helped wipe things up.

Zechariah nodded. "There's something I've been meaning to ask you." His father sounded casual, but Danny had a feeling that he knew where the question was going. "Master Barrydew tells me that a handful of you broke into the Forbidden Archives to use the globe."

Danny winced. "Was that what this was all about this evening?"

"No, no." Zechariah shook his head. "I sincerely just thought that it would be good for the two of us to spend some time together, and the addition of Margot and her father simply made it better. I've simply... You haven't told me what it was, and while I've been trying to respect your privacy and not ask, I'm also dying to know."

"I need to know you're safe, that you didn't get yourself into some sort of trouble."

"If I got myself into trouble, I got the whole Empire into trouble," Danny said.

"See, that doesn't exactly fill me with confidence." Zechariah turned to him and crossed his arms.

"I..." Danny bit his lip. "I had Radiance do all the talking."

Zechariah paused. "Now that actually does give me some hope."

"I thought it might," Danny laughed. "Well, if I can't trust you, I can't trust anyone." He quickly explained what they had done.

When he finished, Zechariah stroked his chin. Slowly, he folded his hands behind his back.

"I wish you'd come to me." He shrugged after a moment. "I could have made sure that Barrydew never caught you at all."

"So you think it was a good idea?" Danny asked.

"I don't think it was a bad idea," Zechariah said. "And I understand why you did things the way you did. You had the idea, and had to act quickly. If the Emperor, or anyone else, had gotten wind of it, it would have been game over."

He paused, then shrugged. "I suppose we'll just have to find out."

Danny flashed a smile at his father, and with that, they slowly turned and started heading toward their beds.

The winds howled outside, but as Danny pulled the covers over himself, he felt warmth welling up within him.

He only hoped that spring would come for the kingdom, and for the Imperial City, soon. If it didn't, and they couldn't lift the threat of the dungeons...

Danny truly didn't know what future the Empire could possibly have.

Auto save - [Savefile: Information]
Health: 100%
Mana: 100%
[Quest]: Help build more towers.
Location: Youngblood Residence
Inventory: Essential Supplies, Basic Armor, Iron Sword, [Sword of the Wasp], [Aquamarine Sword], [Frostbite Sword]
Skills: [Monster Summoner] (Lv. 47), [Flame Combat] (Lv. 2), [Wind Combat] (Lv. 5)
Relationships: Friendly with Margot, Friendly with Obadiah Flamekeeper, Ascended Fire Mage, Family Bond with Zechariah, Ascended Fire Mage
Time of Day: 10:38 p.m.

Thirty-Four

Walls Rise

Spring would eventually arrive, though the harsh winter had yet to relinquish its grip. As the weeks dragged on, the cold deepened, and blizzards buried the Imperial City more than once.

Despite the relentless weather, food supplies never fully ran out. In time, the snows began to melt, and the chill gave way to the first hints of warmth.

During those long months, Danny scouted and established a quarry in the rocky lands to the north. He split his days between the quarry and the various build sites.

One day, a horde of goblins would extract more stone than a human team could manage in a week, largely because safety measures weren't a concern. If a goblin was crushed by falling rocks, Danny simply summoned another.

The next day, his monsters would set the stones in place, working tirelessly.

Over the course of three months, Danny oversaw the construction of fifty guard towers, each spaced a mile apart, forming a vast ring around the city. As the spring rains began to nourish the prairie, he shifted his focus to building the outer wall.

By then, others were eager to join in, inspired by the progress he had already made. Wildflowers dotted the prairie as legions of civilians, eager to escape the confines of winter, poured out to contribute to the monumental construction effort.

Danny focused increasingly on the quarry, extracting dozens of tons of stone each day. These stones were hauled away by carts drawn by the Corp, delivered to the sites where civilians were building the wall, which now soared to a staggering height of nearly fifty feet.

With Danny's bees working to bind the stones together, the wall became a nearly impenetrable fortress, a testament to the power and might of the Empire. Visible from the city itself, the wall inspired hope in those who saw it.

Whether or not that had been the original intent, it was certainly the result.

Buoyed by this progress, the Imperial Corp rallied, driving off wandering monsters with renewed vigor, while the mages joined the effort with everything they had. To further strengthen the wall, mages specializing in plant growth began to camouflage it, covering the lower stones with vines and even tree bark, making it appear as a natural formation rather than a man-made barrier.

Guards took up positions in the towers as sections of the wall were completed, and it was soon reported that the monsters paid the structure little attention. The hope—one that Danny didn't believe was idle—was that once the wall was finished, only a minimal guard presence would be needed, with just a few sentries in each tower to keep watch.

Despite the coordinated effort, estimates suggested it would take nearly a full year to complete the wall.

"Can you imagine what this is going to be like when it's done?" Tess asked, as Danny crossed his arms, overseeing the quarry. She gestured toward the wall, which was rising not far from the quarry itself.

The excavation site, about a quarter-mile north of where the wall would pass, was some distance from the Imperial

City, which could just be seen growing across the distant hills. "I'm trying to picture it."

Danny shook his head and turned back to the quarry which had grown quite large.

It sprawled across the landscape, having taken down several hills. Now, the hole was a good hundred feet deep, more in some places, and covered a good ten acres.

Goblins were working on the northern wall that day, hammering pegs into the wall to cause cracks to form, splitting away massive chunks of stone at a time. The sound of chisels and hammers and breaking stone echoed through the air, even as large blocks of stone were drawn up out of the pit via a complicated series of pulleys that had been set up for the purpose.

At the top, goblins heaved the stone blocks onto waiting wagons, where they were hauled away.

"It's truly going to be remarkable," he said.

"You should come look at the new fields with me," Tess replied. "I've heard they're really cool."

"I'm too busy for that." Danny shook his head and stretched. "They want to finish the next section of this wall by the end of the week, and for that, I'm going to need to keep these things working."

Tess sighed and shook her head. "You're already ahead of schedule, aren't you? Besides, they can keep working without you, right?"

"I mean, you don't have to be right here."

"True, I suppose." Danny frowned, then nodded. "Alright, then. I have been hearing good things about them."

"Great!" Tess beamed. "Let's go."

She turned and mounted up on her horse, and Danny spawned in his own. He added a Goblin Captain to give orders in case any of the lesser summons started arguing, and gave it the ability to spawn in new workers if needed, then rode off.

He and Tess flashed on south, soon passed by the watchtower that would eventually stand at the gate overlooking the northern road, and made their way to the vast sections of fields being cultivated.

While a great many of the civilians were busily working on the wall, a great many more were busy actually tilling up new fields and building new farmsteads. These were mostly on the southern side of the city, which, while not yet protected by the wall, was easily the most fertile ground.

Priority had been given to farmers who had previously farmed the land, or whose farms had been covered over by the tent cities that had grown out from the city. Thankfully, there was more than enough land to go around (most of that part of the country had been pastures, and... Well, all the sheep and cattle had been eaten by the monsters), and all was working out well enough.

Danny and Tess reached the city walls and veered to the right, following the curve of what was now being called the Middle Wall. As they rounded the southern side, Danny's jaw dropped in astonishment.

Before him stretched a vast expanse of land that was beginning to take shape, transforming into something truly remarkable.

Immense patches of fields had been plowed, and even as he stood there, he watched as horses trudged along, pulling plows and makeshift platforms through the soil. Farmers were scattered across the land, diligently sowing seeds and hammering posts into the ground, their efforts creating a patchwork of activity.

Danny whistled softly, and Tess nodded, sharing in his quiet amazement. "Everyone's working together, and it's just... It's working," she said.

Danny slowly rode down one of the many winding paths that led between the individual farms. Farmers here and there waved at him, several calling him by name.

Apparently, he had become well-known in the city. In the distance, he could see the watchtowers standing tall over what would become the wall, in time.

In another year, he could only imagine what it would look like. Ten years? Twenty?

The Imperial City truly was becoming something new, bouncing back against the darkness that had covered the land.

"Hey! Master Youngblood!"

The call came from off to his left. Danny spun his horse slightly to see a woman striding up to him.

She nodded to him, and he swung down from his mount.

"What can I do for you?" he asked, sensing that the woman had some other purpose than simply saying hello. "Something the matter?"

She nodded. "I think so. I spoke with the Corp last night, but they said that I was mistaken. Can you come and look at something, real fast?"

Danny nodded and followed as she led him over to the site where her husband and several teenage sons were working on sawing a large log into lumber. The husband mopped his brow and stepped to the side, pointing at the ground not far away.

"This appeared... Two nights ago," he said.

Danny frowned as he looked down to see large warg tracks. There were scuff marks on the ground near the tracks, likely where the beast had trod but where it hadn't quite been soft enough to make a full print.

He crouched down.

"Did you see it?" Tess asked, switching into full investigation mode.

"No." The man shook his head. "We've been camping with some other families in a hollow, just over the hill. We heard some noises during the night, but nothing came down to the tents."

"Next morning, we found this. The Corp isn't taking us seriously, they said that they haven't heard any other reports of a warg."

He gestured at Tess. "Any chance you're different?"

"The short answer is yes," Tess said. "The longer answer is that Wargs are classified as a Large beast, so unless there are multiple sightings, reports aren't generally to be considered credible."

"We're stretched pretty thin, so we have some fairly strict guidelines on what we are and aren't allowed to pursue. Thankfully, I'm a Commander, which means that I can bend those rules just a smidge."

The man lit up. "We'd sure be grateful."

Danny nodded then snapped his fingers. Most of his mana had been used up summoning the goblins, and it hadn't yet refilled, but he had enough.

With a flash, a small warg appeared, crouched down, and took a few sniffs. With that, it rose up and bounded off.

Danny smiled. "We'll be seeing you."

He then swung back up onto his mount once more, and off they went. The warg flashed across the fields, darting between homes and around large patches of freshly-sown land.

It was going to look truly amazing once everything started to sprout, Danny was certain of that. He could only imagine how stunning it would be once vast quantities of grain were being grown from wall to wall, but that wasn't the point of his investigation.

They followed the warg as it began to move west, crossing over the main road south out of town, and wrapping around toward the forest. There, a great many workers were hacking and chopping at the trees, clearing large swaths of land for future fields, as well as providing necessary lumber for the assorted construction projects taking place throughout the city.

The small warg swept down into the trees, straight past several crews, and meandered deeper into the woods. Danny glanced at Tess, then plowed onward.

"I'm not liking the looks of this," Danny said as the trees grew thicker over their heads. "Something doesn't feel right."

"I agree." Tess' hand slipped to her sword. "Just tell me if you sense something."

"I just did," Danny said softly. "We need to..."

He froze as a soft growl echoed from ahead of him. Suddenly, they emerged to find themselves overlooking a large hollow which just so happened to double as a warg den.

There were almost a dozen of the creatures around, prowling about as if waiting for a signal to attack.

Tess drew her sword as they all turned in her direction, and Danny quickly re-absorbed the warg and raised a hand.

"Stone golem!"

With a flash, a golem appeared... Since he was low on mana, it was only about five feet tall. One of the wargs sprang forward and snatched it up in its jaws, shook it like a rag doll, and smashed it to bits.

Danny gulped and leapt down from his horse, re-absorbing that and transferring it all into another stone golem. This one was a bit better, a good six feet tall, but it collapsed a second later.

"Sometimes, Danny, it's embarrassing to be seen with you." Tess leapt down and held up her sword as the wargs came charging. "Get down!"

She shoved Danny to the side as the first of the wargs leapt at her. She ducked the blow and slashed across its belly, opening a long gash.

She then spun, ducked to the side as another one lunged, and chopped its neck clean through. The body fell in pieces, and she spun and stabbed another one directly in the open mouth.

Danny gritted his teeth, then opened his inventory and scrolled through his mana stones. He didn't have many, but he had a few of them that had a couple hundred mana points.

With a flash, he activated one of them, and held up his hand again.

"Stone golem! A tough one this time!"

A warg lunged at Tess, and she slashed at it... Only for the warg to stop short. Her blade passed a few inches in front of its nose, and the golem holding its tail spun and smashed it into a tree.

"Kill stealer," Tess snorted as she spun and attacked another one.

"Just trying to be less embarrassing!" Danny called out as his golem ripped a sapling out of the ground and speared another warg then kicked it in the head to smash it flat. "That's what you want, right?"

The two friends laughed as the fight raged on. Soon, they stood over a heap of warg corpses as Danny sighed.

"Another day, another good deed," Tess said firmly. "Now come on, we both have real work that we need to be doing."

"That wasn't real work?" Danny protested.

"Not as far as the Emperor or the Corp is concerned," Tess answered.

Danny laughed at that, and they soon walked up and out of the forest. As they left it behind, though, Danny kept glancing over his shoulder.

Somehow... Something really did feel off about it. There was technically no reason why it couldn't have just been natural, just a handful of wargs that had wandered in from the wilderness, but something told him that it was a bit more.

There was more at work than met the eye... He only hoped that they would be able to figure out what it was before it came back to bite them.

Auto save - [Savefile: Information]
Health: 94%

Mana: 1%

[Quest Update] Supervise the quarry

Location: Imperial City Agricultural Area, South-Western Side

Inventory: Essential Supplies, Basic Armor, Iron Sword, Sword of the Wasp, Aquamarine Sword, Frost-bite Sword

Skills: Monster Summoner (Lv. 47), Flame Combat (Lv. 2), Wind Combat (Lv. 5)

Relationships: Friendly with Tess

Time of Day: 12:57 p.m.

Thirty-Five

Redirection

"Master Youngblood, you are cleared to enter."

As the guards slowly opened the doors to the throne room, Danny squared his shoulders and entered. It had become somewhat of a crapshoot whether or not the throne room would be empty or a hive of activity.

At that moment, it was more of the hive variety as aides bustled this way and that. A great many maps were spread out over dozens of tables that now stood throughout the room, depicting the growing wall, the farms, and a great many other things.

Emperor Ezra stood at one of them, arms crossed in thought. Master Barrydew stood with him, and they both looked over at Danny as he approached.

"Ahh, Master Youngblood," Emperor Ezra commented. "I was hoping you could make it."

"When the Emperor gives an order, it's best to jump just about as fast as you can," Danny said.

"If only more people thought like that," Emperor Ezra murmured with a small smile. He gestured down at a map, which seemed to depict a version of the city with the wall stretching around the whole thing excepting the southern side.

Farms were marked as being tilled around about half of the agricultural area, while a handful of other construction projects were noted here and there between the Middle and

Outer walls. "Tell me, Master Youngblood, what would your opinion be on establishing several settlements in this area, particularly along the four major roads that run out of the city?"

He pointed to some of the new constructions being proposed. Danny leaned forward, noting that they were mostly cottages along with a few mills, bakeries, and other such agricultural processing facilities.

"You're wanting to process everything before it comes into the main city?" Danny surmised.

Emperor Ezra nodded. "That's the idea, yes. We would grind the grain into flour, bake the bread, that sort of thing, in the outermost section."

"Then, it would be transported inward. It was proposed to me around a month ago, and we're getting to the point where, if any of it is to be completed before fall, we need to start working on it now."

He paused and gestured vaguely at the map. "That's what this is, an extrapolation for how things could look in September of this year."

Danny shrugged. "I'm not a city planner or an economist to know how that sort of thing would work out. It seems to me like it would be a good idea."

"Less distance to transport things. That can't be bad."

"True." Master Barrydew held up a finger. "I still contend that it will make the inner rings reliant upon the outermost ring."

"While we're technically still all one city, the divisions of the walls will start to have an effect in time. By all estimates, once we get that outer wall up, it'll be decades before we attempt any further expansion or reclamation projects outside the city itself, and that lends itself to becoming complacent, forgetting the monsters and conjuring up ways to become angry with each other."

"Anything we can do now to help ease things will make that part of the process easier."

"Perhaps so." Emperor Ezra paused then turned to Danny. "In any case, this isn't why I brought you here today, it's simply what I happened to be discussing when you showed up."

"You're aware of the planned Third Herd that was supposed to hit the city, sometime in the spring?"

"Yes," Danny confirmed as the Emperor led him over to a nearby map. "What about it?"

Emperor Ezra nodded to Master Barrydew who folded his hands. "We've been tracking it with the globe, and the simple answer is that it hasn't formed up the way that it was supposed to do."

"In part, the herd that you redirected wound up meeting with monsters that were intended to rendezvous with the main herd, and in part, the Deepcorp Mage doesn't seem to have been exerting his influence upon it. There is something large heading our way, and I do think it needs to be taken care of, but it's not nearly the threat that we once assumed it to be."

Danny frowned and nodded. "The mage still hasn't move?"

"Still in the same place, and still just as weak," Master Barrydew confirmed. "As much as I hate to say it... You really did help us there, Danny."

"I don't know what we'd be looking at if you hadn't used the dragon to attack Castle Rock, so... Thank you."

"Not to get off-topic..." Emperor Ezra held up a finger. "Danny, I'd like you to try and re-direct this third herd. Same way you did it with the other one."

Danny nodded. "Where's it coming from?"

"The west." Emperor Ezra pointed at a map of the entire Empire. "It's been moving up the coast, and is now starting to turn down some of these valleys, which will ultimately direct them up toward the Imperial City."

"If you can turn them down into this valley... Here." Master Barrydew pointed at a thin fingerlet that plunged between several of the Western Mountains.

"They'll come out the other side and meander south across the plains, hopefully missing us entirely."

"How long do I have before they get to that fork?" Danny asked.

"One week," Master Barrydew answered. "Give or take a day or so. I'd rather bet on the taking a day and having you wait, than on the giving a day and having you show up late."

"Fair enough." Danny crossed his arms. "When do I leave?"

"Today." Emperor Ezra nodded. "You'll go with Commander Stoneflower, who I believe you already know, along with some of her troops."

"She already has a map, so..." He shrugged. "I wish you luck."

Danny, Tess, and five other soldiers soon rode out from the Imperial City, moving west along the main road. Travel took them almost three days, due largely to the necessity of moving slower in a large group.

When they reached the Western Mountains, they briefly rode up to a lookout from which you could just see the ocean. Danny stood there, looking at the thin grey band along the horizon, wondering if there was any help on the way or not.

There was no way of knowing, and he saw nothing to indicate that anyone was there at that moment. With that, the army broke away and made their way to the designated location.

As they settled in, Danny almost felt flippant about the whole business. It seemed far less serious than it had the last time, though in all reality, it was far more serious.

If the herd wound up making for the Imperial City, there would only be a week to respond before it arrived, less if the monsters became agitated and decided to make a run at it. And the city simply wasn't well-protected yet.

The Middle Wall was crumbling by the day as more and more attention was placed on the Outer Wall, and the Inner Wall was, realistically, receiving just as little care. In any case, as they settled in, he did his best to just focus on the task at hand.

A large, lush valley rose up from the sea, miles away, before forking and splitting into two. The split to the south was by far the smaller target, but Danny wasn't too worried.

He stared out down the length of the valley, and Tess came to stand just next to him.

"What do you think the Deepcorp Lord's plan right now is?" she asked softly. "Do you think he's still counting on the monsters? Do you think he even knows what's happening?"

"I don't know. Wish I did." Danny murmured. He sighed and crossed his arms, watching. Waiting.

"I know I messed him up pretty badly, but... For him to still be so weak, and still in the same place, you'd think he was either dead or close to it, but I just have this feeling that he's not."

He paused for a moment. "You have no idea how much I wish Nicodemus was here. Barbara is apparently bonded to him, so I understand why she's not showing up, but Nicodemus?"

"Why has he suddenly vanished now that the Deepcorp Lord has vanished?" He shook his head in dismay. "I don't know. I'm trying not to think about it."

"I have this feeling that there's something dark afloat, that so many things we're doing are just playing into his hand, but I can't fathom what that's actually going to prove to be. Maybe it'll be something simple, maybe it'll crush us all in a single blow..."

"Maybe he's just going to take over the mind of the Emperor so he can rule again. I don't know."

Danny huffed in frustration, and Tess flashed a smile.

"Well, thankfully, you don't have to deal with that out here. Just focus on the herd, get it turned away, and then we can go from there."

"This is a real threat, you're not wasting time." She frowned and looked out across the trees. "And here it comes."

The company quickly withdrew within the trees, building a blind out of branches that they had cut down for the purpose. In the distance, monsters slowly began to approach, and Danny did his best to evaluate them from a distance.

There were a lot of magical monsters, from wraiths to sprites to elementals to golems. There were also a few drakes, a handful of giants, and more.

It was a menagerie of mayhem, and Danny puffed out his cheeks.

"What do you want us to do?" the soldiers asked as Danny watched the herd slowly meandering into the valley.

"You all just stay put." Danny rose and balled his hands into fists. "I'm going to need to know that I won't be stomping someone underfoot, you know?"

They nodded, then frowned. "Why, exactly?"

Danny merely flashed a small smile. "Watch and learn."

With that, he raised his hand, creating a fire element, which he sent flashing down the slopes of the valley, carving a path across the broader portion of the expanse. Flames soon crackled and raged, hopefully blocking off the direction toward the Imperial City.

With that, Danny slipped down into the trees and just ran.

He created a horse to ride on when he reached the valley floor, though he dismounted as the monsters began to appear around him. None of them were on alert, making it easy (relatively speaking) for him to sneak around between them.

Finally, as he worked his way into the middle of the herd, he turned his attention back toward the fork in the valley, and stretched out with his senses.

He could sense the creatures approaching the flames. If he was lucky, they would turn out of the way and wander down the other way, and he wouldn't have to do a thing.

As it happened, a few of them did do just that, but the larger monsters, as well as the ones made of stone, saw very little reason to bother changing their path. With that, Danny, hiding near the trunk of a tree, slowly raised his hands.

"It worked once. Let's see if we can do it again."

Rockworms spawned across the valley, and massive monsters began to groan and collapse as their bodies failed them. Massive stone golems exploded as the worms happily chewed their insides to gravel, while other creatures simply shrieked and collapsed.

A huge dragon came crashing down out of the sky to flatten a whole company of orcs, and Danny's kill count began to rise quite rapidly.

[Notification: Monster Summoning has increased to Lv. 48!]

[Reward: Mana Increase: 2140 -> 2270]

Danny's Level up notification rang loudly throughout the valley, and the monsters began to roar in anger and agitation. With that, Danny rose up, spawning as large a stone golem as he could.

He allowed himself to be absorbed into it, and suddenly found himself looking out over the tops of the trees.

Only a few of the other monsters were so large, but they were looking back and forth, seeking their target. They all locked on him, and Danny quickly pointed down the length of the valley and started running.

His massive legs crushed trees and brush underfoot, squashing more than a few smaller monsters beneath his gait, and as he reached the fork, he turned down the smaller path. The herd came streaming out behind him, crashing their way through the forest as they ran after him.

The smaller valley was, indeed, quite narrow, only a few hundred feet wide, but it was enough. In the distance, he could see a brilliant light as it opened onto the southern plains, and he put on a burst of speed.

As he reached the location, he caught hold of a ledge of stone and allowed himself to be ejected from the summon. He landed on top of the ledge and scrambled back from the edge as his stone golem raced onward, and with that, everything fell into place.

The ledge was... Well, when Danny had seen it, he had thought it to be the edge of a large cliff reaching back into the surrounding forest. As it turned out, it was little more than a small lip, ten feet deep, with a few scraggly trees that had looked rather different from down below.

He pressed himself up against the cliff wall as the herd surged past him, shaking the ground as it went along. Hours passed, first one, then two, and still it came.

Finally, though the herd didn't diminish in any significant way, it did slow, and Danny let out a sigh of relief.

One way or another, he had accomplished the goal. True, he was stuck on the side of a cliff, and would be there until the herd finally moved along (he didn't dare direct the herd in any other direction), but it was a win in his mind.

The city had been saved from another threat. Now, all that was left to do was figure out what the Deepcorp Lord really was planning... And how grave the true threat would be when it finally came.

Auto save - [Savefile: Information]
Health: 98%
Mana: 5%
[Quest Update] Return to the Imperial City
Location: Western Mountains
Inventory: Essential Supplies, Basic Armor, Iron Sword, Sword of the Wasp, Aquamarine Sword, Frostbite Sword

Skills: Monster Summoner (Lv. 48), Flame Combat (Lv. 2), Wind Combat (Lv. 5)

Relationships: Friendly with Tess, Speaking Terms with Emperor Ezra the Fifth, Friendly with Master Barrydew

Time of Day: 8:27 a.m.

Thirty-Six

Calm

It took almost two whole days before Danny was able to get down from the cliff. The very next day, he caught sight of Tess's regiment on the slope opposite from him.

When they located him, they seemed to breathe a sigh of relief, and both settled in to wait for the herd to pass. When it finally did, Tess and her soldiers slipped down to the valley floor (it was less steep on that side), while Danny spawned in several monkeys that helped him climb down.

When he finally reached the bottom, he was starving, and helped himself to some of Tess's rations before they made a plan.

"From what I can tell, everything went smoothly," Tess nodded to him. "I sent scouts ahead, and they said that the whole thing is just rolling out across the southern plains. You did a good job."

"Glad to hear it," Danny sighed and stretched. Being stuck on a cliff for two days, trying not to move for fear of alerting the herd, had put quite a few kinks in his body. "Let's get moving."

They went back for the horses, and were soon moving back toward the Imperial City once more. This time, they didn't bother going to the ocean overlook, though Danny rather wished that they could have.

Instead, they cut back as sharply as they could, and were soon on the main road passing back into town.

The return trip, less urgent this time, gave Danny the chance to take in the countryside. Though his mind remained preoccupied with concerns about what might be unfolding back at the Imperial City, he allowed himself to observe the abandoned towns and settlements they passed through.

Some, built from logs and mud, had deteriorated so severely that they were barely recognizable as former settlements. Others, constructed from stone, had become overgrown, their windows shattered and roofs caved in, yet still they stood, defying the passage of time.

In some places, doors had rotted away, while in others, locks remained intact, stubbornly keeping the outside world at bay.

Passing through these ghost towns filled Danny with a strange sense of foreboding. He couldn't help but wonder if, one day, people would walk through the streets of the Imperial City with the same sense of loss and decay.

Would that day come in a year? Ten years? A hundred? Or would the city endure for a thousand, even two thousand years, transformed but still standing?

The answers were beyond his grasp, and as a mortal, he knew he would never see that far into the future.

When they finally caught sight of the Imperial City, the immense guard tower Danny had constructed rising into view, the scene was breathtaking. The woodlands dominated the landscape, but even from a distance, he could see the clearings where forests were being gradually pushed back, and the expanding patches of farmland stretching to the south as the city extended its reach.

Progress was visible everywhere.

Things were improving.

The sense of doom and gloom that had haunted Danny began to dissipate as they rode through the city gates, past the tent city that was slowly transforming into a more permanent settlement with small buildings and huts replacing the makeshift shelters. The atmosphere felt less crowded in the central part of the city, with refugees spreading outward, eager to establish new lives in the outer rings.

As they reached the Academy, Danny waved goodbye to Tess before slowly ascending the long stairs leading to the immense doors. As he stepped inside, though, that feeling vanished, due to the fact that Isa was standing there, anxiously bouncing her foot on the ground.

She lit up slightly when she saw Danny, though not in an I'm happy to see you sort of way, more of a I've been waiting forever on you sort of way. Danny frowned as she rushed over to him.

"Danny! I'm glad you're here," she grabbed his sleeve and started tugging him along through the academy. "You're needed in the library immediately."

"How long have you been waiting on me?" Danny frowned, confused. "Everyone knew I was gone, right?"

"True, they did, but you're almost two days overdue," Isa sighed. "We've been watching the herd, we knew you managed to redirect it, but some of us were worried that you might have been caught up in it, or something."

"Why not just use the globe to track my location?" Danny raised an eyebrow.

"Because we've been busy... Oh, you'll just have to see it for yourself."

Danny frowned but followed as she pulled him along and up the stairs. Soon, they reached the library where he was taken in to see Master Barrydew, Zechariah, Obadiah, and Headmaster Bluestream standing and talking quietly.

As they all turned to look at him, Danny frowned.

"I'd ask who died, but pretty much everyone who might have bit the dust is standing right here," he quipped, trying to lighten things slightly. "What'd I miss?"

"What did we all miss?" Master Barrydew licked his lip. "Ahh... We've made a grave mistake, Danny. You, as well as the rest of us."

"Alright," Danny crossed his arms, a sense of doom starting to return. "I've been wondering if something was amiss, but I haven't been able to figure out what it was. Any chance someone's going to clue me in, or am I going to have to start guessing?"

Zechariah turned to look at Master Barrydew, who nodded. Slowly, he turned and walked over to the Forbidden Archives where he performed the customary scan, found nothing, and allowed everyone to enter.

There, two guards stood over the globe, just watching it. The faint light of the Deepcorp Lord still shone in the southern portion of the Empire.

Danny frowned.

And then he saw it flicker.

It was only for a moment, but it did. It faded to nothingness, just like a torch in the wind, but... In that instant, a new speck of light appeared, smack in the Imperial City itself.

Danny felt his blood run cold. The point of light in the Imperial City was brilliant and bright, shining like the northern star, hardly something coming from a weak, barely-living survivor.

"What's going on?" Danny murmured, walking quickly to the globe. It flickered again, then again, then seemed to stabilize in the south once more. "I don't understand."

"Neither do we, entirely," Zechariah said. "Our best guess, though, is that once the Deepcorp Lord fled the attack of your dragon, he likely set up a spell of some sort that showed his bodily presence as being located down south somewhere."

"He may even have stayed there for some time, but... Now, he's come to the Imperial City under the protection of his little cloak, and we've been none the wiser."

"How long has he been here?" Danny asked, though he already knew the answer.

"No way of knowing," Master Barrydew said. "Our guard discovered the deception two days ago. So... On the late end, he came here three days ago. On the early end, it could have been almost six months."

"That's a lot of variety," Danny bit his lip and leaned over the globe, desperately looking down at those two locations. "Have you tried to do anything with the globe?"

"What would you do?" Master Barrydew asked.

"The same thing I've done twice now," Danny turned then paused. "Well... once. Once, for sure. You absolutely didn't catch me doing it a second time."

Master Barrydew gritted his teeth then let out a sigh. "In answer, while I wish that I could tell you we've done nothing, we actually did try to use the globe to ascertain more information. It would seem that your ability to use the globe for such things is tied to your ability to summon monsters, and that wind mages can mostly just use this thing as a glorified map."

"So..." Danny glanced at the mages around him, all of whom looked quite solemn. Isa had her hands folded respectfully behind her back, the others were all in various stages of confusion or frustration.

"Is that permission to see what I can do?"

None of them answered, and Danny slowly took a step toward the globe. When no one stopped him, he bit his lip and stepped up to place his hands on the wooden surface, right where his fingers had already burned twice into the rim of the globe.

He took a deep breath then closed his eyes.

If the Deepcorp Mage was already in the city, and if he really was as strong as it looked like he had become, he certainly knew that the jig was up. He certainly knew that his secret had been discovered, and that meant that the fight to find him was on.

Danny had few options, except to try and flush him out. As the globe whirled around, Danny gritted his teeth.

"I need to see the Deepcorp Lord."

Instantly, he was sucked into the globe, out of his body, and swept across the Empire. A moment later, he stood within a small, stone room, deep beneath the ground in what appeared to be a fortress of some sort.

At the exact center was one of the infinite crystals, flickering and wavering as spell energy floated around it. Danny set his jaw then raised a hand.

"Stop."

He didn't know what sort of spell he was trying to cast, but nothing happened. He tried to summon something, but wasn't able to do so.

Casting a wind spell, or a flame spell, yielded the same results. He snarled softly and marched forward, grabbing hold of the crystal.

Instantly, pain blazed down his arm, and he gasped.

"Is everything alright?" Zechariah's voice echoed distantly in his ears.

"Yes!" he called out. "Let me be."

The crystal blazed within his grasp. He could see his hand as little more than a mist, somehow coming into contact with the item.

Perhaps because it was made of mana? Perhaps for some other reason? He didn't know, but with all his might, he pulled at it, ripping it from its base.

There was a brilliant flash of light...

And with that, he was standing back in the Forbidden Archives. He gasped in pain as his arm went limp, and something clattered to the floor.

Slowly, he looked down to find the crystal on the ground, and slowly bent down to pick it up with his left hand. As he looked down at it, Master Barrydew gasped.

"You... You fixed it."

Danny looked up to see the beam of light now constant in the Imperial City. A grim determination set over him, and he turned and gestured to his injured arm.

Burns ran from his fingers all the way up to his shoulder, and his robes had been partly burned away.

"Does anyone know any healing spells?"

Master Barrydew nodded. "I do, but I'm not sure-"

Headmaster Bluestream raised a hand and fired a burst of orange magic into Danny's shoulder. His arm, while it hardly healed entirely, did regain the use of motion.

Quickly, Danny dropped the black mana crystal into his inventory, then turned back to the globe.

"Is this really wise?" Master Barrydew demanded.

"You're looking at a Master, I should remind you," Headmaster Bluestream's voice was quiet. "A master who's more powerful, in many respects, than every Ascended Mage in this room. He has the rank to do what he sees fit, at least in this case."

"And I'm going to save this academy," Danny gritted his teeth and grabbed hold of the table again. "Show me where he is."

A moment later, he felt himself drawn into the sphere, and then taken down... Down... Down. He plunged through layers of the Academy, layers of stone, past dragons and drakes... And then, with a flash, he found himself standing in a place that he never thought he would see again- the boss chamber of the dungeon located beneath the school.

The Deepcorp Lord stood with his back to him, gazing up into the massive **[Dungeon Core]**. Nearby, the Red Blood Dragon, still bound tightly, glared at him.

Danny nodded to it, once more contemplating the fact that the creature had an infinite amount of health, and then turned to the Deepcorp Mage.

"So, you found me," the mage chuckled softly. "It took you longer than I expected. Longer than I anticipated. You disappointed me, Youngblood."

"I can't say that obtaining your admiration has long been a desire of mine," Danny balled his hands into fists. "Now that I know where you are, I'll-"

"You'll what?" The mage seemed unconcerned. "Come and try to beat me again? If you do that, I'll release this dragon. The Imperial City will burn, the world will be destroyed... Do you really want that?"

"I don't wish to lose, Youngblood, and I won't play fair. If I can't have what I want, then the entire world will pay the price."

"And what do you want?" Danny demanded. "The ear of the Emperor again? Control?"

"No." The mage sighed and slowly stretched out a hand. "Power. Ultimate... Power. Leave me be, and I will drain this core. Not quickly, admittedly, but assuredly."

"Leave me be, and all the problems in the Empire will go away. The monsters will fade. You'll be able to reclaim your world."

"And you'll be worshipped as a god," Danny posited.

"I'll be a god. Worship will be due me, not something that I'll seek," the mage hissed. "I have sought for true power for years, millennia, but... You, Youngblood... You showed me that I could not seek it through mortal institutions, no matter how grounded they may be."

"Don't put this on me," Danny snapped.

"But it is on you," the mage slowly started to turn. "All of this is."

As he faced Danny, he reached up and pulled the hood of his cloak back. In that moment, Danny felt as if a dagger had been driven into his gut.

Nicodemus's face was staring back at him. His eyes were black, his cheeks gaunt and drawn, but it was him.

"I can take anything, or anyone, that I want," the mage thundered. "I am already well on my way to what I want to be. Leave me alone... Or a great many people will suffer."

With that, the mage turned away, and Danny felt himself falling. His mind was sucked upward, until he suddenly blinked to find himself lying flat on his back, looking up at a group of rather concerned individuals.

His hands were seared, his whole body hurt, and he groaned and slowly started climbing to his feet.

"Do you know where he is?" Zechariah asked.

"I do," Danny nodded wearily. The ground gave a slight tremor, and he felt his gut twist. "And I don't think we have long to stop him."

[Auto save - [Savefile: Information]

Health: 71% (capped)

Mana: 38% (capped)

[Quest]: Stop the dark lord

Location: Forbidden Archives

Inventory: Essential Supplies, Basic Armor, Iron Sword, [Sword of the Wasp], [Aquamarine Sword], [Frostbite Sword]

Skills: [Monster Summoner] (Lv. 48), [Flame Combat] (Lv. 2), [Wind Combat] (Lv. 5)

Relationships: Friendly with Master Barrydew, Speaking Terms with Headmaster Bluestream, Family Bond with Zechariah, Ascended Fire Mage

Time of Day: 12:41 p.m.

Thirty-Seven

Storm

Books began to fall from the shelves as the rumblings grew stronger and stronger. Windows rattled, and something smashed loudly in the other room.

Everyone looked at Danny, who shook his hands as he desperately tried to work feeling back into them. His health was low, his mana was low, and the city was shaking.

"What's going on?" Obadiah demanded.

"I don't know exactly, but the Deepcorp Mage is in the dungeon underneath the academy and is trying to absorb the dungeon core," Danny explained. "I'm pretty sure he's trying to make himself into a god."

Screeeeeeeeeeeee!

Something seemed to explode in the other room, and they all bolted out into the main body of the library. A large chunk of the wall was now missing with rubble and debris raining down onto a lower rooftop of the Academy.

Flying out over the city was a large dragon with purple scales. As they watched, it launched a fireball and melted a building into slag.

"What's going on?" Obadiah demanded once more. "Is the dungeon overflowing?"

"No." Master Barrydew shook his head. Screams echoed loudly, and a troll appeared, thumping along through the streets.

"This is called Dungeon Bleed. It only ever happens when someone accesses the dungeon core directly, they have the ability to start flinging shards of dungeon energy outside, which results in... Well, something like this."

"Granted, I've never seen it on this scale before." He shook his head. "What do we do?"

"We fight." Zechariah stepped forward and squared his shoulders. He turned slowly, and looked at the other mages.

"We fight, and we keep everyone safe."

"What about the mage down in the dungeon?" Obadiah demanded.

"That will be Danny's prerogative," Zechariah said. "For the time being, I think he's going to be needed up here."

"I don't disagree." Danny balled his hands into fists. "Once we've managed to save as many people as possible, then I'll go down into the dungeon to stop him."

"Good!" Zechariah nodded. "Obadiah, round up as many people as you can. You've got the western side of the city."

"Barrydew, Bluestream, you get the south. Danny and I will take the middle and the east."

"Isa, go get Tess and have her get the civilians to safety, fighting whoever and whatever she can, and then tell Radiance and her father that they can cover the north."

"Don't be squeamish about stepping on other people's turf. Are we ready?"

Everyone gave a nod, and Zechariah balled his hands into fists.

"Good! Go!"

With that, he charged forward, and leapt out into space. Danny followed, doing the best he could.

His body was still quite damaged, but he jumped after his father, summoning a stone golem around himself. He hit the rooftop a moment later, just behind Zechariah, who created a small bloom of flame that prevented him from striking the stone.

With that, they raced forward and leapt out over the entrance of the Academy, falling down to land on the ground below. Civilians streamed all around, and the two of them raced through the streets.

A huge troll stomped along ahead of them, raising a lamppost as a club. Zechariah launched a fiery spear that punched straight through it, and it fell back against a building, crumbling the stone edifice into rubble.

As it came crashing to the ground, the two mages ran past, angling toward the Imperial Palace.

"I'd bet half the kingdom that the mage will flatten the Emperor!" Zechariah called out. "I'll go save him. Can you handle things out here?"

Danny looked up as the dragon shot overhead once more, and he nodded.

"I think I can manage that."

"Good!" Zechariah turned and flung a healing spell up at Danny. It warmed his bones, and his health rose slightly, if not quite as far as he might have liked.

"You're a good mage, Danny. Don't make me have to bury my child at the end of all this."

With that, he sped off, and Danny looked up at the dragon. He took a deep breath then launched himself upward and onto the rooftop, allowing the stone golem to remain below.

As he landed, his robes drifted in the wind behind him, and he raised a hand. Rockworms burst to life in the gut of the dragon, and it flapped about before tumbling down and crashing onto the roof of the Academy.

Walls crumbled, ceilings collapsed, but it was dead. Danny balled his hands into fists then turned as more and more flashes of light began to appear.

The dungeon underneath the Academy was a dragon dungeon, first and foremost. It was the only dungeon that Danny knew of that held such a status, and as he stood there, dragons filled the air.

Some were small, hardly larger than the average person, and they came shooting down at him, wings folded, sneers across their reptilian faces. Danny drew in a deep breath, then raised a hand and fired a bolt of magic up into the air.

He wanted to draw attention to himself, he wanted the dragons to focus on him and not the civilians. Down below, people streamed through the streets as they sought for any cover possible, but he simply gazed at the beasts, watching as they came closer.

Closer...

"Alright." He gritted his teeth. "You asked for it."

With a flick of his wrist, he began to summon more and more of the rockworms. It was, perhaps, cheesing them, but in that moment, he didn't care.

Dragons jerked and collapsed, their wings went limp and they suddenly became more like falling banners than harbingers of death. A blue dragon flashed down and smashed a horse cart in a street to his right, another one landed just in front of him and crashed through the rooftop.

A particularly massive dragon came flashing down, spreading its wings so wide that it must have covered three city blocks.

Danny raised a hand, summoning a worm in its neck. The worm cut through the flame glands, so that when the dragon tried to launch a blast of flame, instead of heading outward... It cut inward instead.

Immune to flame or not, the fire surged and boiled through the inside of the dragon, causing the beast's blood to boil. A moment later, it had burst asunder.

The head of the dragon flew over Danny's head and crashed into a storefront, utterly flattening the location, but from what he could see, no one had been hurt. The body fell (mostly) onto the rooftops, cracking stone but otherwise not doing much damage.

[Notice: You are being targeted with a Restriction Spell]

"What does that mean?" Danny grumbled.

He raised a hand and reabsorbed all the rockworms, increasing his mana back to the 38% cap.

[Notice: You can no longer summon Rockworms]

"What?" Danny snapped.

It had to have been a trick of the mage. He had never heard of Restriction Spells before, and it was a fine time for such a thing to come about.

Suddenly, a dragon flew up and out of one of the streets next to him. It was a small one, hardly larger than a horse, but it lashed out and caught hold of his robes, lifting him high into the air.

He flailed about as it flew higher and higher into the sky, such that he was able to see the burning city below. Flames and smoke rose here and there, even as blasts of magic pulsed here and there in a desperate defense against the beasts.

"You will fail, Youngblood," the voice hissed in his ears. "You are nothing."

"Can you hear me?" Danny snapped.

There was a pause. "Yes." It responded. "What do you have to say to me?"

"Only this." Danny took in a deep breath. "Nicodemus! You have to fight this. I know you're in there, I know you can hear me."

"Fight this!"

There was a sharp laugh in his ears, and the voice went dead. Danny gritted his teeth in frustration then balled his hands into fists.

He summoned a stone golem around himself as large as he could manage with his cap in place and grabbed hold of the dragon.

Suddenly, he found himself almost twice as large as the dragon itself. The beast screeched as it found itself falling, and Danny set his jaw.

He grabbed hold of the wings of the beast and pulled as hard as he could, ripping them clean off. A moment later, they tumbled down and struck the ground, smack in the old courtyard where he had first spoken to Nicodemus.

Their impact flattened the old fountain and made the walls of the apartment buildings tremble. The dragon shuddered and started to rise, and Danny, weak and weary, stomped on its head as hard as he could.

It collapsed, dead now, and he slowly turned his gaze skyward. More and more of the beasts were joining the fray, and he drew in a deep breath.

"Stone Golem."

He re-absorbed the stone golem around himself then projected it up into the sky, summoning it on the back of one of the great beasts, one of the really big ones. In that moment, he found that he could see, in his mind's eye, through the eyes of the golem.

It bent down and grabbed hold of the wings, twisting it sharply. The beast began to spiral down... Down... Down to the north, down toward the quarry.

He saw the beast smash into the guard tower there, knocking stone blocks asunder, and with that, he absorbed the golem before it could be destroyed, and thus before he could lose out on all that mana.

[Notice: Stone Golem has been destroyed]

He had been just a second too late. "No!"

It was true, he had mana crystals that he could use, but he had been hoping to save them. Quickly, he opened up his inventory and started to scroll through, only for another notification to appear.

[Notification: Monster Summoning has increased to Lv. 49!][Reward: Mana Increase: 2270 -> 2410]

A brilliant flash of light washed over him, and in that moment, he was healed to full health. His mana was refilled entirely, and the caps on both of his stats were removed.

He blinked in surprise, and a smile came across his face.

"Now that's what I'm talking about. Time to do some damage."

He held his hands up, spawning more and more of the golems across the backs of the monsters. With so much mana, even using almost five hundred mana for each golem (which was more than enough to create a golem powerful enough to rip the wings off a dragon), he could spawn in five of them.

Dragons began to fall from the sky all around him, flattening buildings and crushing ancient walls. He did his best to direct their falls, and he did succeed in making most of them fall into the fields around the city, but it was impossible to make for absolute certain.

He also did his best to absorb the golems back into himself before they were destroyed, but he did so with only limited success. It was less than a minute before he lost the first golem, and only another minute until he lost the second one.

Still, though, he was dealing quite a bit of damage, and pressed forward as hard as he could.

Suddenly, a horse shot through the growing chaos. Tess rode on its back, with Radiance sitting just behind her.

Her eyes were wide, and Danny nodded to her.

"What's up?"

"We just spotted something, coming up from the west," Tess shouted. "We need you, now."

Danny nodded then quickly spawned in a horse for himself. The three of them sped off, flashing through the growing chaos.

Monsters stomped this way and that, and Danny continued to summon monsters to fight them. He pulled out one of his mana crystals that held 10,000 mana, and spawned in his Blue Dragon Hatchling, more or less turning it loose on the city.

As he watched, it raced down a lane, threading its way between a handful of rather surprised-looking civilians, and burned three trolls to death in the blink of an eye. Satisfied that something was being done in his absence, he sent the remainder of his stone golems into the city as well, and turned his attention to the west.

They flashed out through the rings of the city and were quickly through the tent city, which was now in utter chaos as the people there began to flee the chaos over the city. From a distance, Danny watched as smoke billowed high, and flames lapped at ancient buildings.

Soon, though, he felt the ground rumbling... And turned his attention westward once more. He could just glimpse something coming up over the hills...

And then, as they sped up through the wooded road, they reached the peak of the hill to find an army sitting on the other side. Both horses drew up short, and Danny's jaw dropped.

Spreading out across leagues of territory was a huge cavalry, with infantry troops marching in the rear. So far away that he could barely see it were supply wagons, all of them winding through the rough terrain.

A man on a grand, white stallion at the front came cantering up, a man that Danny recognized well. The king from across the sea now sat there in grand battle armor, bronze mail that glistened with enchantments and was set with a house crest of a lion.

The other nations of the world had come to help. Now, it was time to see what they had to offer.

Auto save - [Savefile: Information]
Health: 84%
Mana: 2%
[Quest Update] Stop the dark lord
Location: Imperial City Agricultural Area, West Side

Inventory: Essential Supplies, Basic Armor, Iron Sword, Sword of the Wasp, Aquamarine Sword, Frostbite Sword

Skills: Monster Summoner (Lv. 49), Flame Combat (Lv. 2), Wind Combat (Lv. 5)

Relationships: Friendly with Master Barrydew, Speaking Terms with Headmaster Bluestream, Family Bond with Zechariah, Ascended Fire Mage, Friendly with Obadiah, Ascended Fire Mage, Friendly with Tess, Friendly with Radiance

Time of Day: 1:47 p.m.

Thirty-Eight

Nations

"You came." Danny could hardly think of anything else to say.

"Perhaps I should handle formal introductions," Radiance offered as Tess rode up a bit closer. "We're very pleased to welcome you to our city."

Behind her, a loud screeeeeeeeee split the air, followed by a powerful booming noise as a fireball cut through another of Danny's guard towers.

"I'm afraid that you'll find the accommodations somewhat lacking, and... Well, the welcoming banquet is a bit overdone," Radiance said with a grin.

The king simply laughed. "After traveling two thousand miles, across land and ocean, my troops have been spoiling for a fight. It seems like you could well use the help."

"We really could," Radiance said. "Thank you, so much, for coming to our aid. Anything you can do for us would be helpful."

"What's the play?" the king asked. "I only ask so that my soldiers can have a proper understanding of the situation?"

Danny nodded out to the city. "There's an ancient mage in a dungeon beneath the city. He's siphoning the power of the dungeon core, and spawning monsters throughout the city to keep us so busy we can't go down there to stop him."

"Then allow us to handle the situation above the ground so that you can handle the situation below." The king paused.

"Forgive me. My soldiers are powerful, and I have many mages with me, but dealing with evil, ancient mages is something that should best be done by those close to the situation."

"I couldn't agree more." Danny spun around, watching the city closely. "Thank you, again!"

"Prepare for battle!" the king bellowed, his voice echoing over the soldiers. "Kill any monsters throughout the city, and remove civilians to a safe distance. You are to respect all local commanders!"

With that, he drew out a horn and lifted it to his lips. When it blew, the noise seemed to echo in both directions, across the soldiers and across the city.

Danny might have imagined it, but he thought he saw several dragons turn in their direction. With that, Danny flashed down toward the city once more, followed by Tess and Radiance.

And behind them, came the army.

The legions of warriors thundered through the woodlands there, clinging to the road and flashing through the thick trees on either side. The whole forest shook with the ferocity of it... And then they were out the far side, out and racing across the open plain toward the city.

Dragons came swooping down from the air, landing on the Middle Wall, snarling and opening their mouths wide.

"That wall!" The king rode up next to Danny. "How important is it? I only ask because it doesn't exactly seem to have been well-built to begin with, and... Well..."

"If you have to knock it down, do it," Danny ordered. "There are civilians on the other side, so tread lightly, but-"

"Got it!" The king raised another horn to his lips and blew a second blast.

The dragons sneered, and the front several lines of horsemen raised their spears. In that instant, Danny saw patches running down their battle armor that looked rather like the patches that the mages in the Academy wore.

And then, magic pulsed down the length of their weapons. Fireballs and ice crystals filled the air, along with countless wind arrows, blasts of lightning, water strikes, and more.

The dragons were blown clean off the wall, and a moment later, the army struck the poorly-built construction.

Danny wished he could have seen what it looked like on the other side as magic chewed the wall to shreds, and the army came racing through. Civilians screamed, but the horsemen were good and didn't strike a single one.

As monsters thumped through the area, they roared in surprise as the army came flashing past, cutting them down in the blink of an eye. Trolls and orcs fell dead as doornails, along with wargs and wraiths and all sorts of other creatures.

The army slowed as it neared the main gates of the city, and there, things began to break apart.

They were obviously well-trained. A great number of them raced forward, shooting straight through the open gate and pouring into the city.

Others wheeled to the side and dismounted, then began throwing grappling hooks up over the city walls. Some of their mages simply launched themselves over the walls with their magic.

Meanwhile, other units broke off and began to ride around the sides of the city, angling for the other gates. Still more units began to cluster the civilians together, ushering them to safe locations.

"Don't worry!" The king rode up next to Danny. "We can take it from here. Head down into that dungeon and stop the dark lord. I promise, everything up here will be safe!"

Even as he said it, a wagon was wheeled slowly forward. Workmen pulled a tarp back, exposing a latticework of wood and metal.

They pulled it upward, causing a crossbow not unlike Isa's creation to snap together. Within a moment, they had a working weapon.

One of them loaded a bolt into the weapon, and they raised it to point at a dragon flashing overhead. Danny held his breath, and the weapon fired an instant later.

The results were extraordinary. The bolt flashed up into the sky, glowing brightly, only to explode into a hundred separate bolts as it neared the beast.

The dragon screamed as it was pierced by dozens of arrows, and it began to flounder and flap down toward the ground. A dull boom echoed through the city a moment later.

"This is incredible," Danny murmured and nodded to the king. "How can we ever thank you?"

"Swear fealty to me when this is all over, and join my expanding Empire of the East." The king put his hand on Danny's shoulder then burst out laughing. "Please, please! You should have seen the look on your face!"

"In all seriousness, I'd love to have a long conversation about trade routes and things, but..." He sighed. "My nation, and the nations around us, didn't survive by locking ourselves inside and only fighting our own battles. Against the race of humanity, the monsters are a common threat."

"What you see here is a single army made up of volunteers from twelve nations, all of whom left their lives and families to come and rescue yours. Now, please. We can discuss all this later. Go kill the mage that's causing all this."

"Alright, alright!" Danny laughed and turned toward the city. "Thank you again!"

With that, he rode into the city, flashing through the streets as fast as he could go. Everywhere he went, now, the new soldiers were warring against the beasts, getting the civilians to safety.

They were building blockades with the rubble and debris, and were using every means necessary to fight back against the monsters. As Danny closed in on the Academy, he saw Obadiah racing across the rooftops, pursuing a warg that was leaping from building to building, its large claws smashing holes in a great many of the roofs.

A foreign mage appeared a second later, launching a flaming spear through the warg and sending it toppling to the ground. Obadiah followed and speared it as the beast struggled to rise, and Danny saw the two of them shake hands.

With that, on he flew, until he stood at the base of the stairs that led up and into the Academy.

There was a thump-thump from inside, and a second later, the doors were blown open. A massive troll, wrapped in chains, stood there to block his path.

The great beast roared down at him, then drug out one of the chains, which had been wrapped around a large, spiked ball. He swung it down at Danny, trying to flatten him.

Danny dove out of the way, and the ball smashed the Academy stairs to rubble instead. The troll grunted and started trying to pull the ball back, but before he could, a piercing blast of flame shot down from above.

Zechariah leapt into the fray, cutting through the iron chain. The troll staggered backward as the chain gave way, and Zechariah launched a blistering flame arrow attack against its face.

Danny raised his hand and spawned a stone golem just behind it, which reached out and snatched up a large wooden beam. It slammed the beam into the thing's back, using it like a spear.

The wood punched out through the front of the troll a second later, and it groaned before toppling forward. The two mages leapt to the side as it struck, and they charged up into the Academy together.

"And Nicodemus always said that trolls were superior to golems," Danny snorted.

"Nicodemus says a lot of things. Always take what he has to say with a grain of salt," Zechariah said. "Or... Maybe a whole bag of salt. I sure hope he's okay, I really do."

"Yeah, about that..." Danny muttered as they ran through the academy halls. Monsters continued to roar just outside, and they started working their way upward toward the Headmaster's office.

"I might have seen him down in that dungeon, too."

"He's working with the mage?" Zechariah demanded. "I thought you said that you'd seen him about six months ago, and that he was clearly working against the mage."

"I did." Danny paused. "He... Well, he's sorta being possessed by the mage. And then Barbara is bonded to him, and..."

"Right." Zechariah sighed. "All sorts of chaos. So we're going to be fighting my father-in-law. Again."

He bit his lip. "You know, it gets sorta old, sometimes. You're supposed to have issues with your in-laws, that's just life, but this is ridiculous."

Danny laughed. "Maybe I'll just never get married so I don't have to worry about it."

"If you let the Youngblood line die out just because you don't want to have to deal with in-laws, I'm going to haunt you through this life and whatever comes in the next." Zechariah held up a finger.

They reached the stairs that led to the Headmaster's office, and quickly raced up them three at a time. When they reached the massive door, they found it locked, but Zechariah was able to blast through without a second thought.

As they stepped through, they gazed out through the windows over the city... And there, for a moment, they stopped.

Dragons were still swooping this way and that over the land. Bolts of fire lanced up from the oncoming army, shooting them down.

Out beyond the walls, more and more soldiers were still pouring into the Imperial City, warring desperately against the beasts that sought to reduce the city to utter ruin. Smoke rose freely.

Even if they could beat everything back right at that moment, it was going to be a long road to recovery.

"Come on, Danny." Zechariah walked up to the headmaster's desk and raised his hand. "We don't have much time."

Danny nodded and stood next to his father. "I'm sorry. I just..." He paused. "Who would do something like this? What's the point of causing so much death and destruction, you know? What would someone get out of this?"

"A feeling of power," Zechariah muttered. "Nothing more than that. It's an empty feeling, but when you have nothing, the best thing you can think to do is make sure that other people have even less."

With that, Zechariah activated the portal that led down into the dungeon. Lights washed over them, and the two of them were taken away.

Auto save - [Savefile: Information]
Health: 82%
Mana: 3%
[Quest]: Stop the dark lord
Location: Headmaster's Office
Inventory: Essential Supplies, Basic Armor, Iron Sword, [Sword of the Wasp], [Aquamarine Sword], [Frostbite Sword]
Skills: [Monster Summoner] (Lv. 49), [Flame Combat] (Lv. 2), [Wind Combat] (Lv. 5)
Relationships: Family Bond with Zechariah, Ascended Fire Mage, Friendly with King of the Army of Twelve Nations
Time of Day: 2:19 p.m.

Thirty-Nine

Red Dragon

Danny and Zechariah stepped through the portal and down into the lower dungeon. As the portal closed behind them, Danny drew in a deep breath and slowly looked around as shrieks and roars echoed loudly throughout the room.

It was just as he remembered. Singularly enormous, it felt like it was larger than the entire academy itself, hundreds upon hundreds of feet tall and countless thousands wide.

The floor was rough, covered in sharp outcroppings and deep crevices, while small walkways and bridges wove here and there to provide a path to the small building that he knew all too well. High above, stalactites larger than entire buildings clung to the ceiling, pointing downward like enormous teeth.

Danny gulped as the countless dragons that filled the place began to circle steadily downward.

Zechariah asked, "Shall we?"

The two of them charged forward as quickly as they could, racing along the narrow footpath. Below them, huge chunks of stone began shifting around.

They were, of course, monsters instead of actual stone, and Danny gulped as they took on the form of enormous insects, trolls, and other such things.

Neither mage stopped running as they flew, pell-mell, toward the distant shaft that would lead them down to the boss chamber. Dozens of monsters came at them, flashing down from the sky or exploding through the boulders to attack them.

Zechariah let off attack after attack, while Danny mostly kept his head down. Soon, they came crashing into the door of the shack, which Zechariah threw wide open.

They dove through, slammed it shut behind them, and let out a long breath.

"What do you think the odds are that he doesn't know we're here?" Danny asked softly.

"Zero," Zechariah said. "Absolutely zero. Come on. Maybe he's so full of hubris that he'll think we'll give up before actually getting down there."

Danny gave a small nod, and the two of them started down the long flight of stairs. It wrapped around and around, twisting upon itself, endless in its duration.

Danny felt fear gripping his heart, and did his best to contain it. He had a job to do, and he was going to do it.

When they reached the little door at the bottom, Zechariah unlocked it with a wave of his hand, and the two of them slowly stepped through.

The inside of the boss room crackled with energy. The **[Dungeon Core]** hung at the exact center, a crystal that sparkled and blazed with unfathomable energy.

The dragon's muscles bulged as it fought to break free of its bonds, which had held it in place for the previous thousand years, but it was just as captured as it had been in the past. That, at least, was some small consolation.

Standing in front of the **[Dungeon Core]**, so small that he might have been an insect, was the mage. Danny let out a long breath, and the two mages slowly started walking down the long flight of stairs that wrapped around the side of the room.

The dragon's eyes followed them, and Danny did his best to prepare for the coming battle.

"You are more resourceful than I might have guessed," the mage muttered. "Getting another army to come and fight on your behalf? Incredible. Good work hiding it, too. You surprised me, and that doesn't happen very often."

"You flatter us." Danny bowed at the waist.

"When I give someone a compliment, it is far more than flattery," the mage snapped. "I have seen a thousand years of history. If I say that you are-"

"And now he's flattering himself," Zechariah cut in, shaking his head in mock disappointment. "It's sad to see the depth that some dark lords will sink to."

"I am not- Ahh. You are trying to get under my skin," the dark lord sneered. "Well, it won't work."

Danny only shrugged. The mage still wasn't attacking them, and that likely meant that he was having to focus all his energy upon controlling the **[Dungeon Core]**.

The amount of energy being channeled through his body was simply enormous, and if he lost concentration, it would likely kill him almost instantly. Danny would have loved to see that, if not for the fact that the lord had possessed Nicodemus.

As they reached the floor and approached, Nicodemus's features came fully into focus. The mage had left the hood down, allowing Nicodemus to be seen fully.

He had a smile upon his face, basking in the glow of the deadly energy.

"Nicodemus!" Zechariah called out. "Snap out of it!"

"He can't hear you." The mage cackled then slowly turned around. He kept his left hand pointed at the **[Dungeon Core]**, where a blazing arc of energy leapt to his palm, while he turned his right hand toward the two newcomers.

"He's as dead as a doornail, as they say. Well, mostly dead. His mind is in here, I suppose, but he has no free will. All of it was surrendered to me. Me, and me alone, which is what will happen to all of you. To all of the world."

He smiled wickedly. "The whole of the world will bow to me, starting with you two."

A blast of energy shot out and hit Danny and Zechariah in the chests. Danny suddenly felt his knees grow heavy, and he was slowly forced down to his knees.

It felt like a mountain must have landed on his back, driving him to the ground. He groaned softly as his knees hit the stone, and the mage laughed all the harder.

"See? You are pathetic. You are nothing before me," The mage sneered. "You will die, right here, and no one will ever know. Survivors may assume that you failed, but that will be all that they know of you, all that they remember of you."

"And that's the difference between you and us," Zechariah asked through clenched teeth. "You care about being remembered. You hid yourself away for the last thousand years, when all you want to do is bask in the glory of us mortals."

"We, on the other hand, don't care. We care about doing good, here and now, and then will happily perish." Zechariah paused, then flashed a thin smile at Danny. "Provided that he makes sure that the Youngblood line doesn't perish with him."

It was a small joke in the midst of such chaos, but it brought a smile to Danny's face. The mage twisted in rage and anger, and the weight on Danny's shoulders became stronger.

"You will not treat me with such flippant-"

When the mage was distracted in his anger, Zechariah chose that moment to act, launching a flurry of arrows at him. The mage sneered and waved his hand to deflect them, and in that moment, Danny and Zechariah both launched themselves forward.

The arrows were scattered across the floor, and the father and son threw themselves at the dark mage. Danny drew his sword, Zechariah launched a flurry of fireballs.

The mage simply raised another hand and casually deflected them, then flicked a finger and launched a shockwave that smashed Danny and his father into the ground. Danny groaned as the wind left him, and he gritted his teeth as yet another weight began to press him down into the stone.

"Weak fools," the mage snapped.

"Hopeful idiots," Danny countered. A second later, the stone golem that Danny had summoned, in those brief moments, hit the mage from behind.

The Deepcorp Mage screamed as the stone golem plunged through the bolt of energy, grabbed the man, and threw him across the room. The mage didn't actually go that far, he used some sort of magic to halt his forward progress through the air and landed only about ten feet away, but it had served as a distraction enough.

He was no longer connected to the **[Dungeon Core]**, and that meant that he was mortal. The stone golem lunged at him, and the mage casually launched a bolt of lightning that blasted the thing into shreds.

The two mages attacked.

Zechariah stalked forward with a purpose, calling up larger and larger fireballs. They streaked down from the ceiling, from the walls, even up from the floor.

The dungeon trembled from the magical display, and Danny whistled. Truly, his father was every bit deserving of the title of Ascended Mage.

The Deepcorp Mage was forced to use every instant, every last ounce of skill that he had, in order simply to stay alive. Danny drew in a deep breath... Then slowly glanced at the **[Dungeon Core]**.

It hung there, flickering and crackling with energy as a small smile came across his face.

"I need a dragon."

A bolt of light exploded off the core and struck his palm. Energy seared through his whole body, and he gasped as it was subsequently discharged.

A huge, blue dragon appeared behind the Deepcorp Mage and stomped on the man with a massive claw, and Danny groaned as he fell to his knees.

"Danny!" Zechariah snapped. "Don't do that!"

"Yeah, I got that much," Danny groaned. He sighed as he climbed back to his feet. The Deepcorp Mage unleashed a blast of magic that knocked the dragon back, and the huge lizard opened its mouth and unleashed a furious blast of fire.

The two forces raged against each other, which Danny was more than willing to let them do. "We have to do something about it, though. If it stays there..."

"He'll just be able to do the same thing." Zechariah raised a hand and flung a spell at the core. It struck, and arcs of energy began to flare around it.

After a moment, a force field appeared, protecting it from any and all approaches. "The core itself is maintaining the spell. It won't last for long, maybe twenty minutes or so, but that'll hopefully be enough."

"Ahh!" The mage roared and flung a blast of lightning up, killing the dragon.

As it collapsed, he swung back around then roared in fury again.

"Dad, I have an idea." Danny glanced over at his father. "I need to touch him, though."

"I'll see what I can do." Zechariah rushed forward, launching more and more attacks. Fiery bolts of lightning flared at the mage, though the mage simply crossed his arms to block it all.

The force of the explosions drove him backward several feet, and Zechariah leapt through the guard and punched the man in the face. With that, he held out a hand, and a spectral rope flashed out to Danny.

Danny grabbed hold, and Zechariah pulled with all his might.

Danny found himself lifted off his feet, launched toward the Deepcorp Mage with extraordinary force. A moment later, he struck the man, and they tumbled across the ground together.

Danny grabbed hold of the mage's arm... Nicodemus's arm... And squeezed as hard as he could.

"Foolish child!" the Deepcorp Mage snapped. "You are nothing more than a whelp!"

"Then kill me already!" Danny snarled.

"I will!" The Deepcorp Mage began struggling to climb to his feet. "Let go of me!"

Danny gritted his teeth and reached out to grab hold of the Deepcorp Mage with his powers. "Not likely."

He pulled with everything that he had. Physical muscle, magic powers - he poured everything he had into just pulling with every last possible ounce of energy.

There was a sharp rip that echoed through the air and a flash of light more brilliant than anything he had ever seen before.

And then, as lights faded before his eyes, he found a shabby old man standing before him, stooped over and leaning on a cane, a skeletal face peering out from a tattered cloak. Standing at his right shoulder, on the other hand, was Nicodemus.

Nicodemus looked down at his hands then slowly looked at the Deepcorp Mage. He was still dressed in his combat robes, the grand and glorious attire that he had been wearing when they had been hit with the dragon fire.

His eyes were sharp, and he slowly cracked his knuckles.

"Danny." He gave a nod. "Zechariah."

Zechariah raised an eyebrow. "A thank-you might be in order."

"I'll thank you when we all walk out of this alive," Nicodemus answered, then scowled at the Deepcorp Mage. "Well... Most of us."

The mage sneered then raised a hand and unleashed a furious blast of lightning. Nicodemus waved a hand to deflect it all then charged forward.

"Alright, Danny!" he said. "Give me a stone golem, and make it a strong one!"

"With pleasure." Danny snapped his fingers, pouring every ounce of mana he had left into a single construction. The golem appeared only feet from the mage and stomped on him without question.

The mage escaped with a flash of teleportation light, and Nicodemus waved a hand. Magic flared across the stone golem, making it shrink down to the size of an ordinary human (while maintaining all stats, power, health, and more).

As glowing lights of a variety of colors flared from within the monster, Danny smiled.

The stone golem threw itself at the Deepcorp Mage, unleashing a fury of attacks that blasted the man back into the wall of the chasm. The monster followed, punching and striking with extreme prejudice.

The noise was so great that Danny was certain it could be heard all the way on the surface. Finally, the mage broke free and raced away, fleeing as fast as his broken body would allow him to go.

He ran straight at the **[Dungeon Core]**, leaping over the broken stones, a wild cackle upon his lips.

"And where do you think you're going?" Nicodemus stepped in his way, reached out, and caught the man by the throat. He lifted the skeletal figure off the ground, turned, and smashed him down to the stone once more.

The mage's eyes were wide, and Nicodemus sneered. "Never thought it would go quite like this, eh? How many others have you enslaved like me? How many have you used like puppets, how many have you slain over the years?"

"More than you could know." The mage kicked at him, but his magic seemed to be waning. "And I'll do a lot more before this is all said and done. You think you've won, you think you have a chance, but all you can do is delay me. Even killing me will only set my spirit free!"

"Really?" Nicodemus smirked. "Then let's give it a try, shall we?"

Nicodemus pulled a large knife off his belt and gave it a twirl. It was the same knife that Danny had seen Barbara wield earlier.

For a moment, he was confused, then he realized that when the mage lost Nicodemus's body, he had likely lost any items stored on Nicodemus's body. Nicodemus raised the weapon and slashed down, but before it could land, the mage spun like lightning.

All Danny could do was watch as the mage threw off Nicodemus, grabbed his wrist, and twisted sharply. The sound of Nicodemus's wrist breaking echoed loudly through the whole of the cavern, and Danny gasped.

A second later, the mage once more held his knife, and leapt upon Nicodemus like a cat. The blade plunged down, slamming deep into Nicodemus's chest.

The mage gleamed in triumph, and sneered down at Nicodemus.

"And now... Now, you perish. You and the rest of this miserable world." He ripped the blade back out then gave it a twirl.

"Maybe... So." Nicodemus's feeble words echoed softly in the air. "But then... So will you."

Danny gritted his teeth and set the stone golem flashing across the ground toward the mage. The mage looked up and sneered, and in that moment, Nicodemus's head lolled backward.

With a flash of light, he was suddenly replaced by Barbara, who, thankfully, didn't seem particularly bothered by finding herself pinned by a Deepcorp Mage. Before Danny could blink, she sat up and snatched the knife from his grasp.

He had only a moment to look surprised before she slashed it through his neck and his head slowly toppled from his body. Dust exploded up into the air as his spirit ceased to hold the body together, and Danny smiled.

For the briefest of moments, at least.

Suddenly, the dust swirled about, and the Deepcorp Mage's voice laughed brilliantly.

"I told you that I would become more powerful if you killed me!" He laughed. "I told you that I would-"

Danny quit listening, and turned to the massive dragon. It glared at him, and he raised a hand. "Absorb elements."

[Creature Absorbed: Red Blood Dragon]

[Traits: Red Blood Dragon Torso (Lv. 500), Red Blood Dragon Legs, Red Blood Dragon Tail, Red Blood Dragon Head, Dragon Scales (already owned), Dragon Claws (already owned), Dragon Fire Attribute (already owned)]

[Mana to Quicksummon: 1,000,000,000,000]

"Danny?" Zechariah called out. "What are you doing?"

"Something stupid." Danny gritted his teeth and pulled out his black mana crystal. "Better hope this works."

Auto save - [Savefile: Information]

- **Health: 31%**

- **Mana: 0%**

- **[Quest]: Stop the dark lord**

- **Location: Lower Dungeon, Boss Chamber**

- **Inventory: Essential Supplies, Basic Armor, Iron Sword, [Sword of the Wasp], [Aquamarine Sword], [Frostbite Sword]**

- **Skills: [Monster Summoner] (Lv. 49), [Flame Combat] (Lv. 2), [Wind Combat] (Lv. 5)**

- **Relationships: Family Bond with Zechariah, Ascended Fire Mage, Family Bond with Nicodemus, Ascended Monster Summoner, Friendly with Barbara, Archenemies with [Unknown Deepcorp Mage]**

- **Time of Day: 2:48 p.m.**

Forty

An End of Things

Danny gripped the mana crystal as tightly as he could, and in that instant, power blazed through his body. He made certain not to allow any of it to rest in himself, as that would kill him in an instant.

No, he simply let it flow. He didn't want to summon the dragon, exactly, but he did want to show off its attributes.

He had a very clear view in his head of what he wanted to do, and...

Well, it turned out to be just enough.

With a flash, he found himself standing in what could be called a realm of mana. The Deepcorp Mage stood before him just in front of the dungeon core.

In that realm, the mage looked young, scarcely older than Danny himself, though his eyes were hard. Danny gritted his teeth and nodded to him.

"Take one step closer to that core, and you'll regret it."

"You can't stop me," the man snarled. "You can't possibly. You can rage against me all you want, but... You can't stop me."

"Oh..." Danny shook his head as the mage turned away. "I think I can." He turned himself as he spawned the massive dragon just behind him, and saw pure fire roaring through the strange realm.

He stepped out of the way, saw the immense beast shoot past, finally free of the bonds that had kept it contained for the last millennium. Fire crackled and roared, the mage screamed...

And then, with that, he found himself standing back in the dungeon.

He frowned then glanced at Barbara and Zechariah. The whole of the dungeon trembled, rumbled, raged... And then, with a loud crack, the mana crystal in Danny's hand shattered into bits.

A second later, the dungeon core itself began to crack and fracture. Danny felt his gut twist, and Zechariah gasped.

"Danny, what did you do?"

"I didn't think I did anything!" Danny shook his head. "I-"

BLAM!

The noise was impossibly loud... And yet, it also didn't seem to make any noise at all. The dungeon core shattered and exploded, flinging tens of thousands of shards out in every direction.

Danny raised his hand reflexively, only to find them vanishing into thin air long before they touched him. The bindings holding the immense dragon vanished, and the dragon rose, stretched, looked down at them... And toppled over, dead.

With the core gone, there was no energy to sustain it. Distantly, more thuds echoed through the air, and Danny gradually heard the roars of the dungeon going quiet.

"What just happened?" Barbara asked.

"I... I wish I knew," Danny murmured.

Zechariah, though, walked over and clapped his hand on Danny's shoulder. "I do believe that he just closed down a dungeon." He flashed a thin smile.

"Come on. Let's get back to the surface."

"Right!" Danny gasped. "Nicodemus!"

"He's fine." Barbara held up a hand. "He doesn't technically exist at the moment, which means that he's not getting any worse. Don't worry, he'll be alright."

Danny bit his lip and nodded slowly, and they all turned and headed up the stairs. Danny had no way of knowing what they would find when they reached the surface... But he was eager to find out.

As it turned out, there was mostly a great deal of confusion up on the surface, and a great deal of time was spent getting everything sorted out. The vast majority of the monsters in the Imperial City had simply dropped dead in the midst of the fighting, though, admittedly, not all of them.

Those remaining had been hunted down, and from that point, the Army of the Twelve Nations secured the border of the Imperial City and sat back to wait.

Upon returning to the surface, Danny, Barbara, and Zechariah made their way to the infirmary, where, under the watchful eye of a great many nurses, Barbara and Nicodemus were separated once more. Nicodemus was pale and dying when he appeared, and quite unconscious, and the nurses quickly set to work.

Danny refused to leave the room, and simply watched while they worked. An hour went by, then two.

Finally, the head doctor stepped back, wiped his brow, and nodded.

"He'll be fine," he said. "It'll take a month or two until he's back on his feet, but he'll make it."

Danny let out a sigh of relief, and with that, he was escorted from the room. After a bit more confusion, he was taken out from the Academy and whisked across the desolated town toward the Imperial Palace where he was placed before the Emperor.

The Throne Room was in a great deal of confusion, as aides and attendants and all sorts of other people rushed back and forth. Emperor Ezra stood tall, hands folded behind his back, with the other king standing next to him.

As Danny approached, Emperor Ezra nodded to him.

"Master Youngblood! May I present you to King Korlok, of the Nation of the Green Mountains."

"It's a pleasure." Danny knelt before the king then rose again.

"Or it would be, if I truly believed that this was the first time you had met," Emperor Ezra scowled good-naturedly. "Now, would you mind telling me exactly what just happened? Omit no detail, and I do mean that in the most literal sense possible."

Danny nodded and began to recount the tale. When he finished, which took quite some time, Emperor Ezra frowned.

"I see." The emperor didn't say anything for a long time more then finally shrugged. "Well... While I cannot officially condone a great many of the actions that you took, particularly the parts where you went behind my back to conduct negotiations with a foreign nation... I thank you for the result."

"I wish I could take credit for it all." Danny bowed his head. "Truth be told, I have no idea why the dungeon core reacted like that. I've always heard that the first Emperor tried to close down the dungeon core, and that the result was a much larger dungeon core instead."

"I actually might be able to answer that," King Korlok said. "The very simple answer is that dungeon cores, mana crystals... All of it represents tears in the world between the realm of mana and our own realm."

"When he tried to close down the dungeon, he very likely simply smashed it, in a physical sense of the word. This would have resulted in the core trying to heal itself, on both sides of the world, which would have resulted in a much larger core as the pieces were fused back together."

"From what you've described, attacking it from the mana side of the realm, I can only imagine that you more or less closed the gap."

"I see." Danny frowned. "I wasn't trying to attack it, though. Just the Deepcorp Mage."

"Well, perhaps he had already depleted its power." Zechariah suggested. "Flames cause splash damage, if he had already weakened it... I don't know."

"Nor do I." Emperor Ezra sighed deeply. "What I do know is that you, Danny Youngblood... No. Ascended Mage Youngblood, the Empire has you to thank for a great many things."

"You've freed the Empire from a dark force that corrupted the throne for generations. You've rid the world of an immense dungeon, you've re-established trade with our long-lost neighbors, you've... You've done more than anyone else in the history of our nation, excepting perhaps the very first Emperor who forged it."

Emperor Ezra slowly knelt down before him. "Please believe me when I say that, from now on, you shall answer to no one. Name anything you desire, up to half my kingdom, and it shall be yours, from now until my death, and until the death of my offspring, and until the death of theirs, as long as you yourself draw breath, and rest assured that your own children shall bear your own honor."

Danny bit his lip. "Let's not get ahead of ourselves." He paused then slowly folded his hands behind his back. All eyes in the room were upon him, the apparent savior of the Empire.

"Write me an IOU. For now... Let's just get this city rebuilt."

King Korlok smiled, and bowed his head in reverence to Danny. "For that answer, consider yourself to have the same honor in my own nation as well." He clapped Emperor Ezra on the shoulder.

"Now, like he said, let's get to work. I think a statue of me would go great... Right about there, don't you?"

Emperor Ezra frowned, and King Korlok's laugh echoed throughout the room. Danny smiled as well, and started to follow them out.

Indeed, things were going to return to normal.

All he had to do now was see it through.

*****

Ten Years Later...

Danny sighed deeply as he walked out onto the terrace of his home, which overlooked the sprawling landscape of the Imperial City. Grander and more glorious than ever, immense spires rose into the sky, complimenting golden and silver domes that were all the rage over on the great western continent that they had contacted.

Even as he stood there and leaned against the railing, he saw a group of traders walking through the western gates, not far from his home. Their wagons were loaded high with goods, and would be stacked just as high when they returned.

A slow tap-tap echoed through the air, and Danny turned slightly to see Nicodemus walking out, leaning heavily upon his cane.

"You're up." Danny raised an eyebrow. "You should be-"

"Don't tell me that I should be resting." Nicodemus sighed as he reached Danny, and leaned against the railing as well. "I'm old, not infirm." He paused for a moment, then flashed a smile.

"Wonderful, isn't it? I can remember when this place looked half this grand, and we thought it was stunning."

He paused, then shook his head. "Amazing what knocking out one single dungeon will do to a world."

Danny had to nod and laugh at that. When the main dungeon had collapsed under the academy, it had done more than simply kill all the monsters in the city.

Isa had been watching the globe at that moment, and according to her, you could see a wave traveling outward from the Imperial City. It had killed off almost eighty percent of the monsters in the land, and closed almost eighty percent of all the dungeons.

The adjustment brought it into line with the other nations of the world, making the land far more habitable.

Survivors in the Deepcorp Lord's enclaves had come surging out to find a vast and fertile land, while settlers from other nations had come as well. The whole Empire, larger and grander than ever before, had rapidly grown into its place in the world.

The Silver Estate had taken advantage of the chaos to reclaim most of its old land, and was now officially a minor kingdom within the Empire, controlling vast swaths of northern land. Other noble families had done the same, including the Flamekeepers in the south, and the Stoneflowers near the central mountains.

"Where is that old globe?" Nicodemus asked after a moment. "It's been so long since I've had a proper look at it."

Danny flashed a small smile. "It's at the Academy, in the headmaster's office."

"Ahh, the headmaster," Nicodemus scowled. "He's a real hard case, this one."

Distantly, a door slammed, and Zechariah's voice echoed through the home. "Danny? You here?"

"Out here, dad," Danny called.

A moment later, Headmaster Zechariah Youngblood strode out, sighing deeply. "What's up? Something urgent?"

"Depends on how you define it," Zechariah said. "Isa... No. Master Fireworth told me that she detected a flare-up of monster activity on the northern ice. She thinks that the old Ice Cave Dungeon might have overflowed."

"We've gotten sorta lax about patrolling it, I'll admit."

Danny frowned. "You're wanting me to head up and take care of it?"

"It's just an A-ranker." Zechariah paused. "That said, if you'd be willing, I'd like to go with you. Too long since I've seen any action."

"Sounds like it might be fun, taking on another dungeon together."

"You'll have to clear that with the missus," Nicodemus snorted. "Three little boys to watch?"

Danny flashed a smile, and another door slammed somewhere in the home. With that, Jonathan, David, and Solomon came running out, ages 8, 5, and 3, respectively.

Danny smiled as they threw themselves into his arms. Jonathan launched a fireball at David, who quickly blocked it by summoning a goblin holding a shield.

"Hey! No magic in the house." Danny snapped, then rubbed the back of his neck. "Your mother will kill me. Remember when you broke the vase we got as a wedding present from King Korlok?"

Jonathan turned pale, and the three boys ran off once more. Zechariah laughed then clapped Danny on the shoulder.

"In any case, I already cleared it with your wife. She told me we should go and have some fun. We've both been teaching at the Academy too long, not enough air in our lungs."

"And I can help out, too," Nicodemus commented. "As I said, but as everyone keeps ignoring, I'm just old." He snapped his fingers, and an elegantly-dressed goblin appeared next to him.

It bowed deeply. "It can even do the dishes."

Zechariah laughed and started back into the home. "We'll leave tomorrow morning! I've got to go find Barrydew to square some things away with him for our absence."

"Oh, and Abraham has sent me something like forty letters asking me to please return the Diamond Carriage, which he's certain he only lent to us for the christening of Emperor Ezra's son."

"No, I'm quite certain he gave it to us." Danny winked. "Offer it back to him for a token sum of, say... Your weight in gold?"

"Better make it Barrydew's weight in gold," Nicodemus muttered. "Youngbloods are featherweights."

****

The End

We hope you enjoyed following Danny Youngblood's transformation from a young mage to the Empire's savior. If you enjoyed his story, please consider leaving a positive review. This is the life blood of an author and helps basically everything.

Be sure to follow Kal Griffith at https://www.amazon.com/stores/Kal-Griffith/author/B0C5JZT4D3 for more fantasy adventures. Here are a couple of recommendations to keep you entertained:

Blade of the Blue Star

https://www.amazon.com/dp/B0DHD4NXJR

Meet Reinhardt Blazkowicz, an orphan and warrior who unexpectedly becomes the heir to the legendary Blue Star Duchy. Discovered by the Duke on a battlefield, Reinhardt's life changes dramatically as he joins Aegis Crown Academy. In a world filled with magic, combat, and political intrigue, Reinhardt must rely on more than his fighting skills to survive. With loyal friends by his side, he faces challenges from the Legion Arena to the complexities of nobility. Can this seasoned fighter adapt and become the leader he's meant to be?

The Talentless Prince is a Governor - A Lord LitRPG

https://www.amazon.com/Talentless-Prince-Governor-Healing-Hardhome-ebook/dp/B0DHV63NK2/

Follow Heath Shieldmire, the "Talentless Prince," as he takes on the role of Governor in the struggling settlement of Hardhome. With the Governor System at his command, Heath is determined to turn the wasteland into a thriving town. Facing limited resources, relentless monsters, and political adversaries, he must prove he's more than just an exiled noble and demonstrate true leadership. As the town grows, so do the challenges. Will Heath earn his companions' trust and transform Hardhome into a place they can call home? Find out in *The Talentless Prince is a Governor: A Lord LitRPG*.

Thank you for joining us on this journey. Until next time, happy reading!

Made in United States
Troutdale, OR
04/18/2025